NALINI SINGH

ARCHANGEL'S
BLADE

A Guild
Hunter
Novel

BERKLEY
SENSATION

$7.99 U.S.
$9.99 CAN

S EAN

ISBN 978-0-425-24391-6

9 780425 243916

5 0 7 9 9

continued . . .

"Amazing. Fantastic . . . Simmering with both violence and sexual tension, and with vivid worldbuilding that blew my socks off." —Meljean Brook, national bestselling author

"A refreshing twist on vampire and angel lore combined with sizzling sexual tension make this paranormal romance a winner." —*Monsters and Critics*

"Singh provides incontrovertible evidence that she's an unrivaled storyteller . . . This book should be at the top of your must-buy list! Tremendous!"
—*RT Book Reviews* (Top Pick)

"Nalini Singh's Guild Hunter series is a fabulous addition to the paranormal world . . . A definite must read."
—*Fresh Fiction*

"A fully nuanced and startling story from start to finish . . . Nalini Singh should take a bow! *Angels' Blood* is going to leave you hungering for more instantly."
—*Romance Junkies*

"Fans will relish Nalini Singh's excellent first Guild Hunter thriller." —*Midwest Book Review*

Play of Passion

"Compelling characters and wonderfully dense plotting are two reasons why Singh's books continue to enthrall. There is no finer storyteller around!"—*RT Book Reviews* (Top Pick)

"A provocative, captivating, and scorching-hot paranormal romance that fans of the series will absolutely love and newcomers won't be able to put down."
—*Night Owl Reviews*

"Offers everything we expect from Nalini Singh: smart, feisty heroine, delectable hero, and plenty of action. This book is not to be missed!" —*Katidom*

Bonds of Justice

"Sheer genius. Nalini Singh writes with amazing skill . . .
You have to read this book!" —*The Romance Reviews*

"Nalini Singh has the golden touch. An imagination that
won't quit. A writing style that punches you in the gut,
wrings your heart out till there's nothing left."
—*The Good, The Bad and The Unread*

"An unforgettable story. Once again Nalini Singh comes
through and proves why she's on my auto-buy list."
—*ParaNormal Romance*

Blaze of Memory

"Another incredibly strong entry in the Psy-Changeling series, my very favorite in paranormal romance."
—*Romance Novel TV*

"When it comes to delivering stories that grab you by the
throat and don't let go, Singh is in a class by herself!"
—*RT Book Reviews* (Top Pick)

"Singh has really run with her Psy-Changeling world . . . A
standout series among the paranormal romance on the mar-
ket today." —*Fresh Fiction*

Branded by Fire

"Sexy, intense, and riveting, this book was also deeply satisfying. I couldn't put it down." —*Dear Author*

"A superb addition to a winning series."
—*The Book Smugglers*

"An amazingly talented writer . . . She grabs the reader and
doesn't let go until the very end and leaves them begging
for more . . . I give *Branded by Fire* and Nalini an enthusi-
astic 5 hearts." —*Night Owl Reviews*

continued . . .

Hostage to Pleasure

"Singh is on the fast track to becoming a genre giant!"
—*RT Book Reviews* (Top Pick)

"Nalini Singh has penned another keeper . . . If you want a thrilling read with action, danger, passion, and drama, don't miss Nalini Singh's *Hostage to Pleasure*."
—*Romance Junkies*

"An intriguing world that's sure to keep readers coming back for more." —*Darque Reviews*

Mine to Possess

"Fierce . . . Paranormal romance at its best."
—*Publishers Weekly*

"With its intense characters, story line, and scenery, *Mine to Possess* is quite a read. It showcases Singh's talent and shows her to be a writer that will no doubt shine for some time." —*Romance Reader at Heart*

"If you've been looking for a book that will entice and entrance, look no further. The very talented Nalini Singh has yet again proven that her books are gems, true treasures that are intriguing, multifaceted creations that just get better and better . . . Don't miss *Mine to Possess*!"
—*Romance Reviews Today*

Caressed by Ice

"Delivers increasingly inventive worldbuilding, intrigue-filled plotting, and a complicated and satisfying love story—and will leave readers eagerly anticipating the next installment." —*BookLoons*

"The paranormal romance of the year." —*Romance Junkies*

Archangel's Blade

Nalini Singh

BERKLEY SENSATION, NEW YORK

THE BERKLEY PUBLISHING GROUP
Published by the Penguin Group
Penguin Group (USA) LLC
375 Hudson Street, New York, New York 10014

USA • Canada • UK • Ireland • Australia • New Zealand • India • South Africa • China

penguin.com

A Penguin Random House Company

ARCHANGEL'S BLADE

A Berkley Sensation Book / published by arrangement with the author

For information, address: The Berkley Publishing Group,
a division of Penguin Group (USA) LLC,
375 Hudson Street, New York, New York 10014.

ISBN: 978-0-425-24391-6

PUBLISHING HISTORY
Berkley Sensation mass-market edition / September 2011

PRINTED IN THE UNITED STATES OF AMERICA

10 9 8 7 6 5 4 3

Cover art by Tony Mauro.
Hand lettering by Ron Zinn.
Cover design by George Long.
Interior text design by Kristin del Rosario.

*Writing this book was a wonderful journey,
made more so by the amazing people around me.
Thank you, to each and every one of you.*

Before Isis

"*Papa! Papa!*"

"*Oomph, Misha.*" *Catching his son's excited form as the little boy came running down the rough country drive, he settled Misha on his arm—browned, scarred, and muscled from working the fields—and said, "What has your mama been feeding you?"*

A giggling laugh, his son secure in the knowledge that his father wouldn't drop him. "Did you bring me a sweet?"

"I was hungry on the way home," he teased. "I'm afraid I ate it."

Misha's brow furrowed, his dark eyes intent . . . and then he laughed again, a huge and deep laugh for such a small boy. "Papa!" He began to look in his father's shirt pocket, gave a triumphant cry when he found the small wrapped package.

Smiling at his son's joy, he looked up and saw her in the doorway. His wife. With their new daughter in her arms. His heart twisted into a knot that was almost painful. Sometimes, he thought he should be ashamed to love his wife and children so much, until the days when he went away to the markets were a rare anguish . . . but he could not bring himself to believe it.

When other men complained about their wives, he simply smiled and thought of the woman with the slanting eyes and wide mouth who waited for him. Ingrede hated her mouth, wanted a little bow like the wife of their neighbor across the plain, but he loved her smile, loved the crooked tooth in the front, and the way she began to lisp when he talked her into too much of the white fire brewed by the same neighbor's son.

Now, setting down his bag on the doorstep, he cupped her cheek with his hand. "Hello, wife."

"I missed you, Dmitri."

1

Crouching on the concrete pier lit only by the dull yellow glow of a flickering streetlight several feet away, Dmitri tilted the severed head toward him with a grip in the dead male's damp hair, not bothering with gloves. Elena, he thought, would not have approved of the breach in proper forensic protocol, but the hunter was currently in Japan and wouldn't return to the city for three more days.

The victim's head had been separated from his—as yet undiscovered—body with hacking slices, the weapon possibly some kind of a small ax. Not a neat job, but it had gotten things done. The skin, which appeared to have been either pink or white in life, was bloated and soft with water, but the river hadn't had time to degrade it into slime.

"I was hoping," he said to the blue-winged angel who stood on the other side of the grisly find, "for a quiet few weeks." The reappearance of the archangel Caliane, thought dead for over a millennium, had rocked both the angels and the vampire population. The mortals, too, felt something, but they had no true knowledge of the staggering change in the power structure of the Cadre of Ten, the archangels who ruled the world.

Because Caliane wasn't simply old, she was an Ancient.

"Quiet would bore you," Illium said, playing a thin silver blade in and around his fingers. Having preceded Raphael and Elena home from Japan the previous day, he looked none the worse for wear after having been kidnapped and caught in the middle of a battle between archangels.

Dmitri felt his lips curve. Unfortunately, the angel with his wings of silver-kissed blue and eyes of gold was right. Dmitri hadn't yet succumbed to the ennui that affected so many of the immortals for the simple reason that he never stayed still. Of course, some would say he was leaning too far in the other direction—in the company of those who lived only for the piercing pleasure of blood and pain, every other sensation having grown dull.

The thought should've concerned him. That it didn't . . . *that* concerned him. But his inexorable descent into the seductive ruby red darkness had nothing to do with the current situation. "He has nascent fangs." The small, immature canines appeared almost translucent. "But he's not one of ours." Dmitri knew the name and face of every vampire living in and around New York. "Neither does he fit the description of any of the Made who've gone missing across the wider territory."

Illium balanced his blade on a fingertip, the yellow glow from the streetlight reflecting off it in an unexpected spark of color before he began to play it through his fingers once more. "He could've belonged to someone else, tried to escape his Contract, run into trouble."

Since there were always idiots who tried to get out of their side of the deal—a hundred years of service to the angels in exchange for the gift of near-immortality—that was highly possible. Though why a vampire would come to New York when it was home to an archangel, and a powerful Guild of hunters dedicated to retrieving those who decided to run, wasn't as explicable.

"Family ties," Illium said, as if he'd read Dmitri's thoughts. "Vampires that young tend to stay connected to their mortal roots."

Dmitri thought of the broken burned-out shell of a house he'd visited day after day, night after night, until so many years had passed that there was no longer any sign of the small cottage that once stood there. Only the land, carpeted with wildflowers, remained, and it was Dmitri's, would always be Dmitri's. "We've been working together too long, Bluebell," he said, his mind on that windswept plain where he had once danced a laughing woman in his arms while a bright-eyed boy clapped his hands.

"I keep saying that," Illium responded, "but Raphael refuses to get rid of you." That silver blade flashed faster and faster. "What do you think of the ink?"

Rising to his feet, Dmitri tilted the head to the other side. The tattoo high on the dead male's left cheekbone—black marks reminiscent of letters in the Cyrillic alphabet intertwined with three scrolling sentences in what might've been Aramaic—was both intricate and unusual . . . and yet something about it nagged at Dmitri.

He'd seen it before, or something similar, but he'd been alive almost a millennium and the memory was less than a shadow. "It should make him easier to identify." Light glinted off those small fangs. And he realized what he'd overlooked at first glance. "If his fangs aren't mature, he should've still been in isolation."

The first few months after their Making, vampires were scrabbling creatures, little more than animals, as the toxin that turned mortal to vampire worked its way into their cells. Many chose to navigate the conversion in an induced coma, except for certain necessary periods of wakefulness. Dmitri had spent the months after his violent Making locked in iron chains on a cold stone floor. He remembered little of that time beyond the ice of the stone below his naked body; the rigid grasp of the manacles around his neck, his wrists, his ankles.

But what came after he woke as an almost-immortal . . . that he would never forget, not even if he lived to be ten thousand years old.

Wild blue across his vision, the flickering yellow light turning the glimmering threads of silver in Illium's feathers to pewter. "The Guild has good databases," the angel said, closing his wings and slipping away the knife at the same time.

"Yes." Dmitri had ways to access those databases without Guild cooperation, had done so on many a previous occasion, but it might be a good move to loop the hunters into this case so they knew to alert him to any similar incidents—because the instincts honed by close to a thousand years of bloody survival said he needed to handle this himself, not pass it on to the Guild. "Where's the bag?"

When Illium produced a black garbage bag, he raised an eyebrow. "I'd have thought Elena would have taught you something by now."

The angel gave him an unexpectedly solemn look out of those golden eyes tipped with black lashes dipped in blue, an echo of his hair. "Do you think I will fall again, Dmitri?" Memory in his voice, whispers of pain. "Lose my wings?"

Dmitri was unsurprised at the question. Illium wasn't one of Raphael's Seven, the angels and vampires who had pledged their lives to the archangel, because he was anything less than piercingly intelligent. Now he met that extraordinary gaze. "You look at her in a way no man should look at a woman who belongs to an archangel." Illium had a weakness for mortals, and while Elena was now an angel, she had a vulnerable human heart, was mortal in her thinking.

The blue-winged angel said nothing as Dmitri put the head inside the plastic bag. There was no other evidence here for anyone to collect—the head had floated up on the Hudson, been spotted and retrieved by Illium as he flew over the river a mere fraction of a moment before the last rays of the sun were consumed by the night, could've come from anywhere.

"She compels me," the other male admitted at last. "But she is the Sire's, and I would guard that relationship with my life." Quiet, passionate, absolute.

Dmitri could have let it go at that, but there was more at stake here than a dangerous attraction. "It's not betrayal I'm worried about. It's you."

Illium's hair swept across his face in a capricious wind before settling. "In Amanat," he said, speaking of the lost city newly arisen, "Elena said she needed me to protect her against you." A faint smile. "It was a tease, but it does her no harm to have someone in her corner."

Dmitri didn't dispute Illium's implied assessment of his own feelings toward the Guild Hunter who was Raphael's chosen consort. "You're convinced she saved his life when Lijuan attacked?" Illium's report seemed implausible, and yet

Raphael himself had confirmed some of it when the archangel contacted Dmitri soon after Caliane's reawakening.

"Only Raphael knows the truth, but I know what I saw," Illium said, his face strained with remembrance. "He was dying, and then he lived—and the flame in his hands was colored in shades of dawn."

The same soft colors that lingered on part of Elena's wings.

Dmitri remained leery. Elena was the weakest of angels, her mortal heart nowhere near strong enough to survive the world of the archangels. "She's become a permanent chink in his armor." As Raphael's second, Dmitri was never going to accept that, though he had vowed to protect her and would carry that vow through to the very end, no matter what the cost.

"Have you never had a woman create such a chink in your armor?" One of Illium's feathers fell toward the ground but was whipped away and over the water before it could touch the unforgiving concrete. "In all the years I've known you, never have you had a lover on whom you placed a true claim."

"I will watch the roads for you, Dmitri."

Illium was just over five hundred years old to Dmitri's near thousand. He didn't know anything of what had gone on before—Raphael alone knew. "No," Dmitri said and it was a lie he told with centuries of expertise. "Weakness gets a man killed."

Illium blew out a breath as they reached the flame red Ferrari the angel coveted but couldn't drive because of his wings, and said, "Do not lose your humanity, Dmitri. It's what makes you." He flared out those wings of impossible beauty and rose into the air with a grace and strength that foretold what he might one day become.

Watching the angel fly up into the star-studded skies above a Manhattan stretching awake for the dark beat of night, until he was a sweeping shadow against the glittering black, Dmitri's lips curved into a grim smile. "I lost my humanity a long time ago, Bluebell."

Honor was in the subterranean depths of Guild Academy's main building, peering at an illuminated fourteenth-century text to do with one Amadeus Berg, legendary hunter and explorer, when her cell phone rang. Jumping up at the abrupt burst of sound, she grabbed it from where she'd placed it on the table beside her keys. "Sara?" she said, having recognized the number flashing on the screen as that of the Guild Director's personal cell phone.

"Honor." Crisp. No nonsense. Sara. "Where are you?"

"Rare books section of the Academy library." Dimly lit in deference to the age of the books stored here, and kept at a precise ambient temperature, it had become a refuge, a place few ventured.

"Good. You're not too far." The sound of papers rustling. "Tower needs a consult and you're particularly well qualified. When you—"

Honor didn't hear the rest of the director's words because her ears crashed with a thundering rush of blood, her face heating until it felt as if her skin would peel off from the burn, leaving her flesh exposed to the cruel air. "Sara," she blurted out, fingers clenching on the edge of the desk, the bone showing white against skin that had once been a light brown touched by sunshine but was now dull, pasty, "you know I can't." Her terror was greater than any pitiful surviving shred of pride.

"Yes, you can." Sara's tone was gentle but firm. "I won't allow you to bury yourself at the Academy forever."

Her hand squeezed the phone, her heart racing so fast and jagged it hurt. "And if I want to be buried?" she asked, finding the will to fight in the same bone-crushing fear that had sweat beading along her spine.

"Then I'd have to get tough and remind you that you are still under contract as an active hunter."

Honor's knees collapsed, crumpling her into a chair. The Guild was the only home she knew, her fellow hunters her family. "I'm an instructor." It was a last-ditch attempt to claw her way out of this.

"No, you're not." A denunciation no less ruthless for being soft voiced. "You haven't taught a single class in the months you've been there."

"I'll—"

"*Honor.*" A single, final word.

She fisted her hand on the desk, staring unseeing at the

haunting blues and passionate reds of the illuminated manuscript she'd dropped with a shocking lack of care on the polished wood. "Tell me the details."

Sara blew out a breath. "Part of me wants to wrap you in cotton wool and keep you safe and warm where nothing can hurt you," she said with a fierceness that betrayed the generous heart beneath that tough exterior, "but the other part of me knows I'd be helping to cripple you and I refuse to do that."

Honor flinched. Not because the words were harsh, but because they were true. She wasn't whole, hadn't been whole for the past ten months. "I don't know if there's enough of me left to scrape up, Sara." Sometimes, she wasn't sure she wasn't still in that filthy pit stained with blood, sweat, and . . . other bodily fluids, that her current life wasn't an illusion created by a fragmented mind.

Then Sara spoke and the very razor of her words was a welcome reinforcement that this was the truth. Because surely if she'd dreamed herself into a fantasy to escape the brutal reality, she wouldn't have made the Guild Director so unyielding?

"Ransom and Ashwini didn't risk their lives to pull you out just so you could turn around and give up." A reminder of the hands that had undone her bonds, the arms that had helped haul her up into the painful light. "Find the pieces and stitch yourself back together."

Honor's stomach was a churning mess by now, her free hand clenching and unclenching compulsively. "Is this where I salute and say, yes, sir?" Her words held no bite, because she remembered waking time and time again in the hospital to see Sara sitting beside her, a ferocious, protective force.

"No," the director replied, "you say you're heading up to get your ass into a cab. It's only half past eight so you shouldn't have any problems flagging one down."

Chills crawled up her spine; perspiration shimmered on her upper lip. "Is it an angel I'm meeting?" *Please say yes,* she begged in silent desperation. *Please.*

"No, your meet is with Dmitri."

An image of a man with skin of dark honey and a face that was cruel in its beauty. "He's a vampire." It came out a near soundless whisper. *The* vampire as far as this city, hell, this country was concerned.

Sara didn't say anything for a long time. When she spoke, she asked a single shattering question. "Are you happy, Honor?"

Happy? She didn't know what happiness was anymore. Maybe she'd never known, though she'd thought she'd learned something of it by watching the biological children in the foster homes she'd been shuttled around after she left the orphanage at five. Now . . . "I exist."

"Is it enough?"

She uncurled her fingers with effort, saw the half-moons carved into her palms, red and angry. The Guild had paid for a counselor, would continue to pay for one as long as she needed it. Honor had gone to three sessions before realizing she was never going to speak to the lovely, patient woman who was used to dealing with hunters.

Instead, she tried to stay awake, tried not to remember.

Fangs sinking into her breasts, her inner thighs, her neck, aroused bodies rubbing themselves against her as she whimpered and begged.

She'd been strong at first, determined to survive and slice the bastards to ribbons.

But they'd had her for two months.

A lot could be done to a hunter, to a woman, in two months.

"Honor?" Sara's voice, touched with worry. "Look, I'll get someone else. I shouldn't have pushed you so hard so soon."

A reprieve. But it seemed she had some tiny remnant of pride left after all—because she found her mouth opening, the words coming out without her conscious volition. "I'll be on my way in ten minutes."

It was only after she hung up that she realized she'd picked up a pen at some stage . . . and written Dmitri's name over and over again on the writing pad she'd been using for her notes. Her fingers spasmed, dropping the pen.

It was starting again.

2

The Tower, filled with light, dominated the Manhattan skyline, a cloud-piercing structure from which the archangel Raphael ruled his territory. Honor hitched her laptop bag over her shoulder, after paying the cabbie, and looked up. Their wings outlined against a night sky scattered with diamonds, angel after angel came in to land as others departed. She couldn't discern anything beyond the haunting beauty of their silhouettes, but up close, they were as inhuman as they were stunning—though word in the Guild was, you hadn't seen inhuman until you'd found yourself face-to-face with Raphael.

Given their disparate skills, and therefore assignments, Honor had known Elena only in passing, couldn't imagine how the other hunter handled having an archangel for a lover. Of course, right this minute, she'd rather deal with Raphael than the man she was here to meet . . . the man who was both a nightmare and a dark, seductive dream.

Forcing herself to look away from the illusionary escape of the skies, she gritted her teeth and kept her eyes focused straight ahead as she walked down the drive to the Tower entrance—manned by a vampire dressed in a razor-sharp black suit and wraparound sunglasses. Her throat dried up the second she stopped in front of him, her gut twisted, and for an instant, dark spots filled her vision.

No. No. She would not faint in front of a vampire.

Biting down hard enough on her tongue that tears sprang into her eyes, she resettled the strap of the laptop bag and looked into those sunglasses to see her own face reflected back at her. "I have a meeting with Dmitri." Her voice was soft, but it didn't shake and that was a victory in itself.

The vampire reached out to open the door with a strong hand. "Follow me."

She knew she'd been surrounded by the almost-immortals from the instant she entered the secure zone around the Tower, but it had been easier to lie to herself about that fact when she couldn't see them. That was no longer an option. The one in front of her, his shoulders covered by that perfectly fitted suit jacket, his skin holding a cinnamon tone that spoke of the Indian subcontinent, was simply the closest. Several stood near the corners of the foyer of gold-shot gray marble, sleek predators on guard. Then there was the pretty woman sitting at the reception desk in spite of the late hour.

The receptionist smiled at Honor, her almond-shaped brown eyes holding a welcoming expression. Honor tried to smile back, because the rational part of her knew that all vampires weren't the same, but her face felt as if it had been frozen into place. Instead of forcing it, she concentrated on keeping herself together on the most basic of levels.

"She's nonresponsive. Catatonic."

"Prognosis?"

"No way to tell. I know I shouldn't say this, but part of me thinks she'd be better off dead."

Lying awake staring into the dark in a futile effort to fight the rancid horror that stalked her dreams, Honor had often thought that faceless doctor had been right, but tonight the memory incited another emotion.

Anger.

A dull throbbing thing that caught her by surprise.

I'm alive. I fucking made it. No one has the right to take that from me.

Her astonishment at her own fury was such that it carried her through the elevator ride—trapped in a small cage with a vampire who wore an Armani suit and had an aura of contained power that said he was no ordinary guard.

When the doors opened to deposit them on a floor carpeted in thick black, the gleaming walls painted the same midnight shade, she sucked in a breath. There was a sexual pulse to this place that hummed barely beneath the surface—the roses were lavish and bloodred against the midnight where they stood in their crystal vases atop small, elegant tables of lustrous black, the carpet too lush to be merely serviceable, the paint shimmering with glints of gold.

The artwork along one wall was a fury of red that drew her with its cruel ferocity.

Sensual.

Beautiful.

Lethal.

"This way."

Blood pounding through her veins in a way she knew wasn't safe in the company of the Made, she followed two steps behind her guide—so she'd have warning if he swiveled, went for her throat. Her gun was tucked into a shoulder holster concealed under the faded gray of her favorite sweatshirt, her knife in a sheath openly on her thigh, but she had two more hidden in sheaths strapped to her arms. It wouldn't be enough, not against a vampire who instinct and experience told her had to be over two hundred, but at least she'd go down fighting.

Stopping in front of an open door, he waved her through before turning back toward the elevator. She took a step inside . . . and froze.

Dmitri was standing on the other side of a heavy glass desk, the Manhattan skyline glittering at his back, his head bent, strands of silken black hair caressing his forehead as he scanned the piece of paper in his hand. Her mind rolled back. Before . . . *before* . . . she'd been fascinated by this one vampire, though she'd only ever seen him from a distance or on the television screen. She'd even made a scrapbook of his movements—to the point that she'd started to feel like a disturbed stalker and burned the whole thing.

It hadn't gotten rid of the strange, irrational compulsion she'd felt toward him as long as she could remember. Nothing had gotten rid of it . . . until the dank, filthy basement and the terror. That had numbed everything, but now she wondered if she hadn't always been slightly unhinged, she'd been so obsessed by a stranger who was whispered to have a penchant for sensual cruelty, pleasure cut with pain.

Then he looked up.

And she stopped breathing.

Dmitri saw the woman in the doorway in a kaleidoscope of images. Soft ebony hair clipped at her nape, but promising a wildness of curls. Haunting—*haunted*—eyes of deepest green tilted up at the corners. Pale brown skin that he knew would turn to warm honey in the sun. "Born in Hawaii?" he asked, and it was a strange question to ask a hunter who'd come to do a consult.

She blinked, long lashes momentarily shielding those eyes that spoke of distant forests and hidden gemstones. "No. In a nowhere town far from the ocean."

He found himself circling the glass and steel of his desk to head toward her. For an instant, he thought she would stumble backward and out into the corridor, but then she stiffened her spine, held her position. He was aware of the fear—sharp and acrid—skittering behind her eyes, but still he shifted around her to push the door shut.

Allowing her to leave wasn't an option.

When he stepped back to face her once more, the ugly ripple of fear had been brought under rigid control, but her breathing was jerky, her gaze skating away from his when he tried to capture it. "What's your name?"

"Honor."

Honor. He tasted the name, decided it fit. "Hunter-born?"

A shake of her head.

Not surprising. Elena had likely warned the Guild Director about his ability to use tendrils of exquisite scent to seduce and lure those hunters who were born with the bloodhound capability to scent-track vampires. Sara would hardly send him fresh prey. But this woman, this Honor . . . he wanted to use luscious strokes of scent on her until she was flushed and limp, her arousal an unmistakable musk against his senses.

It was instinct to ensure she wasn't lying to him—he

swirled out a drugging whisper of champagne and desire molten as gold, orchids under moonlight, chocolate-dipped berries kissing a woman's skin. Honor shook her head a little, a barely imperceptible movement that echoed the frown lines on her forehead.

So, not strong enough to identify herself, or be identified by the Guild as hunter-born, but enough that she had a slight susceptibility to the scent lure. He was unsurprised by the discovery, having met more than one like her in the centuries since he'd developed the talent—they seemed drawn to the Guild, regardless of the fact that they carried only the merest hint of the hunting bloodline. That, of course, meant he couldn't seduce Honor as easily as he could a true hunter-born . . . but scent wasn't the sole weapon in his arsenal when it came to sex.

Scanning his eyes over her again, he noted the jagged pulse in her neck, but it was the skin covering the spot that held his attention. "Whoever you allowed to feed from you," he said in a smooth murmur he was well aware held a caressing stroke of menace, "wasn't very tidy." Her scars denoted a vampire who'd torn and ravaged.

Her hand clenched on the handle of the laptop bag she'd shrugged off her shoulder. "That's none of your business."

Surprised she'd found the guts to say that to him in spite of the terror that rippled through her, raw and bleeding, he raised an eyebrow. "Yes, it is." He'd bedded many a beautiful woman, left some sobbing with pleasure, others from a sensual viciousness that had taught them to never again attempt to play him. Honor wasn't beautiful. There was too much fear in her. Dmitri might like a little pain in bed, but in most cases, he preferred his partners enjoy it, too.

This broken hunter, with her terror that turned the air caustic, would quiver and shatter like fractured glass with the first touch of his mouth. And still he wanted to run his fingers over that skin meant to be gilded by the sun, to trace the lush curves of her lips, the long line of her neck, the compulsion strong enough that it was a warning. The last time he'd allowed his cock to overrule his head, he'd almost ended up an archangel's pet assassin.

Turning, he walked around to behind the sleek sprawl of

his desk and picked up the garbage bag sitting on the floor. "I assume you have some experience with tattoos?"

Lines on her forehead, confusion momentarily wiping out the far more distasteful dominant emotion he'd perceived thus far. "No. My specialty is in ancient languages and history."

Clever of the Guild Director. "In that case, tell me everything you can about this ink." Using gloves this time, he pulled out the head and set it on the bag, the stump sticking to the plastic with a sucking sound.

The hunter stumbled backward, her eyes locked on the gruesome evidence of violence. When she jerked her gaze back to him, he saw a grim fury on that face that had already shown itself to be so expressive, he wondered if she'd ever won a poker game in her life. "You think that's funny?"

"No." The truth. "Seemed no point in putting him in the freezer when you were on your way."

It was such an inhuman thing to say that Honor had to take a minute, reset her mental parameters. Because the fact was, regardless of his dark masculine beauty and modern speech, she wasn't facing a human. Not even close. "How old are you?" The media speculations ran from four to six hundred, but at that instant, she knew they were wrong. *Very* wrong.

A faint smile that made the hairs rise on the back of her neck. "Old enough to scare you."

Yes. She'd been trapped with vampires who had wanted only to hurt her, bore the scars of their abuse even now, but never had she been in the presence of someone who chilled her blood with his mere presence. Yet though he was known to be a powerful son of a bitch, ruthless as a gleaming edge, Dmitri functioned fine in the human world. Which meant he could mask the lethal truth when he wanted to, but this was who he was beneath the civilized black on black of his suit—a man who looked at a severed head the same way he might a bowling ball.

Keeping that knowledge in mind, she put her laptop bag down on the glass of his desk, since there were no chairs on this side, and forced herself to lean closer to the decapitated head. "He's been in water?" The skin was soaked and pulpy, gone a wrinkled white—an obscene reminder of happy hours spent in the bath.

"Hudson."

"He needs to be looked at by a proper forensic team," she muttered, trying to see the full lines of the tattoo. "I need access to lab equipment so I can—"

Gloved hands in her vision, shoving the head back into the garbage bag. "Follow me, little rabbit."

Heat burned her gut, seared her veins to fill her face, but she grabbed her laptop and did as ordered. His back was solid and strong in front of her, his hair gleaming a rich, evocative black under the lights. When she didn't step up beside him, he shot her an amused look over his shoulder—except the laughter didn't reach those watchful eyes that whispered of ages long gone. "Ah, an old-fashioned woman."

"What?" It was taking all of her concentration to breathe, her body close to adrenaline overload.

"You obviously believe in walking three steps behind a man."

It was beyond tempting to reach for a blade. Or maybe her gun.

Smiling, as if he'd read her thoughts, he strode to an elevator different from the one she'd ridden up in and, ripping off one of the gloves, placed his palm on the scanner. The pad glowed green for a second before the doors opened and he waved her in. She refused to enter. Maybe he was so old that she didn't have a hope in hell of ever defeating him should he come after her—but logic had no chance against the primal animal within, the one who knew the monsters could hurt you easier if you couldn't see them coming.

"And here I was being courteous," he drawled, stepping inside the steel cage and waiting for her to enter before pressing something on the electronic pad to one side.

The elevator dropped at a speed that had her stomach jumping into her mouth, but that didn't scare her. It was the creature in the elevator with her who did that. "Stop it," she said when he continued to stare at her with those eyes of darkest brown. Yes, she'd been fascinated by him once, but that had been from a distance.

Up close, she was very aware it wasn't safe to be alone with him. He was, she thought, capable of amusing himself by tearing her to shreds with nothing but the exquisite silk of his voice . . . before he really began to hurt her.

"The boyfriend," he murmured, eyes dipping to her neck again, "obviously didn't take the care with you he should have."

Hysterical laughter threatened to bubble out of her, but she brazened it out. He had to have tasted her fear, but she'd give him nothing else. "Never left marks of your own, Dmitri?"

He leaned against the wall. "Any marks I leave are very much on purpose." Sensual tone, provocative words, but there was something hard in his gaze as he continued to stare at the ravaged flesh of her neck.

The scar wasn't that bad—just looked like a vampire had gotten a little carried away while feeding. That had been at the end. At the start, they'd tried to keep her as undamaged as possible so she could continue to provide them with pleasure. Those ones, the "civilized" vamps who had been almost delicate about feeding while she was naked and blindfolded, their hands stroking over her breasts, between her thighs, had been the most horrifying. And they were *still out there*.

A wash of cooler air, the doors opening.

Having never taken her eyes off Dmitri, even as her memories threatened to suck her under, she stepped out beside him. Her attention was caught by the glass walls on either side, beyond which lay offices, computers . . . and state-of-the-art labs. "I've never heard of all this being down here."

Dmitri pushed through into a lab. "New addition. Don't talk about it or I'll have to pay you a visit one quiet midnight while you're tucked up nice and tight in your bed."

Every muscle in her body went tight at that almost lazy comment. "I don't make it a habit to gossip."

"Here." He deposited the rubbish bag and its contents on a steel table. The horrific nature of his task should have eroded the allure of sex he wore like second skin—if you liked your sex kissed by blood and pain. It didn't. He remained sophisticated and sexy and very much a creature she did not want in her bedroom any time of day or night.

His lips, the lower one just full enough to tempt a woman with fantasies of sin, curved as if he'd read her thoughts. "Do you need help to peel off the skin?"

3

"No." Her reaction upstairs had been incited by shock at his callousness—she didn't have a problem working with the grisly find on her own. "I'll take the best photographs I can, given the condition of the victim, and I'll mostly work off them. But I want to use the microscope on the tattoo itself, too, make sure I don't miss any fine details."

More at ease now, she slid out the slim digital camera she'd tucked into the side pocket of her laptop bag. "A pathologist should examine the head before we consider removing the skin." She clicked on the camera. "Have you got someone asking around the tattoo parlors?" If they lucked out, she might have a clean photograph to work from.

"Yes." Snapping on a glove to replace the one he'd removed, he pulled the head out of the bag and stretched the skin tight over the man's cheekbone as she took a number of high-resolution shots from different angles. "That should do for now." As he put the head down onto a tray and got rid of the trash bag, she set up her laptop and transferred the photos onto the hard drive.

Her body alert to his every small movement, she was aware of Dmitri placing the head in the freezer, stripping off his gloves, and cleaning his hands. So when he appeared beside her chair without warning, the emotion he awakened was so bone-chilling, so vicious, parts of her mind just shut down. And when he lifted her hair off her neck to touch the sensitive skin of her nape, she—

Noise. A shattering metallic crash. Words.

The next thing she knew, she was standing several feet from Dmitri, a tall stool with legs of beaten steel lying on its side between them. A line of blood marked his cheek, but his eyes were focused on the door at her back. "Out!"

Only when the door shut did she realize that someone had attempted to intervene. Sweat dampened her palms, beaded on her spine. *Remember,* she told herself, *remember.* But the time was gone, a black spot drenched in the panic that was a vile taste on her tongue. "I hit you."

Raising his hand, he rubbed a finger on his cheek, came away with a dark red slick on his fingertip. "Something about me seems to make women want to use knives."

Oh, God. She looked down, realized she was gripping a blade in her hand, the tip wet. "I don't suppose you'll accept an apology." It came out calm, her mind so shocked it was numb.

Sliding his hands into his pockets, Dmitri said, "No, but you can pay for your crimes later. Right now, I need what you can give me on this."

"I want to consult some of the texts at the Academy library," she said, forcing her brain into gear, though her hand refused to release the knife she'd apparently pulled from the sheath on her thigh.

"Fine. But remember, little rabbit, not a word to anyone." He moved close enough that the dark heat of him lapped against her in a quiet threat that made her glad for the blade. "I am not a nice man when I'm angry."

She held her position, a ragged attempt to erase the humiliation of the panic attack. "I'm fairly certain you're not a nice man at all."

His answer was a slow smile that whispered of silk sheets, erotic whispers, and sweat-damp skin. The unhidden intent of it had her heart slamming hard against her ribs. "No," she said, voice raw.

"A challenge." He wasn't touching her and yet she felt caressed by a thousand ropes of fur, soft and lush and unmistakably sexual. "I accept."

Dmitri made the call an hour later, having had to deal with another matter in the interim. "Sara," he said when the Guild Director answered her cell.

"Dmitri." A cool greeting. "What do you need?"

"To know why the hunter you sent me just sliced my face." The wound had already healed, but it made the perfect opening gambit.

Sara sucked in a breath. "If you've done something to her, I swear to God I will get my crossbow and pin you to the side of the fucking Tower."

Dmitri liked Sara. "She's being chauffeured home as we speak." The blood debt was between him and Honor; it would be settled in private. "I gave her a human driver."

Sara muttered something under her breath. "She's the best person for the task."

He stared out at the jewel-bright skyline of Manhattan. "Who did that to her neck?" Cold burned through his veins, a vicious response to the scars of a woman he didn't know and who would simply be another bedmate for so long as she amused him. Because while her resistance was intriguing, would make for an interesting diversion, he had no doubts that she would end up in his bed—and she'd crawl into it with pleasure.

Then Sara spoke, and the cold turned frigid. "The same bastards who kept her chained up in a basement for two months." It was a brutal summary. "She was barely alive when we found her. They'd carried on with their sick games even though three of her ribs were broken and she was bleeding and feverish from wounds that—" Sara bit off her words, her rage a finely honed edge, but Dmitri didn't need anything more.

He remembered the incident. The Guild had requested Tower assistance, been granted it at once. However, involved in the reconstruction of a Manhattan that had been badly damaged by the battle between Uram and Raphael—and, more important, focused on holding Raphael's territory while the archangel spent the majority of his time in the Refuge, waiting for his sleeping consort to wake—Dmitri hadn't taken personal control of the investigation. That was about to change. "Status of her attackers?"

"Ransom and Ashwini killed two of the four they found at the scene. The other two were turned over to the Tower, but they were hired muscle at best, allowed to—" A ragged breath. "The ones behind this were smarter. They left no forensic clues and Honor was always blindfolded. We'll get them." Icy words. "We always do."

Ending the call on that, Dmitri looked out at a city that wouldn't yet slumber for hours. Honor's attackers would all die. That had never been in question. The only difference was, now that he'd felt her blade against his skin, now that he'd tasted the screaming depth of her fear, he'd take exquisite pleasure in personally cutting out vital organs from their bodies before he left them to heal in some hole . . . and then he'd do it over again.

His conscience wasn't the least bothered by the idea of such sadistic torture.

"You shouldn't have been so stubborn, Dmitri." A slender female hand stroking down his naked body to close over his flaccid cock.

Rage bloomed in those eyes of a bright, mocking bronze.

Shifting her hold to his balls, she squeezed until he came close to blacking out, his muscles straining against the chains that spread-eagled his standing body in the center of the cold, dark room at the bottom of the keep. The position left every part of him exposed to her and those she commanded to do her bidding.

As dark spots lingered at the edges of his vision, she kissed him, her fingernails digging into his jaw and her wings spreading out at her back, white as snow but for the wash of shimmering crimson over her primaries. "You will love me."

The first blow came a second later, as she continued to kiss him. His back was ground meat by the time she halted the punishment, the scent of blood ripe and thick in the air.

Lips against his ear, silk against his skin. "Do you love me now, Dmitri?"

A beep.

Turning, he shut down a memory that hadn't come to the fore for centuries upon centuries, and answered the internal line. "Yes?"

"Sir, you asked to be notified if Holly Chang changed her pattern of behavior."

Forty minutes later, Dmitri stood outside the small suburban home in New Jersey where Holly Chang lived with her boyfriend, David. Isolated from its neighbors by a generous yard and high fences, it was nothing she could've afforded if the Tower hadn't stepped in and ordered her to relocate—from an apartment block where she'd been dangerously close to too many mortals.

The human woman had just turned twenty-three when she'd been abducted off the street by an insane archangel. She'd seen her friends butchered, their limbs amputated before the pieces were put back together in a macabre jigsaw puzzle; when Elena tracked her down she was naked and covered in the rust red of their blood.

Holly had survived the horror, but she hadn't come out of it the same as when she went in. Quite aside from the fact that there was some question as to her sanity, Uram had either fed her his blood or deliberately injected her with some of the toxin that had fueled his murderous rampage. They didn't know for certain, because Holly's memories of those events were clouded to uselessness by the blinding fear that had turned her mute for days after she was found. What they did know was that the young woman was . . . changing.

"Remain by the gate," he said to the vampire who had called him, before walking out of the shadows and up the drive to the house lit only by the flickering glow of a television in the front room.

Holly, petite and outwardly delicate, opened the door for him before he reached it. Blood stained her long-sleeved white shirt, rimmed her mouth. Raising her hand, she wiped the back of it over her lips, smearing the liquid. "Have you come to clean up the mess, Dmitri?" In those angry slanted eyes, he saw the stark knowledge that he would be the death that came for her if she lost the battle against whatever it was Uram had done to her. "It was a neighbor's kid. Tasted sweet."

"Careless of you to hunt so close to home." Wrenching her forward with a hand on her left wrist, he shoved up the sleeve of her shirt before she could stop him. The bandage around her upper arm was wrapped tight. "I'm a vampire, Holly," he murmured, reaching up to wipe away a smeared droplet of blood at the corner of her mouth with his thumb. "I know when the blood on you is your own."

She hissed at him, pulling away her arm to stalk back into the house. Stepping inside, he closed the door at his back. He'd been here many times, knew the layout, but rather than following her to the kitchen where he could hear her washing off the blood on her mouth, he turned off the television and checked to make sure they were alone in the house.

When he did finally enter the kitchen, now lit by a bright bulb, it was to see Holly wiping her face on a dish towel, though she hadn't changed out of the bloodstained shirt. "Death by Dmitri," he said, leaning against the doorjamb with a laziness that would've fooled no one who knew him. "Is that what you were aiming for?"

A glare from eyes that had once been light brown, but were now ringed with a vivid green that was growing ever deeper into the irises. The same gleaming shade as Uram's eyes . . . but not as dark as those of the hunter who'd used a knife on him earlier tonight. Honor's gaze held the mystery of forbidden depths, of haunting secrets whispered deep in the night. Holly's, by contrast, held only clawing anger and an overwhelming self-hatred.

"Isn't that your job?" she asked. "To execute me if I prove a monster?"

"We're all monsters, Holly." Folding his arms, he watched as she began to pace up and down the length of the small kitchen. "It's just a case of how far you push it."

Back and forth. Back and forth. Hands through her hair, jagged shakes. Again. "David left me," she blurted out at last. "Couldn't take the fact that he found me awake and staring at him five nights in a row, my eyes glowing." A giggling laugh that failed to hide a terrible pain that he knew had cracked her heart open. "I wasn't looking at his face."

"Have you been feeding?" Holly had a limited need for blood and Dmitri had made certain she'd been supplied with it.

Her response was to kick the fridge so hard she dented the polished white surface. "Dead blood! Who wants it? I think I'll go for a nice, soft neck as soon as I can escape the fucking minders."

Stepping into the kitchen proper, Dmitri walked around to grip her hands, still her pacing. Then he lifted his wrist to her mouth. "Feed." His blood was potent, would fulfill any need she had.

As he'd known she would, she pulled away and slid down to sit, to *hide*, in a corner of the kitchen, arms locked around her knees and head lowered as she rocked her body. Because in spite of her words, Holly didn't want to touch a human donor, didn't want to believe she'd changed on such a fundamental level. She wanted to be the girl she'd been before Uram—the one who'd just secured a coveted position at a fashion house, who'd loved fabric and design, and who'd laughed with her girlfriends as they walked to the movies to catch the late show.

None of those friends had made it.

Turning to the fridge, he retrieved one of the bags of blood he had delivered on a regular basis and poured it into a glass before going to crouch down beside her. He pushed back a wing of glossy black hair currently streaked with cotton candy–colored highlights and said, "Drink." Nothing else was necessary—Holly knew he wouldn't leave until the glass was empty.

Strange, hate-filled eyes. "I want to kill you. Every time you walk through that door, I want to pick up a machete and hack your head off." She gulped down the blood and slammed the empty glass on the floor so hard it cracked along one side.

Using a tissue to wipe her mouth, he threw it in the trash before standing up to lean against a cabinet opposite her. "A woman cut my face today," he told her. "Not with a machete but a throwing blade."

Holly's eyes skimmed over his unmarked skin. "Bullshit."

"I'm fairly certain she was going for the jugular but I was too fast." And Honor had moved with far more grace than he'd have believed her capable of before that little demonstration.

The woman was trained in some kind of martial art, trained at a level that meant she was no helpless victim. And yet she had been made one.

"Too bad she missed," Holly muttered . . . before asking the question that had lingered in the air since the second he walked into the house. "Why won't you let me die, Dmitri?" Her words were a plea.

He wasn't certain why he hadn't killed her the instant she began to show signs of a lethal change, and so he didn't answer her. Instead, crouching back down, he tipped up her face with his fingers under her chin. "If it comes down to an execution, Holly," he murmured, "you'll never see me coming." Quick and fast, that was how it would be—he would not have her go into the final goodnight drowning in fear.

She died afraid, Dmitri. If only you'd given me what I asked for, she would still be alive." A sigh, elegant fingers brushing over his cheekbone as he hung broken from iron cuffs that had worn grooves into his skin. "Do you want the same for Misha?"

"Don't call me that." Holly's harsh voice fracturing the crushing memory from the painful dawn of his existence. "Holly died in that warehouse. Some*thing* else walked out."

It was an attempt to erase herself, and that he would not allow—but it would do no harm to permit her to establish a line between her past and the present. Perhaps then, she would finally begin to live this new life. "What would you have me call you?"

"How about Uram?" A bitter question. "He doesn't need the name anymore, after all."

"No." He wouldn't let her harm herself in such a way, her name itself a poisonous shroud. "Choose again."

She thumped her fisted hand against his chest, but her anger was permeated with pain and he knew she wouldn't fight him in this. "Sorrow," she whispered after a long silence. "Call me Sorrow."

No joyful name that, no hopeful one, but he would give her this one choice when she'd had so many others stolen from her. "Sorrow, then." Leaning forward he pressed his lips to her forehead, her bangs blades of silk against his lips, her bones fine, fragile, so vulnerable under his hands.

In that instant, he knew why he hadn't killed her yet. Age notwithstanding, she was a child to him. A dangerous child, but a child nonetheless, scared and trying so hard to hide it. And the murder of a child . . . it left a scar on a man's soul that could never, ever be erased.

4

Arriving back at Guild Academy after midnight, Honor put her laptop bag down on the small table tucked in beside the wardrobe in her quarters. The bed took up most of the remaining space. The room was adequate, and that was it—most hunters only used the quarters when they needed to do a short, intense session of instruction at the Academy. Honor had been here since the day they allowed her out of the hospital.

It wasn't because she couldn't afford anything better. Given the fees hunters commanded as a result of the high-risk nature of their work, and the fact that she hadn't really had much downtime in which to spend that money, she'd built up a considerable nest egg before the abduction. None of it had been touched during her convalescence, as the Guild covered the medical costs of all its hunters. Truth was, she could move into a penthouse if that was what she wanted.

It just hadn't seemed worth the effort to move out.

Except tonight, the room was suddenly a cage. How could she have been so numb that she hadn't noticed the claustrophobic confines? The realization of the depth of her apathy was a slap, one that made her head ring—but not enough to settle her sharp response to the walls around her.

Beginning to sweat, she ripped off her sweatshirt and dropped it on the bed, but that did nothing to cool her down.

Water.

A few minutes after that thought passed through her head, she was dressed in a sleek black one-piece swimsuit, a toweling robe around her body. The night owls she ran into on her way to the Academy pool stopped only long enough to say hi before continuing on their way—and she was soon sliding into the pristine blue waters that promised peace.

Stroke, stroke, breathe. Stroke, stroke, breathe.

The rhythm was better than meditating. It took ten lengths, but by the end of it, she was calm. However, the feeling of suffocation struck again the instant she returned to her room—now that she'd noticed its tiny size, she couldn't get it out of her head. And there was no way she'd be able to sleep even if she forced herself to bed. Her nightmares—malevolent, clawing things—were bad enough without adding claustrophobic panic to the mix.

Having showered at the pool, she pulled on fresh clothes and picked up her laptop.

The library was quiet at this time of night, but not deserted. There were a couple of instructors working on research papers, and a hunter who looked like she'd come in from active duty.

A single glance at that shining dark hair, those worn boots, and her lips curved in joyful surprise. "Ashwini?"

The tall, long-legged hunter put down the book she'd been examining and swiveled on her heel. Face cracking into a smile that turned her from beautiful to breathtaking, she gave a "Whoop!" and vaulted over a library table to grab Honor in a tight hug. No sign remained of the knife fight that had left her seriously injured not long ago.

Laughing, Honor hugged her back—Ash was one of the rare few people she'd never had trouble allowing close, even directly after the assault. Perhaps it was because the other hunter was her best friend . . . and perhaps it was because Ashwini was the one who'd ripped off her blindfold and shot off the chains that had held her trapped and helpless, her body a piece of meat for her captors.

"I've got you, Honor—the bastards won't touch you again."

"What are you doing here, you lunatic?" she asked, focusing on the fact that her friends had never given up on her, rather than the putrid miasma of a far more vile memory.

A smacking kiss on her cheek before Ashwini drew back. "I came to see you—you weren't in your quarters so I came here to wait." Glancing around when one of the instructors said "Shh" in a loud voice, she rolled her eyes. "Funny, Demarco. Didn't they call noise control on your last party?"

The rangy hunter, his hair the streaky blond of a man who loved the sun, grinned and pointed a finger. "I *knew* you were there, Ms. Flaming Lying Pants."

"This is a library, people," said the last man in the room, scarred boots on a reading table and a leather-bound book open in front of his face.

Ash and Demarco hooted. Because Ransom was the last person you'd expect to find in a library—except word was, he was shacked up with a librarian. *That*, Honor thought, she'd have to see to believe. Now he put the book down in his lap and leaned back in his chair, arms crossed behind his head. "I'll have you know I'm teaching an advanced course in how to deal with the Wing Brotherhood when necessary."

Ashwini sauntered over to play with Ransom's gorgeous black hair, tugging it out of its usual queue to run it through her fingers. "What conditioner you using, Professor Ransom? I'm thinking of changing brands."

"Fuck you." Said without heat as he glanced at Demarco. "I'm hungry."

The other hunter paused, nodded decisively. "Yeah, me, too."

That was how Honor found herself sitting in an otherwise deserted dining hall with three other hunters, talking shit. It was something she hadn't done for months, even pushing Ash away when her best friend tried to draw her out, and now she couldn't understand why. For the first time since she'd escaped that hellhole where she'd almost died, she felt real, a person, instead of a forgotten shade, a translucent illusion.

Stop lying to yourself, Honor.

She'd felt very much real, very much alive, at the Tower. Chilled by a fear that had left her skin sticky with sweat, and by her deep-rooted compulsion toward a vampire who had looked at her with sex—the dark, screaming kind—in his eyes, but alive nonetheless.

Her hand clenched on the handle of her coffee mug. She'd already eaten a toasted cheese sandwich and a banana, truly hungry for the first time in months—though the Guild nutritionist's stringent eating plan meant she'd slowly returned to a healthy weight over the past half year. She'd tasted none of those things, complied only because it was easier than arguing.

Dmitri's gaze had made it clear he appreciated her curves, that he had no problem with the fact that her natural body shape was too much of an hourglass than was currently fashionable. He would, she thought, take exquisite pleasure in stroking his hands over every inch of a woman's body . . . if he wasn't in the mood to hurt her a little.

"Any of you met Dmitri?" she found herself asking during a lull in the conversation, disturbed by the fact that even knowing beyond any doubt that he'd be no good for her, she couldn't stop her mind's eye from tracing the slightly full curve of his lower lip. A dangerous indulgence, a small madness.

"Yeah." Ransom swallowed the bite of Pop-Tart in his mouth. "When Elena went missing. Cold son of a bitch. Not someone you'd want to run into in a deserted alley."

A challenge. I accept.

It would've been easy to tell herself that he'd been playing with her, amusing himself at her expense . . . except she was fairly certain a man didn't look at a woman with that kind of slumberous heat in his eyes unless he was planning to have her naked and helpless beneath him, her thighs spread wide.

"Hey." Ashwini's voice, pitched low to skate under Demarco and Ransom's conversation. "I heard you were consulting for the Tower. Dmitri?"

"I cut him," she whispered, the memory of the actual act still a black nothingness in her mind.

Ashwini's grin was feral. "Good for you. Bastard probably deserved it."

Staring at her best friend, Honor started to laugh and it was the first time she'd done so since Ash and Ransom carried her out of that filthy pit, bruised and violated and bleeding from so many bite marks torn into her flesh that the doctors had put her into an antiseptic bath, not wanting to miss one of the wounds.

Uninterested in sleep that night, Dmitri was standing on the railingless balcony outside his Tower suite when the night-shadow of wings swept over him and then down.

The angel who landed at his side was both familiar and unwelcome. "Favashi," he said, having expected the visit. The archangel's progress had been tracked since she was spotted an hour out from the Boston coast. "Have you come to lay claim to Raphael's territory while he is in the Far East?"

Favashi's serene face betrayed nothing as she folded back wings of a soft, exquisite cream. "We both know he's stronger than I am, Dmitri. And even were he not, you lead his Seven. I would be a fool to stand against you in battle."

He snorted, though she was right. His strength as a vampire, coupled with his intelligence and experience when it came to combat situations, made it certain that no city would ever fall under his watch. And this city? He'd watched over it since long before it was a jewel coveted by many, would never let it slip into enemy hands.

"So you are here to stroke my ego?" he purred, his tone as deadly as the edge of a scalpel. "Pity that I prefer the hands stroking me not belong to a cold-blooded bitch."

Fire in her eyes, a glimpse of the vicious power that lived behind the mask of a lovely Persian princess, elegant and benevolent. "I am still an archangel, Dmitri." A whip of arrogance in the reminder, but then her lips curved. "I was a fool and this is my reward. Will you never forgive a young woman's ambition?"

Dmitri stared at her, this archangel who had made him believe, for one shimmering moment, that he might crawl out of the abyss and stand in the light once more. With hair of a luxuriant mink brown and eyes of the same lush shade, her skin the creamy gold of Persia, and her body that of a goddess, Favashi was a queen who looked the part.

Men had fought for her, died for her, worshipped her. Women saw in her a grace that was lacking in Michaela, the most beautiful of all the archangels, and so they served her with willing hands and loyal hearts, never understanding that Favashi was as merciless as her brethren in the Cadre. "Ambition," he said, "has its price."

Flaring out her wings, as if to expose them to the night's languid caress, Favashi turned her face toward the diamond-studded nightscape that was Manhattan. "Such a stunning place, but so hard. My land is gentler."

"A man could burn to nothing in your deserts without ever being found." He had no doubts that Favashi had buried many a body beneath those rolling sand dunes. He didn't have a problem with that—he'd buried a few bodies himself. What he did have a problem with was the fact that she'd not only fooled him into believing in her, but that she'd expected to lead him on a leash, her own personal guard dog cum assassin.

Once, so long ago it was another life, Dmitri had been turned into a thing to be used. Never again. "Why are you here?"

"I came to see you." A simple answer, but her voice held a soft, exotic music that turned it into an invitation. "Let the past lie where it belongs. I would court you again."

"No." He captured her wrist as she raised her hand to touch his face, squeezing so hard he'd have fractured a mortal woman's bones. "The last time an angel tried to court me," he whispered, leaning down to speak with his lips brushing her neck, "she ended up in bite-sized pieces I then fed to her hounds." It was he who had courted Favashi before—or at least she'd allowed him to believe he was the one leading the dance. The one good thing that had come out of the experience was that he'd never again make the mistake of believing a woman's sweet lies.

Running his lips along the sensitive edge of her ear, he sucked lightly in the way he knew turned her weak, while rubbing his thumb over the escalating pulse in the wrist he still held. "I watched the dogs feed," he murmured, reaching out to run the fingers of his free hand over the curving arches of her wings in the most intimate of caresses, "and I wished I had taken longer to carve her with the blade."

Favashi ripped away her wrist and stepped back from him. It mattered little—her eyes were dilated, her skin flushed. He smiled, touched his finger very deliberately to the rapid pulse in her neck. "The bed isn't far if you wish to be serviced, my Lady Favashi."

No flinch at the mocking appellation. She was an archangel, after all. But her tone held a concern that might've once fooled him into believing she cared. "You are not who you once were, Dmitri. I would not have a man such as you in my bed."

"Pity. I have so many things I'd enjoy doing to you." None of it would have anything to do with pleasure. "Now," he said, having had enough of games, "tell me the real reason you're here."

A strand of mink-dark hair played across her face before falling as the wind fell. "I spoke the truth." Her face flawless in profile, she watched a group of angels angle in to land on a lower balcony, their wings cupped inward to lessen the speed of their descent. "Raphael and Elijah both have consorts and are stable, unlike the others in the Cadre.

"I have decided it's time to join them—you were the only one who seemed a suitable choice." The cool calculation of an immortal. "Whether or not I would ever trust you in my bed, the invitation stands. Consider how much power you would have at your command as my consort." With that, she flared out wings he'd once caressed as she arched naked above him, and swept off the balcony.

Making a call to ensure she'd be tracked out of the country, Dmitri turned his face into the cool night winds that held strands of the Hudson intertwined with the frenetic beat of this wild, living city of steel and glass and heart. Favashi didn't understand and likely never would. The fact was, Elena was weak, far too weak to be consort to an archangel, and yet Raphael loved her.

While Dmitri, as the leader of Raphael's Seven, could not accept such a weakness, the mortal he'd once been, the one who had loved a woman with a wide mouth and eyes of slanted brown . . . that man understood what it was to love so deeply it was a kind of beautiful madness.

Scorching heat.
   Charred flesh.

Screams.
Words she should understand but couldn't.
Pain, searing, blinding . . . but overwhelmed by anguish.
"No, no, no."

Jerked out of the nightmare by the sound of her own voice, Honor touched her face to find a single tear splashed on her cheek. It startled her. Most of the time when she dreamed of the basement, she woke up rigid with terror, nausea churning in her gut. Sometimes she surfaced enraged, her hand bloodless around a weapon. The one thing she did not do, hadn't done since the rescue, was cry. Not when awake, not when asleep.

Rubbing her sleeve over the wetness to eradicate the evidence of her loss of control, she took a self-conscious look around the library. It lay deserted, and a glance at her watch showed her why—it was five a.m. Ashwini and Demarco had left her and Ransom here sometime after one, and she remembered muttering "Bye" to the other hunter as he, too, went to bed after about an hour.

Now, packing up her laptop and the photocopies she'd made from a number of texts, she headed back to her room. Her small, stifling cell of a room—exhaustion or not, she knew sleep was going to be an impossibility. Figuring Ashwini would be up, since the other hunter had left after being called in for a local hunt, she picked up her cell phone.

"Honor, what do you need?"

"Can you talk?"

"Yeah, just got home after pulling in the idiot vamp."

"Already?" That had to be some kind of a record.

"He had the bright idea to—get this—hide at his mom's. Like that isn't the first place we'd look."

It was at times like this that Honor was forcibly reminded that vampires had once been human. The echoes could take decades to fade . . . though she was sure none remained in Dmitri. "You said something about an apartment being free in your building last time you were here," she said, angry at herself for being unable to stop thinking about the lethal, sensual creature who'd looked at her with eyes full of unhidden intent. "Don't suppose it still is?"

"Nope. Because I put your name down for it."

Honor's butt hit the bed. "You knew."

"It's open plan," Ashwini said, instead of answering the implied question. "Glass everywhere, and while that would be a security hazard lower down, you'll be on the thirty-first floor. I might've sort of picked the lock on your storage unit and moved all your stuff in last week, but if you tell anyone, I'll say the gremlins did it."

At any other time, with any other person, Honor would've been angry, but this was Ash, who had understood that Honor needed to escape before she had herself. "I owe you one."

"Want me to come pick you up? I still have the car I signed out for the hunt."

Honor glanced around her room. "Give me a couple of hours to pack up here." She didn't have much, but it was an unspoken rule that the bed was to be stripped, the floor vacuumed, and any trash removed, before departure. "I'll meet you by the front gate."

"Honor?"

"Yes?"

"It's good to have you back."

5

He'd lied to Favashi.

Dmitri maneuvered the Ferrari back into Manhattan, having made an early morning trip across the river to the Angel Enclave—to Raphael's home.

During the time he'd been caged, he had once threatened to feed Isis to her hounds. But in actuality, after he'd stabbed the angel so many times that her heart had been nothing but thick, bloody pulp, Raphael had wrenched off her head with a single vicious pull. Then together, the two of them *had* cut the bitch up into small pieces, but not to throw to her hounds. No, they had burned her to ash in a blaze set in the center of her courtyard. Unlike an archangel, Isis hadn't been powerful enough to return from that.

Dmitri had never regretted the brutality of what they had done. It had been necessary to make sure she would never again rise. He only wished they could've taken longer, made her scream and beg and plead . . . as his Ingrede must have. But Misha had been alone and scared in the cold, lightless place beneath the keep, returning to him Dmitri's number one priority.

"Papa! Papa!" His son, attempting to crawl across the

stone, small hands swollen and bruised from his futile attempts to claw away the manacle around his neck, the unspeakable thing neither Dmitri nor Raphael had been able to remove without hurting him.

"Shh, Misha." He tried to keep his voice calm, to not allow his agony to show through as he took those broken hands into his own, brought them to his lips. "It is only a scratch. Papa is fine."

Having taken the key from Isis, he unlocked the iron that held Misha bound, threw it far away. "I'm here now." His eldest child's small, feverish body in his arms, holding on tight, so tight. "It'll be all right."

Chest taut with a pain that had never lessened, Dmitri pushed the remote that allowed him access to the sprawling parking lot beneath the Tower. Silent and fast, the gate opened at once. The Ferrari purred into its usual spot, and a couple of minutes later, he was out and heading toward the elevator, his memories contained behind walls no one had ever breached.

Just as the doors opened, his cell phone rang, the receptionist advising him of Honor's arrival. A dark anticipation hummed through him, intense enough that there was no chance he'd set her free before satiating his hunger. "I'll escort her up," he said.

The receptionist looked up at him the instant he exited onto the lobby floor, tension around her pretty mouth. "Sir, there's—"

"Dmitri." An airy, breathy female voice.

Turning, he found a voluptuous blonde pushing off the wall where she'd apparently been waiting. "Carmen," he said, conscious of Honor standing a couple of yards away. "Do you have business in the Tower?" He waved off a guard who approached—the reason why Carmen had been allowed to make it to the lobby was the reason why she was Dmitri's problem to handle.

The stunning human, her hair tousled as if she'd rolled out of bed a second ago—though her lips were painted to perfection, her big blue eyes outlined in kohl—put her hand on his chest, stroking down to curl her fingers into his lapel. "I have business with *you*." Nothing if not elegant in her sultry sexuality, she angled her head a fraction to the left.

He didn't miss the invitation. Placing his hand on her wrist, he pulled off her own with a gentleness she mistook for care. Until he said, "We fucked once, Carmen. It's not happening again."

Her face colored, eyes glittering with an emotion that wasn't anger, but ran as hot. "God, you're a bastard." A flush across the creamy tops of her breasts, exposed by the deep neck of the businesslike sheath that encased her body. "I'll do anything you want."

"I know." It was part of the reason he'd never again take her to his bed. She'd been too willing from the start; and while Dmitri had nothing against willing—liked his women soft and wet with welcome—Carmen wanted more than sex.

Dmitri didn't. Not with her. Not with any woman. "Go home, Carmen."

She pushed herself into him instead, her nipples pressing through the dove gray material of her dress to make it clear that, elegantly sexy or not, she wasn't wearing a bra. "Just once more, Dmitri." Thudding hunger in her pulse. "I want to feel your fangs breaking through my skin." The shudder that rolled through her was almost orgasmic. "Please, just once."

"Any vampire will do, Carmen. We both know that." She'd become addicted to the pleasure a vampire's kiss could bestow, something he hadn't realized until after he'd taken her to bed. "I don't fuck and feed from the same woman." It was an ironclad rule.

Her hands clenched on the lapels of his suit. "*Anything,* Dmitri."

"You don't want to say that to me." He allowed the cold, dark predator within him to rise to the surface, to fill his eyes as he lowered his voice to hold pure, silken menace. "I don't play nice and I never stop when asked." Raising his finger, he touched it almost delicately to her cheekbone, the violence in him a pitiless blade as a result of the memories that had suddenly begun to surface. "Do you want me to hurt you?"

Carmen went white, didn't resist when one of the vampires on watch put a hand on her arm at Dmitri's minute nod.

Watching her go, he turned to Honor. "Now, you," he murmured, having never lost awareness of the staccato beat of her pulse, the jagged spike of her breath, the subtle complexity of her scent. "You, I want to say those words to me."

A sucked-in breath. "I don't sleep with men who get off on making me bleed." A biting anger in those words . . . and something older, richer, darker.

Having reached her, he smiled and knew from the look in her eyes that he'd let a little too much of himself bleed through, the blade too lethal. "Good," he murmured. "It'll make it sweeter when I do have you."

Spots of color on her cheeks, though he could hear her heart beating like a small, trapped creature's, panicked and stuttering. "I don't fuck."

"You," he said, wanting to place his mouth over her pulse and suck, "I wouldn't fuck. Not the first time anyway."

Regardless of the words he'd chosen, Honor wasn't sure Dmitri was talking about sex at all in that dark purr of a voice that was both the most sinful decadence and a deadly warning. He'd terrified Carmen with quiet, calculated menace, was feared by every other vampire in the city—and yet she found herself standing her ground, her courage coming from some hidden part of her she didn't entirely understand.

Maybe she'd collapse into a gibbering mess when she was alone, but she *would not* break in front of this vampire who'd looked at a former lover with the same detached distance as another man might an insect. "If you want to know what I found out, get the hell out of my personal space."

He didn't move. "Pity you're not one of the bloodhounds."

"Scent," she said, breath catching as she felt the faintest caress of black fur and diamonds entangling her senses, "Sara told me you can lure with scent." It made her wonder how many hunters he'd called, naked and willing, to his bed with nothing but the intoxication of his ability. "I'm not hunter-born," she argued, though it had just become clear that she may well have had one of them in her lineage.

And Dmitri knew it.

Those beautiful lips setting in the slightest curve, he angled his head toward the elevators. "Come, little rabbit."

Gritting her teeth, she forced herself to follow—though her heart threatened to punch out of her chest at the thought of being trapped in an elevator with him. Unfortunately, escape wasn't an option. There was nowhere she could go in this city where he wouldn't track her down.

And he would, because she had what he needed. The fact that he wanted to sleep with her was an adjunct, a diversion. "Did your people discover anything else about the victim?" she asked, sweat beading along her spine as they reached the elevator.

"He died perhaps a day before the head was discovered." Dark, *dark* eyes lingering on every curve and shadow of her face. "You need to slow down your pulse, Honor. Or I'll take it as an invitation. And we both know just how much you'd enjoy my fangs."

Her stomach clenched, roiled. "Carmen was right. You are a bastard." In the pit, one of the vampires had used his fangs to pump something into her bloodstream that was meant to make things pleasurable for the donor, forcing her to orgasm over and over again—a wracking rape of her senses that she couldn't fight.

She'd vomited after he finished, much to his disgust. Ice-cold buckets of water thrown over her had been her punishment. "I'd rather eat nails than let you near me."

"A colorful analogy, but I don't have to force my food." Extending his arm to keep the elevator doors from closing, he waited. "As you saw, it comes begging to my door." He continued to hold the elevator even when it began to beep.

No way in hell would she let him win.

He smiled when she stepped in, and again, it was the smile of a predator. Without warmth or any hint of humanity. "So, the quivering rabbit has some spine left."

The doors whooshed shut.

"How's your face?" she asked, hand itching for a blade.

He turned so she could see the cheek she'd cut. The dark honey of his skin was smooth and warm with health once more, the kind of skin that invited touch . . . if you forgot the fact that he was as dangerous as a cobra watching its prey.

"The tattooed vampire," he said, leaning lazily against the wall, his voice a languid stroke, "was barely-Made. Two months old at most. He shouldn't have been out of containment."

Frowning, she bit the inside of her lip. "Hunters don't usually have anything to do with vampires that young. I've heard they're relatively weak."

"Weak is one word." Glancing toward the doors as they opened, he nodded at her to step out.

She locked her feet into place. "After you."

"If I wanted to go for your throat, Honor," he said in that same deceptively lazy voice, "you'd be pinned to the wall before you saw me move."

Yeah, she knew that. Didn't change things. "I can stay here all day."

Once again, Dmitri held out his arm to block the door from closing. "Who were you before they got to you?"

It ripped at the pride Honor hadn't thought she still had that he knew how she'd been debased and degraded, how she'd been made less than an animal, but she found her voice in a rage that had grown in brittle silence since the day she stumbled out of the pit. "I have a question of my own."

A raised eyebrow.

"Why the fuck are the worst of them still out there walking around?" While she was trapped in this body that couldn't forget the bruises, the broken bones, but most of all, the agonizing loss of her right to make a choice, to allow or not to allow a touch.

A cold, cold *something* swam behind Dmitri's dark eyes. "Because they don't know they're dead yet." Icy words. "Would you like to watch when I make them scream?"

Her blood froze in her veins.

Dmitri smiled. "What fantasies have you been having, little rabbit? Stabbing out their eyes, perhaps, letting them grow back so you could do it again?" A terrible, sensual whisper. "Breaking their bones with a hammer while they're conscious?" Not waiting for an answer, he stepped out of the elevator.

Following, she stared at the black suit jacket that sat so very perfectly over broad shoulders graceful with a liquid kind of muscle. Nothing about Dmitri was less than sophisticated. Even his violence. And yet he'd come scarily close to guessing at the vicious dreams she entertained when she thought of having her attackers at her mercy—in a cold room devoid of light as they'd had her.

"I know," he said, as if he'd read her mind, "because I once cut out the tongue of someone who had held me prisoner."

Something slumbering in her stretched awake, some waiting, *old* part that hungered for his answer to the question she was compelled to ask. "Was it enough?"

"No, but it was satisfying nonetheless." Pushing through the door to his office, he walked over to the windows. "Those who say vengeance eats you up are wrong—it doesn't, not if you do it right." Glancing over his shoulder, he gave her a razored smile that both fascinated and terrified. "I'll make sure to invite you when I track them down."

"You sound certain you will."

He didn't answer—as if it was a given he'd hunt down his prey. "Come here, Honor." A command twined with the faint taste of some exotic spice that made her breasts swell, her breath catch.

It was a good thing she appeared to have only the merest drop of the hunting bloodline. "Even before the attack," she said, digging her nails into her palms, "I wasn't the kind of hunter who played with vampires." While she had nothing against those of her brethren who took vampiric lovers, she knew herself well enough to know she needed commitment of a kind the almost-immortals couldn't give. Their lives were too long, love an amusement, fidelity to a mortal laughable. "Being food has never appealed to me."

Dmitri turned to lean against the plate-glass wall that looked out over Manhattan, his masculine beauty starkly outlined by the piercing light of the sun at his back. "Ah, but I think you'd be a delicious snack."

Dmitri watched the hunter across from him tug her laptop bag off her shoulder and place it on his desk before pulling out the slim computer. Her face was flushed, her breasts pushing against her sweatshirt, but there was nothing less than unyielding focus in her words. "We can play games all day, or I can show you what I've found."

"Dmitri, stop playing games."

Words spoken in a distant language, as clear to him as the sunlight. She'd been angry with him that day, his Ingrede. And yet in the end, he'd tumbled her into bed, stripped her down to her skin, and kissed every inch of her small, lush body. He'd loved sinking into her, of having his hands full of her breasts, his thighs wedged between her softer, plumper ones as he sucked and licked at her mouth, her neck. That was the day Caterina had been conceived, or so Ingrede had always maintained.

"That's why she is such a bad-tempered child, your daughter."

"Dmitri?"

Lashes lowering, he fought to hang on to a memory that held nothing of the pain or horror that was to follow, only to have it flitting out of reach. "I'm listening," he said, eyes on Honor.

Her gaze lingered on him and, for an instant, he felt the most disconcerting sensation—as if he had been in this moment before—but then she blinked and looked down and it passed. "The tattoo isn't in our database. However, I've sent out some discreet feelers along the international hunter network."

Dmitri had also put out the word amongst the network of high-level vampires who either worked in or with powerful courts. The cooperation at that level was much more prevalent than believed by most people. It was only when issues of territory and power became involved that things got problematic. "Have you had any success deciphering the lines of text?"

Her eyes sparkled, the first time he'd seen such a light in them. It fascinated him, the sudden, brilliant life of her. *This*, he thought, *this* was who she had been before she'd been broken . . . before she'd learned to taste fear in her every breath. He understood what it was to break, better than she could imagine.

"Watch, Dmitri."

"No, don't!" Pulling against his chains until his wrists bled. "I'll do whatever you wish—crawl on my hands and knees!"

Laughter, beautiful and mocking. "You will anyway."

"No! No! Please!"

6

"The language"—Honor's voice intertwining with one of the most painful moments of his hundreds of years of existence—"is close to Aramaic, but not quite. It's almost as if someone took Aramaic as the base, then wrote their own . . ." A puff of breath that lifted the fine tendrils of hair that had escaped the clip at her nape. "I'd call it a code. The lines are a code."

Drawn by the softness of her, he walked closer, saw her stiffen. "Can you unravel it?"

"It'll be difficult with so small a sample," she said, holding her position, "but yes, I think so. I've already begun."

He was about to ask for more details when his cell phone rang. Glancing at the screen, he saw it was Jason, Raphael's spymaster and a member of the Seven. "You've found something," he said to the angel, his attention on the curls in Honor's hair.

"In a sense—I'll be there in five minutes to discuss it."

Hanging up, Dmitri glanced at the skies beyond the glass, searching for Jason's distinctive black-winged form. He didn't find it—not a surprise, given that Jason had a habit of flying high above the cloud layer and then descending in a burst of speed. Looking back to Honor, he caught her staring at him. "Usually when a woman looks at me like that," he murmured in deliberate provocation, "I consider it an invitation to take whatever I want."

Hand clenching around the pen in her grasp, she stood to her full height. "I was thinking that you looked like a man who could break my neck with the same inhuman calm as you might a cell phone."

Dmitri slid his hands into his pockets. "I'd be more worried at losing my cell." He said it to shock her, but part of him wasn't certain it wasn't in fact the truth.

Honor's gaze lingered on his face, those midnight green eyes full of secrets too old to belong to a mortal . . . except this one had lived an eon in the months she'd spent trapped at the mercy of those who had none. "Everyone," she now said, "knows vampires were once human. I'm not sure you were."

"Neither am I." A lie, made so by his awakening memories, memories that incited the same rage, horror, and anguish he'd felt so long ago that the time was nothing but an ancient legend to mortals. However, Honor had no right to that knowledge. Only to Ingrede would he have laid his soul bare, and his wife was long dead, ashes on the unforgiving wind.

Dmitri.

I'll meet you on the balcony, Jason. Though their ranges and specific abilities varied dramatically, every member of the Seven could communicate on the mental plane, an incalculable strategic advantage in certain situations. "Don't leave just yet, Honor. I wouldn't want to have to chase you down."

Honor watched Dmitri prowl out through the small door that led onto the balcony. An angel with wings as black as the endless heart of night swept down to land with quiet grace on the very edge of the open space an instant later. Honor sucked in a breath as she saw the tattoo covering the left-hand side of his face—swirling lines, dots arcing along the curves to create a striking piece of art. Beautiful and haunting, it suited a face that carried the compelling strength of the Pacific intermingled with other cultures she couldn't quite identify. His hair, tied back in a neat queue, reached to midway between his shoulder blades.

Dmitri, with his flawlessly cut black suit paired with a

vivid blue shirt, his hair just long enough to invite the thrust of a woman's fingers, was as urbane and sophisticated as the angel was rough around the edges. But one thing was clear—both were honed blades, blooded and ruthless.

Jason glanced through the plate-glass window. "Honor St. Nicholas," he said. "Found abandoned as a newborn on the doorstep of a small church in rural North Dakota. Named after the nun who discovered her and the patron saint of children. No known family."

Dmitri wasn't surprised at Jason's knowledge—there was a reason the angel was called the best spymaster in the Cadre. "I assume you didn't come here to talk about Honor."

The angel tucked his wings in tighter as a swift wind swept across the balcony suspended high above the frenetic beat of the city. "There's something in your voice, Dmitri."

It was odd how good Jason was at picking up cues about people, though he was an angel who preferred to keep to himself. "Unless you have intentions toward Honor," he said, "it's not something you need to worry about."

Jason didn't speak for a long moment unbroken by any sound but for the wind whispering over his wings. "Do you know what was done to her?"

"I can guess." Unlike Jason, he had intimate knowledge of the bloodlust that lived within the Made. Dmitri had had control of his from the start—perhaps because he'd stabbed his rage into Isis's body, or perhaps because he'd been determined never to become a slave to anyone or anything—but that didn't mean it didn't exist. "She's stronger than she appears."

"Are you certain?"

"Why the sudden concern about a hunter?" Jason saw everything, but preferred to keep his distance from those he watched.

Jason didn't answer. "I've had some news from Neha's territory."

The Archangel of India was powerful and, ever since the execution of her daughter, walking the edges of sanity. "Is it something we need to worry about?"

"No. It doesn't seem connected to anything else." He

tracked a chopper coming in to land on a roof outside Tower territory. "An angel appears to have gone missing. A bare two years from the Refuge."

Dmitri frowned. "She can't know anything about it." Angels that young were habitually put under the command of a senior vampire or angel.

"No. The vampire—Kallistos—who did have a care of the angel, says he assumed the young one went back to the Refuge."

That wasn't suspicious in and of itself. A senior vampire in an archangel's court had a lot on his plate, and it wasn't unusual for young angels to bolt to the security of the hidden angelic stronghold after their first taste of the wider world. "You've alerted the Refuge?"

"Aodhan and Galen are making inquiries," the black-winged angel said, naming two of the Seven.

Dmitri nodded. Territorial borders aside, the young ones were always looked after. "I'll speak to the other seconds in the Cadre, see if they can shed any light on the matter."

"Angels do not just disappear."

"No, but I've known the occasional youth to go a little wild after first leaving the Refuge." Jason dealt mostly with the oldest of the angels, archangels included, but Dmitri continued to have contact with the younger angels because he liked to take a look at everyone coming into Raphael's territory. "I once tracked a young male to a 'party island' in the Mediterranean." He shook his head at the memory. "The boy was sitting there in a tree, watching the revelers—he'd never imagined that level of hedonism."

"Such innocence." Jason stepped to the very edge of the balcony. "Astaad," he said, "there's something there. Maya hasn't been able to get any details but she's working on it."

Astaad was the Archangel of the Pacific Isles and one who did not appear to play political games. "I thought his behavior was connected to Caliane's awakening." There were always side effects when an archangel rose to consciousness, and Raphael's mother was one of the most ancient of Ancients.

"It may be nothing, rumors begun by another source." Eyes on the city, dazzling under the sunshine, he said, "You're older than me, Dmitri."

"Only by three hundred years." A joke between two men who had lived longer than most could hope to imagine.

"I asked Elena what it was like to be mortal. She said time is precious in a way an immortal will simply never know."

"She's right." Dmitri had been both, and if he could go back in time, destroy Isis before she ever came near him and his own, he would do so in a heartbeat, though it would mean he would die in a few short decades. "I felt more as a mortal than I have in the centuries since."

"Will you love me when I'm fat and unwieldy with our babe?"

He put his hand on the curve of her belly, touched his lips to her eyelids, the tip of her nose, her lips. "I will love you even when I am dust on the wind."

IIonor watched Dmitri walk to stand beside the black-winged angel and hissed out a breath at how close he was to the unprotected edge. Unlike the angel, he had no wings should he fall, and yet he stood there with a confidence that said he wasn't the least worried about the eventuality.

A change in the air at her back.

Swiveling, she discovered the vampire with the wrap-around shades in the doorway. "Dmitri's outside."

He headed through to the balcony without a word, just as the black-winged angel stepped off the edge. Those incredible wings disappeared for a moment before he rose up at dizzying speed. On any other day, she would've followed the trajectory of his flight, but today her attention was locked on Dmitri—whose face turned to granite after hearing whatever it was the other vampire had to say.

Stalking in, he said, "Leave that. We're heading out."

An arrogant command, but she read the tension in the air, made the connection. "Did you find the rest of the body?" Even as she spoke, she was removing the data card from the laptop in case she couldn't immediately return to retrieve it.

"Yes." Dmitri's phone rang as they entered the elevator, but clearly the signal didn't drop because he had a quick, curt conversation.

Meanwhile, the other vampire turned to look at her. He said

nothing, and those mirrored sunglasses made it impossible for her to get a reading on him. Wanting to distract herself from the fact that she was trapped in a steel cage with two deadly predators, she said, "Sunglasses in the dark as a fashion statement went out with perms."

He flashed his teeth—but not his fangs—at her. "You don't want to see what's behind the shades, sweetheart." The last word was a mockery of an endearment that made every hair on her body rise in defensive warning.

"Venom."

The vampire turned to face the front again, but the corners of his lips continued to tug up at the corners. "You want me to drive?"

"No, we'll take the Ferrari. Take another car so I can leave you there."

"I might make it faster on foot and it'll give me a chance to observe the crowd without them being aware of it."

"Go."

Stepping out into the artificial light of an underground garage had never felt so good—she was fairly certain that without Dmitri to hold his leash, Venom would've shown her his fangs in more ways than one. "Now I know you're important," she said when the currently open-topped Ferrari proved to be parked in the spot nearest the elevator.

"If it took you this long, Honor, you're dimmer than you look."

As a taunt, it was only mildly irritating, especially when it was clear Dmitri wasn't paying full attention. Sliding onto the butter-soft leather of the passenger seat, she looked over to where Venom had exited the garage. "What's with the sunglasses?"

"You haven't heard? He's been in the city long enough to have come into contact with a number of hunters."

"I didn't work in the country much . . . before." She took her first real breath in what felt like an hour as Dmitri drove them out of the secure Tower zone and into the music of Manhattan—complete with beeping horns, yelled-out insults, and a thousand cell phone conversations taking place at once. "Had no reason to interact with Tower personnel when I was in the city."

"In that case"—an amused tone—"I'll leave it to Venom to surprise you."

The city picked up in volume the farther they got from the Tower. New York had overwhelmed her when she'd first arrived—fresh off a bus from North Dakota. This wasn't home—no place was home, really—but at least the Guild was here. Ashwini and Sara lived here. So did Demarco, Ransom, and Vivek. Friends who had searched for her with relentless persistence, who would die for her if it came down to it. That was something. And it gave her an anchor when everything else was spiraling out of control. "Where did they find the body?"

"In Times Square."

Disbelief was followed by a sudden mental connection. "The same spot where Raphael punished that vampire?" The incident was legend. The archangel had broken every single bone in the vampire's body, then left him in the center of Times Square for three long hours. Cold, calculated, brutal, it had been a punishment no one would ever forget.

At the time, she'd felt pity. Now she knew exactly how sadistic the almost-immortals could be, their minds capable of thinking of the most depraved, dehumanizing of horrors. Now she understood that Raphael's punishment might have been nothing but a warning.

"Close enough." Swerving around a delivery truck, Dmitri ignored the cussing of a cabdriver—who bit off his tirade midword—and stared at a suited business executive about to jaywalk across the road. She froze in place, her coffee dropping unheeded to the asphalt. "Condition of the body parts says he wasn't dropped from the air," he said after they flew past the woman, "so the pieces had to be carried in."

Parts. Pieces.

Not such a surprise, given the decapitated head. "Surveillance?" she asked as they hit the edge of the wonderland of flashing billboards and crushing humanity that was Times Square.

"It's being pulled." Parking illegally in the middle of a street that had been blocked off, the crowd pressing at the police cordon, he got out. Everyone within a foot of him moved back . . . and kept moving as he walked through to the scene.

Honor followed in his wake, saw people's eyes take in the knife strapped to her thigh. The tense expressions disappeared, to be replaced by wary smiles. Hunters were generally well enough liked by the general public, since folks knew that if it all went to shit and the vampires bathed the streets in blood, it would be the Guild that would ride to the rescue. Even the weaker vamps in the crowd gave her friendly nods—law-abiding citizens had nothing to fear from the Guild.

A minute later, she ducked under the police tape to find herself looking at a scene more suited to a slaughterhouse than the chaotic, vivid center of one of the most well-known cities in the world. A thousand scents surrounded her—the sweet, sweet taste of sugar from the chocolatier across the street; coffee, bitter and rich, from the place on the corner; tobacco smoke and car exhaust mixed with the sour tang of human sweat—but none of it could overwhelm the ripe, wet smell of rotting flesh.

7

The police had left the majority of the body parts in the large sports bags in which they'd been found, but even a cursory glance at the top half of the torso—which appeared to have fallen out of a bag, likely when someone got curious—showed that the vampire had been dismembered with the same hacking slices she'd noted along the neck. "Either someone was really angry or they just didn't give a damn."

Dmitri crouched down by the torso. "Don't ascribe human motives to this, Honor."

Memories of slaps that had split her lip as a child, carefully aimed punches where teachers and social workers wouldn't see the bruises, the slice of her knife into fatty flesh as the bedroom door opened late one night. "Humans can be as vicious." She wasn't sorry for what she'd done to protect herself and others as a child—she'd decided the first time a foster "father" looked at her in a way no man should look at a child that she'd never be a defenseless victim.

And she hadn't been . . . until the basement and the softly mocking laughter as elegant, manicured hands roamed her naked body.

Fuck them, she thought, the anger that had awoken inside

her the previous night blazing ever brighter. Whatever happened, she wouldn't give the bastards the satisfaction of seeing her curl up and die.

"Yes," Dmitri said as she let that vow settle into her very bones, "but this has the touch of an immortal." His hair gleamed blue-black under the sunshine, a sensual invitation. Her fingers were halfway to it before she realized what she was doing.

Face burning, she retracted her hand, clenching it into a fist. What was *wrong* with her? Forget the fact that they were about as much in public as it was possible to get; she was certain he was capable of doing things to her that would make the basement seem like child's play.

And still she wanted to touch him, until she could almost feel the cool silk of his hair sliding through her fingers.

"Have you seen anything like this before?" she asked, giving herself a hard mental slap to snap the seductive thread of compulsion.

"Dismemberment isn't new," he said with the cool pragmatism of a man who had lived through the dark ages of both mortal and immortal. "But this isn't about how the body was torn apart—that, I think, was a practical exercise."

Easier to transport, to leave in such a public place. "So it's about the spectacle."

Dmitri's nod sent strands of hair sliding across his forehead. "That and a challenge. Why else go to the trouble of dumping the body here, in the heart of Raphael's territory?"

She saw it then, akin to pieces of an ancient language coming together in her mind to form a perfect sentence. "But Raphael is famously not here right now, Dmitri. You are."

He went motionless, in a way a human being simply couldn't. It was as if every part of him went quiet. He didn't breathe, didn't so much as blink. "Very good, Honor. Seems like it was a good idea to keep you around."

Perhaps it was a taunt. Or perhaps it was nothing but the arrogance of an almost-immortal who had lived centuries, seen empires rise and fall, fought on blood-soaked fields of battle, and seen a million, billion human lives extinguished under the inexorable march of time. It was a thought both fascinating and disconcerting. Unsure why she was so . . . disturbed by the idea, she rose to examine the other body parts as well as she could—she was no pathologist, but she'd had the basic training all hunters received.

The flesh had begun to decompose, maggots crawling in several of the pieces. "Not refrigerated, even though it appears as if the body was dismembered soon after death," she said. "If this dump was planned—and it had to have been, for so many pieces to have been left here at one time—I'd have expected the murderer or murderers to have taken better care of the body."

"Why?" Rising to his feet, Dmitri stripped off and disposed of the gloves he'd grabbed from one of the cops. "The whole point was to create a show. I'm fairly certain hunks of human meat crawling with maggots had the right impact."

He was right. It wasn't hard to guess that the scent of decomposition had been critical to the early discovery of the remains—and that spoke not of rampant madness but of a sly kind of intelligence. "I'd like to know if the pathologist finds any other markings." The more text she had to work with, the easier the decoding process.

"I'll arrange it." He took out a cell phone. "Do you want the skin or will photographs do?"

Such a beautiful male. Such a pitiless question.

"Photographs will do for now," she said, wondering if he was capable of the raw depths of human emotion any longer, this creature formed for seduction and honed in blood, "but they should preserve the skin if possible."

"It'll be done."

Not long afterward, he drove her to the Academy. "Your quarters are here?"

She shook her head. "I moved out this morning." Another step out of the pit, another "fuck you" to the bastards who had hurt her.

Dmitri's smile was slow, dangerous. "Good."

Her hindbrain screamed a warning even as her abdomen clenched in visceral sensual awareness. "The building has security."

He raised an eyebrow.

Yeah, she didn't think that would stop him either.

Getting out, she took in the picture he made in that car, a

gorgeous, sexy creature, his skin kissed to warm perfection by the sun, the stunning blue of his shirt an exotic contrast. "You look like some rich playboy." If said playboys were sharks.

"And?"

"And playboys prefer the glossy model type, in bed and out. It's a rule."

"While you're in the library, look up a painting titled *Asleep* by Gadriel," he said, slipping on a pair of sunglasses. "That's my idea of the perfect woman."

Of course it was the first thing she did—and felt an electric current of wicked heat singe her blood when the computer screen filled with the nude image of a couple asleep in bed, the man on his back, the woman lying on top of him, his hand fisted in her abundant ebony hair. There were tangled sheets aplenty, but none covered the woman's honey-colored skin. Her heavy breasts were crushed against the man's chest, his free hand lying proprietarily on her lush bottom, her body all curves and softness.

But for the lack of muscle that underlay every hunter's form, it could've been a painting of Honor.

Returning to the Tower with his mind full of images of what Honor would look like in place of Gadriel's model, Dmitri headed up to his office. "What have you got?" he asked Venom when the vampire returned from his duties overseeing the removal and transportation of the body parts. His question, however, had nothing to do with the morning's find.

"The vampires who took Honor were clever," Venom answered, removing his sunglasses to reveal eyes no human would ever, *ever* possess. "They used weaker, younger vamps to do the dirty work, and it was those vamps the hunters cornered when they went in."

Dmitri knew the two survivors had been shot and sliced all to hell but left alive. However, according to the vampire who'd had charge of the case till now, neither had provided any information of value. The mastermind behind the kidnapping had kept them scrupulously out of the loop.

Dmitri decided he needed to pay them a personal visit. This was his hunt now. "Keep on it."

His private line rang just as Venom left. Answering, he found himself talking to Dahariel, Astaad's second. "What news of Caliane?" the angel asked.

The query wasn't unusual, given the fact that the oldest of the archangels was allowing only Raphael and those he called his own through the shield around the newly risen city of Amanat. "Concerned with helping her people make the transition from sleep to wakefulness." Those people, mortals and—it had been discovered—a number of immortals, had slept more than a millennium beside their goddess in a city of stone gray now sparkling under the light of a foreign sun.

From what Raphael had told him in their last conversation, the residents of Amanat were content to re-create and live in the time in which they had gone to sleep, filling the gardens with blooms, the fountains with water. They would not hear of modern things, had no curiosity to explore a mountainous new homeland far from the place where they had last walked.

"She holds them in thrall," Raphael had said of his mother. "But she did not sing them to it—their devotion is true."

"Does she wish for more territory?" Dahariel asked in a tone some would call emotionless, but that Dmitri recognized as icily practical.

"No. Land, it seems, has never been the source of Caliane's madness." The archangel had sung the adult populations of two bustling cities into the sea in order to protect the world from war, creating "a silence so deep, it echoed across eternity"—words Jessamy had written in her histories of Caliane's reign.

"I spoke to Jessamy," Dahariel said in an uncanny echo. "There has never been an awakening such as this."

And so no one knew the rules of engagement. "We're immortals, Dahariel. Time isn't our enemy." Better to wait, to learn the truth of Caliane's sanity or lack thereof before preparing for a war that would drench the world in blood, turn the rivers red, make the sea a silent graveyard. "How's Michaela?" Astaad's second was the archangel Michaela's lover, a clash of loyalties that made Dmitri wonder exactly who Dahariel served.

"Some women," Dahariel said in that same hard tone devoid of any hint of humanity, "get under a man's skin until digging them out makes you bleed."

Hanging up, Dmitri wondered at the undertone of violence in Dahariel's statement. Dmitri knew about loving a woman, but he'd never wanted to rip Ingrede from his heart, no matter the associated pain. Favashi hadn't ever made a place for herself that deep. And Honor . . . yes, she was getting under his skin, but it was a compulsion that would end when he took her to bed, had her naked and writhing beneath him.

But first he would fulfill his promise, lay the screaming, bloodied remains of her abusers at her feet. Vengeance, as he'd told her, could taste sweet indeed.

"I will give you your freedom, never look your way again." Attempting to be regal even when her eyes fell on the blade in his hand. *"Wealth beyond imagining, it'll be yours."*

What he wanted, Isis could never return to him. "The only thing I desire," he whispered, touching the tip of his blade to the skin above her heart, "is to hear you beg for your life. So beg."

The knife slid home.

I**t was just past eight, the world swathed in cool darkness,** when, dressed in jeans, a T-shirt, and a long black coat he'd had for years, he turned into the Angel Enclave estate held by the angel Andreas. Andreas had been given charge over the interrogation and punishment of the vampires Honor's rescuers had left alive.

"Dmitri." Andreas's wings—a dark amber streaked with gray—flared behind him as he greeted Dmitri in front of a home that was all glass and hard angles, unusual for an older angel. "Why the sudden interest in these two?"

Because it was personal now. "We'll talk after I've spoken to them."

The aristocratic lines of Andreas's face didn't shift into an expression of affront. The angel was powerful, but Dmitri was more so. The only reason Dmitri didn't rule a territory was because he preferred to work in the Tower . . . and in the shadows. His position as Raphael's second had never been boring yet.

In what he thought of as his "adolescence," angry and full of a helpless pain, he'd once left to work for Neha. The Archangel of India hadn't been pleased at his decision to return to what had been the beginnings of Raphael's first Tower the minute he completed the term he'd agreed to serve in her court. But then she had smiled.

"So wild, both of you." A shake of her head, those deep brown eyes holding the amusement of an archangel who had lived millennia. "Of course you find my court too genteel for your taste. Go, then, Dmitri, but should you wish for civilized company, this court's doors will always be open to you."

Neha had been a gracious queen then, with her consort, Eris, at her side and laughter in her eyes at what she considered the folly of youth. Now Eris hadn't been seen for hundreds of years and her daughter Anoushka's execution had turned the Queen of Snakes, of Poisons, into a cold-blooded creature akin to those she kept as pets.

"This way." Andreas swept out before him.

As they passed through the wide-open central core of the house, Dmitri saw a handsome if slender man of Asian descent working at a small desk in the corner. His eyes narrowed. "Is that Harrison Ling?"

Andreas stopped. "Yes. You know him?"

"He's Elena's brother-in-law." The fool had attempted to escape his Contract, been dragged home by Elena herself. Dmitri doubted Harrison had any idea of just how big a favor she'd done him—Andreas wasn't known for his mercy toward those who broke their Contracts. The longer Harrison had remained amongst the missing, the worse the price he'd have had to pay.

"Harrison," Andreas said with an echoing darkness in his voice, "has done very well in learning the meaning of loyalty."

The male looked up at that instant and the fear that crawled, oily and slick, behind his eyes was a slithering thing. Dmitri felt no sympathy for him. Unlike Dmitri, Harrison had chosen to become a vampire—and he'd made that choice not knowing whether the woman he professed to love would be able to follow. As it turned out, Beth, Elena's sister and Harrison's wife, was incompatible with the toxin that turned human into vampire; she would die, while Harrison remained forever young.

"The prisoners," he said, dismissing the pathetic male from his mind.

Andreas led him outside and to a small grove of evergreens

behind his home. The naked creatures hanging from the branches of two separate trees keened in terror the instant they heard the rustle of angelic wings.

Holly . . . Sorrow had the same primitive reaction. She might mouth off to Dmitri, try to play power games that gave her an illusion of control, but put her in a room with an angel and she went close to catatonic. She refused to talk about what Uram had done to her, but Dmitri had seen the carnage in the warehouse, the torn limbs and blood-slick floors, the gaping mouths full of organs plump and wet, the staring, blind eyes.

"Do they still have their tongues?" he asked Andreas, noticing the fact that both men had been turned into eunuchs, their penises and testicles removed with what appeared to have been dull blades. They were vampires. The parts would grow back—which was when Andreas would order their removal once more. Without anesthetic.

"I was planning to have them cut out again tomorrow."

Dmitri felt no disgust at the brutality of the ongoing punishment, not when he had an excellent idea of the horrors these males had inflicted on Honor for their sexual gratification. "Leave it for now. I might need to question them again."

Andreas inclined his head. "Do you wish for privacy?"

"Yes."

Waiting until the angel disappeared through the trees, he prowled to the vampire closest to him. "So," he murmured, "you enjoy taking what is not yours by force?"

8

The male's keening turned into wild panic as he recognized Dmitri's voice. Since he was missing his eyes, his eye sockets huge black holes in his face, sound was the only thing left to him. "I don't know anything! I would tell you if I did!"

Dmitri believed him—the vampire was weak, would have broken at the first sign of pain. But there was a chance he'd glimpsed something without knowing it. "Tell me everything," he said, speaking to them both. "From the first instant you were approached. If it proves useful, perhaps I won't take over your punishment."

Terror turned them incoherent for several minutes. He simply waited it out. Cold of heart, Favashi had once called him. But since she was a bitch who had wanted only to use him, her words held no power. Still, the accusation was true—his conscience rarely troubled him, and never when it came to retribution for those who had brutalized women or children.

"Enough," he snapped when they continued to sob and plead.

Silence, as they choked on their very breaths. Almost half a minute later, the one he'd first spoken to opened his mouth. "I was working as a private security guard when I got a call one day. Man on the other end said he'd seen me at a big party, liked the job I'd done, and did I want to earn some money on the side with an off-the-books gig."

"Which party?"

"He never said, but we mostly worked the premier events—wealthy vamps."

That didn't give Dmitri anything new, but he'd put someone on rechecking the guest lists of the parties this male had worked. "And?"

Jerking out a leg when something big and black landed on his exposed flesh, the vampire twitched violently. "It was so much money, I said s-sure." Swallowing. "Then I asked Reg if he'd like in since the client said he needed two people."

Reg, a thin blond male, was still crying, but silently. "I wish to fucking hell I'd said no."

Now he did, Dmitri thought. He'd had no problem with it when he'd torn into Honor's flesh, when he'd touched her in a way no man had the right to touch a woman without consent. Walking across to the blond, Dmitri backhanded him hard enough that something fractured with an audible crack. "Do you really think I give a shit?" he asked in a quiet, contained voice. "Now answer the question I asked."

Spitting out a tooth, the vampire blubbered out the next series of words. "Leon had the contact. I just did what he said."

Leon began to speak before Dmitri could remind the vampire why it wasn't a good idea to keep him waiting. "Always by phone." Gasped out. "Never had any face-to-face contact. Money was deposited into my account and I gave Reg his cut."

Dmitri didn't say a word.

"The client," Leon continued, stumbling over his own tongue, "said she was his girlfriend, that it was some stupid sex fantasy of hers to be snatched and . . ." Thudding heartbeat, twitching skin, as if he was chillingly conscious of what Dmitri would like to do to him. "He said it was her fantasy."

Dmitri heard the quaver beneath the irritating whine. "What was your first clue that it wasn't?"

Reg was the one who answered. "When she broke Leon's nose! I told him something was wrong, but he was pissed so he punched her, knocked her out."

Dmitri spread his hand, his fingers flexing. "You're older, Reg. Why didn't you stop him?" he asked in a tone as soft as fresh-fallen snow.

Reg began to retch.

Dmitri said nothing until the spasms passed. Then he walked over to stroke his hand over the vampire's face. "Answer my question."

Sweat trickling down his temples, the blond swallowed. "The money. I wanted the money."

"Good." He patted the vampire's cheek, left him quivering as he walked over to Leon.

Who was trying to break his wrists away from the rope in a futile effort to escape, a broken marionette. Reaching into the inside pocket of his coat, Dmitri removed a filleting knife, pressed the cold metal to the new pink skin in front of him. "Tell me the rest." He cut a deep line down the center of Leon's chest.

Blood, dark and red, seeped out of the cut as the vampire whimpered. "We weren't supposed to damage her and I gave her a black eye. So we tied her up and left her where the directions said and got the hell out."

"You didn't stay out." Another cut, this one horizontal, and deep enough that it brushed Leon's internal organs.

But the other vampire kept talking, because he knew Dmitri could do far worse. "Seven weeks later, client calls me again, gives me an address, says maybe we'd like to join in the festivities."

Twisting the blade, Dmitri pulled up, collapsing a lung. "Keep talking." Vampires of Leon's age didn't need to breathe . . . much.

"We got there"—harsh, gasping attempts to take in air— "the place was empty except for the hunter, but it was clear more than one vampire had fed from her. Client left us a note to enjoy ourselves. Note's gone. I threw it away."

Dmitri removed the knife. "And did you? Enjoy yourself?" They were rhetorical questions—these two had been found with Honor over a week later, their mouths smeared with her blood. "You invited your friends, too, didn't you?" The two vampires killed during the rescue had worked for the same security company. "Who else?"

"No one," Leon answered. "I swear. Just the four of us."

They were too terrified to lie, so Dmitri accepted that. "Good."

The screaming stopped when he removed their voice boxes. But he left them alive. Raphael had told him something once, a long time ago. Something his mother, Caliane, had said.

"Three days in the span of a mortal lifetime can feel like three decades."

Raphael's mother might yet turn out to be an insane Ancient, but on this point, Dmitri agreed with her completely. So he would make sure Andreas knew not to let Reg and Leon die. As for the others . . . they would wish for death every single night for the next two centuries once he found them.

Two months, after all, was a lot longer than three days.

Nine at night, and Honor didn't know what she was doing here. "Sorry about canceling our other appointments. Thanks for coming in so late."

Anastasia Reuben smiled, her steely gray hair pulled back in a neat bun. "I've worked with hunters for two decades, Honor. I know going to see a therapist is worse than getting your teeth pulled."

She laughed, or tried to, the sound an awkward rasp. "So, how does this work?"

"There's no pressure, no rules here," Dr. Reuben said, eyes gentle. "If all you want to do is talk about the latest episode of *Hunter's Prey*, then that's what we'll do."

Honor had the feeling that wasn't a hypothetical example. "I came because . . ." Shaking her head, she jerked to her feet, adrenaline racing through every cell in her body. "I'm sorry to have wasted your time."

Dr. Reuben rose, too. "I'm glad you came." Reaching into a cupboard, she pulled out a small book covered in gold and white swirls. "Some hunters never talk, but I've found that putting words down on paper can help."

Honor took the notebook, having no intention of using it. "Thanks."

"It's for your eyes alone. Burn it afterward if you want."

Giving a nod, Honor strode out of the small, discreet office two blocks from Guild HQ.

It wasn't until she was back in her apartment, laptop open to the tattoo file, that she allowed herself to think about why she'd gone. Perhaps it had been the slowly awakening anger inside of her, a cold, bright thing that was all teeth and gleaming edges. Then again, perhaps it had been the knowledge that, stupid or not, she wanted to taste the dark sin of Dmitri's lips. Or perhaps it had been the nightmares.

All her life, she'd felt alone, rootless. Even now, when she had friends, loyal and strong, there was a huge hole deep within—as if she'd lost something terrible and precious. As a child, she'd thought she must be a twin, that her mother had kept one and given away the other. However, as an adult, she recognized the sense of loss as something *other*, outside of herself. That strange, piercing loneliness was never more prevalent than after a nightmare—whether waking or sleeping.

"Enough," she muttered. "Time to work."

And work she did, until the city began to pulse with a quieter beat, the sky that impenetrable opaque shade between midnight and dawn. She shouldn't have given in to sleep but she was tired, her eyes gritty from the parade of sleepless nights, and oblivion hit before she knew it.

It was the sound of a woman's endless, ragged screams that jerked her awake. Her body was curled up into a tight ball on the sofa, wracked by dry sobs, the lingering echo of the woman's torment ripping holes in her soul. Unable to bear it, she stumbled to the bathroom and threw ice-cold water on a face ravaged by an anguish so deep, she'd never felt its like. How could that be? She'd been tortured and broken . . . but this desolation, it came from another place, so very, very deep that it had no name.

Swallowing the burn in her throat before the sadness could recapture her in its aching grip, she stripped off her clothes and stepped into the shower. It was barely five a.m. but the three hours of sleep she'd gotten tonight were better than the hour the previous night. Washing off the sweat, she pressed her head against the tile and simply let the water roll over and off her.

She'd always loved water. Part of the reason she'd ended

up in Manhattan was because it was surrounded by water. It had been a considered decision to apply to the Academy. She'd wanted to study ancient languages and knew that the Guild would cover her fees if she signed a contract to remain active on the roster for at least four years after graduation.

The four-year mark had come and gone, but she'd never even considered leaving. Not only had the other hunters become her family, but her expertise in ancient cultures and languages was a skill in constant demand, given the fact that theirs was a world ruled by immortals. The thought circled her mind back to the Tower and to the vampire who had always been her darkest, most secret weakness.

Switching off the shower, she stepped out to dry herself off, forcing her brain to focus on the task that had left her with a splitting headache the previous night. Whatever it was that had been tattooed on the vampire's face—and on the back of his right shoulder, according to the photos she'd received from the pathologist—was so idiosyncratic as to defy logical explanation. And yet she knew there had to be one. Because regardless of how the head had come into Dmitri's hands, the body had been an unmistakable message.

Dressing in jeans and a plain white tee, she headed out into the kitchen area, which flowed off the lounge, to prepare some tea. The view from the entire front section of the apartment was the same—the Tower. Brilliant with light against the dark early morning skies, it drew the eye like a lodestar.

Walking to the glass wall, tea in hand, she watched a solitary angel come in to land. He was only a silhouette from this far out, but even then, his grace was extraordinary. Not one of the "normal" angels, she thought. This was someone akin to the black-winged angel Dmitri had spoken with on the balcony outside his office.

The knock on her door was so unexpected that she didn't startle, just stared. When it came again, she put down the tea, pulled her gun, and walked on silent feet to the peephole. The vampire on the other side was a sleek predator she should've shot at first glance. Instead, she opened the door. "Dmitri."

Dressed in black jeans, a T-shirt of the same color, and a butter-soft leather coat that reached his ankles, he looked like the most sinful fantasy she'd ever had, the kind that left a woman damp and slick and ready. Drawing in a deep, shuddering breath, she caught the tendrils of sumptuous pleasure and blade-sharp sex in his scent.

Not the reason for her response, but the lush addiction of it certainly didn't help. It was a good thing she wasn't a true hunter-born—because he was potent. "You usually visit around this time?"

"I was passing." He leaned against the doorjamb, lifting the large manila envelope in his hand.

The blades in his scent grew razored, cutting across her senses with deadly eroticism. Suddenly all she saw in his eyes was a menace as sensual as a caress in the dark and as lethal as a stiletto. "What have you done?" The question escaped every filter of social nicety and convention.

"Nothing that didn't need to be done." Pushing off the doorjamb when she released her death grip on the edge of the door and stepped back, he walked into her apartment.

She tugged the envelope from him the instant the door was closed, sliding away her gun even as she allowed herself to indulge in the wicked, beautiful scent of him. "Further photos of the victim's tats?"

"No."

Opening it, she pulled out several sheets of paper, along with a number of blown-up photographs. At first, she didn't understand what it was she was seeing, and then she did and her blood boiled. "This is my medical report." Specifically, from the humiliating examination after her rescue. The doctor and nurse had both been gentle, kind, but there in that examination room, there had no longer been any way to pretend that it hadn't happened, that she hadn't been turned into—

Choking the river of memory, she focused on the here and now, on the anger so incandescent in her vision. "Where did you get this?" Her hands trembled with the need to hurt him, this vampire who played with her as if she was an amusing toy.

Stalking to the window where she'd stood only moments before, he said, "That's not really a question."

No, it wasn't. "You bastard," she said, throwing everything onto the coffee table, the edge of pleasure she'd taken in his presence eradicated by the ice of his voice, an unforgiving reminder that he was *not human*, that he had no conscience as she knew it. "What right do you have to invade my privacy?"

"I wanted the images they took," he said without turning.

Her stomach roiled. "I knew you liked pain, but I didn't realize you got off on torture."

A glance over his shoulder. "Of the bite marks, Honor." Her name sounded like the most decadent of temptations, touched by a sensuality that was as natural to the male in her apartment as breathing . . . even when he was coated in the ice of what she belatedly recognized was rage, tempered and deadly.

Bite marks.

Her own anger chilled by the cold of his, she picked up the stack of paper and photos, flipped until she came to the pages that listed the bites on her body, with associated images. "There's nothing you can learn from this." At the end, they'd torn at her as if she was a hunk of meat, shredding and ripping.

"You'd be surprised." Shifting on his heel, he shrugged out of the coat, throwing it over the back of one of her sofas to reveal muscled arms free of weapons . . . but for the long, thin blade angled in a sheath across his back. Somehow it didn't surprise her that he was a blade man, though from the gun she was certain he had in an ankle sheath, she knew he didn't have a problem with modern weaponry either.

She stood her ground when he came to stand next to her, though the force of her clenched jaw sent pain shooting down the bone. No more fear, she vowed, even knowing it couldn't be as simple as that, the primal core of her brain scrabbling at her to run—or to fight, shooting and cutting and kicking.

The heat of his body insistent against her skin, Dmitri pointed out a set of three bites that were small and evenly spaced. They'd survived the violence later because of their location—the only mercy was that they had healed without leaving scars, so she wasn't constantly reminded of how they'd come to be. "Back of my left thigh—"

"—a few inches up from the knee," Dmitri completed.

Small, fine-boned hands on her body, delicate fangs sinking again and again into that one area. "Blood Ruby," she whispered. "The vampire always smelled of Blood Ruby." The fashionable perfume had been an opulent cage around her senses, and it brought up her gorge still—a stranger on the street, in a store, it didn't matter. She caught a whiff of it and bile coated her throat as a cold sweat broke out over her body. "I used to dream of slitting her throat and watching her flop about at my feet while I drowned her in that stuff."

Dmitri's eyes—dark, so, *so* dark—met hers. "Would you like to pay her a visit?"

9

Silence. In her mind. In her soul. An endless stillness.

"You've seen her feed before." The words shattered the quiet, had her dropping the papers in her hand. They floated to the carpet with a strange, serene grace.

"She's five hundred years old—peculiar habits tend to get around. Feeding from the femoral artery in the thigh isn't unusual." A dangerous pause. "Not between lovers," he corrected, and it made her wonder if that was how he preferred to drink. "But from the back? It's muscle."

"It hurts," Honor said, not knowing why she admitted that. "That's why she does it. It always hurts." Looking down at the gun somehow in her hand again, she said, "Will you stop me if I shoot her?"

"No." Not even the slightest hesitation. "But you might want to wait until after I finish questioning her—it'd be a bitch to wait for the bullet wound to heal."

Part of her wasn't sure if he was joking, but she read the cutting anger in his eyes well enough. She knew it had nothing to do with her. No, what had him ready to mete out the most brutal punishment was the fact that an old vampire he likely trusted to maintain order had been playing some very nasty games. Honor didn't much care about his motivations if it got her to within killing distance of one of the creatures who had turned her into their own personal "blood pet" for two interminable months.

They pulled up to the gates of an estate in Englewood Cliffs just as dawn was streaking the sky in watercolors of peach, pink, and golden blue. Dmitri had stored her laptop in the trunk of his Ferrari and put down the top. She found a welcome freedom in the crisp whip of the wind, using the time to gather her defenses, to ready herself for the thick, nauseating scent of Blood Ruby.

The gates, tall and ornate and covered with dark green ivy, swung open with stately grace the instant the guard saw the car. The drive was dappled in sun and shadow from the oak trees that lined it, and the house, when it came into view, spoke of another century—a heavy and ostentatious one. "Not a vampire who believes in moving with the times."

"No." Dmitri brought the car to a halt in front of the shallow steps that led up to the entrance. "In certain periods, it was the done thing to keep your 'cattle' within easy reach. Valeria continues to hold to that practice, though it's come to be considered an archaic one by most of her contemporaries."

Valeria.

Her hands wanted to grab the huge hunting knife in the sheath at her ankle and rush through the door, gut the vampire, but she forced herself to wait though her pulse beat only a single word—vengeance. "Did the cattle volunteer?"

"There are always those who volunteer." He pushed open his door and stood to strip off his coat, revealing the soft black cotton of his T-shirt.

She thought of Carmen, how the blonde had debased herself before Dmitri, until Honor had been humiliated for her. "You've never had any trouble."

Dmitri didn't answer until they met in front of the car. "There are different kinds of trouble."

She saw something unexpected in him at that moment, a

quiet, dark thing as raw and painful as that which lived within her. "Dmitri," she began, just as the door of the house opened to reveal a maid in a crisp black and white uniform.

"It's time."

Her entire body going hot then cold at his words, she walked up the three wide steps with him. The maid stepped aside as they neared. "The mistress is in the morning room, sir."

Honor had no idea what a morning room was, but Dmitri gave a clipped nod. "We won't need you. Take the day off. The Tower will contact you tomorrow."

The maid paled, but said only, "Yes, sir. The cook is also here."

"Tell her she doesn't need to be. Valeria's cattle?"

"In the guesthouse."

"Get them out. You have five minutes."

"Yes, sir." Bobbing her head, the maid bolted down the hall.

That was when Honor realized she'd caught a glimpse of fang. "She was a vampire." Yet Honor felt no fear; the other woman was obviously so much weaker than her, regardless of her vampirism.

"Young," Dmitri answered, shutting the door with a quiet snick. "Serving out her Contract. I'd say first decade."

"No wonder she seemed so human."

"Some of the weak ones never lose that core of humanity." With that, Dmitri led her down the corridor—it was lined with carpet of deep burgundy, the walls covered with the most exquisite cream paper embossed with a subtle motif. Near-immortality did give the Made longer to gain wealth, but Honor had known vamps hundreds of years old who'd never reached this level of affluence. So either Valeria had begun with wealth or she'd created it through a combination of power, will, and ruthless determination.

Dmitri entered a doorway to the right, a shadow in black.

"Dmitri, darling," came a smoky voice that made Honor's body fill with cold terror. Then she caught the dark, musky scent of Blood Ruby. Freezing with her back to the wall beside the doorway, she tried to get the tremors to stop, to control the nausea that threatened to bring up the tea that was all she'd had for breakfast.

"Valeria," Dmitri drawled, even as he twined tendrils of exquisite chocolate and rich liqueur around Honor's senses. The potency of it overwhelmed the musk of Valeria's signature perfume, allowed Honor to draw in a breath.

Dmitri spoke again before the woman in the room could respond. "Did I get you out of bed?"

A low, intimate laugh. "That's one thing you're always welcome to do."

Another sickening jolt. She'd never thought to ask Dmitri if he'd slept with the female vampire. Anger followed hard on the heels of the roiling ugliness of the supposition, a hard, vicious bite that made her want to stab him in that muscular back. The very strength of her reaction was a slap, grounding her once more. Wiping her palms on the thighs of her jeans, she pulled out her gun.

Dmitri seemed to sense the instant she steadied, because he straightened and said, "I've brought you a visitor."

"Oh?" A curious question as Dmitri shifted aside to allow Honor to step into the opening.

Valeria was reclining on a cream-colored chaise lounge set in front of a window, dressed in a crimson satin robe that stopped midthigh—the belt tied loosely enough at her waist that the inside curve of one perfect breast was artfully exposed. She'd angled her head to ensure the early morning light hit it at the ideal angle to heighten her already stunning features. Long golden brown hair curled over her shoulders to bounce against nipples gone hard and ready where they touched the satin.

As an invitation, it couldn't have been clearer.

Until that deep blue gaze turned from its appreciation of Dmitri's body to fall on Honor. Suddenly Valeria was limbs in motion, fury a red flush across the creamy skin of her face as she rose to her feet—but Honor glimpsed a split second of the most vicious hunger beneath the rage. Valeria was recalling how she'd used Honor, debased her. And she wanted only to do it again.

"Well . . ." Calculation in those stunning eyes that spoke of immortal beauty. "You brought me a snack. You always were a sweetheart."

Honor saw Dmitri tense and—without thinking—reached

out to touch him on his back out of sight of Valeria. *Not yet.*
Coiled tension, taut muscle, but he didn't strike, this beautiful
predator with death in his eyes. "This is a nice room," he murmured instead in that silken voice Honor never, ever wanted to
hear in the dark.

Lines marred the smoothness of Valeria's forehead. "What?"

"Small windows, though," Dmitri continued, his back flexing slightly under Honor's spread hand. Startled to realize she
was still touching him, she dropped it. "Means," he added,
"there's only one exit."

Honor had always known Dmitri was ruthless, but it was
when she glimpsed the dull haze of fear creep over the lake
blue of Valeria's gaze that she understood exactly where he
stood in the food chain. The female vampire glanced around,
her eyes wild when she faced them again. "It was just a bit of
fun, Dmitri. You know how it is."

"Hmm. Tell me."

Valeria seemed to take the slow purr as encouragement.
"Life can get so tedious after centuries of excess. It was a
naughty little thrill to have the hunter at our disposal." Walking forward, sleek thighs exposed in teasing glimpses through
the crimson satin, she ignored Honor to stroke her hand down
Dmitri's chest, slow and with unhidden pleasure.

Honor's fingers clenched on the gun. It took teeth-gritting
control not to put a bullet right between those blue eyes so
wide and alluring.

Dmitri simply raised his hand, closed it over the vampire's.
"An intriguing game," he said, his voice dropping as he tugged
Valeria ever closer, until he was speaking with his lips brushing her ear, her breasts flush against his chest. "I wouldn't
have thought you that creative." He fisted his free hand in the
brunette's hair.

Valeria's eyes closed, her body shuddering from the contact with his muscled body. "I would take the credit"—a husky
whisper—"but you'd find me out."

Dmitri's laugh would've made Honor thrust a blade in his
gut and run as far as humanly possible. But Valeria smiled,
opened her eyes. "I got an invitation." A greedy look over at
Honor. "Her fear was so potent by the time I got there, but she
wouldn't scream or beg. Not for weeks."

Dmitri jerked Valeria's face back toward him, the act ungentle. "You kept the invitation, didn't you?"

"Yes. It was a memento." Lips trailing over his jaw. "Did you bring her for me, Dmitri? Can I have her all to myself?"

Honor touched her hand to Dmitri's back again, not knowing why she believed that would do any good, not even knowing why she thought she could possibly read this vampire so old and powerful it made her bones ache to think about it.

"First tell me who you shared her with," he whispered, ignoring the fact that Valeria had tugged open the tie of her robe to expose creamy skin framed in crimson. "I want to know who else has your tastes."

"But I want her to myself." Petulance.

"Valeria."

The woman all but orgasmed at the command in that voice full of knife blades and midnight screams. "They say you make it hurt, Dmitri."

In response, he used his grip on her hair to pull her head back so hard it made tears form in her eyes. She licked her lips, made no effort to cover the dark pink nipple exposed by the shift of satin over skin. "Tommy. I saw Tommy there once when I ran late during my turn with her."

Honor remembered that day, remembered the elegant female voice arguing with the deeper male one as Valeria cajoled the man into allowing her to stay.

"We'll play together." The sound of clothes brushing up against each other, the wetness of a slow kiss. "You know you like the way I play."

The man—Tommy—had eventually folded. Together the two of them had . . . they'd made Honor scream. Her hand clenched on Dmitri's T-shirt as he moved the hand not in Valeria's hair to close around her throat. "Just Tommy?"

"There were others, but I never saw. We had our own times." Breasts rising and falling, lips parting.

"The invitation, Valeria." Unvarnished command. "Tell me about the invitation."

The brunette shaped the rigid muscle of his chest with possessive hands Honor wanted to break into a thousand pieces. "In my bedroom, in the top drawer of the little table beside the bed." Fingers trailing down to tug up his tee, revealing skin of a warm, dark tan. "I'll show you when we go up." Again, her eyes shifted to Honor. "I want her."

That was when Dmitri smiled, arched Valeria's neck again . . . and slit her throat with about as much emotion as might be expected from a hunting cat taking down prey, the heavy blade a sleek silver shimmer in the morning sunlight.

As the female vampire clapped her hands around her throat, he gripped her by that throat and pinned her against the wall with the blade thrust into her neck. "Don't pull it out," he ordered when Valeria went to do exactly that. "Or I'll cut off your hands."

Honor had jerked up her gun at the first slice, but now her eyes met Dmitri's as he raised an eyebrow. She shook her head. "I can't shoot her now." Not when the vampire was pinned like an insect, the red satin of her robe a wetter, richer shade, her skin bloody cream.

Dmitri moved toward Honor, and she realized that aside from the hand he'd used to grip Valeria's throat, he'd managed to avoid getting any blood on himself in spite of the arterial gush—which led to the very scary conclusion that he'd done this before. "You," he said, touching her chin with the fingers of his clean hand, before ripping out the roses from a vase and upending it to wash the bloody one clean, "are too human."

Yes. It was a welcome shock, a confirmation that she'd retained the core of herself no matter the horror of that dark pit where Valeria and Tommy and their grotesque friends had used her until they tore her very spirit to tatters. Walking past Dmitri to face the brunette vampire, she said, "Anything else you'd like to share about my kidnapping and assault?" to the monster with the wide blue eyes.

Dmitri took a seat on the chaise, reaching over to choose a chocolate from the crystal bowl on a nearby table. When Valeria bared her teeth at Honor, refusing to answer the question, he shot the other woman through the thigh, in almost precisely the spot where the female vampire liked to feed.

Valeria screamed, high and shrill.

Honor understood that the punishments used for immortals, their bodies able to recover from brutal injuries, weren't the same as for mortals. But she'd never been up close and personal with the merciless reality of it. "Does it bother you at all?" she asked Dmitri when Valeria's screams died out into sobs.

He shrugged, shoulders moving with muscled grace beneath the thin cotton of his T-shirt. "No." Putting his gun down beside the crystal bowl, he said, "Valeria, be a good hostess and answer Honor's question," before popping one of the chocolates into his mouth.

"I don't know anything else," the vampire sobbed, her eyes rimmed red with her tears. "J-just about T-Tommy."

"Oh, don't worry," Honor said, remembering how Valeria had sipped at her own tears, how she'd giggled when Honor screamed so much her throat turned raw, her voice gone, "we'll get to Tommy." She didn't know what Valeria heard in her voice, but the vampire suddenly looked afraid in a way Honor would have never expected in a vampire of her age and power.

"He did everything, remember?" Valeria said, hands rising to her throat again as the wound began to heal around the heavy hunting knife.

"I wouldn't." Dmitri ate another chocolate.

Dropping her hands in spasming fear, Valeria continued to speak to Honor, eyes shimmering with tears. "He was the one who hurt you—I just wanted to feed."

Yes, Tommy had hurt her, as only a man could hurt a woman. But only because Valeria had egged him on. Before that, his physical assaults had been relatively minor in the scheme of things—the bastard had enjoyed her blood more than anything else. Valeria, however, had always been very inventive when it was just her and Honor in the dark.

"Oh, did that hurt?" A whisper-soft laugh. "Naughty me. But a girl has to feed."

"Dmitri," Honor said, "I've changed my mind."

And then she shot Valeria through the other thigh.

10

It worried her a little that she didn't hesitate, but this woman, who now screamed because it was her own flesh on the line, had *tortured* her. Who the fuck was anyone else to say what would make her feel better . . . because putting that bullet in Valeria sure as hell did. "I'm done." Never again would this pathetic creature stalk her in her nightmares.

"See if you can find the invitation." Dmitri rose to his feet. "Valeria and I need to talk in private."

Holstering her weapon, she turned to him. "Don't kill her." It would be too quick, not enough. And from what Valeria had done to her, her expertise in certain kinds of pain, Honor knew she was far from the vampire's first victim.

A lazy smile that made the hairs on the back of her neck rise. "Trust me."

The strange thing was that she did. Perhaps that made her a self-deluding fool, but it didn't change the fact of it. Leaving him with the terrified vampire, who was already whimpering and attempting to cajole a man Honor knew no female wiles would ever influence, she strode out and up the stairs.

The theme of opulent elegance continued on through the rest of the house, the artwork on the walls displayed in frames gilded with gold, but tastefully so, the runners handmade in tones that didn't break the flow of the decor, an exquisitely carved marble banister bordering the curving staircase to the second level. The bedroom boasted a massive four-poster bed of dark wood with curtains tied neatly back at the corners. The sheets were finest Egyptian cotton, tumbled from Valeria's early morning wake-up.

It was as she was opening the bedside drawer that the first scream reverberated through the house, so high-pitched that Honor couldn't imagine what Dmitri was doing to Valeria. Pity stirred within her, but she set her jaw and kept going. Because if Dmitri showed mercy here, then other vampires would soon begin to give in to their darkest lusts and the world would turn bloodred.

There.

The invitation was a silver card folded in half.

Ennui is such a bore, is it not, Valeria? Words written in black ink in a graceful hand that could've been either male or female. *I have an entertainment that should satisfy even your jaded appetites.*

Below that was an address, a list of three dates and times, and a note that said: *Should you wish to indulge, come at the same times on the same days in the weeks following.*

There was no signature, and though Honor had handled the note with care, she knew there were unlikely to be any fingerprints. Still, she went down to the kitchen, to the accompaniment of another chilling scream, and found a plastic bag. Not Ziploc, but it would do for now. Placing the card inside, she walked back to the morning room, the halls full of a lingering silence broken only by the sound of Valeria's whimpers.

She stepped inside to find not a speck of blood on Dmitri's body or clothes, his bronzed arms catching her eye as he tucked his gun into an ankle holster with the unhurried actions of a man who knew he was the most dangerous thing in the room by far. Valeria by contrast, was somehow . . . diminished.

"I have it," she said.

"Good." He angled his head toward the drive. "Illium will watch Valeria until Andreas's men arrive."

Valeria made a low, pleading sound just as Honor looked out the window—to glimpse the astonishing sight of an angel with wings of silver-kissed blue coming to land on the verdant green of the lawn. "He's . . ." Her breath rushed out of her. She'd seen still photos, even television images of the blue-winged angel, but none of it had done him justice. None of it could.

The impact was even more startling up close. Staring at him as they met by the car, she took in the eyes of Venetian gold, the black hair dipped in shimmering blue, the face that was so pure in its beauty, he should've been too pretty. He wasn't. He was simply the most beautiful male creature she had ever seen in her life.

Meeting her gaze, he said, "I'm Illium."

Her lips threatened to curve at the unashamed curiosity in those golden eyes. "Honor."

Dmitri, having taken a quick call on his cell phone, opened the driver's-side door. "Valeria tries anything," he told Illium, "cut her arms off."

The blue-winged angel didn't look the least disturbed by the order. Added to Dmitri's obvious trust in him, it made it clear that, beauty or not, Illium was no pretty ornament. Though, she thought, catching the acute intelligence in that face as he spoke to Dmitri, he was fully capable of using the impact of his looks to his advantage.

"Elena and Raphael are on their way," he now said. "Be landing around six tonight."

Giving a crisp nod, Dmitri slid into the car. "Honor. Stop flirting with Illium. It only encourages his vanity."

"He's right." Illium walked around to open the passenger-side door for her. "I'm also a gentleman, unlike some people."

As she got in the car, their eyes met and she wondered who he was beyond the startling beauty and the charm, this Illium with his wings of blue. "Thank you."

His responding look was assessing . . . almost gentle. "You're not like the others."

"What?"

Dmitri roared away before Illium had a chance to respond. When she glanced back, it was to see him watching them with a distinctly considering expression on his face, his wings spread to catch the early morning sunlight. Silver threads glittered, turning him into a living mirage. "I thought," she said, after he disappeared from view, "angels were higher up in the food chain than vampires." And yet Illium had taken orders from Dmitri.

"He's one of the Seven, Raphael's elite guard," Dmitri told her as they turned out of the gates. "I lead them."

Raphael's second. The reason for the title was suddenly so much clearer. "I've never met an angel like Illium." Regardless of his stunning appearance, he had seemed more "human" than any other immortal she had ever met.

A hard glance. "Flirt with him if you want, Honor, but you're mine."

The blunt words were a shock . . . and not. "I don't know what *this*—between us—is," she said, acknowledging the dark fire that had burned between them from the start, "but I do know that for my mental health, I need to stay far, far away from you."

"Too bad." Said with the same lack of emotion with which he'd shot Valeria.

It scared her. A sane response. What wasn't sane was that she wanted to reach out and touch the brutal angle of his jaw, soften him somehow. Impossible. "If it comes down to it, I'll die to hold on to my freedom," she said, letting the wind whip her hair off her face. "I won't ever be a prisoner again, yours or anyone else's." It was a vow she'd made as she lay a broken doll in a hospital bed, one she'd spill the dark red of heart's blood to keep.

Dmitri shifted gears with the ease of a man used to power. "I don't intend to break you, Honor." The harsh edge replaced by black silk, sinful and tantalizing as the rich scent of chocolate seeped into her very bones. "I intend to seduce you."

A burst of heat low in her body, a pulse of attraction that followed no rules of rational behavior . . . and an obsession she couldn't fight. "Ever had a woman say no to you, Dmitri?"

"Once." He turned the corner with a smile that made her want to cup his face, trace those beautiful lips with her own. "I married her."

Dmitri wasn't certain why he'd told Honor that, when he spoke of Ingrede to no one. Raphael alone knew, and the archangel respected his wish to keep silent on the matter, on the wound that had never healed. "Tommy," he said, changing the direction of the conversation when Honor opened her mouth as if to ask him about the only woman in his long, long life who had ever held his heart, "is Thomas Beckworth the Third."

Honor's gaze lay heavy on him but she took the cue. "Tommy is a common name."

"Valeria confirmed." When she'd realized that begging and pleading wasn't going to work, the female vampire had attempted to hold the information hostage. It had only taken a couple of broken bones to end that. Dmitri had made certain those breaks echoed the half-healed fractures he'd seen on the X-rays taken after Honor's rescue.

"Please, Dmitri," Valeria had cried. "Don't turn into a monster because of a mortal."

It had made him smile in genuine amusement. "Dear Valeria, I was a monster before you were born." He'd become one the instant the cottage burned, taking the best part of him with it.

"According to a search I asked Venom to run while you were upstairs," he said, glancing away from a memory that would haunt him for all eternity, "seems like Tommy's gone to ground."

A whisper of scent, wildflowers in bloom as Honor shifted in her seat. "He can't know we're onto him."

The scent of her wrapped around him, touching him on a level he didn't permit any woman. "No," he said, hand tightening on the steering wheel, "but he's connected enough that he must have realized you were working for me."

Honor caught the lines of tension around his mouth, had to curl her fingers into her hand to stop the urge to lean over and stroke them away. This madness, it might just get her killed.

"We'll go to Tommy's home," he continued when she didn't interrupt, "see what we can discover."

That home proved to be as ostentatious within as Valeria's had been elegant. Ornate scrollwork on the moldings, wallpaper so ugly it had to have been bought more with reference to cost than taste, the furniture clunky and covered in floral fabric as hideous—and undoubtedly as expensive—as the wallpaper.

But the bedroom was what took the cake.

"Wow," Honor said, staring at the enormous circular bed covered in pink satin sheets as well as thousands of bloated pillows edged in white fur. "I didn't think people actually had beds like this outside of a porn set on steroids." Unable to stop herself, she looked up. "A mirrored ceiling. I'm shocked."

Dmitri began to laugh, and it was a wild, beautiful sound that cut off with harsh abruptness. "Honor, leave the room." An order coated in frost.

Her stomach clenched. It would've been so easy to turn on her heel, to allow him to shield her—and that was what he was attempting to do, this dangerous creature who would never be human—but to do so would be to give in to the bastards who had tried to destroy her. "No more running," she said, keeping her tone calm through vicious force of will. "Show me."

A taut moment, dark, dark eyes examining her. "Honor."

"Some battles," she said softly, holding that gaze full of secrets so very *old*, "a woman has to fight on her own."

His cheekbones cut against his skin as he said, "Behind you."

The blown-up black-and-white photograph covered the entire wall facing the bed. It was of a naked woman hanging from heavy chains by her wrists, her legs spread and manacled to the floor. Her head was slumped, her hair falling around her face, the side of her breast bleeding where a vampire had fed.

It was Honor.

Walking across to that image that threatened to catapult her back into a nightmare, she took out a blade and slowly, methodically, began to cut it to pieces. "I forgot," she said, swallowing her rage when it threatened to drown her, "that he took pictures."

Click. Click.

The sound had humiliated her anew when she had thought herself hardened to everything her abusers could do to her. "Then he began bringing the video camera." Which meant there were recordings of her somewhere, recordings where she tried not to scream as Tommy hurt her. That was why she'd forgotten—because she couldn't bear the shame of knowing others, perhaps her friends, would see her trapped and helpless and degraded . . . but of course, she had never *truly* forgotten.

"We'll find the original images and recordings." Dmitri began going through the bedroom with quiet, focused fury, ripping out drawers, emptying shelves. "He'll have kept them for
himself, a secret thing, because as soon as they got out, he
knew I'd slit his throat."

"You can't know that." A pain in her chest, so huge, so
heavy.

Dmitri walked over to help her pull off the last piece,
watched in silence as she tore it into even smaller shreds. "No
matter what," he said, when the last scraps fluttered to the
ground at her feet, a thousand black and white moths, "those
images will never see the light of day."

In his eyes, she saw a chilling prophecy of death.

Tommy wasn't the smartest of men—they found the memory cards holding the photos and videos in a wall safe. Dmitri
said nothing when she disappeared to the car—and to her laptop—to check that the images gave no clues that could lead to
the identification of the other members of this sick little group.

"I'm going to destroy these," she said to him when he
walked out, having found nothing else useful in the bedroom.
It was evidence, should be handled with care. Except it was
her. Naked and bound and dishonored. Rational or not, she
wanted the images gone, so no one else could ever see them.

Walking around to the trunk, Dmitri opened it to pick up a
small hammer from what turned out to be a sleek toolkit. She
used it to smash the memory cards into dust, then took the pli-
ers he held out to cut the metal components into tiny, tiny bits.
Dmitri was a cool-eyed audience throughout, but that cool was
edgy by the time they finished going through the house—
Tommy had left no clues as to his whereabouts.

"Honor." Dmitri angled his body to face her as he brought
the Ferrari to a stop in front of Guild HQ. Holding her gaze, he
reached out to touch a curling strand of hair that had escaped
the clip at the base of her neck, taking care not to brush any
other part of her. "So soft," he murmured. "Feminine, beautiful, and tough to break."

The pain in her chest, that horrible thing, it didn't lessen.
But right then, she could've kissed him. He wasn't human,

wasn't even good, but he had just given her back a piece of her pride that Tommy's evil had stolen. "I'll call you as soon as I have anything," she said, and it almost sounded like a promise.

Rather than going up to see Sara once she entered the Guild building, she went down to the Cellars. The underground hidey-holes served a dual purpose—as a place for hunters to take cover when things got too hot, and a home for the Guild's sophisticated surveillance and data collection systems.

All of it run by a brilliant mind trapped in a body that had been crushed in a childhood accident. Vivek only had feeling in and above his shoulders, but if anyone thought that stopped him from being the best damn "information analyst," a.k.a. spy, in the Guild's worldwide operation, they were probably going to get a rude surprise one of these days.

"Honor," he said when she cleared his security protocols to enter the bunker that housed the computers from where—according to Guild rumors—he ruled the world. "Dmitri after you already?"

11

Startled, she stared . . . and glimpsed the lines of concern on his face. "I'm not hiding from Dmitri."

"Oh, good. Though if you do piss him off enough for that, try not to attempt to shoot him in broad daylight. Sara still hasn't forgiven Elena for that."

Honor had heard of the incident; she'd even looked up the newspaper reports online. "I think a bullet wound might hurt him for a while, but I'm fairly certain he's too old to be killed by it even if you blew out the heart."

Vivek winced. "Oooh, Elena doesn't know that." Turning his chair around with a soft vocal command, he rolled over to the main computer panels to investigate a flashing alert. "So, did you come down here for my cheery company?" A sarcastic statement, but Honor had spent her childhood wrapped in loneliness—she understood the emotion better than most.

"I'm sorry I haven't visited," she said. "Truth is, I probably wouldn't have left the Academy even now if Sara hadn't forced me into it." It seemed impossible that she'd been that weak, beaten creature, but she had, and it was a truth she couldn't ignore. Because never again was she going back to that.

Vivek shot her a penetrating look. "It's safe, isn't it? People don't understand needing that."

She thought of him here in his bunker, protected from a world that had discarded him when he became less than perfect. Except—"You have far more courage than I ever will, V." Abandoned in an institution by his family, he'd literally made himself through the sheer, stubborn refusal to surrender.

"I was a kid when this happened," he said, voice raw. "I had a lot of time to get over the self-pity as I lay rotting in that hospital bed, so don't give me kudos I don't deserve."

Honor shook her head, but kept her silence. Then she asked what she'd come down here to ask, though the horror of it continued to be a jagged brick crushing her chest from the inside out. "I need you to do a search." Anger and panic and nausea roiled in her stomach. "For images or video clips of me."

Vivek's eyes flared with a rage so deep she might've been startled if she hadn't known he was hunter-born—wheelchair bound or not, he had the same instincts as the rest of the Guild. Now, turning to focus on his computers, he began to issue vocal commands so fast across so many different screens that she couldn't keep track.

A drop of ice trickled down her spine as she watched the hits come in one on top of the other. Swallowing the bile burning her throat, she forced herself to wait until he'd completed the search. "Show me."

Image after image filled the screens.

She scanned every single page of results, with Vivek doing a double check. "Is that it?"

"Yes. I dug down as far as you can go, used multiple and wide-ranging search terms."

Shuddering, she collapsed into a chair. "They're all file photos released when I disappeared, or candid shots taken after my rescue."

Vivek continued to talk to his computers for the next ten minutes as he checked and rechecked. "Net's clean, Honor. Whatever images the bastards took, they haven't uploaded them." A gleam in his eye. "I'd say they're too scared of the Tower."

"They're right to be." She should've been happy, but finding Valeria and discovering Tommy's identity had only reinforced the fact that the others who had treated her like a piece of meat were out there walking around, mocking her by living their lives free of terror or fear. "I won't stop," she said so low that it didn't reach Vivek, her hand fisting on her thigh. "And neither will Dmitri." A reminder that she had someone infinitely more dangerous and relentless on her side than any of Valeria's sick friends.

I don't intend to break you, Honor. I intend to seduce you.

Of course, that man also wanted to take a bite out of her. Not a little bite either. No, Dmitri wouldn't be satisfied with anything less than total, carnal surrender.

N<small>ine hours after he'd last seen Honor</small>, with night blanketing the world, Dmitri had just finished speaking to Galen via a satellite link when Venom strode into the room. "Sorrow slipped her security." The vampire had had no trouble switching to Holly's new name—perhaps because he'd once embraced a new identity of his own. "At least an hour ago."

Dmitri didn't swear. "I'll find her." He'd also be having a chat with the guards, because while Sorrow was highly intelligent and not quite human, she was also less than a quarter of a century old to their hundred and fifty–plus.

Venom shook his head, his hair falling across his forehead. "Look," he said, shoving it back with an impatient hand, "you're dealing with this other situation. I'll—"

"No. She's my responsibility." Elena had tracked her, but he was the one who'd coaxed her out of that tiny guard shack where she'd been hiding, her entire body encrusted with blood. "I know the places she goes."

Venom didn't budge, his willingness to stand up to the others in the Seven part of the reason he'd been accepted into the group in the first place. "You're getting too close, Dmitri. If . . ." The vampire's black pupils contracted, hard points against the searing green of his irises. "If she has more of Uram in her than she has of her humanity, execution might become necessary."

"That won't be a problem." He'd broken the neck of his own son, after all.

"It will be all right, Misha. I promise." He told the lie with
a smile, kissed his son on the forehead, that fine baby-soft skin
so hot against his lips. *"Papa will make it all right."*

The Ferrari got several "oh, yeahs!" from the boys hanging
out at the curb when he slid it into a No Parking spot in front
of a dingy little building with a neon sign proclaiming it *The
Blood Den*. Since the number plate made it clear the car belonged to Dmitri, he didn't bother with warnings. Anyone stupid enough to touch his car deserved what was coming to him.

A wide-eyed bouncer who outweighed Dmitri by two hundred pounds—and who wouldn't be able to stop him for so
much as a second should Dmitri find himself annoyed—
opened the door to the club before Dmitri reached it.

"Five-foot-four woman of Asian descent," he said to the
shaven-headed male. "Black hair streaked with pink, brown
eyes"—for the moment at least—"pasty skin." Sorrow
shunned the sun, not because it hurt her but because she
thought she was a creature who belonged in the dark.

"I noticed a chick going into one of the booths with a guy
when I went in for a break," the bouncer said. "Could be her."

Striding to the booth after the bouncer pointed it out, he
pulled open the door to expose a twenty-something white
male with his pants around his ankles. He had his hand on a
turgid cock, was jerking off, a glazed look in his eyes.

Sorrow, sitting on the bench opposite, curved crimson-
painted lips. "Come to join the party?" A mocking question
that held nothing of sex, though she was dressed in a tight
black dress with spaghetti straps that ended high on her thighs,
her legs covered in boots of liquid black.

Not saying a word, Dmitri slapped the male. The man
blinked, looked down, back up. "Wha—"

"Get out." Dmitri held open the door.

Cock deflating, the man pulled up his pants and left, stumbling over his feet in his rush to vacate the room. Shutting the
door, Dmitri leaned on it and watched as Sorrow threw back
what looked to be a large tequila before slamming the glass
down with a look of disgust. "Do you know I can't even get
properly drunk?"

"Your metabolism's altered." Along with so many other things.

A bitter laugh. "Yeah, and I can make men whip out their cocks and jerk off in front of me. Great superpower, huh?"

In point of fact, it was. Along with that ring of hypnotic green around her eyes and perhaps a murderous insanity, Sorrow had gained the ability to mesmerize people for short periods. Right now, she could only get them to commit acts they were already predisposed to engage in, but Dmitri didn't think it would stay that way for long. In the time since Uram had bitten her, *infected her*, the changes in Sorrow had progressed at phenomenal speed.

Aware of her frustration at his lack of overt anger, he watched as she uncurled from her seat, graceful as a cat, and walked over to press herself against him. "Why haven't you ever bled or fucked me, Dmitri?" Glittering eyes. Hard words. "Not good enough for you?"

"I don't sleep with little girls."

Her head snapped back, eyes heavy with makeup slamming into his. "I'm no child."

Dmitri didn't bother to argue the point. Instead, taking her hand, he opened the door.

She resisted. "I—"

"Enough," he said in a quiet tone that sliced through the pulsating music as if it didn't exist. "I cut small, precise pieces out of a vampire today." Honor hadn't realized that Valeria was missing most of her heart beneath her robe by the time Honor walked back into the room. "I'm planning to do a lot worse to another. So I wouldn't mess with me."

Sorrow sucked in a breath, but didn't speak again until they were out on the street, the late spring air brisk enough to raise goose bumps on her arms. "How long did it take?" she asked in a voice that trembled.

"What?"

"To become . . . inhuman?"

"Three months after my Making was complete." That was how long Misha had screamed and sobbed in the chains across from him, how long Caterina's ashes had lain exposed to the elements beside those of her mother.

"I'm sorry, Ingrede." Standing beside the burned-out shell

of the cottage, his dead son's body cradled in his arms, the most precious of burdens. "Forgive me."

Striding to the Ferrari, he wrenched open the passenger-side door. "Get in."

Sorrow obeyed, her defiance crushed by the brutality of his mood. Suddenly she looked heartbreakingly young, but Dmitri wasn't about to cut her any slack. She'd had over a year of it. "Using vampiric abilities on mortals without approval can get you sentenced to the earth." The punishment involved being buried alive in a coffin, given only enough blood to survive.

Her lower lip quivered.

"My coat's in the back."

Twisting, she pulled it over herself, shrinking down in the seat. "Are you going to put me in the earth?"

"No. That particular penalty's been taken off the books." Raphael had done it for Elena, a gift from an archangel to his consort. "I've been tasked to come up with a replacement."

Sorrow tugged his coat tighter around herself. "I'm sorry." The hesitant, scared words of the child he'd called her.

Sighing, he drove them over the Harlem River and cut across Manhattan to traverse the George Washington Bridge, before bringing the car to a stop on a clifftop outlook that faced Manhattan. The cityscape was a spread of gemstones against the black of the sky, the angels sweeping across it cast in silhouette. "I'm putting you under Contract, Sorrow." It was the only way to teach her control. "Doesn't matter if you were Made without your consent, you won't be free until I decide you're not a risk."

Having unzipped and pulled off her boots during the drive, she curled her legs under her on the seat. Tiny as she was, it didn't take much effort. "Will you teach me what I need to know?" A plea.

"No. Venom will take care of it." The girl was becoming dependent on him.

"I'm cold."

"I know, Misha. You're being a very brave boy."

"They hurt Mama and Rina." Valiant attempts to fight his sobs. "They hurt Mama and Rina, Papa."

The sound of Misha's cries still haunted him. He wouldn't,

couldn't, add another voice to that. "Venom will also start teaching you how to control your talent." Though Sorrow didn't know it, Venom's ability to mesmerize put hers in the shade. "I expect you to follow his commands."

"I will." A pause filled with things unsaid after that quiet acknowledgment. "What am I becoming?" she asked at last.

He could've lied to her, given her false hope, but that would only get her dead. Turning, he reached forward to tuck a wing of slick raven hair, streaked with color stolen by the night, behind her ear. She flinched and he knew she'd felt the cold blade of his anger. "No one knows. But the one thing I will not allow you to become is a problem. Do you understand?"

Her throat moved as she swallowed. "Yes." A whisper before she turned her face into the hand he still had brushing her cheek. "I'm scared, Dmitri."

"Papa, I'm scared."

Sorrow wasn't Misha, small and defenseless, but she might as well have been. And so, in spite of his vow to maintain his distance, he didn't tell her that she *should* be afraid, that almost everyone believed her chances of surviving this were beyond limited. Instead, he caressed the dark silk of her hair and thought of the soft black curls he'd once felt under his palm as his son's body lay wracked with convulsions in his arms.

"Please! No! Stop!"

Honor shoved off the sheets and rolled out of the bed, her heart thudding triple time. A glance at the clock told her it had been a bare three hours since she'd collapsed, after having worked on the tattoo past midnight. Trouble was, she kept remembering what Valeria, Tommy, and their friends had done to her.

Except that nightmare . . . she could've sworn it had had nothing to do with the pit. Maybe it had been an echo of the childhood night terrors that had been the reason she'd never been adopted, though infants were always in demand. Apparently, she'd screamed and screamed and screamed, until she wore herself out—only to start again as soon as she woke. The screaming had continued until she was four or five, after which she'd tended to wake herself up when they began and spend the rest of the night fighting sleep.

Abandonment issues, one child psychologist had called it. Honor wasn't so sure. What she'd felt when she woke from those childhood nightmares had been too huge, too vast, a terrible darkness filled with utter desolation. The same thing that had her throat so thick now, her heart pounding deep and hard enough to bruise. Rubbing her hand over her chest to dispel the feeling, she headed to the shower.

Dressed in fresh clothes afterward, she picked up the phone and input a number she'd never expected to use at four a.m. on a cool spring morning, the sky a smoky black broken by a scattering of light-filled offices in the high-rises.

A dark male voice came on, asking her to leave a message.

Hanging up, she rubbed her palms over her face and went to spread the blown-up photographs of the tattoos on the small dining table beside the window. She'd made a breakthrough, or what she'd thought was a breakthrough, just before she'd fallen exhausted into bed. Now, her mind clearer, notwithstanding the nightmares, she began to retrace her line of thought.

Yes, that was definitely it. The key. Or part of the key.

She didn't know how long she'd been working but her writing pad was covered with several pages of notes, when there was a knock on her door. Frowning, she glanced at the wall clock.

Half past four.

Body tensing with a strange exhilaration because it could only be one person, she picked up her gun and looked through the peephole.

12

She slid away the gun—odd, given who she was about to let in—and opened the door.

"You called?" Dmitri was wearing a white shirt open at the collar and black suit pants, his hair tumbled just enough to make her think he'd been running his hands through it.

It made her own fingers curl into her palms. "Come in," she said, a vivid image of what he might look like sated and lazy in bed forming full-fledged in her mind. Though she knew Dmitri was far more likely to be a lover who would take total control even in the most intimate of dances, her mind insisted on seeing him sprawled relaxed on his back, a teasing smile on his face—the way a man might look at a familiar lover.

The idea was so tempting that she had to force herself to ignore it, to remember the truth of him as a sophisticated vampire who'd tasted every sin—and who wouldn't stay with the same woman beyond the time it took to satisfy his curiosity.

"I married her."

One woman at least, had awakened more in him than a fleeting sexual attraction. Honor had the most unquenchable desire to know everything about that woman, a hundred thousand questions she wanted to ask. However, for one question she needed no answer: it was patent that Dmitri had spoken his marriage vows long, long ago. That man didn't exist anymore, had likely not existed for centuries.

"I have something to show you," she said, unable to understand the strange ache inside of her.

He followed her to the table, listened in silence.

"I'm near certain," she said after explaining the process by which she'd come to her conclusion, "this is a name." She touched a particular grouping of symbols. "The sample I have to work with is so small that it's possible I could be way off, but I *think* the sound is something like Asis or Esis."

Dmitri went very, very quiet. "Isis."

A skeletal hand gripped her throat, squeezed. "Tell me about her." Dmitri's face was all hard lines when she glanced up after making that demand, his eyes so remote that she saw nothing and forever in them. "Dmitri." Somehow, her hand was on his forearm, his skin hot through the fine linen of the shirt, his tendons taut.

His face, however, showed nothing. "You shouldn't be touching me right now, Honor."

She jerked away her hand, but the fear she felt had nothing to do with him. It was in her very bones, brought to life by a name that meant nothing . . . and yet it incited not only fear but an anger beyond rage, beyond fury. *"Tell me."*

Dmitri's voice remained oddly flat as he said, "Isis was the angel who Made me. I stabbed her in the heart and cut her into pieces for it."

Pleasure, vicious and wild, intertwined with a haunting despair, roared through her. Shocked, she dropped the pen she'd been using to explain her reasoning and stumbled backward from the table.

Dmitri's eyes didn't move off Honor as she shoved her hands into her hair, pulling it loose from the messy bun at her nape, and made her way to the kitchen with jerky steps. "That's where I saw this code." On Isis's writing desk—at the start, when she'd taken him to her chambers. "She called it her little secret, but her courtiers and friends had to know it because she wrote notes to them using the code." Too many immortals to single out a name, but he would set that line of investigation in progress.

Right now, it was Honor who held his attention.

As he watched, she began to make tea with the methodical motions of a woman who had often done the same task—and yet who now took care with each and every step of the process. The kind of thing Ingrede had done when she needed to calm herself.

"What," he murmured, leaning on the bench that separated the kitchen area from the dining and living areas, "do you know of Isis?"

The space was open on both sides, so he couldn't block her in, but Honor, skittish as she was, didn't seem to want to run from him. At this moment, as she poured boiling water into a glass teapot, her bones pushing white against her skin, she seemed to be fighting only herself.

"Nothing," she said, putting down the hot water jug and setting the pale red-orange tea to steep. "Yet I want to dance on her grave."

The naked emotion in her voice found an echo inside him. "There is no grave," he said, looking into those deep green eyes full of secrets. "We made sure nothing of her remained." Except it seemed something *had* survived, some tainted piece now attempting to take root.

"We?"

He saw no harm in sharing the truth—it had never been a secret. "Raphael was there. We killed Isis together." The bond forged in that pain-soaked room beneath the keep, and in the blood and viscera of Isis's death, was one nothing would ever break.

Honor braced her hand on the counter. And then she met his gaze with those eyes that belonged to an immortal, and asked a question he would've never expected from the scared woman who had first walked into his office. "Who were you before Isis, Dmitri?"

"I broke it." A disconsolate whisper.

"Let me see."

"Will you tell Mama?"

"It'll be our secret. There, it's fixed."

"Dmitri, Misha, what are you up to?"

"Secret things, Mama!"

Laughter, sweet and feminine and familiar, followed by In-

grede's quiet footsteps. Heavy with child, she kissed first her giggling son, then her smiling husband.

"I was another man," he said, put on edge by the forceful draw he felt toward Honor. He may have led a life of debauchery after his world burned to ash, may have blackened his soul and indulged in every vice there was in an effort to numb the pain, but he had never, ever betrayed Ingrede where it mattered. His heart, it had remained untouched, encased in stone.

"I will love you even when I am dust on the wind."

This hunter shattered on the innermost level was not likely to tempt him to break that promise . . . but there was no denying that there were hidden depths to her. Depths he was compelled to explore. "You're an excellent shot," he said.

A shrug. "I practice, and Valeria wasn't exactly a moving target." Lines marred her forehead. "I should feel bad about taking advantage when she was pinned up like a butterfly, but I don't. What does that make me?"

"Human. Flawed."

"Strange how that actually makes me feel better." She reached to open an upper cupboard. The motion pulled her gray sweatshirt a fraction tighter over her full breasts, but nowhere near enough to showcase a body that Dmitri was damn certain was meant to be showcased.

Hmm . . .

Turning on his heel, he began to prowl around her apartment. When he turned in the direction of what he guessed was her bedroom, she said, "That's private, Dmitri."

He ignored her.

Heard her swear a blue streak.

But he was already at her closet by the time she ran around the counter to follow. "What do you think you're doing?"

"Seeing who you were before Valeria and Tommy." He pulled out a short scarlet dress with a plunging neckline and no back. "This, I *like*."

Honor, her cheeks as red as the dress, grabbed the hanger from him. "For your information, I never wore this. It was a gift from a friend."

His enthusiasm cooled. "That's the kind of dress a man buys."

"Or a girlfriend who likes to jerk my chain," she muttered, shoving the dress back into the closet. "Now get out."

He reached in to pull out a number of other items instead, throwing them on the bed. Shirts and simple tops, for the most part, but all of them fitted. Nothing like the shapeless tees and sweatshirts she'd taken to wearing. Throwing them on the bed, he said, "Get dressed properly and I'll show you something you've never before seen."

Glaring at him, she started to put the clothing back. "I happen to be working—the rest of the ink won't decode itself."

A cold burn of anger invading his veins at the reminder of Isis, he shut the closet doors with deliberate care. "From what I saw," he said in a tempered voice, "you've been going around in circles."

A blown-out breath. "I've almost got it. It's there on the tip of my tongue."

"A break will help." While she dressed, he'd make a few calls, including one to Jason. If someone was attempting to revive or revere Isis in any way, shape, or form, Dmitri wanted to know. So he could crush the repugnance.

Movement, Honor walking to the vanity to pick up a brush. "Where are we heading?"

"You'll find out when we get there."

Narrowed eyes. "Leave so I can get dressed."

"Don't take too long." Striding out to her glare, he began to make his phone calls. Jason hadn't heard even a whisper of anything related to an angel named Isis, but promised to alert his network. Dmitri also contacted Illium, instructing him to brief the rest of the Seven. His final call was to Raphael.

The archangel's response was simple. "You're certain?"

"Yes," he said, understanding the question. "I'll handle it." Isis was his nightmare.

Hanging up, he was staring out at a Manhattan still swathed in the graying kiss of night, the Tower dominating the skyline, when the scent of wildflowers in bloom grew stronger. It tugged at long-buried emotions in him, that scent, made him remember the mortal he'd been so many years ago that entire civilizations had risen and fallen during his lifetime.

"Let's go."

He turned to see Honor dressed in ill-fitting jeans and a

loose white shirt. "I said properly dressed." He knew full well what she was doing with her shapeless clothing, and it turned him merciless. "Just because the predators can't get a good look at you doesn't mean they don't consider you fresh meat."

Fury spotted red high across her cheekbones. "Fuck you, Dmitri."

"Right now?" He gave her a deliberately taunting smile. "Come over here, then, darling."

He saw her hand twitch, knew she was fighting the urge to go for her gun, drill him in the heart. "You know what?" she said. "I think I'd prefer my own company. Get out."

"Pathetic, Honor," he said, well aware of the painful buttons he was pressing. "Valeria—if she still has her tongue, which is doubtful—would be laughing at what she's made you."

Honor went motionless. "I think I'm starting to hate you."

"Doesn't bother me." There was strength in hate. It was why he'd survived that dungeon. "It'll make it even sweeter when I have you naked and wet for me."

Not answering, she slammed her way into her bedroom. Ten long minutes later she stepped back out. This time, her hair pulled back into a tight ponytail, she was dressed in skin-tight jeans tucked into knee-high black boots, topped with a close-fitting black tee over which she'd thrown a hip-length leather jacket in the same shade. He'd been right—her breasts were luscious, her body a knockout.

Walking over to stop bare inches from a female form that was all but vibrating with rage, he reached out to touch her, the compulsion undeniable. A blur of movement, an elbow to his chest, his legs being kicked out from under him, and suddenly he was crashing onto the floor, looking up at an Honor who was no victim.

Dmitri laughed.

Honor didn't know what she'd expected, but that laugh, deep and masculine and hotly *real*, wasn't it. When he lifted a hand toward her, she ignored it . . . though it was troubling, how much she wanted to straddle that beautiful body and lean down to kiss those sensual, laughing lips—as if he hadn't just cut into her with the pitiless blade of his voice.

His laughter faded into a smile that was very, very male. "Come here."

She walked to the door instead . . . but she was no longer so sure that when it came to this madness inside her, a madness that bore Dmitri's name, that she'd emerge the winner.

Honor froze when Dmitri brought the car to a halt around the back of a discreet black building in Soho. "You bastard," she said, her voice so soft it was almost not sound. Erotique was the club of choice for the more high-ranked vampires. Its hosts and hostesses—mostly human, but with the occasional "new" vampire thrown in—were trained to know how to deal with the older almost-immortals. Some called the dancers within its exclusive walls the geishas of the West.

Bracing his hand against the back of her seat, Dmitri shot her a glance that appeared darkly amused . . . if you didn't look into those eyes, cold and brutal. "There is a high chance," he said in a voice that was black satin over her breasts, "that at least some of the vampires you'll meet here tonight have already had a taste of you."

"Come on, hunter. Scream a little more. The blood tastes better when you do."

Spots in front of her eyes, her breath strangling in her chest. Her gun was in her hand and pointed at Dmitri's head before she was aware of pulling it from the shoulder holster. "I'm leaving."

Dmitri moved at lightning speed, and suddenly her gun was in his grip, that sensual face an inch from her own. "Taunt them with your survival, Honor. Or run like a scared rabbit. Your choice."

The violence within her body needed release—she wanted to hit Dmitri, bloody him. "Why do you care?" It was a harsh whisper. "I'm just a new diversion for you."

"True." Touching the nose of her gun to her cheek. "But I find there's no fun in playing with someone who's already half dead." He put the weapon in her lap and pushed open his door to step out. "Strange," he murmured, snicking the door shut, "how you sometimes remind me of her, and yet you don't have even a glimmer of her spirit."

She stared at his retreating form as he headed toward the back entrance of the club, leaving her alone in a panther of a car, gun heavy in her holster as she slid it back in. His words had been calculated to incite a reaction, but they still hit. Hard.

"You're no fun anymore, hunter. I expected more resistance to this game."

Vaulting out of the vehicle, she stalked after Dmitri. He glanced over his shoulder, waited for her to catch up. "Try not to shoot anyone." A low purr that stroked her senses with an intimacy as lush as the sinuous scent of midnight roses. "We need people to talk."

They'd reached the door by then, a door the bouncer was already holding open. "Sir," he said, keeping his eyes scrupulously off Honor.

"He looked surprised," she said once they were inside the back corridor. "Not usually your scene?"

"No." Angling his head in her direction as they turned toward the throaty sound of a jazz singer coming from the left, he said, "They'll assume I have you in my bed."

13

Closer, the singer's voice tangled with the music of soft conversation. The voices were elegant, cultured . . . just like the ones she'd heard in the basement. "I know," she said, determined not to let this drive her back into the dark, "but since you have a reputation for enjoying pain, I'm sure they won't be surprised if I give in to the need to stab you."

A gleam of laughter in those eyes so dark and old, but he said nothing as they walked through the doorway into what appeared to be a very genteel bar, complete with a chanteuse in a glittery green dress on a low stage to the side. The lighting was soft, the groupings of tables intimate, the clientele dressed in immaculate formal clothing. "A bit early for cocktails."

"Or very late," Dmitri answered. "Time means little here."

All the men and women in her line of sight were old enough that vampirism had worked its magic, honing their looks to a level of beauty only possessed by the rare mortal. "I expected . . ." In truth, she'd never thought that much about Erotique, but what she had heard focused on an aspect that was missing here. "The dancers?"

"In another section," Dmitri told her. "There's an entire

floor below us, as well as a number of other more intimate areas similar to this one."

"Dmitri." A stunning woman in a clinging black dress that reached her ankles and showcased her assets with sensual elegance crossed the room to them, her steps quick. "I didn't know you were coming or we'd have set up a private room for you and your guest."

"Get us that corner table, Dulce." His voice was that of a man who expected instant obedience. "Champagne. And find Illium."

The barest flicker of . . . something on the perfect bones of Dulce's face, gone as fast as it had appeared. "Yes, of course."

Honor saw the couple already at the corner table move with alacrity when they saw the hostess heading toward them. There was more than a little fear in their movements. Aware that vampires of a certain age had preternatural hearing, she leaned up to speak against Dmitri's ear. With any other man, any other vampire, she'd have been close to throwing up by now . . . but whatever inexplicable alchemy existed between her and Dmitri, it allowed her to breathe in his scent, say, "Do you keep them afraid on purpose?"

His hand only just brushed her lower back. "Means I have to execute fewer of them."

She didn't say anything else until they were seated and Dulce had melted away after serving the champagne. "Dulce isn't human." It had been the eyes that had given her away. An intense deep purple, jewel bright against raven black hair. No human had eyes that color—and the contact lenses hadn't been invented that could mimic that kind of otherworldly beauty.

"No. She manages Erotique, has done so for the past ten years." A raised eyebrow. "You didn't think I'd be greeted by anyone less than the manager, did you, Honor?"

She didn't take the bait. "Why are we here?"

"Look in the corner diagonally opposite."

Following his gaze, she saw a tall, sandy-haired vampire with a curvy brunette in his lap. Neither had noted Dmitri's arrival—and the reason why was clear. The vampire's pale hand lay on the shimmering silver of the woman's ankle-length gown, dangerously close to the full curves of her breasts, his lips nuzzling the long line of her throat. They both went motionless an instant later, and then the vampire was feeding, his throat muscles moving, as the brunette threw back her head in silent orgasm.

Honor's hand clenched around the champagne flute in front of her. Scanning the room, she realized more than one vampire was feeding—and they weren't all male. An ethereally lovely woman with Hispanic features was stroking her hands into the hair of a slender blond male, the crystal blue sharpness of her nails dramatic points against his skin as she wrenched him down to feed just above the pulse point in his neck.

"I thought," she said, throat dry, "this was a club, not a feeding orgy."

Dmitri's laugh was a rope of fur twining around her senses. "So innocent, Honor." He took a sip of his champagne. "Some vampires come here because they know they'll find a willing partner should they need one, partners who know what to expect. But most of the others are lovers indulging in a little harmless exhibitionism."

Obviously noting her gaze on the female vampire, he said, "That's Amalia. She likes them young—but he's legal, adult enough to make a choice." There was something in that statement, something old and buried and *so* angry.

"You're watching the vampire with the attractive brunette," she said, knowing that even if Dmitri did get her into bed, that's all it would ever be—sex. Erotic, sinful, dangerous sex, but nothing beyond a physical coupling. No secrets would be shared, no bonds forged. "Why?"

"That is Evert Markson. Tommy's best friend."

Her head jerked up. "You knew he was going to be here."

"Evert has the rather distasteful habit of feeding at Erotique on a regular basis."

It was hard not to stare at Markson, but she kept her attention on Dmitri. "You just told me vampires come here to feed."

"Only now and then, when they don't have a regular lover or donor. Perhaps if they are visiting from out of town." He placed his champagne flute on the table. "The reason Evert needs to feed at Erotique is that he hurts his lovers so badly that not even the worst of the groupies will go near him now. The hostesses here only acquiesce on the condition that he feeds in public, where he can be monitored."

Heart in her throat, Honor looked back at the brunette in Markson's arms, seeing what she'd missed earlier—the shallow breaths, the white lines bracketing full lips pursed tight. "She's not orgasming, is she?" The urge to get up and tear the vampire off the other woman had every muscle in her body tense to breaking point.

"He's making it hurt."

"Dmitri"—releasing the fragile stem of her own flute before she broke it—"if he's Tommy's best friend, then . . ."

"Yes. Exactly." His gaze shifted to the doorway. "Bluebell's here."

The silver filaments in Illium's wings caught the light as he walked over. The women in the room—and more than a few men—went motionless, watching his progress with eyes full of wonder and *want*.

Anger, a bright, sharp thing, continued to sing a piercing song in her blood, but she said, "Hello, Illium," when he grabbed a chair from another table and swiveled it to sit with his arms braced on the back, his amazing wings sloping down to brush the floor.

"Hello, Honor St. Nicholas." His eyes, those beautiful golden eyes tipped with the most impossible lashes, locked on her. "You look like you want to use a knife on someone's flesh, watch the blood bead on their skin."

"Yes," she admitted, "but I have to wait."

Illium stole her champagne, took a sip, shuddered. "Never did like that stuff." Putting the flute back on the table, he turned to Dmitri. "Word is, Tommy's gone underground because he's scared of someone. It was before Honor was assigned to the Tower, so it's not you."

Dmitri's eyes never shifted off Evert Markson. "Do me a favor. Fly to Evert's home and see if you find anything interesting."

The blue-winged angel left without further conversation.

Beside her, Dmitri smiled and it was a cold, cold smile. She knew who he had in his sights before she turned her head and saw Evert. Swallowing compulsively as he shoved the brunette off his lap without care, his eyes skittered between Dmitri and Honor. The recognition in those eyes was a stabbing confirmation that Tommy had taken his best friend into the game.

When Dmitri did nothing to stop the vampire from leaving, she began to rise. He clamped a hand over her wrist. "Let him stew in his fear, Honor." Dmitri's murmur was a brush of silk over her senses. "Evert isn't as smart as Tommy. I know where he's going."

It was hard to sit back and watch one of the men who had tortured her walk out of her sight. "You could be wrong."

A thumb moving over her skin. "I'm not."

She looked down, startled to realize that he was touching her . . . and she had no urge to pull away. "Is it only the scent thing you do, Dmitri?" she asked, feeling a languorous warmth invade her blood. "Or do you have other compulsions at your command?"

"I'll leave that for you to figure out." Stroking her once more, he stood. "Let's go play with our prey."

Honor held her words inside until they were driving through the misty gray skies painted by the last edge of night, the wind cool, with a bite that hinted at rain. "I don't want to become that cold." To lose her humanity. "I don't want to take pleasure in the pain of others."

Shifting gears with ruthless ease, Dmitri began to head toward the Manhattan Bridge. "Sometimes there is no choice."

The ancient darkness of his words wrapped around her. She'd already told herself he was a man who would never share his secrets, but she couldn't *not* ask, couldn't not attempt to see beneath the deadly, sophisticated surface when it came to Dmitri. "What did Isis do to you?" Instinct—primal, visceral—told her that that was the genesis of what he'd become—a predator who had very few moral lines he would not cross.

His hair whipped off his face as he took them onto the bridge, the car purring sleek and dangerous over the wide span. "I'm not beautiful like Illium, but I'm a man women want in their beds."

Yes, she thought. To look at Dmitri was to think of sex. Rich, dark eyes, black hair, skin of a tempting, warm shade between honey and brown, lips that spoke of pleasure and pain, a body that moved with a lethal grace that incited sexual fantasies of how he might move with—inside—a woman. "But you're not a man who can be owned." To try would be both foolish and dangerous. "You'll choose your own lovers."

"Isis didn't think so." No change in his expression. "I was mortal then, weak. She wanted me and when I said no, she took me."

"Whoever it was that took you, hunter"—a long, slow lick along her inner thigh—*"I owe them my thanks."*

She curled her hands into fists. "She hurt you."

No answer.

It was perhaps twenty minutes later that he brought the car to a silent stop down the street from a modern dual-level home set behind a small green hedge. Painted what appeared to be a stylish black, the window frames and the roof were picked out in a deep red striking even in the monochrome shadows before dawn.

"This can't be Evert's place." He'd been wearing a platinum watch, an Italian suit. Not the kind of man who'd be satisfied with a small, albeit fashionable home.

"It's owned by his former mistress," Dmitri answered after they'd exited the car and begun to head toward the front of the house. "Evert believes Shae continues to have a soft spot for him." He produced a key. "He's wrong." Unlocking the door, he entered on silent feet.

Honor followed, reaching back to snick the door closed. The hallway was devoid of light except for the subtle glow of the small wall lamp by the staircase, but the house wasn't as quiet as it should've been at this time of the morning. Retrieving her gun, she held it by her side as they climbed the stairs, Dmitri with the grace of a panther, her with a more mortal stride.

". . . I'm sure." A placating feminine voice. "Do sit down, Evert darling."

"He was staring *right at me*." Gasping, jagged words. "And the hunter was with him!"

That *voice*. Honor knew him now, remembered exactly what he'd done, how he had laughed that high-pitched laugh more suited to a teenage girl.

"What hunter?"

"Tommy promised she was finished, good as trash. Knew nothing, he said. Bastard lied to me."

"That can't be true. He's your best friend." Rustling sounds, as if Shae had risen to her feet. "Why don't you call him—"

"Don't you think I haven't tried?" A rasping shout, followed by the unmistakable crack of flesh meeting flesh.

Rage, hot as blood, hazed Honor's vision.

Shae, however, didn't sound cowed when she said, "I'm sure it's a misunderstanding. If Dmitri wanted to harm you, he wouldn't have let the public location stop him."

"Yes, yes, you're right." Relief, spurts of girlish laughter. "Maybe he's just fucking the bitch. She is a sweet piece of ass."

Honor clicked off the safety on her gun. Across from her, Dmitri shook his head, and she remembered that, age notwithstanding, she'd sensed no hint of true power in Evert Markson. A heart shot might kill him—and they needed him to talk. Forcing herself to back off from the edge, no matter how satisfying it would be to turn the bastard's heart into fleshy shrapnel, she followed in silence as Dmitri opened the bedroom door and walked inside.

Dressed in nothing but pink lace panties and a white baby tee, a short woman with café au lait skin, her hair a storm of tight curls, stood facing the door. The instant she saw them, she ran into the bathroom at her back and shut the door, depriving Evert of a hostage. Swiveling around, the vampire screamed and launched himself at Dmitri, hands out like claws.

Honor shot him through the knees.

Dmitri glanced at her as the ghost-pale vampire crumpled in a spray of blood and bone. "I didn't need the help, sweetheart." A mild statement.

"I know." Markson had hurt her in ways that had caused internal damage it had taken the doctors months to fix—seeing him scream wasn't enough to erase the memories, but it was something. And . . . he'd been trying to hurt Dmitri. Honor wouldn't allow that. *Not Dmitri.* "Neighbors probably heard that."

"No, they didn't. Evert had this house soundproofed, didn't you, Evert?"

"I don't know anything, I swear." Sobbing words, snot running out of his nose.

Dmitri smiled, as gentle as a dagger sliding between the ribs.

And Evert folded. "He has this rough woodland cabin upstate—in the Catskills. No one thinks to look for him in a place like that." Wiping away his tears, he struggled up into a sitting position against the bed, his wounds already beginning to heal. "He's not picking up his phone, though."

"Number?"

Evert rattled it off, hazel eyes too innocent to belong to this creature, jumping to Honor before swinging back to Dmitri. "I thought you were in on it," he whispered, rubbing the sleeve of his suit jacket across his nose. "I thought you okayed it."

14

Even before Honor had learned what Isis had done to Dmitri, she had never—not for an instant—considered that possibility. Didn't now. Because if she had always understood one thing, it was that Dmitri didn't share what was his. "Why?" she asked instead. "What possible reason could you have for thinking that?"

"When Tommy invited me," Evert said, his breathing no longer choppy, his eyes awash with tears, "he said it was a new game *all* the high-level vamps were playing."

"If you thought I was in on it," Dmitri asked in a silken whisper, "why did you run from the club?"

Eyes jerking back and forth, tears mingling with the sweat pouring down his face. No more words. No more lies. Suddenly Honor didn't care what happened to him—he was too pathetic. "Do what you have to," she said to Dmitri, stepping close enough that he had to bend down so she could whisper in his ear, the masculine heat and primal sin of him stealing into her lungs to infuse her blood. "But he's not worth a piece of your soul. Don't give him that."

His breath whispered over her cheek, his words a low murmur that wrapped her in lush intimacy, making her feel oddly protected . . . safe. "You sure I have a soul?"

"It might be battered and scarred, but it's there." Many would call her a fool for believing that, but there was nothing rational in her when it came to Dmitri. Just instinct, primitive and unrelenting. "So don't waste it on this bottom-feeder." Pulling back, she strode to the door of the bathroom and knocked.

Evert's ex-mistress opened it at once. Having put on a white terry-cloth robe, she followed Honor down the stairs, before taking the lead to bring them out into a small, paved backyard. "I'm Shae."

"Honor."

"Evert broke my jaw once." The pretty woman sat down in one of the outdoor chairs placed around a square wooden table. "For fun."

Grabbing a seat opposite, Honor focused on the ugly mottled mark forming on Shae's otherwise unblemished skin. "Why stay with him?"

A shrug. "I was only seventy when I met him."

Honor's spine twitched at the realization that Shae, petite and with those bruised human eyes, was a vampire. "Dashing older man, right?" she said, forcing herself to remain relaxed. Shae was no threat, her power so muted as to be negligible— the reason her body hadn't yet been able to heal the damage caused by Evert's vicious slap.

"Yes." The other woman shook her head, her curls catching on the terry cloth. "Stupid, but hey, we're all stupid once in a while." A penetrating glance. "Dmitri, huh? No offense, but talk about stupid."

Yes, it was. Probably the worst mistake of her life—but walking away wasn't an option. Not anymore. If it had ever been. "You sound very certain we're involved."

"*Puh-leeze*, as my great-niece would say." Shae shoved her hands through her hair, either agitated by the events of the morning or constitutionally incapable of staying still.

So young, Honor thought, so vulnerable, and it was a curious thought to have about a woman who had more than half a century on her. But then, time wasn't everything. Dmitri would've been a force to be reckoned with soon after his Making. Shae would always be the quarry, rather than the hunter.

Eternity, Honor thought, was a long time to spend as a victim. "What do you know about Tommy?"

"Prick friend of Evert's. He's four hundred years old and still has that smarmy, sweaty look that says a man's thinking about getting you naked—and not in a nice way." The vampire tugged her robe tighter around herself. "Evert wasn't lying about the cabin. They took me there once." Her silence was heavy with secrets too terrible to be voiced.

Neither of them spoke for long moments filled with the cheerful sounds of birds scolding one another, their day long begun.

"I'm so afraid," Shae said when the birds scattered with a bright chorus, fine lines pinching out from her mouth, "that that's what I'll become as I age. Depraved, finding pleasure only in the humiliation and suffering of others." A look of unhidden concern. "Even Dmitri . . . he's barely on this side of the line, you know that, don't you?"

"Yes." He was no innocent, would never be one. "Tell me more about Tommy."

"He's good with money so he has financial power, but is otherwise weak." Fingers playing with the lapels of her robe, dropping to twist the ends of the belt at her waist. "They like to pretend to be big men, but they're sheep, him and Evert both."

"Yes." Dmitri's deep voice from behind Honor as he stepped out through the kitchen. "They were minor pawns in the scheme of things."

For the first time since she'd met him, she didn't angle her body to keep him in her line of sight. Instead, she allowed him to come up behind her, to place his hand on the back of the wooden chair where she sat, brush his thumb over the skin of her neck.

Terror, visceral and gut-deep. Her heart rabbiting against her ribs.

Gritting her teeth, she held her position, a small rebellion, a tiny reclaiming of who she'd been before the pit. "No screams," she said, the words husky.

"I had my orders." Continuing to play his thumb over her

now fear-dampened skin, he spoke to the other vampire. "Evert won't bother you again. Someone will be picking him up in about twenty minutes."

Shae shuddered. "I—Will—" Her eyes landed on Honor, not Dmitri. "Will you stay? If he wakes up . . ."

"Yes," she said, caught by the irony of Shae looking to safety from a woman who was currently fighting not to choke on the rancid taste of her own terror.

Dmitri tugged at a tiny curl of hair at her nape. "Look up, Honor."

Illium was a stunning sight against the lightening sky, his wings sweeping through the air with a grace that made him seem a half-forgotten dream. When he landed in the courtyard, his wings flaring out for an instant, he was at once very much a man, physical and sexual, and an unattainable fantasy.

She could never see herself falling for such a beautiful man. No, it seemed her tastes ran darker, rougher, edgier. But she could admire him . . . and she could wonder about the shadows beyond the gold, shadows that resonated with something hidden inside of her. "Bluebell," she said, remembering from Erotique. "Pretty name."

"I call Dmitri Dark Overlord."

"Shae," Dmitri said and the female vampire rose at once to walk quickly into the house. "Now, pretty Bluebell"—another languid stroke across her skin—"tell the Overlord what you discovered."

Grinning, Illium perched on the wooden table, one of his wings a bare inch from Honor. "I found this." He passed over a textured cream-colored envelope. "It was on the nightstand, put there by the maid. Came tonight."

Honor reached up to grab the envelope before Dmitri could, running her finger under the flap to unseal it. Inside was a single sheet of heavy paper with a very simple message.

The second hunt begins soon. I hope you will find this prey as delicious as the first—the Guild has the most appetizing personnel.

Honor put the letter on the table. Seeing its contents, Illium and Dmitri exchanged words, but their voices were drowned out by the crashing thunder inside her head. "No one else," she whispered and it was a vow. "The bastards get no one else."

Dmitri's response was a simple "They won't." His hand curved around her nape . . . and she didn't jerk away.

Ten minutes later, just after he'd finished speaking to one of his men in the vicinity of the Catskills, Dmitri got a call from Sorrow. "I think I did something, Dmitri."

Long-dormant instincts struggled to wake at the fear-thinned sound of her voice. He crushed them—he couldn't afford to think of the young woman the way he'd thought of Misha and Caterina. "Where are you?"

"The park near my house, by the big birdbath." Shaken words, a spirit close to broken. "I'm sorry I sneaked out. I just wanted to go for a walk, that's all."

"Stay where you are," he said, those old, buried instincts attempting to surface once again, harsh and ragged from centuries of disuse. "Illium's going to fly to you—he won't land," he added, because he could feel her panic through the phone lines. And whatever else he might be, he wasn't bastard enough to terrorize her in such a way. "I'll be right behind him."

Illium rose into the air as soon as Dmitri gave him the details. Dmitri then called Sorrow's watch detail to tell them where to locate her. "Don't approach."

"Shae," Honor said when he hung up. "She's scared."

He saw compassion in those midnight-forest eyes, was rocked by her ability to feel the tender emotion. But he wasn't like her—everything good in him had burned as his son's tiny body burned in the ruins of the cottage he'd built for his bride. So fast Misha had disappeared, so impossibly fast. The crackle of the flames, the whistle of the wind, none of it had drowned out the echo of the last words his son had ever spoken to him.

"Don't let go, Papa."

"Good," he said, shoving the memories back in the steel box that could no longer contain them, "fear will keep her from being stupid." Striding through to the living area where Shae hovered, he grabbed her chin. "Say a word about what you learned here tonight, and you'll be joining Evert as Andreas's guest."

The vampire went sheet white. "I w-won't. N-never."

"Dmitri."

He released Shae because she'd gotten the point, and headed out the door just as the retrieval team drove up, a furious Honor by his side. "There was no need to terrify her." The scent of wildflowers hit him hard as he got into the driver's seat of the Ferrari, scraping against the raw wound that was the memory of Misha's funeral pyre.

"She's a victim." Honor slammed her own door shut.

Feeling vicious, he didn't bother to sugarcoat his opinion as he guided the car away from the curb. "She's weak, a parasite. A year, maybe not even that, and she'll have found another Evert to bleed."

"You're talking about a woman with all the hallmarks of abuse," Honor argued, stubborn in her belief, so like another woman who had once fought with him, wild passion in her voice. "It'll take her time to break the cycle."

He heard what she didn't say—that it had taken her months to crawl up out of that dark pit into which she'd been thrown. "Shae," he said, punching the car into higher gear, "has had the span of a mortal life to find her spine. She hasn't, and she never will."

Honor sucked in a breath. "That's brutal."

"It comes with the territory." He'd stood over a dead schoolgirl's body not long ago, tugged the sheet over her small, innocent face. "Vampires who don't fear consequences create carnage."

"I know—I wasn't born yesterday." Reaching back, she tightened her ponytail.

He wanted to fist his hand in that luxuriant ebony hair and kiss the temper right out of her. The only other woman he'd ever been tempted to do that with had bitten him hard on the lip and told him he deserved it. Later, after her anger had cooled, she'd turned to him in bed and kissed him, hesitant and sweet, his new wife who was too shy to make the first move.

A caress of wildflowers, the past and the present colliding as they were doing all too often since Honor walked into his life. But these memories . . . they were some of the good ones. "Tell me," he said, because he heard a story in her voice, and he had the driving need to know everything he could about Honor St. Nicholas.

A long, cool silence.

Unexpectedly, he found his lips curving. "Illium did warn you I'm no gentleman."

A feminine snort, but she began to speak. "One of my first hunts was an older vampire. He wasn't under Contract, so it wasn't about that."

Intrigued because an infraction by a vampire who had served out his Contract was considered an internal matter, Dmitri said, "What did he do?"

"Stole something from his angel—an ancient artifact." She tucked an escaped strand of hair behind her ear, the act so familiar that Dmitri felt as if he'd watched her do it a thousand times. "The angel had no one close to the small village where he knew the vamp was hiding, but I wasn't very far away, so the Guild asked me to keep an eye on him until the angel's people got there."

Dmitri said nothing when she went silent, almost able to touch the heavy black that painted the tones of her voice, in stark contrast to the vibrant blues and white-gold of morning, the touch of rain having passed out into the Atlantic.

"One of his friends," she said, "had called ahead to warn him that he was being hunted. He took out his rage on the villagers. The ground was sticky with blood when I arrived, the air so full of iron I could barely breathe. He'd butchered everyone—men, women, children, *babies*." A shake of her head. "That was the first time I understood that vampires were no longer human, even if they'd started out that way."

Dmitri remembered the case. It hadn't been in Raphael's territory but in Elijah's, the archangel who ruled South America. "That vampire was found shot through the heart multiple times and staked to the ground with knives." He'd been a power, the second in one of the courts that reported to Elijah.

"I didn't have a control chip," Honor said, referring to the weapon that immobilized vampires, "and he was on his way to another village when I tracked him down. Only way to stop him was to shred his heart and then, while he was down, pound so many knives into him that he couldn't pull them all out before help arrived." She rubbed her face. "I went through five clips—he kept reviving before I'd gotten enough knives into him, and then, afterward, when I thought he'd pull the blades out."

"Beautiful and deadly," he murmured, bringing the car to a halt by the park where Sorrow waited. "I find that an intoxicating combination."

Honor got out, falling into step beside him as he headed into the park. "Every other man I've seen since the assault has winced after mentioning something that might be considered an innuendo, and you continually say things like that."

"Some people," Dmitri said, "survive. Others don't. You did." He knew because he knew what it was to stand in a place beyond desolation.

Wild blue flickered through the web of leaves in front of them at that moment and Dmitri's priorities shifted. Stepping into the small clearing, he took in everything with a single glance. Illium, coming to land out of sight of Sorrow. The young woman herself sitting on an old tree stump with her arms locked tight around herself, her eyes diverted from the corpse on the grass in front of her.

The male's fly was open, his genitals spilling out. His head rested at an angle that told Dmitri it had been broken with force, while his mouth was caught in an expression akin to that of a blowfish. "What happened?" he asked Sorrow, while Honor went to crouch beside the body.

"I was walking"— rapid, staccato, as if she'd been hoarding her words—"and the next thing I remember, I'm standing here, watching his body slam to the ground." Her eyes, eyes that bespoke the man—the monster—who had Made her, met his. "I'm becoming like him. A butcher." The tang of her fear was unmistakable, but she held his gaze, this woman who had become Sorrow. "You have to do it, Dmitri." A whisper. "End me."

15

"Not yet." His eyes went to the man's exposed penis, shriveled and wizened in death. A normal man didn't walk around with his cock hanging out. But with Sorrow's memory a blank, there was no way to know if she'd enticed or mesmerized the human to come close enough that she could murder him, or if she had reacted in self-defense.

That was when Honor rose to her feet, a grim smile on her face. "I thought I recognized him." She passed over her smartphone.

Taking it, Dmitri glanced at the newspaper article she'd pulled up about one Rick Hernandez, rapist out on parole. His mug shot had been printed as part of the paper's policy of alerting neighborhoods about violent offenders in their midst. A further scan of the article showed that the two women he'd been convicted of assaulting had both been small boned and of Asian descent.

Handing Sorrow the phone, he watched as she began to shake. "I'll handle this." He put a hand on her hair and felt something fundamental in him break, reshape itself. "Venom will drive you home."

"Venom isn't here," Honor said. "I am. Give me your car keys."

"Sorrow isn't human."

"The fact that she snapped the neck of a man twice her size was my first clue." Folded arms, but there was no aggression in those eyes full of mysteries. Instead, he saw a quiet strength and an inexplicable tenderness that twisted around his heart, barbed wire that made him bleed. "I'm armed and she's young."

"Stay with her until Venom arrives." Dmitri threw her his keys.

Instead of skirting around the other side of Sorrow's dead assailant, she walked close enough to him that the backs of their hands touched. It was the first time she'd made a conscious effort to touch him skin to skin.

His body burned.

The trip to Sorrow's house didn't take long. "Come on," she said to the young woman, who sat quiet and shaken, a doll with its strings cut. Honor saw herself in her, as she'd been before Sara's call . . . before Dmitri. The rough heat of his skin lingered on her own, and she wondered if he understood what it meant to her to know that her need to reach him was deeper than the scars left by her abduction. "Let's go in and have some tea."

"I don't have any." A pause, the dull, glazed look lifting a fraction, as if she was fighting to break free of the shock. "I have coffee."

"That'll do."

Sorrow's movements continued to be jerky and uncoordinated as they walked into the house, where the woman who wasn't quite human began to make coffee with quick, jagged movements. "Uram," she said without warning. "I was one of his victims." Ground beans into the coffeemaker, water reservoir being filled. "He took us as we walked to the movies."

According to the media, the archangel Uram had entered New York in an effort to take over Raphael's territory. But, if Honor was remembering it right, there *had* been a low-level hum of speculation that he'd had something to do with the string of disappearances that had taken place in the city around the same time. However, that speculation had died down the instant a more viable suspect was found. No one wanted to believe such madness of an archangel. "You were the sole survivor," she guessed.

"Yes." A laugh as bitter as the coffee dripping into the glass pot on the counter. "Though I'm not sure you'd call this surviving. I wasn't always Sorrow." The coffeemaker switched off on that haunting comment. Pouring out a cup, she slid it across to Honor before pouring one for herself. "I've never killed a man before."

Honor took a sip of the hot liquid before answering, feeling eons older than this girl, though the actual age gap between them was probably closer to six or seven years. "It takes something from you," she said, because Sorrow didn't need lies, "something you never get back."

The first person Honor had stabbed hadn't died, but the feel of her knife slicing into fat and flesh, the sharp scent of iron in the air, it was nothing she would ever forget. "But," she continued, "some people need to be killed." That man had intended to hurt her—she'd seen it in his yellowed smile the instant the social worker left.

He'd had the nerve to call the cops afterward, screaming at them to arrest her. Except the chain-smoking detective had zeroed in on the fact that the "victim" had been stabbed at three a.m. in a young girl's bedroom. Sometimes, the system worked.

A perfunctory knock at the door, then firm footsteps walking into the house—the vampire she had never seen without his sunglasses, dressed in another sleek black suit, this time with a shirt of gunmetal gray.

"There you are, Sorrow." An almost gentle comment, with the finest razor-sharp edge of mockery. "Looks like I'm going to have to keep a closer eye on you."

Sliding her gun back into her shoulder holster, Honor watched as he slid off the shades. Slitted and bright green, his eyes were those of a viper. "Okay," she said, not fighting the urge to stare, "that, I wasn't expecting." They had to be real, the reason for the sunglasses, but even knowing that, her brain had trouble processing the sight, it was so alien.

A slow smile, his cinnamon-dark skin holding a warmth at odds with the eyes of a creature whose blood ran ice-cold. However, the words he directed at Sorrow were merciless. "Next time you slip your guard, I'll find you nice, comfortable accommodation in a cell somewhere. Or maybe a cage would work better."

The young woman's mouth tightened. Then she threw her half-full cup of coffee at the vampire's head. "Go bite yourself, Venom."

Dodging the missile with a reptilian burst of movement, the vampire hissed as the cup hit the wall and shattered, the coffee spraying out to splash his slick suit. At that instant, there was nothing human in him—only a predator on the hunt. Honor had her gun leveled at him before he rose from the crouch he'd fallen into after avoiding the cup. "Enough," she said, directing the statement to both of them. "Sorrow, clean up the mess. Venom, get out."

The vampire, strands of black hair falling over a face that was shockingly handsome in its eerie *otherness*, smirked. "A toy gun isn't going to do you any good." Suddenly he was in front of her, long, strong fingers closing over her rib cage, though she hadn't so much as seen him blink.

It was too much.

She pulled the trigger.

The sound was huge in the enclosed space, Sorrow's scream a reverberating echo. Venom went down, clutching at his thigh. Tucking her gun back into the holster, Honor picked up her coffee again, surprised at her own calm. "No touching. Ever."

The vampire grimaced, pulled himself into a sitting position against the wall, his hand clamped over a thigh pumping blood at a speed that would've promised death for a mortal. "Do you know how much this suit fucking cost?"

On the other side of the counter, Sorrow leaned against the sink, wild color in her cheeks. "I want to learn to do that," she said, staring at Honor. "To defend myself."

A snort from the vampire, who was already beginning to heal. "I hear you did a mighty fine job of defending yourself today, kitty." Sorrow's snarl filled the air. "You should've ripped his nuts off before you killed him, you know," Venom said in a considering tone. "Would've hurt like a bitch."

Honor's lips twitched. "Good advice." Putting down her coffee, she watched as Sorrow went to clean up the mess she'd made, glaring at Venom when he picked up a broken piece to give to her.

"It wasn't conscious," the young woman said after a while. "I don't know how I did it—I'm just a stupid kid on my own."

No woman should ever be helpless.

The thought came from deep, deep within her. "I'll teach you," she said, and it was a decision that took no thought.

Venom pushed himself upright, though he continued to favor one leg. "You sure you want to invest the time? Sorrow here might have a very short life span."

Dumping the broken shards she'd collected into the trash, Sorrow gave Venom a look that was eerie in its own way, a thin line of green *glowing* around the dark brown of her irises. "Someday," she said in a voice as serene as a high mountain lake, "I'm going to break your neck. Then I'm going to saw it off with a hacksaw so I can take my time."

Venom's grin creased his cheeks. "I knew you had it in you, kitty."

Dmitri had dealt with the Hernandez situation and was in his office by the time Honor drove the Ferrari into the Tower garage. Watching her enter the room, all feminine power and intriguing strength, he couldn't imagine the terror-crippled woman he'd first met. Yet that terror lived inside of her—he'd tasted the ugliness of it in the air as he stroked his thumb over her skin that morning. "Sorrow?"

"Doing better than I expected." An incisive look. "Venom is highly intelligent."

"He's one of the Seven for a reason." Spreading a number of colored printouts on his desk, he motioned her over. "I just received an e-mail from the man I sent to investigate Tommy's cabin." The images were self-explanatory.

Honor's body brushed against his own as she came to stand beside him. He wondered if she would dare remain so close if she knew how much control it was taking for him not to bend his head and kiss the delicate skin of her nape. She'd taste of salt and wildflowers, intermingled with an earthy femininity that sang a siren song to the man beneath the civilized surface.

"His attacker," she said, her attention on the photo of Tommy's head nailed up like a hunting trophy on his front door, "really wanted to shut him up."

"Literally." Satisfying himself with the thought that he *would* have her, he moved his gaze off the vulnerable skin so close and tapped the image. "They cut out his tongue."

Her body pressed a fraction into him as she leaned over to pick up another photograph. "The place is a bloodbath."

Weaving a curl of sin, rich as brandy and just as heady, around her was as natural to him as breathing. "I've got a team examining it."

"Dmitri." Husky censure, but no anger. "I'll get ready to head—"

"You're exhausted." He took in the black circles under her eyes, the pallor, felt the ice of ruthless anger. "If you came up against one of them today you'd end up their blood pet all over again."

Streaks of color high on her cheekbones. "You might order your people around, but don't even try it with me."

Some men liked women who knew how to submit; others, women who fought back. Dmitri didn't have a preference either way. To do so would be to care for a female beyond a fleeting sexual connection. Yet when it came to Honor, he wanted to strip her bare in more ways than one, unravel the mystery of who she was to him. "A single phone call," he murmured, gaze lingering on the full curves of her mouth in conscious provocation, "and Sara will deem you unfit for duty."

That mouth flattened. "You think that'll stop me?"

"No. But the fact that you have no idea of the location of Tommy's cabin will." His lips curved when he caught the calculation in her. Such an expressive face, had Honor, one that would never be able to hide anything from a man who knew how to read her. "Don't bother to ask Vivek to dig it out for you unless you want him to become a permanent guest of the Tower."

"Threats now, Dmitri?" It was somehow an intimate question, his name pronounced with an accent so perfect, it was a caress.

"You always knew I wasn't a nice man," he said, wanting to hear that voice in bed, in the warm hush of a pleasure-drenched night. "Go home. Sleep. Be a good girl"—he leaned close enough that their breath mingled, close enough that kissing her would take only the dip of his head—"and I'll let you come on the chopper tomorrow morning."

"If what you told me about Isis wasn't bullshit," Honor said, her voice vibrating with the force of her emotions, "then you know *exactly* how I feel right now. You know."

Dmitri's response was pitiless. "I also know that if the bastards slip through your grasp because you're too weak, the regret will make you bleed worse than any wound."

Folding her arms, Honor stalked to the window. "Could you have slept?" It wasn't about reason, about anything so sane.

"I didn't," he said, walking to stand behind her, dangerous, muscled, immovable. "But I wasn't mortal." No emotion in his voice.

Isis, she thought, had done far worse to Dmitri than a forced Making and bedding. "I came to tell you," she said, feeling a deep, inexorable anger that had nothing to do with their fight and everything to do with a long-dead angel, "that I figured out the tattoo on the way back from Sorrow's home."

Turning, she looked into that sensual face that had haunted her since the first time she'd seen it and knew there was no way to protect him from this. Why she felt a desperate need to try, until it was a tearing agony within her, she didn't know. "It says, 'To remember Isis. A gift of grace. To avenge Isis. A rage of blood.' Someone's out to take vengeance for the death of a monster."

Honor didn't go up to her own apartment when she arrived at her building. Her emotions were a kaleidoscope of shattered pieces—anger, pain, aggravation, that strange, piercing desolation . . . and a *need* that seemed to be growing ever stronger. Realizing Ashwini might still be in the city, she knocked on the other hunter's door and found herself invited in for ice cream and a movie.

"Hepburn," Ashwini said, digging into the quart of mint chocolate chip she'd threatened to defend to the death with her spoon if Honor so much as looked in its direction. "Classic."

Frustration churned within her at being forced to wait to continue the hunt, but though it galled, Dmitri was right. Her bones were tired, her mind fuzzy after days of nightmare-ridden sleep. So she dug around in Ash's fridge for the butter pecan that was her personal favorite, and, boots abandoned by the door, sprawled on the ridiculously comfortable armchair her friend had had for as long as Honor had known her. "We've seen this one before."

"I like it."

"Why are you in your pajamas?" The other hunter was dressed in an old gray T-shirt and a pair of faded fleece pants with dancing sheep on them. "It's two in the afternoon."

"I'm on vacation today."

No sounds except that of ice cream being seriously eaten and the repartee on the screen. It would surprise many people how tranquil being with Ashwini could be. Most had never seen the other woman without the prickly emotional armor that Honor had recognized the instant they met at a Guild bar in Ivory Coast, didn't understand that she was one of the most accepting people Honor had ever met. Flaws, scars, none of it scared her.

Scooping up more mint and chocolate, Ash said, "You won't believe what Janvier did this time."

"Can't be too bad since you're not inviting me to his funeral." Ashwini and the two-hundred-something vampire had a complicated relationship.

Reaching over to the side table, Ashwini picked up and passed a small box to Honor. It proved to hold a stunning square-cut sapphire pendant set in platinum, the setting a little jagged, a fraction off center . . . as if the person who'd commissioned it knew that nothing too smooth, too perfect would've suited Ash.

Point to you, Cajun. "Are you going to wear it?"

"It'll only encourage him."

"Oh, so it's okay if I ask him out?" she teased. "He is hella sexy, *cher*."

"Funny." Ash stabbed her spoon at her. "Tell me about Dmitri."

Of course her best friend had figured it out. "I feel like a moth drawn to the flame." Contact would hurt, might be fatal, and yet she couldn't stop herself. Obsession or compulsion, she didn't know, but she did know that before this was over, she'd either end up in Dmitri's bed . . . or one of them would bleed darkest red.

16

Dmitri wrapped Elena in tendrils of whiskey and night-blooming roses, rich and seductive, as the Guild Hunter walked into the library of the home she shared with Raphael in the Angel Enclave, the white-gold tips of her wings brushing along the carpet.

Her jawline firmed, pale eyes narrowing. "Weak effort, Dmitri."

It had been, his attention on another woman. "I was being polite." Elena was more sensitive to his ability than any other hunter he'd ever met, likely as a result of the horrific massacre that had ended her childhood.

Dmitri would have sheltered and protected the child she'd been, but he couldn't, wouldn't, have mercy on the adult—because he wasn't the only vampire who could lure with scent. The other members of the Cadre wouldn't hesitate to use Elena's vulnerability to this most insidious of weapons against her. And Elena was Raphael's heart.

"I heard about H— Sorrow." A solemn expression, quiet words. "How is she?"

"Uncertain." The girl's future remained a fragile thing that could be destroyed with a single, brutal act. "She acted in self-defense today, but she seems unable to harness or channel the violence."

Elena's head turned toward the door an instant before Dmitri sensed Raphael's approaching presence. Spreading out those wings of midnight and dawn behind her, she walked to touch her hand to Raphael's chest, something silent and powerful passing between the archangel and his consort.

It remained incomprehensible to Dmitri how Elena, an angel with a weak mortal heart, had formed such a bond with Raphael. But he had taken a vow and he would defend that bond to his last breath. "Sire," he said when the two drew apart, "I would speak to you." *It's about Isis.* He didn't know how much the archangel had told his consort.

I see. Eyes of an intense, infinite blue met his before shifting to Elena. "Your indulgence."

Elena glanced between them, gaze perceptive. "I need to call Evelyn," she said, naming her youngest sister. "I'll do it from the solar."

"Wait." Dmitri and Elena agreed on little, but he'd never questioned her loyalty to those who were hers. "You may want to talk to Beth as well. It appears Harrison has been forced to seek alternative accommodation." Andreas had mentioned it during their meeting after he spoke to Leon and Reg.

Now Elena's mouth tightened. "Good on Beth if she's kicked him out." A pause. "Thanks."

Dmitri held his silence until she left. "She doesn't know." He didn't find that the least surprising. Raphael was well into his second millennium of existence. A being that ancient had many memories.

"She will before this night is out. I won't have her vulnerable." The archangel walked with him to step out on the sprawling green of the lawn that led to the cliff and the constant rush of a Hudson tinged red-gold by the setting sun. *I will not speak that which is yours to tell.*

I know. He agreed with Raphael's decision to brief Elena, because while he couldn't accept the weakness she represented in the archangel's defenses, he understood that once a man claimed a woman, it was his task to protect her. Dmitri had failed in that task, failed his Ingrede, and it was a failure for which he would never forgive himself. "Did she truly save

your life against Lijuan?" he asked, wrenching his mind from
the raw agony of the past and the memory of a woman with
eyes of slanted brown who had trusted him to keep her safe.

"Do not sound so disgruntled, Dmitri."

"I merely find it an impossible truth." And yet it was a
truth, so he would add it to what he knew of Elena. "Isis . . . it
seems we left a stone unturned." He told the archangel the full
details of the dead vampire's dismembered body, the tattoo.

"Bold and stupid both." Wings of white streaked with gold
spread a fraction.

Dmitri took a step back, examined the feathers. "Your
wings, the gold is spreading." His primaries were almost to-
tally metallic, the sunlight playing off the filaments in glittering sparks.

"Yes," Raphael said, strands of hair lifting off his face in
the early evening breeze. "It became apparent the night after I
confronted Lijuan. Elena thinks I am evolving in some way.
We shall see."

The last time an archangel had evolved, she had raised the
dead. But Raphael had never committed the atrocities that
stained Lijuan's hands, and he was the son of two archangels.
His evolution couldn't be predicted.

"I've compiled a list of all those who remained loyal to
Isis till the end," Dmitri said, even as he considered the tacti-
cal advantages of obscuring the truth of why Raphael's wings
had altered in color. "Jason is tracking down their whereabouts." None had been seen entering the country, but that
meant nothing.

"I'll speak to him. I've kept a discreet watch on certain
people through the centuries." A glance out of those eyes of
inhuman blue. "As have you, Dmitri."

"None of them could have done this." He'd already made
certain of it. "However, games," he said, "no matter how vicious, are something I can handle with ease." Even if those
games attempted to awaken the ghost of an angel who hadn't
deserved the quick death they'd dealt her. "It's the second situation that's become more critical."

Raphael listened in silence as Dmitri laid out the facts of
the mortal "hunt." "This Honor," the archangel said when
Dmitri finished, his tone icy with anger, "she is competent?"

"Yes." Brilliant mind, human heart, ancient eyes.

"Elena is a better tracker."

Impossible to dispute, since Elena was hunter-born, a bloodhound as far as vampires were concerned. "That skill isn't necessary at present." And this was Honor's hunt, as Isis had been Dmitri's. "We're digging out the snakes, not chasing them."

"An apt analogy." Wings rustling as he folded them tight to his back, Raphael turned to look Dmitri straight in the eye. "Many believe such depravity is exactly what you would savor."

Dmitri knew that, understood full well how close he was to crossing lines that could not be uncrossed. "It seems even I am not yet that degenerate."

You would never harm a woman in such a way, Dmitri. The archangel's voice in his mind, the purity of it almost painful. *We both know this. It's why I allow you to push Elena in ways for which I would kill another.*

Some would say you trust me too much, Sire.

And some would say you are wasted as a second when you could rule your own territory.

It seems neither of us cares much for the opinions of others.

Together they walked back into the library and down the corridor that led to the front entrance. "Venom will need to leave the city soon," Raphael said. "Galen is strong, but I want him to have another of the Seven in the Refuge. Naasir must remain in Amanat."

Dmitri blew out a breath. "Aodhan is serious about coming to New York?"

"Yes."

"He'll cause chaos." With eyes of fractured glass and wings of diamond brilliance, Aodhan stood apart even amongst immortals.

"He is apt to fly so high that mortals will glimpse only a shadow that splinters light."

Dmitri nodded. Aodhan had an aversion to touch, one Dmitri understood. He'd been in the Medica when the angel had been brought in two hundred years ago. Raphael had carried Aodhan's emaciated and dirt-encrusted body in his arms, laid him down with the utmost care so as not to crush his wings, which were nothing much more than a few slivers of tendon hanging on to bone.

It had been, Dmitri thought, the last time anyone had held Aodhan in any way, shape, or form. "I'll work out the transfer." He rubbed his jaw. "I need someone on Sorrow, and Aodhan won't be suitable."

"Janvier."

"Yes." The smooth-talking Cajun was no longer under Contract, but he'd given his loyalty to Raphael and it was a loyalty that went to the core. "I'll contact him closer to the transfer date."

"Dmitri."

"Sire."

"Are you well?"

Dmitri knew what the archangel was asking. "Isis is dead and buried, this sycophant nothing but an irritation." The ghosts who haunted him were far gentler . . . and cut so deep that he bled inside without surcease.

The dream wasn't a nightmare. That fact startled Honor enough that she almost woke, but the pleasure, oh, the pleasure was too much to resist.

A strong male body over her own, a rough-skinned hand on her throat as he kissed her with a lazy patience that she knew could turn demanding without warning. But today, today he wanted to play. And she was his willing plaything. "Open," he murmured and she parted her lips, let him slide his tongue inside.

It was a wicked, decadent act, one she'd allowed him early on in their courtship, her resistance to him so flimsy as to be smoke. Her reward for such sin had been a pleasure that had stolen her breath, the taste of him an addiction. Now that beautiful mouth explored hers with open possession as he thrust his thigh between her own, pushed it up to rub against the softest part of her.

She cried out at the feel of the crisp hairs on his leg, the hard flex of muscle. Bare to the skin as she was—he'd made her strip for him, made her go slow as he devoured her with the only eyes that had ever seen her thus—no part of her was safe from the proprietary heat of his touch. Moving the hand on her throat down to a breast that had grown heavy and even fuller over the past spring, he squeezed. Not too hard for the sensitive flesh. Just hard enough.

"Please," she whispered, knowing he would have no mercy on her tonight.

A husky chuckle that vibrated through her body. "We've just begun." Tugging at her nipple, twisting it a little. She bucked against him, his skin slick and damp where it pressed against her. Reaching down, he insinuated one hand between his thigh and her swollen flesh. "Is this what you want?" A flick over the hot nub at the apex of her thighs.

"Oh!" It was a frustrated cry as he slid his fingers through her sensitive folds before withdrawing. "More."

Smiling at her in the musky dark, he brought those fingers to his lips instead, sucked deep. Her womb clenched, because he used that sinful mouth to suck her most intimate flesh as deep when the mood came upon him. Tonight, however, he seemed content to pin her to their simple bed and tease her to fever pitch with callused hands that knew her every secret, her every fantasy—he had talked her into whispering them in his ear this past winter, as the world lay quiet around them. And then he had told her his own.

When his mouth descended on the stiff peak of her breast, she almost sobbed at the relief of it. He rolled her nipple in his mouth, bit down a fraction to remind her he was in charge . . . before sucking so hard that she rubbed herself against his thigh with frantic need, no longer shy with him, not now. Right when she would have gone over, found that secret place he'd shown her on a sun-golden field three summers ago, he withdrew his thigh.

She shuddered. "Beast." He'd been so careful with her that day, so gentle, even as he seduced the most good of girls into lying down with him in the grass, his hand stroking up under her dress to touch her in ways no one had ever touched her.

She'd been shocked at the raw pleasure he'd coaxed from her with hands rough and marked from a life carved from the earth, his skin dark from the sun. He'd sipped at her tears, caressed her through the trembling, and then he'd stroked up her dress and bared her to the sun, to the kiss of his eyes . . . his mouth. Yes, he was a beast.

Her beast.

Now, still smiling, he lowered his head to her neglected breast, pushing upward with a thickly muscled thigh at the same time, to grind her delicate flesh in the most exquisite of ways. Oh, yes. Gripping the black silk of his hair, she arced up into his mouth as her body trembled and broke in a burst of liquid heat.

"There," he murmured against her mouth when she could see again, when she could hear again, though her chest continued to heave, "now you will behave, will you not?"

Stroking one hand down his stubbled jaw, she tugged him down. "Kiss me, husband."

"Husband." Honor woke with the word on her lips, the images from the dream as vivid as the tiny spasms low in her body. She moaned at the realization that she'd orgasmed, her thighs clenched tight around a pillow. But instead of jerking away, she rubbed herself against it, trying to hold on to the vestiges of a dream more erotic than any real-life experience she'd had—a dream that returned a sense of sexual pleasure to her she'd thought forever stolen.

"There, now you will behave, will you not?"

Her nipples tightened to near-painful points, aftershocks rippling between her legs. "Oh, God."

The strange thing was, she'd never been drawn to dominant men in bed, wouldn't have expected to find the dream so very sexy—especially after the assault. If she did have sex again, she'd assumed it would be with some man who'd be gentle and patient with her fears.

A brutally beautiful face, dark eyes with an edge of menace.

Yes, Dmitri wasn't gentle in any sense of the word, but there was no doubting the sexual energy between them. He was, she was forced to admit, the likely inspiration for her faceless dream lover. Her hand fisted on the sheets at the sensory memory of her lover's weight on her, so heavy and rough, the feel of his callused hand molding her breast, the clever wickedness of his mouth, the hard ridge of a sizable erection pressing against her.

Muscles low in her body clenched, wanting that thick heat pushing inside her.

"Cold shower time," she muttered, shoving off the sheets to see that she was naked.

Panic spiked and she went to reach for the gun under her pillow—until she saw the clothes strewn on the floor, as if she'd thrown them about in the night. Laughing, she said, "Some dream." One she wouldn't mind repeating, if she was being honest. Being tormented to orgasm by a man her dream self clearly trusted . . . yeah, it was far better than remembering that black pit filled only with pain.

The clock showed that she'd actually slept for a serious amount of time—it was half past five in the morning, and she'd fallen into bed at six the previous day. Showering, she got dressed, weapons included, and was about to call Dmitri when her cell rang.

She picked up to find Sara's deputy, Abel, on the other end. "There's some kind of a situation in Little Italy," he said. "Can you check it out?"

Every part of her hungered to get to the Catskills, but she was a hunter and that meant something. "Signal's going to drop in the elevator," she said. "Call you back when I reach the ground floor."

Once there, she headed out onto the street. "So, details?"

"Yeah, not so much," Abel said. "Cops are out there. No one's quite sure what's happening, but if you think it's ours, call me back and I'll assign someone—your Tower contract takes priority. Here's the street." He read it out.

"Got it," she said, hailing a cab and sliding in. "I'll call you after I've had a look at the scene."

The cabbie began to drive. "Hunting?"

She nodded and gave him the address. It felt oddly comforting to be pegged as a hunter, because for months after the abduction, she hadn't been. "Fast as you can."

The cabbie's eyes flicked to the rearview mirror, down, back again. "Hey, aren't you that hunter that was missing?"

Her gut twisted. "Yes."

There was lurid speculation in the eyes in the mirror this time. "I heard you came into the hospital covered in vampire bites."

The Guild had done everything in its power to tamp down the gossip after her return, but there'd been nothing they could do about the non-Guild personnel involved in her recovery. Add in the numerous tests she'd had to undergo to find out if the bastards who'd taken her had left her with anything other than bruises, bites, a body on the edge of starvation, and more than a few fractured bones as well as a number of internal injuries, and she'd been seen at her weakest by dozens of people.

Most of those people had been good and kind. Some had been like this cabdriver.

The cabbie's gleaming eyes, his lips half parted, threatened to shove her back into the pit, those ugly, probing hands violating her until there was nothing left. A month ago, she'd have curled into herself and gone silent. A month ago, she hadn't shot bullets into two of her attackers. "Vampires' tongues," she said, sliding her finger carefully over the blade she'd pulled from the sheath on her thigh, "grow back when you cut them off. Humans, unfortunately, don't have that ability."

He whimpered and dropped his head. Sweat was rolling down his temples when they arrived at her destination, and he couldn't even get the words out to ask for the fare. Swiping her credit card, she paid and got out.

Never again would anyone drag her into the dark.

17

"Nicholas!"

Glancing up at the sound of her name, Honor saw a big black cop with distinctive salt-and-pepper stubble that appeared to be a permanent fixture.

"Santiago," she said, having worked a case with him a couple of years back, one of the rare few times she'd been put on a situation in Manhattan. "What do you have?"

"This." He ducked under the barrier of crime scene tape to crouch down beside a body lying half on, half off the sidewalk. Lifting away the tarp that covered the victim, he nodded at her to have a look.

"Looks like he got attacked by a dog." The young male's neck was shredded, as if it had been gnawed on.

Santiago grunted. "Yeah, except the only places he's been gnawed are the neck and the inner thigh."

The carotid and the femoral arteries.

Leaning in close, she visually examined both wounds. The victim's pants were bunched around his ankles, but he still had on his underpants, so the attack had been about the blood—though his attacker had wasted a great deal of it, from what she saw around the body. "I'm no pathologist, but looks to me like the wound is too degraded to determine if this was a vampire." The fang marks had been obliterated in the mess of flesh.

"One of the hunter-born could scent the skin," she said, "see if they catch a vampiric scent. Ransom's in the city, not sure about Elena—I'll call the Guild, ask if one of them can swing by." Everything about this scene felt off. Another hunter's input would be welcome. "Blood splatter makes it clear he was killed here," she murmured after making the request. "Pretty public at night."

"Yeah, but this street's almost all daytime businesses, no restaurants, one hole-in-the-wall bar," Santiago said, salt-dusted eyebrows heavy over eyes of faded brown. "Bar staff had cleaned up and were out of here by three thirty, according to the manager I just woke up. Launderette down the street opens at six thirty. Given the time our anonymous tipster called in the body, I'd put money on this going down between four and five."

"Before it would've been light." Honor nodded. "Otherwise, there's probably a few folks who'd cut through to the subway entrance."

"Yeah, I'll have my men canvass the area tomorrow morning, see if we can catch any of the regular foot traffic." He looked up as a shadow swept across them.

An instant later, an angel landed beside them, her wings the most stunning black, segueing to midnight blue and indigo, then to a gleaming shade that reminded Honor of the dawn, until the primaries were a shimmering white-gold. Tall, with lithe muscle over her frame, Elena had the kind of grace that came only with knowing how to move your body against opponents who were usually stronger and faster.

Honor had seen the photos, of course, but the reality of a fellow hunter with wings was surreal. "I know I'm staring," she said into the hush that had fallen, "but, Elena, you have *wings*."

Elena laughed, her eyes appearing silver in this light, her damp, near-white hair pulled back into a neat French braid. "I still wake up surprised some days," she said, her face losing its shine when she turned toward Santiago. "I'll check the scent." Those incredible wings spread out on the dirty street as she knelt on the asphalt.

Elena didn't appear to worry about it, peeling back the tarp to examine the neck, then the thigh wound. "No scent on him that might possibly be vampiric." Her voice was decisive. "I'd expect something strong, given how long the attacker had to have spent with the victim." She glanced up at Honor, frown lines marring the deep gold of her skin. "This one's weird. Human with filed-down teeth, maybe?"

Filed-down teeth.

It was the cue Honor's mind needed, flicking back to a short article in a Guild newsletter she'd read while in the hospital. "Santiago, can we move him just enough that I can see the back of his right shoulder?"

"Yeah, no problem." Placing his gloved hands under the body, he shifted it to the side. Elena quickly gloved up, too, so she could help hold the body as Honor went around to push up the victim's T-shirt. Neither the cop nor the winged hunter said a word, but Honor could taste the tension on her tongue, it was so pervasive.

Deciding to pretend she hadn't noticed what was clearly a private rift, she managed to bare the victim's shoulder. "Damn, I didn't really think I'd find it."

Two heads twisted around to examine her discovery. It was a small tattoo—the letter *V* in a ring with a wing coming out from each side. Elena scowled. "I've never seen that."

"That edition of the Guild newsletter came out while you were off growing wings."

"You actually read the newsletter? I thought people like you were urban legends."

"Kinda just saw it out of the corner of my eye," she said with a grin that felt natural. "This 'movement' "—she tapped the tattoo—"apparently originated in London. Looks like it's crossed the Atlantic."

Lowering the body back down, Santiago rose to his feet, his joints creaking like old timbers. "Tell me about this."

Honor stood, too, aware of Elena pulling her wings tight to her back as she followed. "My info is out of date, but it's an underground clique started by older teens and people in their early twenties. They emulate the 'vampire lifestyle.' " Shaking her head, she looked down at the lump beneath the tarp, saddened by the loss of a life hardly begun. "Mostly it's an excuse to have sex."

"Aren't most things at that age?" Santiago muttered.

Honor hadn't ever been that young, couldn't imagine such innocence. "Yes, it's fairly harmless—except some of the adherents take it one step further and drink blood from one another."

"You're shitting me," Santiago said.

"Afraid not."

"Vampires can drink from any donor because their bodies process out any problems in the blood," Elena said, scowl darkening her eyes to storm gray. "These kids are messing with who knows what diseases."

"If they can even digest it," Honor said, unable to see the lure of a life ruled by blood.

Santiago pushed back his jacket, hands on his hips. "You saying we should look for vomit?"

Elena was the one who answered. "It would depend on how much he or she actually drank, but yeah."

"Great, that'll make some uniform's day."

"Could be some of these kids start to think they *are* vampires," Honor added as Santiago called over a young officer, who curled up his lip at the task given him but began to circle out from the scene. "I'd take a look at who this boy's friends were. Seems to me he was playing donor to someone else's vamp and things got out of hand."

"From the location of the bites," Elena said, "I'd bet on sex being in the mix."

Santiago rubbed a hand over his face, his stubble scraping on his palm. "Good old-fashioned sex and violence."

Honor was about to agree, when her phone vibrated with an incoming message. "Excuse me." She stepped a small distance away, but could still hear Santiago and Elena.

"I got the harness," the cop said with a sort of gruff curtness.

A pause before Elena replied. "I didn't expect you, too."

"Yeah, well." The rustle of cloth, the scrape of a shoe on the asphalt. "I guess it's about adapting—some old dogs might be able to learn new tricks."

Elena's answer was quiet. "Thank you."

A longer pause before Santiago said, "This case is the last thing I need," in his normal tone of voice. "We've got that cross-jurisdictional serial sucking up resources."

"The one who's targeting young mixed-race women?"

"Yeah. No bodies, but my gut says they're dead."

When Honor joined them, the tension was gone, to be replaced by a cautious familiarity—two people who'd often worked together trying to find a new balance. Looking at them both in turn, she said, "I have to head to the Tower."

Dmitri's message had been simple. *I hear you're awake. So am I. Let's go.*

The cabin was located in the middle of thick woods, an almost cutesy place built of logs, complete with a rocking chair on the porch. That chair was motionless now, the woods so silent not a single leaf appeared to stir. It was as if the trees themselves knew the horror that had taken place in this charming setting straight out of a holiday greeting card.

In autumn, she thought, the ground would be covered with leaves the innumerable shades of fall, but it was deep into spring, the leaves bright green overhead. Gold shimmered high above but the heavy canopy meant the light was diffuse by the time it reached the ground, adding to the bleak gray of the atmosphere.

"When I was a child," she said to the vampire who walked beside her, "I used to dream of going on vacation to a place like this. It seemed like the kind of thing families did."

Dmitri glanced at her, the shadows of his face harder, more defined in this light. "Did you ever attempt to trace your parents?"

"No." By the time she'd had the resources to mount a search, she'd known that nothing good could come of it, no happy ending that would take away the loneliness of her childhood, erase all those school plays and sports days where she'd watched other kids' parents clap and cheer while she stood by and pretended it didn't hurt.

The decision not to search hadn't filled in the hollow space inside of her, but it had set her free to live her life without being hamstrung by thoughts of what could've been. "Do you still remember your parents?" she asked as they reached the cabin.

Dmitri skirted the bloodstains on the steps where it appeared Tommy's beaten body had been dragged up, and glanced at the similarly stained rocking chair. "Whoever executed Tommy," he murmured, "set him down, questioned him, after making it clear defiance would result in pain."

It was what Dmitri would've done with a pompous asshole like Tommy—the vampire might have survived for four hundred years, but only because he stayed out of the way of the predators, playing the big dog within his coterie of similarly useless friends. "Makes you wonder what made him a target."

"He might've brought Evert in without permission," Honor said, staring at the door on which Tommy's head had been pinned, a thick blade shoved into his mouth and out through the back of his skull. "I get the feeling the game was meant to be by invitation only."

"So, the second invitation notwithstanding, we probably saved Evert's life." Somehow he didn't think the vampire would be grateful for the long years he would live in Andreas's care. "My parents," he said, pushing open the door, "are as clear in my mind as if I saw them yesterday. Perhaps it's an effect of immortality, but certain faces will never fade."

"Dmitri!" Laughter, hands pushing on his chest. "Behave or you'll wake Misha and the baby."

Deep green eyes connected with his own even as warm brown lingered in his memory, the impact far more visceral than it should've been. "I see so much pain in you," Honor whispered, "so much loss."

He wasn't a man used to being read. "Don't fool yourself about me, Honor," he said, because while he intended to have her, he wouldn't do it with false promises. "The human part of me died a long time ago. What remains isn't that different from Tommy." Stepping over the threshold, he took in the splatters of blood that decorated the walls, the rugs, the varnished floor.

"After he—or she—questioned him," Honor said from behind him, picking up a PDA that looked as if it had been

crushed under a heavy boot, "the attacker brought Tommy in
here and played with him."

Played.

Yes.

If this had simply been about an execution, the entire cabin
wouldn't have been splattered with red congealing to black—
more to the point, handprints wouldn't have streaked the floor and the
walls. "He was allowed to believe he could escape." The vampire's panicked fear would've been even greater when he was
wrenched back.

Dmitri waited to see if he felt any kind of pity. No. "Here,"
he said, pulling out a tiny plastic case from his pocket when
Honor put down the damaged PDA. "Copy of the memory
card. My people are mining it for data."

Taking it, she slid it into her jeans. "I'll go through it, too.
My mind has a way of seeing patterns." She scanned the room.
"The violence appears random, but it was structured to inflict
maximum terror."

"The vampires who abused you," he said, glimpsing what
appeared to be a fingernail embedded in the wall, "did any of
them betray this kind of behavior?"

Boot swiveling on the wood of the floor, Honor walked out
and down the steps into the trees. Closing the cabin door behind himself, Dmitri followed at a slower pace, heading toward
the gentle sound of water. He came out on the pebbled shore of
a small stream—Honor stood only a couple of feet to his left.

Today, she'd teamed a fitted khaki shirt with sleeves to the
elbows with those jeans that skimmed her form, well-worn
boots on her feet. Simple and strong and beautiful. But even
the strongest of women had nightmares that couldn't be con-
quered in a day or even a year.

Saying nothing, he crouched down on the pebbles, picking
up one and rolling it between his fingers. The water was clear,
the air crisp and touched with the scent of a hundred thousand
leaves, the space above the stream wide enough that the light
was bright, the sky a searing blue. A lovely place in which to
consider the most unspeakable violence. "Isis," he said, ac-
cessing a section of his memory that had grown dusty with
age, "was used to being adored, considered one of the most
exquisite women in the world."

That had been no lie—with skin of finest cream, hair of shining gold, and eyes of entrancing bronze, Isis had embodied the mortal ideas of the angelic race. Men and women both had run to see her when she'd stopped in his village on what he didn't realize until later was a well-planned journey to avenge herself against Raphael.

"Do you know my crime, Dmitri?" Raphael's voice, echoing in the cold stone chamber beneath the keep. "I was overheard to say that I would prefer a snake in my bed to Isis."

Vain and cruelly intelligent, Isis hadn't been satisfied with simply capturing and torturing Raphael for what had been nothing but a passing comment. No, she'd intended to corrupt Raphael's mortal friends until they joined her in hurting the angel; she had chosen Dmitri because the archangel's friendship with his family went back generations.

Then she'd seen Dmitri.

"At first she took my polite refusal to her offer with good humor. She thought I was playing a game, wanting a courtship." He dropped the pebble but remained in his crouching position. "It amused and delighted her that I was so apparently proud. Gifts of exotic meats, precious spices, tapestries such as had never been seen in my small village, it all arrived day after day."

18

Honor had covered the distance between them as he spoke, until she stood right by his side, close enough that his shoulder touched her leg. "I sent them all back, but she didn't take offense." Isis had believed he wanted more, considered himself worth more. "Hunks of pure gold, jeweled swords, a cascade of treasures that would've made a dragon proud, began to land on the simple doorstep of the home from where I farmed the land."

"Dmitri, I never even imagined such beautiful things."

He looked up, saw raw fear in those familiar eyes of darkest brown. "Ingrede, you are my wife, not Isis." Anger that she'd doubt him made his tone harsh.

"I know you won't break your marriage vows, husband." Trembling hands tucking the blanket around the baby. "But I'm afraid of what this angel will do to possess you."

He'd shrugged off Ingrede's concern, because, after all, he was a farmer, no one important. "I thought she would eventually tire of my refusals and move on." He had been a fool, an innocent in a way he couldn't comprehend now. "But like Michaela," he said, naming the archangel most people considered the most beautiful woman in the world today, "Isis was used to getting anything and everything she wanted."

Her vampires had taken him as he returned home after a trip to the markets, a sweet for Misha tucked safely in one pocket, a pretty ribbon for his wife in the other. For the baby, such a small thing she was, he had bought a piece of scented wood with which to make a rattle. He'd seen Isis's creatures coming, had had time to give Misha his sweet, caress his sleeping daughter's cheek, and kiss his beautiful, strong wife good-bye.

He would never forget the words she'd said to him that day, the love she had wrapped around him—though she had known he would soon be in another woman's bed, committing a terrible betrayal of the vows he'd made to her one bright spring morning a turn of the seasons before Misha's birth.

"Will you forgive me, Ingrede? For what I must do?"

"You fight a battle." Her hand touching his cheek. "You do this to protect us. There is nothing to forgive."

"If I'd said yes at the very start," he said now, swallowing the rage and anguish that had never died, "I think Isis would've used, then discarded me. I could've gone home." To the only woman he had ever loved, to his son, his daughter. "But because I'd made it clear that I didn't want her, she played with me as a cat does with a mouse." First she'd taken him to her bed, viciously pleased by the knowledge that he couldn't say no.

"Such beautiful children you have, Dmitri. So young . . . so easily broken."

Later, after she'd had her fill, he'd been dragged to the cold, mold-lined bowels of her great castle, where she Made him with methodical care. Only after the conversion was complete, his body stronger and more able to bear damage, had he been stripped naked and chained in a spread-eagle position, every part of him exposed. "She started with a whip tipped with razor-sharp metal."

"Stop, Dmitri." A hand clenching in his hair. "I can't bear it."

He heard the tears, was astonished by them. Honor had almost shattered in that hellhole she'd been held in for two interminable months, but according to her psych records, she'd

never once cried during her months in the hospital. *Not once.*
Her doctors had been highly concerned, worried she was in-
ternalizing her emotions, would implode. But as she knelt
down on the stones in front of him and cupped his face in a
way he'd allowed no woman to do for near to a thousand
years, her eyes were awash in dampness.

Reaching out, he traced the path of one tear over her cheek,
down to her jaw, where he caught the droplet, brought it to his
mouth. The salt of it was strange, an unfamiliar thing. Dmitri
hadn't cried either. Not after the day he broke his son's neck.
"In my time," he said, "they believed in witches. Are you a
witch, Honor, that you make me say these things to you?"
Causing him to rip open wounds that had stayed safely
scabbed over for so long that, most of the time, he managed to
forget they existed.

Her hands, so very, very gentle, continued to hold his face
as she tugged him down until their foreheads touched. "I'm no
witch, Dmitri. If I was, I'd know how to fix you."

Such a strange thing to say when she was the one who'd
been fractured.

Perhaps he should've been angry at her arrogance, but his
emotions toward this hunter were nothing so simple. "Tell
me." An order.

Dropping her hands, she got to her feet and walked to stand
at the very edge of the stream, the water kissing her boots as it
worked its way down the slight slope and deeper into the
woods. He stood, too, taking a position beside her. It took her
long moments to speak, but what she said returned him to a
time in which he'd lived for the blade alone.

He'd learned to fight at Raphael's side, a simple man of the
land become one who knew only the dark caress of death.
Nothing else would quench the fury within him, not for decades, not for centuries. The sole mercy was that he'd been
Made in a time of blood-soaked battle between immortals, his
sword never lacking for fodder—that time was long gone, but
Dmitri had lost none of his deadly skills.

"There was one man," Honor began, staring out over the
water but seeing nothing of the spring green wood shot with
golden light. "The one in charge." Blindfolded, the sole thing
she'd been able to sense of him had been the pine of his after-

shave . . . and the ugliness of his presence. "He taunted me with the possibility that I might be able to convince him to let me go."

Instead of shutting up, she'd made the decision to keep talking, because her voice had been the only weapon she'd had. "As he walked out the first day, he slapped me so hard my ears rang." She'd been stunned by the unexpected blow, the inside of her cheek bleeding into her mouth. "I didn't see him for what might've been an entire day." She'd spent it naked and bound on the concrete floor, tethered to a metal ring set into the concrete.

Furious in her determination, she'd spent the entire day attempting to free just one of her hands, had even made the conscious choice to try to break her wrist. But the restraints had been too tight, too well constructed.

"The next time, he apologized, loosened the tension in the chains after he hung me up from my arms once again; and he brought me something to drink." She'd gulped it with focused greed, aware she'd need every advantage if she was going to survive this. "He wanted to condition me to the point where I would begin to be grateful to him for allowing me to live." But Honor had gone through the compulsory and rigorous psychological warfare course at the Academy, been prepared for the eventuality in which she might find herself a hostage.

Even that might not have been enough, given the duration of her captivity, but she'd also grown up across thirty different foster homes. Some had been good; most livable; others horrors. But the experience had taught her one thing—always, always look beneath the surface for a person's true face. "I don't know how many days he took that tack. I lost my sense of time fairly quickly."

Since her prison could only be reached by an internal staircase, she hadn't even been able to count on a burst of light when the door opened, to orient herself. "I tried to play along, but he figured out I was manipulating him." She forced herself to tell Dmitri the rest. It was the first time she'd spoken of the ordeal to anyone, and that it was Dmitri . . . but maybe it was always going to be him.

"He fed from me, from my throat. His hand . . . he touched me." In a foul travesty of a lover's caresses, the gentleness of his touch making it no less a violation. "Afterward, he whispered to me that he knew he'd been my first." That, too, was true. She'd always had a revulsion against allowing anyone to feed from her. It hadn't been a mere dislike, but a deep, nauseating abhorrence of the act, inexplicable in its intensity. "I think that's why he chose me."

"Planning," Dmitri said, his voice glacial, "and the patience to carry it through. Put that together with his knowledge of the appetites of Valeria, Tommy, and the others, and it means we're looking for a strong vampire of at least three hundred. Anyone younger would find it difficult to gain their trust."

"Yes." His pragmatic manner made it easier, made her feel a hunter, not a victim. "I got that impression from his speech—it was modern for the most part, but he'd occasionally use old-fashioned words or phrasing."

"How did he dress?"

Honor's gut clenched as her mind brought back the sensation of her attacker pressing against her, his aroused body making what little food she'd had rise into her throat. "Doublebreasted suits." She could still feel the buttons cutting into her skin.

"That would seem to eliminate several of the old ones from the equation"—no hint of emotion—"but I won't disregard them just yet."

"Yes, he's clever, could've altered his normal style." Seeing the banded tail of a Cooper's hawk riding a thermal wind overhead, she followed its progress over the trees. "The house where they found me, it was in the middle of an abandoned housing project about an hour out of Stamford."

"I read the file."

She shifted to face him . . . and almost stumbled backward at the untrammeled rage in those dark eyes burning with black flame. "Dmitri."

He didn't respond, his hair lifting in the breeze that whipped through the trees, exposing the brutal lines of a face of such sensual beauty, she understood how an angel had hungered to possess him. But then, that angel had *hurt* him—the idea of it made an incandescent rage form in Honor's soul, so deep it was as if it had been a part of her since the moment of her birth.

"I need to return to Manhattan," Dmitri said at last, turning to head back in the direction of the clearing where the chopper waited. He looked beyond remote at that moment, a man who followed no rules but his own. But he waited for her at the edge of the wood, shortened his stride to match her own. She didn't make the mistake of thinking that meant she had any kind of a claim on him. Whatever it was that drew them to one another, it was a fragile, almost brittle, construct.

Dmitri was anything but that; a man who had been formed in rivers of blood.

Yet once he'd lived in a small village, made his living from the land. A simple life, but one for which he had turned down the offers of an angel renowned for her beauty. Most men would have accepted such an invitation, if only for the novelty of it. Perhaps he'd been too proud to be an angel's fleeting plaything . . . or perhaps his heart had already belonged to another.

A shimmer over her skin, a sense of indisputable *rightness*.

However, she swallowed the question on the tip of her tongue—about the woman whose memory had brought an intimate cadence to his voice the one and only time he'd mentioned her. Not just because this wasn't the right time or place to ask, but because whatever the answer, it could be nothing good. Not when Dmitri walked alone. "Any word on the tattoo?" she asked instead.

"The three master tattooists we consulted were of the opinion that, regardless of the surface intricacy, it was an amateur job."

"Damn." It would make the doer so much more difficult to identify. "And those who might be loyal to Isis?"

"Her name appears dead, forgotten." Turning to face her, he stopped in the shade of a tree with almost dainty branches hung with shivering leaves, the area around them relatively clear. "Whoever it is that seeks to resurrect her, he's kept his intentions secret."

"Devotion?" Her eyes locked with his, and in them she saw a thousand secrets, potent and swathed in velvet shadows formed of violence and pain. "If he—or she—has revered Isis this long, he must consider her his goddess." Too precious to stain with the scrutiny of those who might look on her with a more jaundiced eye.

"Perhaps." Not breaking the intimacy of the visual connection, Dmitri touched his hand to the side of her face.

It was no longer strange, no longer jarring, the rough heat of his skin against her own. And though her heartbeat accelerated, it did so as any woman's would at the caress of a man so sinfully compelling. The decision instinctive, she cupped his face in her hands when, an erotic rain of bitter chocolate and liquid gold cascading over her senses, he angled his head and bent to press his lips to her own.

A flicker of black, of nothingness . . . and she was on the other side of the clearing. Glancing down at the blade in her grip, then at Dmitri, she bit back a scream. "How badly did I cut you?" A harsh question, twisted through with anger and despair and a wrenching sense of failure.

He held up a hand painted red by a diagonal cut across his palm. "Nothing major."

The same injury might well have cost a human man the use of the nerves in his hand. Shoving the knife back into her boot after wiping it on fallen leaves, she thrust her hands into her unbound hair, her chest heaving as if she'd run a mile. "Well, that answers that, doesn't it?" The divide between dreams and reality was a gaping chasm.

A single thick drop of blood running down his fingers, to hit the ground in crimson silence, Dmitri raised an eyebrow. "It tells me only that I need to be faster."

Her laugh was jerky, bitter. "You *are* fast." A vampire of his age and strength could snap her neck before she ever saw it coming. "You're letting me hurt you."

"No, Honor. I don't let anyone hurt me." Black silk across her skin. "I was, however, looking at your lips, not your knife hand. Next time, I'll strip you of your weapons first."

The sheer arrogance of the statement cut through the barbed ugliness of her emotions to incite a languid heat in her veins. "Yeah? Well, maybe next time, I'll cut off that hand," she said, though the sight of his blood, it did something to her, birthing a visceral repudiation.

"So long as you understand"—stalking closer, his finger brushing her lower lip, smoke tangible as a lover's touch stroking her in places that made her gasp—"that there will be a next time."

Honor didn't know what she would've said to that announcement, because a strong wind swept over them at that instant, to be followed by an angel with wings of white-gold landing a bare three feet away. Her heart stuttered—most mortals who met the Archangel of New York ended up dead.

That was when eyes of absolute, unrelenting blue fell on her, beautiful beyond bearing . . . and utterly without mercy. The moment hung suspended in time, and she knew she was being judged. Her death, she thought, would mean as little to him as that of an insect. *Dear God.* How could Elena call this inhuman being her mate, take him to her bed?

"Raphael."

The archangel shifted his attention to Dmitri, his feathers sliding against one another as he folded back his wings. "There's been a second incident."

Honor, drawing in air to ease a painful chest, snapped up her head as Dmitri said, "Another public location?"

"No. The victim was left in a warehouse run by a vampire who still has ten years to go on his Contract."

"No chance of the body not being immediately reported to the Tower." Dmitri spoke to the archangel with a familiarity that made it clear their relationship was nothing so simple as lord and liege. "You could've contacted me without flying here."

Raphael glanced at Honor. "Leave us."

No one had ever before spoken to her in that tone. "I might," she said, not certain where she found the guts to challenge this being who made every tiny hair on her body rise in an alarm so primal, it came from the part of her brain that was without sentience or reason, "be able to help."

The Archangel of New York looked at her for a long, chilling moment. "Perhaps. But that is not for you to decide."

Dmitri's lips tugged upward a fraction at whatever he saw

on her face. "Go, Honor. I'll make sure you get to examine the body."

It was galling to realize she'd been dismissed, an overly ambitious child, but she was smart enough to know it was nothing personal. Raphael might have taken a hunter for his consort, but he wasn't, and never would be, anything close to mortal. Turning on her heel, she headed for the stream once more. As for Dmitri—she'd settle that account later.

19

Raphael's eyes followed Honor's progress. "Be careful, Dmitri. She has more spirit than all your other women put together."

Dmitri watched that strong, lithe body disappear into the trees, the strength of her even more compelling for having been reborn from the ashes of brutality. "Do you think me in danger, Sire?"

"No. But then, I did not think myself in danger either." Allowing his wings to brush the carpet of fallen leaves, he returned to the matter that had brought him here. "This time, the message was unhidden."

Dmitri had guessed as much. "Tell me."

"The male was branded with a glyph. The sun hiding a sickle moon."

"There now, lover. You will never forget me."

His chest muscles tightened. "We've been unable to confirm the identity of the previous victim," he said, strangling the memory. "Is this one ours?"

"No." *Dmitri.*

I can handle seeing the body. The memory was a vicious one, but it didn't cripple. "The fangs?"

"Near translucent."

"A report came in from the lab early this morning," he said, turning toward the stream. "There was a problem with the first vampire's blood." *Honor should hear this.*

Raphael fell into step with him as they headed toward her. "Tell me about your hunter."

"I have a feeling you already know."

A faint smile. "You're protective of her."

Dmitri thought back to the last time he'd felt protective of a woman. It had been an eon ago. So long ago that he hadn't recognized the feeling until Raphael pointed it out. "It seems so." Such protectiveness wasn't an emotion he welcomed, speaking as it did of ties beyond the raw physicality of sex.

Sinking into a woman's hot, wet sheath, playing with his bedmate until she whimpered and begged, it was an amusement. Pleasure and pain, sex or blood, none of it touched the quiet, hidden core of his heart, where he continued to honor his vows to his wife.

"I can take care of this, Dmitri."

"No." They might have killed Isis together, but the angel had been Dmitri's nightmare. "The message was addressed to me. I'll find its author."

Honor's form appeared out of the trees on the heels of his declaration. She was standing with her body angled slightly toward them, as if she'd sensed their approach, her expression one of cool consideration.

"The first vampire's blood," he said to her, intrigued by the realization that she was calculating a reprisal aimed at him, "was not what it should've been."

"Vampiric blood is distinctive." Lines marring her forehead. "What was wrong with his?"

Dmitri couldn't tell her about the toxin that built up in the bodies of angels, that was used to turn humans into vampires. That was a secret so profound Illium had been stripped of his feathers for speaking it to a mortal, a woman who had long since turned to dust. But he could give Honor the result. "The conversion process was incomplete."

Hereto hidden strands of mahogany in her hair caught the light as Honor angled her head. "An amateur attempt that went wrong?"

He would fist that hair around his hands when he sank into her. "Yes." Involving an angel unaware that the toxin in his blood hadn't yet reached the threshold for a successful Making.

"I can talk to the other hunters, see if they've heard of anything similar." Folding her arms, she looked down at the pebbles, back up. "Thing is, the body drop in Times Square, the butchery, it's not something you'd do your first time around. There must be evidence of previous practice efforts."

"We are speaking of immortals," Raphael pointed out. "His practice could have spanned centuries."

"Especially," Dmitri added, "if he was a disciple of Isis." A disciple Dmitri would not allow to live. The bitch would never come back to life, not even as a remembered goddess.

"Yes, but," Honor argued, displaying a quiet strength that had begun to fascinate Dmitri, "the fact that he hasn't mastered the Making process says he's new at this aspect of things even if he isn't new at the violence."

"Yes." Dmitri frowned, recalling something another member of the Seven had said to him. *Sire, are you able to reach Jason?*

No, he's out of range.

Taking out his cell phone, Dmitri glanced at Honor, using his gaze to caress lips he wanted to debauch and corrupt. "Try not to get killed while I'm making this call."

Her eyes flashed fire, stirring parts of him he'd believed entombed in that field of wildflowers that was a memorial to his Ingrede and their children.

Honor saw the shadow that swept across Dmitri's face before he stepped away to make his call, wanted to reach out and wipe it away, the need an ache inside of her. However, not only did she not have that right, she was being examined by a male whose face was so flawless, it almost hurt to look at him. "I saw Elena this morning," she said, wondering how she'd ended up making conversation with an archangel.

"My consort has a way of finding trouble." Raphael's hair, black as the night, gleamed in the forest light. "Dmitri helps you seek vengeance."

"I think it's more the fact that these vampires are breaking the rules." Fooling herself about Dmitri's motivations would only make the eventual fall harder.

"Perhaps." He joined her at the water's edge, his wings bare inches away, the gold filaments glittering under the sunlight. "The Guild is important to the balance of the world. Its hunters must not become prey."

"If it had been another mortal," she found herself asking, though it might have been safer to keep her thoughts to herself, "one not associated with the Guild?"

"Mortals have a part to play in the world, too."

She didn't know how to read his words, this lethal being who was capable of breaking a man's every bone and displaying him like a macabre doll. Then she glimpsed Dmitri walking back. Dark and dangerously intelligent, with a body that had been sleeked to gleaming purity in battle, and a moral compass that was undeniably skewed, he was no less inhuman than the man he called Sire.

Perhaps he was even worse.

Where Raphael was remote, removed from humanity, the violence that was so much a part of Dmitri hummed just below the surface of his sophisticated skin. Blood and pain, she thought, that was what drove Dmitri. Why that should cause her heart to clench in unrelenting sorrow was a question to which she had no answer.

The body lay on the concrete floor of the warehouse, the young male's arms and legs splayed in a way that was nothing natural. Jeans covered his legs but his upper half was unclothed, better to display the brand seared into a chest that bore lines of muscle development as yet incomplete.

Dmitri had repudiated the same mark with blood-soaked violence, using a knife he'd taken from Isis's home. It was only fitting, he'd thought as he stripped off his rough shirt and pressed his back against one of the beams that had survived the fire that had taken everything from him.

The point of the blade was so sharp, it caused a bloody droplet to appear the instant he put it to his skin.

Gritting his teeth, he began to cut, thrusting deep enough to excise the scar tissue. He was a vampire now. The skin would heal whole and unmarked.

But vampires still felt pain.

Blackness engulfed him when he was less than a quarter of the way around the brand. Picking up the fallen blade with blood-slick hands the instant he awakened, he began again. And again. And again. Until there was no more trace of Isis on his body and his heart had grown so weak, he could feel death whispering in sweet, dark welcome.

A shadow of wings, a glimpse of searing blue. "Dmitri. What have you done?"

"Leave me." It was the only thing he had the strength to say.

"No." A wrist being thrust in front of him, his head pushed forward by an unyielding hand. "Drink."

Dmitri resisted.

Cursing, Raphael used that same blade to slice open his vein, pushing the bleeding flesh to Dmitri's lips without warning. A single taste and the newly awake predator within him took over.

He fed.

He hadn't healed that day, or in the days that followed. He'd been too young Made, the same reason why Raphael had been able to overwhelm him. But he did heal. At least on the outside.

"So young," Honor said, squatting beside the dead male, her sadness a poignant thread in her voice.

Compelled by the sound, he watched her put a gloved hand on the protovampire's jaw, open his mouth. "We already know of the fangs."

"No, I'm looking for something else." Leaning in, one hand continuing to hold the victim's jaws open, she reached back to pull a slender tube off her belt. "Would you hold the flashlight so I can see into his mouth?"

He came down on his haunches beside her, his focus on her rather than the male on the concrete. The lines of her face were elegant, her eyes not bitter or hard in spite of what she'd suffered. She'd survived with her soul intact, still had the capacity to feel compassion for the loss of a life.

Dmitri couldn't say the same. The tattered remnants of his soul had burned up in his son's funeral pyre. Such golden flames around his boy, such a wild blaze for such a small child. It suited him, Dmitri had thought as the final piece of his heart broke, suited his Misha with the deep laugh and the hunger to explore.

"Dmitri."

Glancing up, he saw too much knowledge in the mysterious green eyes that watched him, too much tenderness. "Don't you know to keep your distance, Honor?" He was a predator, would strike at her weaknesses, take every advantage.

A slight shake of her head, curls escaping the rough braid she'd done on the flight over. "I think it's too late for that." Breaking the eye contact with that quiet statement, she said, "Do you see?"

Dmitri followed her gaze. "He doesn't have his wisdom teeth." While such a lack wasn't an absolute indicator of age, when paired with his baby-faced appearance it was another sign these vampires were being Made outside of any accepted structure—the Cadre had long decreed that no mortal who had not lived a quarter of a century could be Made.

"He was vulnerable," Honor said, reaching out to brush the victim's hair out of his eyes with quiet care. "A target who could be controlled once he'd been hooked by the idea of immortality."

Again Dmitri looked at the victim's face. He wasn't completely heartless—he mourned for the young—but this manchild was old enough to have made his own decisions. At that age, Dmitri had been working the fields and courting a woman with sunshine in her smile and eyes that told him he was beautiful without her ever saying a word.

"Leave him," he said, rising to his feet. "There's nothing you can do to discover his identity." The Tower's own technicians would fingerprint and otherwise process the body.

Honor, however, didn't get up. "Anyone looked at his back?"

"It matters little." But he bent down to pull the victim's shoulders off the floor for her.

"Nothing," she said in open disappointment. "I was hoping for another tattoo. Might've given us more clues."

Standing, Dmitri waited for her to join him. They didn't speak again until they were outside the gleaming metal of the warehouse, the late afternoon sun a gentle warmth in comparison to the shadows within. "There was no need for any such marking, Honor. The brand is message enough."

Hearing the brutal cold in Dmitri's tone, a whip that spoke of a vicious pain that might strike out at anyone in the vicinity, Honor nonetheless said, "Will you tell me about it?" because it *was* far too late to stand back, be rational.

"No." A single flat word, a sudden reminder that the stark intimacy of those moments by the quiet music of the stream had been an aberration. "I think it's time you went home."

She should've let it go, but her response was instinctive, springing from the same wild, dark core as her emotions toward him. "You really think you can just set me aside when I become inconvenient?"

"You're under contract to the Tower and that was an order." With that, he turned on his heel and headed back inside.

Furious at the realization that she'd been shut down for the second time that day, she twisted with the intention of confronting him . . . when she remembered the memory card in her pocket. She had no doubts the Tower had the best computer experts at its command—but the Guild had the best of the best, and, unlike with the Tower personnel, neither Vivek's nor Honor's attention would be divided by other pieces of evidence.

Vivek was in a foul mood when she arrived. He snapped at her to slot in the card and then said nothing for almost twenty minutes. Then: "I've cracked the encryption. Data's coming up on the screen to your left."

Swiveling her chair to face it, she began to scroll through the information. Most of it seemed to be business related, so Tommy had, in fact, done some work amid all his depraved play. Not much of it, though. That wasn't necessarily anything to note. A lot of the older vamps had so much accumulated wealth they spent the majority of their time in indulgent excess. The idea of it made Honor's skin itch. What was the point of near-immortality if you weren't going to do something with it?

"It *is* polite," Vivek muttered, "to thank someone after they do a task for you."

Blinking, she looked up to see him staring at what looked like grainy surveillance footage. "What? Oh. I thought I could cook you dinner when this was all over." When she could lay the nightmare to rest, sleep knowing her tormentors would never hurt her or anyone else again.

Vivek shifted his wheelchair to glare at her. "Feeling sorry for the cripple, I see."

"Knock it off, V." In no fine mood herself, she returned the glare. "If we're comparing the right to indulge in self-pity, I think I've got you beat."

"I was abandoned by my family."

"At least you had a family for a while. I was abandoned almost the instant I left the womb."

"I can't walk."

"I was tortured for two months and can't stand for a man to touch me in a sexual way, even a man I find wildly attractive." Until the erotic, decadent taste of him was in her every breath. "Despite my better judgment."

"It's Dmitri, isn't it?" A whir of sound as Vivek brought his wheelchair closer.

Returning her attention to the data, she let her silence speak for itself.

"First Elena and then you." A blown-out breath. "I want to show you something." Not waiting for an answer, he went to another computer and cued up a video clip on the large wall screen in front of the consoles. "Watch."

20

She watched, because Vivek, mood or not, would never waste her time, not when he knew how important this was to her. The clip turned out to be a traffic report from one of the local television stations—and then suddenly, the bubbly blonde reporter was yelling at her cameraman to zoom in.

When he did, the first thing Honor saw was the brilliant near-white hair of the woman racing through the streets, her legs long, her grace extraordinary. An instant later, the reason for her urgency came into focus: a sensually beautiful masculine form giving chase, as fast and ruthless as a panther, his shirt splattered with the viscous red of blood.

Honor had been out of the country at the time of the infamous chase across Manhattan, and while she'd read about it, she'd never seen the actual footage. As she watched, Elena pulled out a gun, turned as if to shoot Dmitri—just as a sleek black motorcycle screeched to a stop at the corner, only a couple of feet away.

Jumping on, the hunter held on tight to the driver as the motorcycle powered away from danger. Dmitri, meanwhile, his chest barely moving in spite of the intensity of the chase, stood at the curb . . . and blew Elena a kiss.

"That," Vivek said with solemn concern, "is the man you've got the hots for. Ellie said she slit his throat and he liked it."

Goose bumps over her skin, a chill sweat breaking out along her spine. "Sometimes," she said, thinking of the violence she'd witnessed in Dmitri, the casual cruelty, "logic doesn't work."

Vivek parted his lips, then seemed to think better of what he'd been about to say. "Just, be careful. And if you ever need to disappear, all you have to do is ask." He headed to one of the computers before she could respond. "I'm copying the data over here, too. I'll run search algorithms through the whole file using key words while you go through the e-mails."

It was twenty minutes later that Honor saw it. An e-mail string hidden amongst all the other business ones, the subject header an innocuous project name. The only reason she'd even scanned it was because it appeared at the beginning of her period of captivity.

The first message said: *Did you get an invitation?*

The response was as simple: *I'll call you.*

Two days later: *I haven't felt this alive in over a century.*

The response: *I'd forgotten what it was to hunt down my prey.*

Except the cowards had done no hunting. They'd simply taken advantage of a trapped woman laid out for their ugly pleasure. Pulse pounding in her temples, she checked the e-mail address of Tommy's friend. It didn't surprise her in the least when it proved to identify the writer. "They never even considered anyone would come looking." After all, Honor hadn't been meant to leave that pit. Ever.

"Leon and his friends aren't as sophisticated as my guests." A lingering kiss that made her empty stomach revolt. *"It'll be interesting to see what remains after they've gorged themselves. But first . . ."*

Icy jets of water hitting her, creating bruises upon bruises. The pungent scent of bleach in the room, the spray shifting to the concrete for long minutes. Her mouth being wrenched open.

"Now, let's clean you up. I wouldn't want your body to betray me when they find it in the trash."

* * *

It only took Vivek a couple of minutes to match a physical address and bio with the e-mail she'd found. "Jewel Wan," he said, bringing up a picture of a woman of Chinese ethnicity, the centuries of vampirism having worn away all traces of humanity to leave her a stunning sculpture carved in ice, her eyes gleaming black diamonds that matched the ones she wore around her neck.

"She's a society fixture," Vivek continued. "Spends a significant amount of time with humans."

Glossy, straight hair stroking over her skin as small feminine hands caressed her ribs. "So much muscle even now." A sweet kind of a voice, intrinsically feminine. "The boys are so rough, aren't they?" Touching her with a delicacy that sought to lull. "I'll make sure it doesn't hurt."

But it had.

Honor hadn't known it was possible to fight the pleasure in a vampire's bite before her abduction, but she'd learned to do it in that torture chamber after the first three times the architect of her capture sent her into an orgasm that had her throwing up afterward, the rape no less painful for having being done through her blood.

Jewel Wan hadn't been pleased at her defiance.

Laughter, soft and vicious. "I will enjoy breaking you. When I'm done, you'll call me mistress and beg for my touch."

A cold, cold thing sliding through her veins, engulfing her chest. "Give me her address."

Vivek twisted his chair around. "She's four hundred and fifty years old, Honor." Unhidden alarm in his voice. "Not powerful for that age, but more than powerful enough to snap your bones regardless of her size."

Cutting pressure against her side, nails pushing in until they pierced the flesh. Fingers curling around her rib. "Now"—a malicious whisper—"who is your mistress?"

Her rib twinged where Jewel Wan had fractured it. The hole in her side had healed, the scar so tiny she didn't even notice it usually, but today it pulsed a rigid lump. "I'll look it up myself." It wouldn't be difficult, considering the vampire's social status.

"No, wait. Here." Vivek brought up the address. "Please don't be stupid."

Her mind was screaming at her to stop, to think, but overwhelming that was the sensory memory of those sharp-nailed hands, that hair of liquid silk. Touching her. Hurting her. Bile rose in her throat but she forced it down, memorized the address, and left. Vivek called out after her, but she wasn't listening, the roar inside her a violent thunder.

Jewel Wan lived on an estate in the Hudson Valley, which meant Honor would need a car. However, when she went upstairs to requisition one, she was told a freeze had just been placed on her ability to access Guild resources.

Vivek.

Not bothering to argue, she strode out into the heavy but flowing traffic before rush hour. It took only seconds to hail a cab, direct it to the nearest car rental place. She swiped her credit card, filled in the paperwork with impatient hands, and fifteen minutes later she was on her way out of the city in a small, maneuverable SUV.

Be rational, Honor. You go there and she'll kill you.

The thought was barely complete when another part of her mind said, *Not before I put a few holes in her.*

What about the others? the tiny, still-coherent part of her asked. *The ones you won't find because you're dead?*

"I'll fucking well find *her!*" The voices went silent, overwhelmed by the red haze of a rage so vicious, Honor hadn't known until that moment that she could hate with that depth of fury.

Two hours and a hundred ignored phone calls later, she looked down the evening-grayed straight of the empty road and saw a helicopter sitting in her path. "No. *No!*"

Braking to a halt, she shoved open the door and strode out to intercept the man walking toward her. Dressed in black, he appeared a darker piece of the falling night, but his chest felt very much real when she slammed her hands against it. "Get that thing out of my way!"

Dmitri's eyes were full of a quiet, simmering anger when they met her own. "I thought you had a brain, Honor."

"Yeah, well, seems I don't." Seeing his unyielding expression, she stalked back to the car. There were other ways to get to Jewel Wan's showcase of a home.

Except Dmitri slammed the car door shut before she could reach it. "Jewel allows trained attack dogs to roam free on her estate and has a standing guard of four who all carry substantial weaponry."

"Take your hand off the door." Sliding out her gun, she pushed the barrel into his heart hard enough to bruise. "At this range," she said, flicking back the safety, "I'll do enough damage to put you down for hours."

"Why this one?" A quiet question that cut her like a knife, destroying the ice that had carried her this far. "Valeria you handled with preternatural calm. Jewel drives you to insanity."

Her muscles spasmed. Wrenching away the gun before she shot him by accident, she flicked on the safety and turned to look at the road she'd driven down only minutes before. When he came to stand at her back, she knew he was blocking the pilot from seeing her. That small act, it shattered her. "She didn't hurt me." A rough whisper. "Not until the very end."

"Yet your hatred for her is so deep it blinds." He touched his hands to her bare forearms, and she was startled when she didn't pull away, when she allowed him to align his chest to her back, the masculine heat of him seeping through to her very bones.

It did nothing to wipe away the shame and humiliation that had her stomach in knots, but it melted the final fragments of ice, leaving her acutely exposed, vulnerable. "Except for the leader and his games at the start, the others," she said, shivering with a cold that had nothing to do with the temperature, "no matter what else they did, only tried to force pleasure on me with their bite."

Dmitri rubbed his hands down her arms, his breath hot at her temple.

"Everything else," she continued, sinking into his heat, "was about power, about control." When that failed to crush her, they'd amused themselves by making her scream instead. "But Jewel, she injected me with something . . . and then she touched me." So delicate, so gentle, so horrifying.

It was near impossible to get air into her lungs now, her

breath jerky, her blood pumping in erratic bursts. But she said the words, because the shame was too huge a thing to keep inside any longer. "She made me orgasm. Over and over." Her body's betrayal had broken something deep within her, taken the last shred of defiant pride.

Dmitri's hands clenched tight on her arms. "It's not only men," he said, his voice rigid with control, "who can be aroused against their will."

Shuddering, she turned into his embrace, pressing her face against his chest. Except for Ash's quick hugs, it was the first time she'd allowed anyone to hold her since the abduction, the first time she'd been able to bear it. Maybe it was because her humiliation was so strong she had no room for fear . . . and maybe it was because he understood in a way no one else ever would.

"I *hate* her, Dmitri." It was a hard, jagged thing inside of her, this hatred. "More than anyone else."

Dmitri stroked his hand over her hair, bending his head to whisper a dark promise in her ear. "I can do to her what she did to you." Black satin around her senses. "It would be nothing to break her until she was a whimpering, crawling shell."

Her response was immediate—and violent. "*No.* You don't *touch* the bitch." Then, perhaps because she was half mad, she added, "You do and I swear I'll shoot off both your hands at the wrists." He was hers, and she didn't care if that was the obsession speaking, didn't care that she'd told herself not to make a claim. Dmitri was *hers.*

A vibration against her chest. Dmitri's laughter.

He drove the rest of the way, though the chopper would've been faster—they decided the extra time would allow her to calm down. That proved impossible, but she did manage to get a grip on her emotions to the extent that she was no longer blind to the stupidity of rash behavior on her part in the up-coming confrontation.

It was as they were heading down the last stretch of road—one devoid of streetlights—that her phone rang again. This time she picked it up. "Vivek."

"Honor, are you all right?"

"You ask that after you sicced Dmitri on me?"

A strained laugh. "Not my fault you have friends in scary places."

"I'm fine." He'd saved her life, and she wasn't going to be an ass about it. "Thanks."

He tried to hide his relief, but she heard it nonetheless. "Yeah, well, now you owe me two dinners." A beep. "Hold on." Then, "Jewel Wan is on the move. I hacked into her security company's system, got access to the cameras on the estate. Looks like she's packing up and getting out of Dodge."

"Guards?"

"Two in the front car, two with her, from what I can see. Visuals aren't that clear, so there could be more."

Hanging up, she relayed the information to Dmitri. "Is this the only road out of the Wan estate?"

His answer was a chilling smile.

Following his gaze, she saw car headlights flash in the darkness before disappearing as the oncoming vehicle curved around a corner. A second flash came on the heels of the first. She said nothing as Dmitri parked the rental in a way that blocked the road, slid out in silence as he did the same.

They were part of the thick blackness of the trees beside the road when the first car stopped, a gun appearing out the window. Dmitri said, "I wouldn't," in a quiet tone that sliced through the night air.

The gun hesitated, but didn't pull back, though it was clear the vampire didn't know where to aim.

"I did warn you." With that, Dmitri was gone, a shadow in the dark.

As she covered him, he smashed the nearest car window to reach in and pull out the vampiric driver, throwing him to the ground with such force that his skull cracked. The man's partner began shooting. Unfortunately, he was aiming where Dmitri no longer was. It was as she was kicking away the weapon of the unconscious driver that she heard the distinct *snap* of a neck being broken.

It had all happened so fast that the second car only started reversing in screeching panic after both the front vampires had been disabled. Picking up the machine gun she'd kicked aside, she aimed at the gleaming Town Car, blowing out the tires, then the windshield.

Glass shattered, smoke rose, and the vehicle slammed backward into trees that shook from the force of the impact but didn't give ground.

Dmitri was already on top of the vehicle, ripping away the roof in a feat of strength that made it patent he wasn't human. The guards inside, their bodies peppered with bullet wounds, made no attempt to defend their cargo. Dragging a screaming Jewel Wan out of the backseat by her hair, Dmitri dumped her in the patch of road spotlighted by the damaged Town Car's headlights.

21

"Anyone," he said in a quiet voice after ordering Jewel to shut up, "who wants to come out of this alive, get out and wait at the estate. If you'd like to make me very happy, try to run."

The guards staggered out and—to their credit—went to check on the other two. They left the one whose neck Dmitri had broken, which meant he was too young to have survived that, but pulled up the driver to drag him away. All of it in absolute silence. Jewel Wan, meanwhile, shoved back her hair and got unsteadily to her feet, her knees bleeding below the hemline of a tight black silk dress, her palms scratched from where she'd broken her fall.

None of it did anything to diminish her haughty elegance. "There you are," she murmured to Honor. "Such a pretty morsel."

Honor wanted to shoot her so badly that her entire body trembled, but she didn't. "I won't kill you and make this easy," she said, forcing herself to walk up and take a seat on the hood of the Town Car that no longer had a roof, the headlights blazing below her. "Dmitri?" When he moved to brace his hand against the hood, his body angled toward her, she said, "Not a single piece of your soul."

Close as she was to him, her cheek brushing the slight roughness of his own, she saw him smile . . . saw, too, the terror that erased Jewel Wan's tattered elegance. But the vampire was a businesswoman. "I can give you information."

"You say that as if it's a bargain worth making." Dmitri leaned up against the Town Car, his shoulders fluid with muscle, the wicked sin of his scent in her every breath. "We both know you'll tell me anything I want to know before this is over."

Jewel flashed her fangs. "I'm a vampire of four hundred and fifty. You intend to sacrifice so much experience for, what, a little mortal amusement? I've had her, and she's not that—"

Dmitri moved to backhand the vampire so fast and hard, she slammed up against a tree, crumpling to the ground with blood pouring out of her nose, a deep cut on her lip. "Now," Dmitri said in a voice so rational, it raised the hairs on Honor's nape, "tell me everything. And maybe I won't order Andreas to give you some extra-special attention."

A pained plea from the woman who looked unthreatening, fragile. Except Honor knew that was a lie. Jewel would always be a monster. Simply one in a package that had the ability to appear harmless. To offer her any mercy would be to sentence another victim to the horror Honor had barely survived. "Dmitri," she said, because lethal, dangerous creature that he was, he was still hers and she would fight for him, "what did I tell you?"

"Sorry." He grinned and it was shocking how very beautiful he looked even surrounded by the acrid scent of fear and blood. "Got caught up in the moment." Returning his attention to Jewel, he said, "Why aren't you talking?" in a voice that was only mildly interested—the same way a lion was only mildly interested in the prey it planned to rend when it got hungry.

"I got an invitation," the vampire said at once, dribbling blood. "It's in my study at home. On the desk." She reached up to wipe away the blood trickling from her nose, smearing dark red across the porcelain of her skin. "Tommy was one of them. He insinuated something at a party and I had him followed. Stupid man never took precautions."

Which was why, Honor thought, Tommy's invitation had been permanently retracted. "You aren't giving us anything we don't already have."

The vampire's eyes snapped to her. "Shut up, mortal."

Walking back to lean against the hood, Dmitri glanced at Honor. "Can't I touch her a little?" His smile when he looked at Jewel was pure sex—if you liked your sex with a *great* deal of pain . . . if you liked to scream until your throat was raw. "Your skin, Jewel, so very soft," he murmured, and while there was nothing overtly threatening about his words, if he'd been speaking to Honor in that tone, she'd have pumped him full of bullets and run like hell.

And then he took out the knife.

Jewel shoved herself back against the tree, began babbling. "Evert had to know. He and Tommy do everything together, but they weren't part of the center. The one who organized this, he made very sure to keep his identity contained, but there's a rumor in certain circles that he once worked at the Tower. How else would he know about the appetites of so many?"

"Certain circles," Honor said, putting her hand on Dmitri's shoulder, a silent reminder that Jewel wasn't worth even a fragment of his soul. "Who?"

A single smile from Dmitri and the vampire gave up three names.

Fifteen more minutes of questioning later, it was clear she knew nothing else. While Dmitri hadn't laid another finger on her, she was so petrified, her teeth were chattering, her eyes darting this way and that.

For an instant, Honor felt pity. "Enough, Dmitri."

Moving with preternatural speed, he snapped Jewel's neck before the vampire even had the chance to draw in a breath to scream. "She's not dead," he said after it was done. "At this level of strength, she'll rise again unless I decapitate her. Venom can fly her to Andreas in the chopper."

Shocked at the brutal swiftness of the punishment, she said, "I thought it would make me feel better, the idea of her being tortured, but it doesn't."

"There can be no mercy here." The words of a man who had seen centuries pass, rivers of blood soak the earth. "The instant word gets out that we're doing clean executions, the Made will lose the fear that ensures they don't dare things such as this more often." He sent a message to Venom as he spoke. "For the old ones, death is no threat. But pain . . . everyone fears pain."

She understood what he was saying, certainly had no loyalty to Jewel, and yet— "It seems so . . ."

"Inhuman?" A grim smile. "We aren't mortals, Honor. We never will be."

She wondered if he was giving her a warning. If so, it was unnecessary. "I've always seen you, Dmitri." No matter if she believed there was more to him, this vein of darkness was also an integral part of his nature, couldn't be ignored or wished away.

Chopper blades sounded at that instant, and soon Venom was landing the machine. The vampire whistled when he saw the carnage, but said nothing, picking up Jewel Wan's body and stowing it with all the care you might show to a sack of potatoes. "You want a ride?"

"No, we'll drive."

Venom slanted Honor an assessing look, but said nothing as he got into the helicopter and lifted off in a wild rush of air.

Leaving the abandoned Town Cars where they were, she and Dmitri got back into the rental. A couple of calls later, and Dmitri had organized a cleanup crew both for the cars and for the guards.

"What will happen to them?" she asked.

"Nothing to the two who didn't lift a weapon against me as long as they prove to have had no knowledge of Jewel's actions. The other one will suffer a punishment." His eyes met hers for a second. "By disobeying me, he disobeyed Raphael. That can't be permitted."

The instant it was, Honor knew, many of the Made would break their bonds, surrender to bloodlust, begin to hunt living prey. "The three names she gave, do you know them?"

"Yes. They're part of the same social circle as Jewel and the others."

"She's enough of a bitch that she might have snuck in a name that doesn't belong, out of spite."

"We'll find out soon enough—I've sent instructions that

they're to be watched. They'll be brought to the Tower for questioning tomorrow morning."

Releasing a long breath, she said, "I just want to finish this." Wanted to get on with the life she'd decided to live.

"You will."

Sitting in the passenger seat with Dmitri tangling her in fur and chocolate and sin, luscious and irresistible, Honor watched the miles pass by, the motion soothing, lulling her into sleep . . . into dreams.

"You are my wife."

"And you are a jealous man." *Shoving her hands into her hair she blew out a breath.* *"If anyone has cause to be jealous, it's me."*

"You know I would never touch another woman."

"And you think I would touch another man?"

Silence, his face harsh with shadows. *"Other men covet you."*

Shaking her head, she reached out to lay her palm against his stubbled jaw. *"I'm no great beauty."*

His fingers closed over her wrist, his other hand coming to lie at her waist. *"You don't see it, but I'm a man. I do."*

Sometimes she wondered what she was doing with him, this beautiful creature every woman in the village watched with admiring eyes. It was as if they knew how he moved when inside a woman, how he could play a woman's body until she would do anything he desired. Except she knew they didn't. For he had waited for her, though his body had to have demanded satisfaction, offers no doubt coming his way from women who did not honor their husbands.

"You are my heart," *she said, taking his hand and placing it over the beating organ.* *"It doesn't matter if another man should give me a thousand promises, it's to you that I belong."*

"Always?"

"Always."

"Honor."

Ignoring the masculine voice that tried to pull her into the waking world, she fought desperately to hold on to the dream—because the woman she was in that hazy place, she was loved, loved so deeply that it was a little terrifying.

"Honor." A caress of orchids and gold, decadent, luxuriant, enticing.

She jerked upright in her seat to find that they were driving into the parking garage beneath her building. "I fell asleep." In a car. With a man. With a vampire.

"You were smiling."

"Just a dream." One so vivid she could almost feel the stubble of her dream lover's jaw on her palm. "Do you dream?"

Reaching across after parking the SUV, he stroked a finger over her cheek, where she could feel lines caused by sleep. "In sleep, I remember memories, times long past."

She caught his hand against her cheek, had a disorienting sense of déjà vu. "Good memories?" she asked, the feeling shimmering out of existence as quickly as it had awakened.

Thick black lashes coming down, rising again. "There are times when even good memories aren't welcome." Remote words, but he didn't break her hold.

Lights cut across the garage behind them an instant later, destroying the intimacy of the moment . . . and yet neither of them moved. "Come upstairs." It wasn't an invitation she would have even considered making a bare few weeks ago. But she'd been another woman then.

Dmitri rubbed his thumb across her chin before dropping his hand, but she didn't need words to read the dark heat in his expression, his lips suddenly softer, erotically tempting. Pulse hammering in her throat, she got out of the car and led him to the elevators, aware of him twining fine tendrils of exotic scent around her. Not susceptible enough to be coerced by it, she allowed herself to luxuriate in the sensation.

He got a call just before they entered the apartment. She wasn't able to figure out anything from listening to his half of the conversation, but he told her the details after he hung up. "Venom's confirmed a watch on two of the names Jewel provided, is tracking the third." Putting his cell phone on her coffee table, he said, "It might be better to keep an eye on them for the time being."

Satisfying as it would've been to rush things, continued surveillance made sense. "I called Sara after we found out about the second hunt. All Guild personnel have been warned." Honor had personally sent a message to Ashwini and been relieved to learn that her best friend was currently working a case with Demarco. Two hunters would be far, far harder to take.

Dmitri nodded. "I'll make sure Venom keeps the Guild Director updated." Sprawling on a sofa, he crooked a finger. "Come here."

Kicking off her shoes and socks, she arched her back in a languorous stretch—both to loosen up tight muscles and to enjoy Dmitri's eyes on her, hooded and dark and open in their appreciation. Stretch complete, she returned the favor. There was a delicious amount to admire. Black jeans, a plain belt with a tarnished buckle, a simple black tee—the stark shade threw the raw sensuality of his looks into even cleaner focus.

No woman, she thought, would kick him out of the house, much less the bed.

Padding across the carpet, she stood between his legs. "I'm going to freak out," she said, and, yeah, it bruised her pride to admit that—but the only other option was to hide and Honor was through with being the rabbit Dmitri had called her.

He pointed at the shoulder holster and the knife sheaths. "Off."

She'd had a weapon on her every waking or sleeping moment since the attack—under her pillow, hidden down the side of the nightstand, on the back of the headboard. The idea of deliberately stripping herself of weapons with a vampire as powerful as Dmitri? It made her heart skitter against her ribs, her mouth turn dry as dust, her throat fill with grit.

"Want to keep a knife?" It was a low murmur of a question.

Honor gave the offer serious thought as she removed her gun and harness and stepped back to place them on the coffee table. The thigh sheath and the flashlight tucked into her back, along with a razor-fine blade worked into her belt, went next. She put the whole lot, belt included, beside the gun. Dmitri gave an intrigued look when she reached down her spine and removed a long knife from a hidden sheath, the blade as thin as the width of the nail on her pinkie. The single blade left was in the sheath she wore around her upper arm.

Touching it, she looked at the sensual, dangerous man on her sofa. Thought about cutting him again . . . and was kicked by a sense of rejection so deep, it would've shaken her if she hadn't already been caught off guard by so many inexplicable reactions when it came to Dmitri. "No weapons," she said as she placed her last knife on the table. "Give me yours." Vampire or not, Honor knew she was smart enough to turn his own weapons against him.

Dmitri began to hand them over. It was her turn to stare.

After they were both done, the pile of knives and guns on the coffee table looked like they'd cleaned out an armory. "I think we have a problem, Dmitri."

"I'm not finished." Unbuckling his belt, he began to pull it out.

Her eyes dropped. Maybe it was because she'd been blindfolded while Tommy and the others tortured her, but she had no trouble admiring a beautiful male body. And Dmitri's . . . oh, yeah. "Same as mine?" she asked, stroking him with her eyes, his T-shirt pulled tight over rock-hard abs.

"Have a look."

Taking the belt, she saw the thin wire worked into the leather. It could be pulled out with a single tug, used as a fatally efficient garrote. "Clever."

"Illium gave it to me a couple of years ago."

"I'd say he doesn't seem the type"—she ran her thumbs over the leather softened by constant use—"but I've known my share of hunters who come across as harmless."

"Put down the belt, Honor." A sexy smile. "Unless you plan to use it."

Stomach clenching, she dropped the belt and stepped back between his spread legs. "I had a feeling you'd be into belts and ropes."

When she reached forward and pushed up his tee, he remained in his sprawled position, a pasha waiting to be served. His skin was the same dark tan shade on his abdomen as it was on his face. "Is your skin this tone all over?"

"Only one way you're going to discover the answer to that."

22

Looking up, she saw hooded eyes, lips curved just enough to tell her he was enjoying himself . . . and a sensuality as lethal as the weapons on the table behind her. Not a man who would be kind to a woman in bed. "Take off the T-shirt."

He did it with a few economical movements—to reveal muscled shoulders, abs she wanted to lick, and a thin line of hair leading down into his jeans. "Orders already?" he murmured, dropping the T-shirt to the carpet. "I think maybe you'd like to wield a whip."

"Maybe I would."

A wicked smile.

Stepping back, she nudged his legs together and moved up to straddle him. He let her do as she would, and she knew why. If Dmitri wanted her flat on the floor on her back, she'd be there before she saw him move. But this wasn't about force or pain. It was something else altogether. What, she didn't quite know, but she knew it was important.

He felt quintessentially male beneath her, his thigh muscles rock, his body heat stroking her with a languid intimacy so slow and undemanding that she didn't fight it—though she knew nothing was that simple with Dmitri. He was a man who would take advantage of every vulnerability.

Touching him with the lightest of fingertips, she began to explore this darkly sexual creature who should've driven fear into her heart—and who did still scare her at times with his brutal inhumanity—and yet who also made her feel safe in a way she couldn't explain. Irrational as it was, she trusted Dmitri.

When she ran her index finger along the top band of his abdominal muscles, he flinched. Only just, but she caught it. So she did it again—and saw the faintest hint of a smile as dangerous as it was sensual.

"Such patience," she said, leaning forward with her forearms braced against his chest. "I guess immortality gives a man time to learn many things."

His gaze lingered on her mouth. "Kiss me."

She shaped his lips with a fingertip, lingering on the slight fullness of the lower one. She'd seen that mouth cool with anger, curved in amusement and in mockery. Through it all, she'd wanted to taste it. There was just one thing. "They fed from my mouth."

Those dark chocolate eyes turned a sudden, deadly black, but all he said was, "Inefficient."

"Yes." It had been more about slashing her with their fangs, making her hurt.

Dmitri shifted slightly, muscles rippling in a reminder of his strength, but again, he left the next move up to her. She didn't make the mistake of thinking it an act of tenderness on his part. No, Dmitri was a predator—and she was being stalked. Slow and easy and determined.

"Stay still," she said, leaning in until their breath mingled. His face betrayed nothing, so much so that she might have thought him unaffected if she hadn't been able to feel the tension in that body made for woman's damnation.

The first touch of her lips against the firm warmth of his was a mere whisper. Her heart thudded and it wasn't panic. So she sucked slightly at his upper lip before releasing it to run her tongue along his lower, indulging herself with this man who was her own personal aphrodisiac.

His chest rose and fell under her hands, his breathing no

longer even. The feminine heart of her stirred in satisfaction. She didn't have to be able to see into the past to know that Dmitri had tasted every sensual act there was, luxuriated in every decadent sin . . . and yet he reacted to her. The response, she knew, was genuine—Dmitri wasn't the kind of man who'd bother to pretend.

Pulse beating in every inch of her skin, she opened her mouth over his, taking the taste of him deep within as she slid up her hands to cup his face.

She always did that, Dmitri thought, recalling the way she'd stroked those long, capable fingers over his cheek, his jaw, during that aborted kiss in the forest—and earlier, beside the stream. Only one other woman had he allowed the tender intimacy.

"Why do you kiss me so, Ingrede? As if I'll break?"

Laughter, husky and familiar. "I'm not kissing you, husband. I'm loving you."

Honor's hands pressed a fraction tighter as she licked her tongue across the seam of his lips and into his mouth. Dmitri could feel his muscles straining to painful tightness—being passive in a sexual situation was no easy task for a man who was always the aggressor. But to attempt that with Honor would be to lose her . . . so he remained motionless, patient as a hunting wolf. She would be his soon enough, and then he'd play.

That was when her tongue brushed across one of his fangs.

His cock, already rigid, grew almost painfully hard . . . and Honor froze.

"I want," he murmured in a tone calculated to entangle her in fantasies as dark as the scents he stroked over her body, "to do such things to your mouth, things that would make you blush."

"I don't blush." A soft whisper, muscles relaxing.

"Oh?" He laid out one of his plans in exquisite erotic detail, indulging himself as much as her.

Heat on her skin, but it wasn't a blush. "I want to do that." Shuddering, she very deliberately licked across his other fang. Her body tensed again, but her muscles weren't as stiff, and when she broke the kiss to draw in a breath, the emotion that glittered in her eyes had no connection to fear. "You," she said in that quiet, intimate tone between lovers, "have an addictive kind of taste."

He curved one of his hands over her hip. "That might make up for the fact you aren't as susceptible to the scent lure as you should be."

A husky laugh that tangled with one of his oldest memories. "That would hardly be a fair fight." Making a low, deep sound of pleasure at the caress of fur he teased over her skin, she surprised him with a second kiss, this one not as hesitant. Her breasts pushed full and firm against his chest, her nipples hard points he wanted to grip between his teeth while he fondled her soft flesh.

By the time she broke the kiss with a suckling taste of his lower lip, her breath was ragged. His own wasn't particularly steady either—but that he'd expected, given the violent craving he'd had for her since the instant she walked into his office. If he'd had a fraction less control, and if she'd been a fraction less terrified, he'd have ripped off her jeans and pinned her to the door of his office before he even knew her name, his cock buried inside her, his fangs sinking into her neck.

Soon.

He dropped his head back against the sofa when she dipped her head to kiss her way down his throat, luxuriating in the lush weight of her on his thighs, the wet softness of her mouth on a part of his body that was exquisitely sensitive, and yet one he never allowed his lovers to caress. He didn't trust anyone's teeth that near his carotid. Then she flicked her tongue over the small depression at the base of his neck.

His hand squeezed down on her hip.

A single jerking move later and she was at the other end of the room, having managed to pick up one of the knives on the coffee table in the process.

It enraged him to see such fear in her, this strong, sensual woman who touched him with a knowledge that belied the fact they were lovers new, but he kept his tone tempered, run through with a lazy sexuality. "Obviously we need to put the weapons farther away next time."

The glaze of nightmare took several long seconds to retreat from the haunting green of Honor's eyes. Staring at the blade in her hand, she gave a little scream and threw it to lodge in the wall above his head.

"Giving up so soon?" He crooked a finger once more.

A look that held a thousand unnamed terrors, but she strode back to retake her earlier position astride him, the weight of her lusciously female, her body built for a man's . . . for Dmitri's pleasure. When she went as if to kiss him, he shook his head. Raising a finger, he traced the taut line of her jaw, the rigid tendons of her neck.

"Women," he murmured, "might want to hurt me on occasion, but no one's ever said that kissing me was a punishment." Though he could make it one—immortality had given him a long time to perfect the ability to be a bastard.

"Damn them." Honor collapsed against his chest with that quiet statement that held trembling fury. "It infuriates me that Valeria and the others have made me into this weak, pathetic creature." Her breath puffed against his neck as her hand clasped his shoulder, nails digging into his skin.

The feel of her full breasts pressing against him stirred his darkest sexual instincts, but immortality had also given him the ability to delay gratification, to find pleasure in every step of the most intimate of dances between male and female. And Honor's trust, it was an exquisite thing, to be savored.

Running his hand over her hair, he twined the soft locks around his finger. "Yet," he said, rubbing the strands between his fingertips, "you're in the lap of a vampire who is their nightmare."

Her entire body went oddly motionless. "Part of me thinks you must've influenced me in some way," she said, "because it makes no logical sense that I trust you as much as I do."

Dmitri unraveled a curl, twined it around his finger again. "When I first developed the scent lure," he said, "I found it amusing to seduce the hunter-born." His cynicism had grown on the jagged edges of his anger. "I'd start with the scent, then fade it until it was no longer there. By the time I actually took them to bed, they just thought it was—it gave them permission to indulge in sex with a vampire, to pretend I made them do it."

Honor took several seconds to reply. "It's what the hunter-born fear, that they'll fall to the scent lure."

"No one ever complained."

Honor heard cool arrogance in those words, and yet the fact that he'd shared the truth with her said he understood that, shades of gray or not, he'd robbed those hunter-born of choice, at least at the start. "Why did you stop?"

He kept playing with her hair in that lazy way that made her want to cuddle up to him and close her eyes. "It was too easy." A shrug. "I discovered the conquest meant nothing—especially when certain hunter-born began to seek me out."

"Like a drug." She could taste the dark eroticism of him on her tongue, her body primed to the satin and champagne and fur of his caresses, could well understand the compulsion that had driven those hunters to return to him over and over.

"The lure," he said, "is not addictive."

No, she thought, that was Dmitri.

Dmitri dreamed that night, of a woman with sunshine in her smile and love in her every breath.

"Dmitri." A shy word, her hands smoothing down her skirts. "You shouldn't be here."

He wanted to touch her, kiss her, adore her. But she wasn't his. Not yet. "I brought you these."

Her eyes, those brown eyes uptilted at the corners, filled with unhidden joy at the sight of the wildflowers he'd clambered all over a mountainside to collect, feeling like one of the goats who roamed the same range. Yet if she asked him to go out and gather more of the wild blooms, he'd do so without question. Because that smile, it was the reason for his heartbeat.

Taking the bouquet, she half laughed her delight. "Thank you." A sucked-in breath, a look of absolute determination.

Running forward, she kissed him on the lips, only reaching him because he was already bending toward her.

Stunned, he didn't have time to raise his hands, keep her with him.

She was gone the next instant, her skirts whipping past his legs in a burst of color, the scent of her a blend of sunshine and those wildflowers she adored. He dreamed every night of having the right to press his nose against the delicate skin at the curve of her neck, to breathe in that scent as he drowned in the wild, feminine taste of her.

As it was with dreams, the colors shifted without warning until he was no longer standing in a rough barn but inside the walls of the small cabin he'd built with his own hands, a lovely dark-haired woman standing, shy and uncertain, in front of him, her back to his front. He'd touched her between her thighs until she was slick and pink with welcome, kissed her there in spite of her shocked cries, licked up the exquisite musk of her pleasure . . . but never had he claimed her as he hungered to do. Such a thing would have dishonored her.

"Ingrede." Closing his hands over her upper arms, he tugged her against his chest. "Are you afraid?"

Her response was a whisper, her body trembling until he wanted only to stroke her, slow and easy. "Yes."

Kissing the soft curve of her neck in the exact place that he knew made her weak in the knees, he found himself pushing his aroused body against her, his control in tatters. Clawing it back, though it was a precarious hold at best, he rubbed his lips over her skin. "I'd never hurt you." He would tear out his own heart before putting a bruise on her.

Making that little moaning sound in her throat that he loved, she angled her head to give him easier access. "You know so many things." Husky words. "I know only what you have taught me."

He shuddered as she pushed herself against him. Control lost, he bit at her pulse as he reached around to cup her breasts with a boldness he'd never before dared, afraid she'd shy. But now . . . now she was his wife, and though her skin burned with color, she didn't pull away. "You are so beautiful." He shaped her through the fabric of her clothing, indulging himself in a way he'd dreamed about for years, often waking with his cock hard between his legs.

"And I know," he said, licking out at her skin because the taste of her was a searing pleasure, "only what we've learned together." Touching another woman—he'd never even considered it, no matter the invitations he'd received. "Anything else is simple imagination on my part."

Ingrede gave a startled laugh, her breasts warm and heavy

under his intimate caresses. "Your imagination is a dangerous thing for a woman."

"For you," he corrected. "I want to see you, wife." Releasing her breasts only because he intended to have his fill of them when he'd bared her to the skin, he began to unlace her gown, aware of her breath getting ever faster, her pulse a thudding beat.

But she didn't raise a hand to stop him, this small woman with ripe curves who had been his fantasy from the day he'd looked up from helping his father in the fields to realize he was no longer a child and neither was she. When he pushed her dress down her arms, she tugged it the rest of the way with a shy touch, the material bunching at her hips.

23

A single push, a small tug, and she was naked in front of him, her back pressed to his chest still. Shuddering with possessive hunger, he stroked his hands over her thighs, along the soft curve of her abdomen and up to cup her breasts again, her skin creamy against his scarred hands.

Full and taut and topped with dark nipples he'd tasted when he'd seduced her into allowing him to tug down her top one hazy summer day, they made his mind spark with ideas he was certain the village elders would term extremely unacceptable. He didn't care. When it came to exploring what felt good between him and Ingrede, he never had.

"I dream," he whispered in her ear, "of sliding myself between your breasts." Using his forearm to plump them up, he sucked his finger to wet sleekness, then inserted it into the warm valley of her breasts to illustrate his meaning.

His wife's body shook in reaction, her hand clenching on his arm. "My mother warned me you wouldn't be a manageable kind of a husband." Turning, she rose on tiptoe to kiss him the way she'd discovered drove him to a glorious kind of madness.

Sucking on his tongue, she jerked when he ran his hand

down to the delicate curls between her soft thighs, but refused to part her legs. Having played this intimate game with her before, he pushed in regardless, rubbing his finger over the hard little nub that he wanted to suck. She'd shoved away his head the last time, unable to stand the pleasure . . . but she wouldn't be able to do that if her hands were tied.

"Spread your legs," he ordered when she broke the kiss to breathe.

Shaking her head, she squeezed her thighs even tighter, a red flush high on her cheekbones.

His own pulse was thunder in his veins. Dropping his head, he sucked one of her nipples into his mouth without warning, drawing hard and deep. She cried out, thrust her hands into his hair, spreading her legs instinctively to maintain her balance. "I claim victory," he said, releasing her nipple.

Her answer held a wickedness no one else ever saw. "Will you make me suffer?"

"Oh, yes."

She was hot and wet to his touch—it would feel like heaven when he sank into her. But it would also hurt her. He'd had his fingers inside her as they lay alone and aroused on a sun-golden field one festival day and later in a dark corner of her father's barn, knew how very tight she was.

His cock throbbed at the idea of the pleasure that awaited, but he would not have it entangled with her pain. "Lie down on the bed." Picking her up before she could respond, he placed her on their simple bed, then—stripping off his own clothes—settled himself with his head between her thighs, pulling her legs over his shoulders.

Her fingers clenched in the sheets, but she didn't stop him when he parted her soft folds to kiss her with a slow, intent ferocity he hadn't dared unleash on her before they were man and wife. She screamed, squirmed, sobbed, but it was pleasure that colored her responses, pleasure that had her tugging at his hair with frantic hands.

Instead of stopping, he found that little nub of flesh he'd discovered the first time he slid his hand under her skirts, and he sucked. Her hands tore at his hair, but he continued the torment until the finger he'd inserted inside of her was drenched in the liquid heat of her need. "Now," he murmured, rising

*above her, his cock a turgid length, "I will make you mine."
Fitting himself to the wet silk of her opening, he closed his
hand over the curve of her hip.*

*Driving into her was the most excruciating pleasure he had
ever felt. When she whimpered in pain, he tried to stop but he
was young, his control shredded, and for an instant, he panicked that he would take her when she did not want to be
taken. It froze the blood in his veins. Locking every one of his
muscles, he tried to find his mind.*

*Her fingers on his chest, her hand on his shoulder, tugging
him down to meet her mouth. "Don't stop, Dmitri. Don't
stop."*

*It was the only thing he needed. Pushing into her until he
was buried to the hilt, her nails digging into his arms, he
kissed her. And kept on kissing her as he began to move inside
the hot, wet sheath that held him with such possessive tightness. She didn't find her pleasure again before his own release
thundered over him, arcing down his spine in a lightning bolt
that had him spilling inside her, but he couldn't curse himself
for that. Not when his blood was seared with the liquid burn of
pleasure. Not when he roused to find a woman with a wide
smile lying under him, cupping his face with loving hands.*

*"I am now," she whispered, "thoroughly debauched, hus-
band."*

Dmitri's eyes opened to see the wall of his Tower office. He
rarely slept—it seemed a waste of time when he needed very
little to survive. But after returning from Honor's apartment,
he'd sat down at his desk, his mind on the hunter who threatened to make him feel things that had long gathered dust in his
soul. Minutes later, he was asleep and dreaming of the only
woman who had ever owned his heart.

Though he had taken her as a man takes a woman on their
wedding night, Ingrede had always been his, their families'
farms side by side. They'd tumbled in mud together as children, gorged themselves on summer fruit on lazy days gilded
by the sun, and taught each other the things one knew and the
other did not.

When she had smiled at him that day over the wildflowers,

the emotion that had burst within him had been incandescent. And it had stayed true as the years passed, as they grew. Looking back, he couldn't imagine he'd ever been that innocent boy who'd gotten up before dawn to clamber up a mountainside, except that his love for Ingrede still felt as deep, as true.

A woman's husky laugh.

It wasn't Ingrede's.

Pushing off his desk, he stalked to the plate-glass window that faced out into the hush of a Manhattan caught between night and day, the steel buildings soft gray shadows rather than glittering bulwarks. It was perhaps the only time the city was quiet, a mere two hours between the end of the nightlife and the beginning of the daylight rush.

He'd lived here for hundreds of years, seen it grow from nothing to a city whose heartbeat spoke to millions far and wide. He'd considered leaving it at times, had done so during his sojourn in Neha's court, young and still filled with an anger that had had no outlet. And then, of course, there had been Favashi. Lovely, gracious Favashi who had been a queen in the making, her home filled with music and art and warmth—the perfect trap for a man who had sought solace for centuries and found none.

Why have you never asked me more about Favashi? he asked the angel he could see coming toward the Tower, his wingspan distinctive, the gold filaments bright even in the dull light.

Raphael's reply was brutally honest. *It didn't seem a subject you cared to discuss.*

You could at least have called me a fool, he said as Raphael landed on the balcony outside, *beaten some sense into me.*

"There was," Raphael said, walking into the room even as he folded his wings to his back, "no need. Favashi was a good choice of mate for someone of your strength."

Favashi had never wanted a mate. "If I wanted to be turned into her personal menace."

"You are mine after all." A slight curve of his lips.

"That's just a bonus." As he spoke, he realized more had changed in Raphael than simply his wings. The archangel had been his friend for centuries, but he'd become a remote, distant being over the past two hundred years.

Dmitri hadn't really paid attention to the transformation because he'd been on the same path. But now the blue of Raphael's eyes was touched with humor and he spoke to Dmitri as they once had on a field far from civilization, two very different men who'd found common ground. "She came here while you were away," he said, wondering what it said about him that he'd not just noted the difference in Raphael, but responded to it.

"As she is not injured or dead, I take it you controlled yourself."

"Without difficulty." The truth was, while his pride had been pricked by the way Favashi had played him, his anger toward her had always been a cold thing. If Honor did anything similar, he realized, told him lies of love with such a sweet face, there would be no cold, only the most deadly of blood fury.

A rustle of wings. "If we are asking questions," Raphael said, "then I have one of my own. Why have you never blamed me for Isis's interest in you?"

"Because," Dmitri said, "Isis's madness was her own. And if there was any penance to be paid, you paid it in that room beneath her keep." Chained to the wall opposite Dmitri, Raphael had been forced to watch Dmitri's violent, forced conversion, to witness Isis's other atrocities, to listen to Dmitri's shattering scream as Isis whispered of what she had done to Ingrede and Caterina.

And he'd been there at the end, a silent guard, when Dmitri had held his son's tiny body in his arms and cried until he had no tears left inside him, his self that of a hollow man. "I thought I died in that room," he said, his hands fisting with the memory of how very fragile Misha's bones had been, how effortless it had been to snap them.

The archangel said nothing for a long time. When he did speak, it was nothing expected. "I thought you had, too."

Dmitri met those eyes of pitiless blue. "Why keep a dead man walking, then?"

"Perhaps I knew what you would one day become." The cold answer of an archangel. *Or perhaps it was because you weren't the only one who made a vow in that place of horror.*

Dmitri shoved a hand through his hair. "You should laugh

at me, Raphael. I warned you against becoming involved with a hunter, and yet I find myself in much the same position." Honor was becoming too important, a compulsion that wasn't only sexual, wasn't only physical.

"It is no hardship," Raphael said. "To have a hunter by your side."

But she wasn't simply a hunter. She was the woman who awakened memories of a life he'd lost an eon ago. Ingrede's laughter . . . it had been so very, very long since he'd heard it, but when Honor laughed, he felt as if he could almost reach out and touch his wife. A strange madness and one he had no will to fight—his heart ached with a need that had survived immortality, survived his every depravity, survived his own will.

"Have you had her blood tested?" Raphael's question was pragmatic. "A sample should be simple to acquire, given that the Guild keeps units of stored blood for all its hunters."

Ignoring the pain in his chest, Dmitri glanced at the archangel. "So certain?"

Raphael didn't answer, because no answer was needed. They wouldn't be standing here having this conversation if Honor wasn't important. "I would not," he said instead, "have you lose another mortal."

"Sometimes there are no choices." He thought of Illium, who continued to be drawn to mortals, though he'd lost the human woman he loved, seen her marry another man. The blue-winged angel had watched over her family until she passed, and then he had watched over her children and her children's children . . . until they spread out across the world, and the small mountain village where his love had been born ceased to exist.

There are always choices.

"No, Raphael," Dmitri said in response to that ice-cold tone in his mind. "I've stood by you for centuries, but if you touch her, it will cost you my loyalty." *And I will do my best to kill you.*

A hint of some unnameable emotion in the inhuman depths of those eyes that had seen a millennium and more pass. "So, she is not only important. She is yours."

Stalking closer to the glass, he stared out at a city beginning to shine silver bright in the dawn light. "I don't know what she is." *But she is compatible.* He'd obtained her blood, had the test done days ago, driven by unknowable need. The toxin that turned mortal to immortal would not drive her insane; it would not leave her a broken shell of the fascinating, compelling woman she was today.

You know you have but to ask. There will be no Contract for your chosen.

I know. He and Raphael had fought over the centuries, had fallen out, but they were tied by bonds so deep that the bindings had held even as they became ever older, ever more inhuman. *The problem is, I think the last thing Honor would ever want to become is a vampire.*

Another silence between two men who had known each other long enough not to fear it. Dmitri was the one who broke it. "What did Naasir say?" The vampire, one of the Seven, was currently posted in the newly risen city of Amanat, once a jewel in the archangel Caliane's crown, now her home.

"That my mother treats him as a beloved pet." Raphael's tone held a dark amusement threaded through with something more dangerous. "It appears likely she has realized what he is."

"It's no secret." Though Naasir's origins and abilities were not widely known beyond a small, tight circle. "At least she's accepted him." Giving them a constant flow of information from Amanat without Raphael having to be there. "And the angel Jason left in his stead?"

"Caliane ignores Isabel, which is as good an outcome." The archangel's wings glittered in the first rays of the sun. "You've always been my blade, Dmitri. Tell me—should I have killed her?"

Dmitri met the inhuman blue of those eyes, centuries of friendship and pain between them. "Perhaps," he said, his mind on a woman with a husky laugh and a smile that haunted his memory, "there are second chances."

Honor sat at her small dining table, the notebook Dr. Reuben had given her now closed, dawn shimmering on the horizon beyond. A few buildings still sparkled with light-filled offices, but the day was coming, the sun a warm glow in the east. The Tower stood outlined against it, appearing somehow softer in this strange, fragile twilight.

Dmitri, she thought, would never appear soft.

Her body continued to smolder from the slow burn of his kiss, his touch. Not even the fact that they'd gone little further after her flashback could mute the impact of it. His sensuality was potent, as raw as it was sophisticated, as dark as it was patient.

Lulling her. Seducing her.

Honor knew full well he was managing their encounters, accustoming her to his touch, his kiss, his strength. She had no quarrel with exploring her sensuality with a man who knew more about pleasure than she could imagine; she trusted him in bed. Of course, she thought with a smile as she got up to prepare breakfast, she had no intention of allowing him to continue to lead the dance once they became lovers in truth.

She'd finished her cereal and was walking to refill her tea when someone knocked on the glass wall that fronted her apartment. Twisting on her heel, she went for the gun tucked into the back of her jeans . . . and saw wings of silver-kissed blue backlit to brilliance by the rising sun. Illium jerked his thumb over his shoulder, toward the Tower.

Nodding, she watched him drop down, then sweep over the city in a breathtaking show of color even more startling against the dawn sky. When his wings were joined by those of midnight and dawn, she drew in a stunned breath, still utterly fascinated by Elena's transformation. Rather than holding a hover beside Elena, Illium executed a sharp vertical dive that had Honor's heart in her throat, before he turned to rise, then fly back up at the same speed to circle around and beside Elena, a playfulness to his movements that said the two of them were friends.

That was one wake-up call she'd have to share with Ashwini, she thought with a grin as she headed to change into a less ragged T-shirt, having showered when she woke. But when she stepped into the bedroom, she found herself discarding the T-shirt in favor of a short-sleeved, scoop-necked top that painted itself to her body and was a bright, stop sign red. It wouldn't impede her movements, didn't even show much cleavage, but it was the sexiest thing she'd worn since after the assault. It felt good. Brushing on a bit of makeup, including poppy red lipstick over her mouth, she pulled her hair back into a tight ponytail and strapped on her weapons.

It was too hot to cover the shoulder holster with a jacket, the temperature having spiked overnight, so she shrugged and left it at that.

There was a topless red Ferrari idling at the curb when she stepped out of her building. "I didn't realize I rated the pickup service," she said to the vampire in the driver's seat.

24

Dressed in a crisp white shirt, open at the collar, and black suit pants, he looked like some high-paid executive on his way to a breakfast meeting, his eyes shaded by mirrored sunglasses she wanted to rip off so she could read his gaze.

"I haven't gotten what I want out of you yet."

It could've been a joke. It could also have been the absolute truth.

"Have you eaten?" he asked, pulling out into the traffic.

"Yes." Speaking of breakfast— "Who do you feed from?"

"Careful, Honor." A tenor to the words that rubbed her the wrong way. "I might start to think you were the jealous, possessive type."

She never had been, but then, he was the only man who'd become an obsession. In the early morning hours today, she'd dreamed not of her faceless dream lover, but of Dmitri, with his experienced hands and sinful touch. "Yes," she said, knowing she was asking for something he might be incapable of giving. "I think I am."

Swerving to miss a Town Car that was attempting to nose its way out into the manic traffic, he took his time replying.

"There was a particularly luscious blonde on offer last night. She called me after I left your apartment."

Honor's hand tightened on the door frame, her arm braced along the edge. She knew he was provoking her on purpose—he was in a mood, that much was clear—and yet she couldn't fight the primal possessiveness of her response. "I'd have thought," she said with manufactured calm, "that you'd have learned your lesson about blondes with Carmen."

He turned, taking them toward the Lincoln Tunnel rather than the Tower. "Ah, but the sweet, hot taste of blood can mask the most unattractive qualities." Displaying no impatience with the traffic backed up before the tunnel, he pulled off his sunglasses to place them in a compartment below the dash. "Honor."

Anger a burn in her veins, she turned her head to find herself sucking in a breath at the intoxicating sensuality of him. The dawn sun, the traffic, none of it did anything to mute the intensity of those dark eyes, the harsh planes of that beautiful face.

"I," he said in a tone that was pure rough silk, "am possessive, too, little rabbit. Lethally so."

Her anger transformed into something far more visceral. "That doesn't scare me," she said, laying her hand on his thigh, the hard strength of muscle flexing under her palm. "But I've seen how vampires your age operate."

"How is that?" A low purr of a question that might as well have been a stiletto slicing over her skin.

"Moody, aren't you?" No answer, as he nudged the car forward. "I know," she continued, "the sexual mores are much more . . . relaxed." She'd once walked in on an orgy in progress during a hunt. Limbs tangled in sexual abandon, necks arched for a bite, and sighs whispering into air perfumed with the musk of sex, it had been erotic as hell, but she'd had not the slightest inclination to join in—even when propositioned by a pair of ripped Scandinavian-blond male twins, something straight out of a naughty fantasy.

"That's not me," she said, because while such fantasies were fun, in reality she fell *very* solidly into the fidelity camp. "This, between us, has crossed a line." A line that gave her the right to demand what she was about to demand. "I'll never accept that you might have other lovers—whether for blood or sex—and if you expect it, then we have to stop this right here, right now."

Walking away from Dmitri would destroy something vital inside her, but worse would be to watch him bend that dark head over the neck of some other woman. "However long we're together"—and she wasn't naïve enough to think she could hold a man like Dmitri forever—"it needs to be exclusive."

When she would've withdrawn her hand from his thigh, he covered it with his own for a second, holding her to him. "Blondes, it seems, have lost their appeal," he said, increasing speed as the snarl eased.

"Not good enough."

"No one else for the duration, Honor." An unambiguous promise . . . followed by a warning. "For either of us."

Her chest hurt and only then did she realize she'd been holding her breath. Releasing it, she said, "I know it's unfair, when I might not be able to allow you to feed from me." A vampire had once told her blood from the vein was as different from stored blood as the most decadent chocolate cake was from a rice cracker.

But Dmitri shrugged those shoulders she wanted to see naked again. "Blood is easy enough to come by." Clearing the tunnel, he took them out into the suburbs. "It's the sex I might die without."

She dug her nails into his thigh, choking on her laugh. When his lips curved in a slow smile that made her think dangerous thoughts, she decided to play him at his own game. Moving her hand, she danced her fingers up the zipper of his sedate black pants. He cursed, but managed not to swerve.

It did something to her that he'd hardened immediately under her touch, made her even bolder. "Try not to drive beside a semi or a pickup," she said, closing her hand over him and squeezing just enough that his jaw turned to granite, "or they'll get an eyeful."

"Fuck that." He punched something on the dash and the car's roof unfolded over them with a smooth electronic hum, locking into place in under half a minute. A second press and the windows were up and opaqued.

Good God. "How much is this car worth?"

Putting his own hand on hers, he urged her to pick up the pace. "You can't have it. Not for a hand job. Maybe if you use your mouth."

Her toes curled, desire igniting liquid and hot in her abdomen. "You can't come," she warned, pumping him with her hand. "Or you'll have to drive all the way back to change."

Clenching his fingers on the steering wheel, he hissed out a breath. "I won't forget this, Honor." It was a threat.

One that made her nipples go tight, rubbing against the lace of the sexy bra she'd slipped on under the top. However, she didn't even consider stopping this—she wanted to do it, to seize an experience the broken woman she'd been at the start of this hunt would have never contemplated. "There," she said, "it's the entrance to some kind of park." Green grass, a few picnic tables.

Wrenching the wheel, Dmitri pulled into the small parking lot. This time of day, it was too late for the dog walkers and joggers and too early for anyone else. Unsnapping her safety belt without removing her hand from his lap, she snapped his open and leaned over to nibble at his ear. When he shivered, she knew she'd hit another one of those hot spots on his body. "Don't suppose the windshield turns opaque?"

Without a word, he reached out to touch something on the dash. The windscreen was a smoky black a second later. "Is that even legal?" Licking at his earlobe, she insinuated her free hand through the open collar of his shirt to play her fingers over the hollow at the base of his throat, felt his muscles lock.

"The offenses are mounting up." Dark, dangerous words.

They made her thighs clench, images of the most erotic of punishments running through her head. Dmitri would be no easy lover—like the faceless man she'd seen in her dreams, he would demand and control and possess. "You," she murmured, using both hands to undo his belt, "are the sexiest man I have ever met." He made her think bad thoughts simply by breathing.

Undoing the button on his pants after successfully releasing his belt, she pulled down the zipper. And slid her hand inside to close around hot, rigid flesh covered with velvet-soft skin. He threw his head back against the headrest, one hand

still on the steering wheel, the other curving around her body
to fist in the back of her top. The taut line of his throat was an
irresistible temptation. Continuing to caress him with firm
strokes that had the tendons in his neck turning white against
the warm seduction of his skin, she kissed her way up one of
those tendons . . . and then she bit him.

His hand flattened on her back in a single, sudden move
before fisting in her top again. An instant later, they were kissing. It was no light brush this time, no exploring touch. This
was all tongues and teeth and wicked wetness as he kissed her
like a man who had rough, sweaty, dirty sex on his mind and
didn't care if she knew it.

Gasping in a breath when they parted, she fisted him,
stroked hard and fast. Once. Twice. His eyes glittered. "If I
didn't know better," he said, "I'd say you'd been taking lessons in how best to please me."

"I should stop this right now for that comment, but you're
in my blood, Dmitri." Not giving the fear a chance to rise, she
dipped her head and took him into her mouth.

"Fuck!" His hand fisted tighter in her top but he made no
move to shove or otherwise direct her head, as if he knew how
thin a line she was walking.

Dmitri had tasted every sexual pleasure there was to taste.
He'd slid into empresses and queens, rolled out of beds with
more than one other body in them, been pleasured by the most
experienced of courtesans and the most dissolute of immortals. For a short, sharp instant of time, the depravity had made
him forget.

Then it had become a game, to see how far he could go,
how much excess he could indulge in without destroying himself. However, for the past hundred years, even the erotic had
failed to satisfy—he'd played the game, but with cold calculation, little heat. Yet at this moment, he couldn't imagine he'd
ever been consumed with such ennui. It was all he could do to
not fist his hand in Honor's hair, teach her exactly what he
liked.

Keeping his hands where they were was an exercise in the
harshest self-restraint. He didn't dare look down, see that gor-

geous mouth working him with lush confidence. Then Honor
hummed in the back of her throat and his body arched, his
spine curving as pleasure arced from his cock to crash through
him in a brutal cascade.

She didn't take her mouth off him as he came apart, lap-
ping up his seed with a sensual openness that made him wonder who she would be when she was fully whole, no more
fractures in her psyche. No longer breaks, he thought, chest
heaving as she stroked her mouth off him with a final lingering
suck, but fine hairline scars.

Bracing herself with her hands on his thigh, she faced him.
Her cheeks were flushed, her eyes a deep, passionate green,
her lips plump and red. Releasing his hold on her top to set
himself to rights, he watched her watch him. The instant he
finished doing up his belt, she twisted over the console between the seats to curl up in his lap, her head on one shoulder,
her hand tracing designs on the other through the fine fabric of
his shirt.

He curved one arm around her, placed his free hand on her
thigh. "The last time I made out in a car, there were no cars."
It had been in a cart loaded with vegetables. Somehow he'd
talked his scandalized new wife into the back, where he'd
tumbled her most thoroughly and satisfactorily.

But his favorite memory was of Ingrede turning up in the
cart on her own one sunny day, an invitation in her brown
eyes that she'd never enunciate. Not then. Later, when they'd
been together several years, when Misha was walking, then
his wife had sometimes whispered the most sinful of wel-
comes in his ear.

As another woman now nipped at his earlobe and said, "I
want your mouth on me, Dmitri," in a low, husky tone that was
as good as a touch. "I dreamed about it, woke up with the
sheets tangled around my legs and my hand between my
thighs."

Stroking his own hand higher up her thigh, he insinuated it
between her legs. She trembled, but didn't fight him. Instead,
she did that thing she did—sliding one arm around his shoulders, she used the other to cup his jaw as she tugged his head
toward her.

He made the kiss a slow, languid seduction as he pressed

up with the heel of his hand, pushing the seam of her jeans against her clitoris. Just that. No other intrusion. A simple, inexorable pressure that had her breath changing, her body attempting to ride against his touch. "Want me to rub, Honor?" he asked, lessening the pressure. "Be a good girl and say the words."

She bit down on his lower lip. Hard. Mouth curving, he began to rub—tiny, tiny up-and-down motions that had her squirming, the hot scent of her rising to infuse the air inside the car. Sensitive as he was to scent, he'd catch hints of her for days to come. He was fairly certain his cock would go rigid every single time.

"Dmitri." Her hand gripping the side of his neck, she went stiff.

He could almost see the ripples of pleasure rolling up over her body, made a note to watch her come as she lay naked in his bed one day soon. When she went limp against his arm, he propped that arm against the door, letting her sprawl across both seats, one long leg bent and braced on the passenger seat, the other on the floor. The flushed curves of her breasts rose up and down in a ragged rhythm that was the most potent of seductions.

Seeing that her eyes were drugged to near blackness with pleasure, he spread his hand over her abdomen. No flinch, no hint of fear. So he slid that hand up to cup her breast, maintaining eye contact the entire time so she would know this was him, no one else. A jagged breath, her hand clenching on his side. "Like to push, don't you?"

"If I don't," he purred, leaning down to kiss her while he plumped and shaped her breast with a proprietary hand, "how will I ever get you to a point where you'll let me tie you up and use a whip on you?"

25

Her nails dug into the back of his nape. "A whip?"

"A velvet whip," he murmured, kissing his way up over her jaw, but not down her throat. She wasn't ready for that yet. "I'll stroke it so soft and easy over your skin, cause only the most exquisite pleasure-pain."

Deep green eyes filled with a sense of *age*, of knowledge no mortal should possess. "You've always been like this, haven't you?"

Fascinated by the enigma of her, he held that haunting gaze even as he stroked and petted her, getting her used to his touch, his body. "Like what?"

"Ready to mix a little pain with your pleasure." She made a deep sound in the back of her throat as he rubbed his thumb over her nipple. "It doesn't have anything to do with your vampirism." Her words awakened another memory, wrenching him back to a past that no longer seemed content to remain buried.

"Dmitri . . ." A nervous tremor in the voice of the naked woman laid out like a sacrifice before him, her breasts taut and high, her hips wide, her body all soft curves and temptation—and her hands tied to the posts of the bed he'd carved knowing she'd share it with him.

"Shh." *Lying down fully clothed beside her, he gentled her, his hand on her breast, his fingers tugging at her nipple with sensual knowledge gleaned over their courtship and marriage.* "I'd never hurt you."

"I know." *The absolute confidence of her statement would have made him hers if she hadn't already owned his soul.* "I just . . . No one ever talks about such things."

Moving his hand down to push between her thighs, to discover her folds plump and wet for him, he touched her with leisurely strokes, felt her hips begin to rise and fall for him. "Are you telling me," *he said,* "that you discuss our bedroom play with the other wives?"

Red filled her cheeks, but she continued to move against his hand, as generous with her sensuality as she was with her heart. "Of course not. I'm not sure anyone would believe me about you."

He laughed and kissed her, this woman who was willing to indulge his need to play games that might well have driven another woman to fainting hysterics. Of course, he'd never wanted to play such games with anyone else. Only Ingrede.

Tangling his tongue with hers, he raised his hand from between her thighs and laid a soft, playful slap on that same delicate flesh. She whimpered . . . raised her hips for more. He gave it to her. Gave her everything. Because while she might have been the one with her hands tied, he was the slave.

Her slave.

"Yes," he said, answering Honor's question even as he curved his hand over her thigh. "The vampirism simply allowed me to refine it, indulge it to the nth degree." As the seasons changed, as the ruin of the cabin disappeared into the mists of time, the sexual playfulness had become touched with a deep vein of cruelty.

His bedmates went home with whip marks more often than not and came back begging for more. Sometimes he tortured them in bed because it pleased him. Sometimes he did it because it amused him. But never did he do it because it gave him the same gut-clenching pleasure as when he'd tied up his wife in their simple bed in a cottage on a forgotten field where the wildflowers now bloomed.

"What was her name?" Honor sat up, raw emotion burning

her throat at the terrible bleakness she'd glimpsed. "The woman who puts that look in your eyes?"

"Ingrede." Nothing in his voice, and that was an answer in itself. "We have to get going."

She clambered back into her own seat, reaching up to redo her ponytail. "Ingrede," she said, unable to drop the subject, "she was your wife, wasn't she?"

He stared out of the now-clear windscreen, but whatever he saw had nothing to do with the verdant grass beyond. "Yes." Then, when she thought he'd add nothing else, he said, "My wife . . . and mortal."

D mitri's business with Sorrow took only a few minutes, and Honor had the feeling he was checking up on the young woman more than anything else. "I haven't forgotten," she said to Sorrow when Dmitri stepped aside to speak to Venom. "About the self-defense lessons."

"I can wait." Sorrow's expression was fierce, her eyes vivid with a ring of brilliant green. "I hope you find each and every one of the bastards who hurt you and make them scream."

Back in the car, she turned to the vampire beside her —the vampire who had once had a wife. A wife he'd loved with such devotion that he protected her memory with vicious strength even now. His expression had shuttered the instant after he spoke of Ingrede's mortality. It was clear he regretted telling her even that much.

His loyalty . . . it staggered her.

Honor had never been loved like that, never even believed it possible. "Venom found something?" she said, conscious he'd give her nothing more about Ingrede. Not now.

"The first one of the vampires Jewel named," he said, his tone once again that of the most sophisticated of creatures, "has a long-term male lover and has never shown any interest in women." A shake of his head that made his hair gleam blue-black in the piercing sunlight. "I'm not sure how that slipped past me, but quite aside from that, the vampire is far too 'bourgeois,' as Valeria would've put it, to have been offered an invitation."

"Translation: he's happy with his lover and doesn't need to abuse someone else to beat the boredom."

Dmitri gave a clipped nod. "The second individual did nothing of note while under surveillance, but from what I know of his habits, he may well have been involved. I've sent Illium to question him."

"Illium seems far too pretty to be dangerous." Dmitri's male beauty, by contrast, was a darker, edgier thing.

"No one ever expects him to take out a blade and slice off their balls," he said with lethal amusement in his tone as he drove them toward the George Washington Bridge. "He does it with such grace, too."

Honor wasn't shocked, because while what she'd said was true, she'd long ago learned that appearances could be deceptive. "Did you cultivate your reputation on purpose?"

He laughed and it was a thickness of fur across her breasts, her body seeming to have become more sensitized to the scent lure. "I was too busy soaking battlefields in blood and fucking women who were drawn to violence to cultivate anything."

Honor didn't even consider letting it go, because as of this morning, they belonged to each other, even if that belonging would be a fleeting thing. "You're so *angry*." Honed and blindingly sharp, that anger was a cold, cold thing. "Tell me why."

A long, still silence. "My memories are my penance, Honor. To share them is pointless."

"I'm never going to be an ornament, or a bedmate content to stay in that sphere." She couldn't be, not when the depth of her draw toward him was nothing sensible, nothing rational.

"And I," he said, reaching out to grip her thigh, "am never going to be—"

"—manageable," she interrupted in a sudden burst of humor. "I guess I can't say I didn't know that going in."

Dmitri gave her the strangest look as they stopped for a red light. "Why choose that word?"

"It seemed to fit." Realizing there was no way he'd reveal any vulnerability until he trusted her on a level it would take time to develop, she decided to return to their earlier topic of discussion. "What about the third vampire?"

Taking his eyes off her after another probing look, he eased the Ferrari onto the bridge. "That's who we're going to see—she's out in Stamford," he said, explaining why they were heading back into Manhattan. "It appears she's been bunkered down in her home for at least five days. Been feeding off blood junkies who come to her door."

"I don't know that term." Though she'd heard "vamp-whore" used to describe those who were addicted to the kiss of a vampire.

"Blood junkies come in pairs," Dmitri explained. "The only way they can get aroused enough to have sex is if a vampire feeds from either one or both in turn. So in effect it's a threesome—only a subset of the Made finds this even mildly attractive."

Honor nodded. "The majority of mortals don't come close to the beauty bestowed by vampirism."

"The deal breaker is that the vampire is relegated to being a conduit, not the center."

No old vampire would enjoy that. "The woman we're going to see—"

"Jiana. She's not known to be into the junkie scene, but there's no doubt she's been indulging lately," he said, making his way to the Bronx once they cleared the bridge. "Look in the dashboard."

Reaching forward, she opened the compartment to reveal an envelope. Inside were a number of large, glossy black-and-white photographs. "When were these taken?"

"Early this morning."

The first one was of a fresh-faced twosome, blond and scrubbed, straight out of a casting call for the "All-American Couple"—the only thing missing was the dog. Hand in hand, they walked up the steps of a gracious old home, wisteria falling from the balconies and the world swathed in black.

The next shot was of the two leaving the house. Both were flushed, their lips swollen, hair messed up—the man's shirt was buttoned wrong while the woman was missing her thin floral scarf. "Is this something a wife does for her husband and vice versa?"

"They have their own subculture," Dmitri told her. "Marry within it. Makes everything go smoother."

Putting away the photos, she tried to get her head around the idea as Dmitri drove them out of the Bronx into Westchester and toward Connecticut. It was as they were passing from Greenwich into Stamford that she remembered something she'd meant to mention about another strange subculture. "I had an e-mail from Detective Santiago," she said, realizing she felt no dread in spite of the fact that she'd been held and brutalized a bare hour outside of this city—the area was so different as to be on another planet. "They've already arrested someone for the murder yesterday morning."

"The victim's boyfriend and another member of the club," Dmitri said. "I made it a point to keep an eye on the situation."

Honor knew that that subculture would soon be getting a visit from the scary kind of vampire. "Old-fashioned sex and jealousy, according to Santiago." All three had been involved in a sexual relationship with each other.

"And a good dose of stupidity." With that pitiless statement, he turned in through a set of open gates that fronted a long, winding drive lined with mature sycamores. The Ferrari was almost to the door when it opened to disgorge another couple. Honor winced.

Catching it, Dmitri laughed. "Appetites don't decrease with age, Honor. You should know that."

"It's easier to accept with vampires," she murmured, watching the elderly pair get into their aging car. "I always think of the younger ones as having an extended adolescence." Stepping out after the couple drove away, she drew in a breath of the fresh spring air. "It's a pretty place." More trees backed the house, while the drive featured a delicate fountain. Landscaped lawns and gardens flowed off on both sides and into the distance, beds of colorful blooms nodding in the wind that whispered down the slight rise to the right.

"Michaela, too," Dmitri said, coming around the car to join her by the fountain, "has the most gracious of homes."

Honor had only ever seen the female archangel in the media, but there was no denying that Michaela was both beautiful and vicious. "What about Favashi?" she asked and it was only because she was looking right at Dmitri that she caught the tightening of his jaw.

"That one looks soft and gentle, and all the while, she's grinding her enemies beneath her boot." A brutal summation.

Not long ago, she'd discovered Dmitri had once had a wife he had loved. Now she realized he might have had an archangelic lover. "Bad breakup?" Jealousy turned her words razor sharp.

A raised eyebrow. "Perceptive, little rabbit."

Yes, he knew how to push her buttons. But oddly enough, she knew how to push his, too. "I guess being dumped by an archangel would bruise the male ego."

"I didn't realize rabbits had claws."

The door to the house opened before she could reply to that amused comment. Looking up, she saw a tall, thin vampire with the bones of a supermodel, the pillowy lips of a screen siren, and mocha skin that glowed in the sunlight—all of which was displayed to perfection in a lace and satin robe of exquisite bronze that barely hit midthigh. "Do none of these women own clothing?" she muttered.

"We did interrupt her during a feed," Dmitri drawled as they walked up the steps.

Jiana blanched at their approach, but she wasn't staring at Dmitri . . . and the knowledge in her eyes was damning. "I didn't know." A whisper, her hand clenching on the doorjamb. "When I accepted the invitation, I didn't know. And when I saw you there, I didn't hurt you. Please, you have to remember."

Honor put a hand on Dmitri's forearm, stilling his forward motion. "That scent." Rich and sweet and speaking of wealth. "Yes, I remember."

"I'm sorry. Here, would you like some water?"

Drinking because her captor, the one who controlled the others, hadn't bothered to give her any water or food that day, she took in as much as she could. "Thank you."

"No, it's nothing." Muted sobs. "I can't help you. Please don't ask me to."

Honor heard the panicked tremor of fear in that voice, knew there would be no deliverance at those slender hands. "Who are you afraid of?"

"Who are you afraid of?" she asked again, meeting eyes dark as onyx.

Jiana seemed to collapse in on herself. Hugging her arms around her trembling body, she stepped back in silent invitation. Inside, the house was as elegant as the grounds were harmonious, the décor relatively modern—light dominated, the walls painted a lush cream.

A skillful portrait of Jiana hung on one wall. It was a nude, beautifully done in its languid eroticism and framed with a simplicity that drew the eye to the art, not the surroundings. The décor flowed flawlessly from the hallway to the room into which Jiana led them, bright splashes of color provided by the furniture.

Collapsing on one of those jewel-toned sofas, Jiana braced her elbows on her knees, her head in her hands. "I haven't slept since the day I left you there."

Honor experienced the same strange mix of anger and pity she'd felt in that basement. "I was the one who was tied up, but you were weaker." Even now, it seemed impossible. Then, it had made her laugh in near-hysterical amusement.

Dmitri leaned against the armchair on which Honor took a seat, a tiger on no leash but his own. He said nothing, but from the expression on Jiana's face, the female vampire knew exactly what she faced.

"Always so weak when it comes to him," she whispered, tears rolling down the sublime perfection of her features. Her despair made her appear even more vulnerably feminine.

The hairs rose on the back of Honor's neck. Was she being expertly played? Or was Jiana's startling attractiveness nothing but a distraction to the grief that seemed to be tearing her apart?

"Even when I saw what he'd done," the woman continued, "I couldn't betray him."

"Who?" Honor asked. "You can't keep his secret any longer, Jiana. He's planning to do it again."

A sob rocked through the vampire's thin frame. "I know." Wiping her tears, she reached into the drawer of a little end table to pull out the by-now-familiar textured envelope. "He sent me this."

Honor knew what she'd find, but she took it and slid out the enclosed card anyway.

Perhaps this one will be more to your liking. I haven't told the others, but it is to be a pair, a man and a woman. You will enjoy that, will you not, Mother?

26

Honor's voice came out a whisper. "Mother?" Vampires were fertile until about two hundred years of age, and the children they sired or bore to that point, mortal. But Jiana was at least four hundred.

It was Dmitri who solved the question of how a child of Jiana's could have survived to perpetrate such atrocities. "Jiana was a young vampire, still under Contract, when she gave birth to Amos. Her son was Made on his own merits. He's highly intelligent, was meant for the Tower."

Her blood ran ice-cold, even as her earlier suspicion that Jiana was a gifted actress died a quick death—a mother's love was nothing rational. "Please tell me he's not there."

Dmitri touched her hair, the caress unexpectedly tender. "No."

"Was he always so—" She swallowed the term she wanted to use at the hollow blankness of Jiana's eyes.

"Amos was . . . changed in ways he shouldn't have been when he was Made."

Jiana gave a cracked laugh. "He went insane, Dmitri. Like some do, the ones we never talk about." Pushing back thick black hair streaked with fine threads of brown and red, the motion jerky, she locked gazes with Honor, her own holding a sudden, violent anger. "Did you know that, hunter? A small minority of the Made go mad during the transformation."

Like every hunter, Honor had heard the rumors, but this was the first time it had been confirmed. "If that's true, I'd have assumed the angels would have eliminated the problem." The angelic race didn't hold power because they played nice.

Jiana's anger faded as fast as it had awakened, a poignant pain carving deep grooves around those lush lips. "Amos's madness was not a bold thing. It was a quiet, creeping taint. He was a hundred years old before he began to show the first signs, two hundred before I could no longer deny them." She wiped her cheeks for the second time, seemingly unaware that her robe was gaping open at the top to expose the inner curves of her breasts, high and taut. "By the time he reached three hundred, I knew nothing could be done. I dedicated myself to curbing his excesses so they wouldn't lead to execution."

To Honor's surprise, Dmitri walked across to hunker down in front of Jiana, taking the woman's long, fine-boned hands in his. "He is your son. You protected him. But he knows what he's doing is wrong and he's choosing to continue to do it."

A true psychopath, Honor thought, remembering how Amos had crooned to her after punching her in the stomach.

"You shouldn't have made me angry." A hand stroking down her back in a mockery of care. "I didn't bring you here to hurt you." His lips along her jaw, over her throat. "So be an obedient pet and do as you're told."

She'd bitten his ear instead, hard enough to almost tear off a chunk. He'd punched her so violently for that, she'd blacked out . . . and woken to find herself bleeding.

"It's the madness." Jiana's tremulous voice cut through the horrific memory, her tone a plea. "That's what drives him."

Honor wasn't so sure. Amos had struck her as coldly intelligent, a man who—as Dmitri had said—had chosen to revel in his sadistic urges rather than attempting to fight them. Not only that, but he'd consciously nurtured the sickness in others.

"He was spoken to when his leanings became clear"— Dmitri's voice was gentler than Honor had ever heard it—

"given both warning and an offer of assistance. He chose to walk away."

Jiana's lower lip trembled, and then she was falling into Dmitri's arms, her cries so primal her entire frame shook as if her bones would fall to pieces. Honor's own heart ached, her eyes burning in maternal sympathy.

She was a mother, she understood what it was to need to do everything in her power to protect her child.

Honor blinked, physically shaking that eerily familiar voice out of her head. Familiar, but not her own—she had never borne a child, never nurtured a life within her womb. Yet her emotional response to Jiana's pain was so deep that she couldn't not be torn by it, even knowing that the depth of her understanding was an impossible thing.

Dmitri's broad shoulders were rock steady in her vision as he held Jiana, and she knew. She *knew.* Dmitri had had a child. No, that was wrong. He'd had *children.* Unsettled by that almost angry mental correction, she rubbed at her temple, but the thought stuck, seemed so very *right* that she couldn't unthink it.

"Where is he, Jiana?" Dmitri asked after Jiana's sobs quieted into painful silence.

The gorgeous vampire shook her head, her hair sliding over her face as she pulled away. "I haven't seen him for three weeks. He has done this before, gone away. But he always contacts me to tell me his whereabouts. This time, there is only silence." Her eyes went to the envelope. "Except for that. It came five days ago."

Terrible as it was, Honor could understand Jiana's maternal instincts overriding all else—even when faced with the malevolent reality of her son's evil. However, there was one thing that made no sense to her. "Why are you in seclusion?" So much so that the vampire had had to feed from the blood junkies. "From that card, it looks like he wants to please, not hurt you."

"Yes." A tight smile. "I hate this, prostituting myself to stay alive."

Again, her response made no sense—surely Jiana had enough contacts that she could've arranged something more palatable. *Oh.* "You're punishing yourself."

Jiana gave a shaky smile. "I asked him to stop—they found you so soon afterward, I believed he'd played some part in that. Then the card came . . ." She tugged the edges of her robe closed over her breasts, her words fading as her eyes turned distant. "I guess you always hope. Against all reason."

Dmitri's hair shone silky and touchable in the sunlight as they stood on the front steps of Jiana's gracious home. "Jewel Wan," she said to him, "might've given you Jiana's name but you knew it couldn't be her." He'd treated the other vampire with courtesy since the second they arrived.

When he said nothing, she clamped her hand on his arm. "How long have you suspected Amos?"

Dark eyes pinned her to the spot, told her nothing. "What good would it have done you to know who I had in mind?"

"Stop protecting me! I don't need it anymore!"

Dmitri's expression shifted, the stone becoming a piercing arrow. "When have I ever protected you?"

"What?"

I know you will always take care of me.

She clasped her hands to her temples. "That voice." So deep inside of her.

"Honor?" Dmitri's hand on her lower back, his breath lifting the curling tendrils of hair along her temple as he leaned close. "Tell me what's wrong."

"No, it's nothing," she said, because to give any other answer would be to acknowledge the aural hallucination. "Just the . . . echo of a dream." Seeping over into her waking life. "You should've told me."

"I'm almost a thousand years old." His hand moved in slow, circular motions on her back, but his words were as calculatedly harsh as his touch was tender. "You're so young it's laughable. You have neither the strength nor the right to question my decisions."

With those words, he negated the commitment they'd made to each other. Perhaps he didn't see it as such, but she couldn't be with a man who expected to maintain that chasm of distance between them. "Do you know how to find Amos?" she asked, putting aside the hurt she felt, though it was a raw, tender thing. Giving up wasn't an option. However, she needed time to regroup, to sit down and figure out if Dmitri was *ever* going to be ready for the kind of relationship she needed.

The idea that the answer might be no . . . it caused a crushing blackness in her soul.

"I've already checked his normal haunts and bolt-holes." His gaze lingered on her face, as if he'd read her very thoughts, but thankfully that was one ability he didn't possess. "He'll eventually surface. In the meantime, my men will continue to watch this house—he's always had an unhealthy attachment to his mother."

"Yes." No normal son would think of inviting his mother to join in a sexual game, to attempt to please her with his choice of victims. "What will you do with her?"

"That's up to you. You're the victim."

"No, Dmitri, I'm a survivor."

"Yes." No hesitation. "But recompense is still yours."

"That woman is going to punish herself for the rest of her very long life. Let her be."

"I'll speak to her." He turned to walk toward the entrance. "Are you coming?"

"No, I think I'll stay here." But she didn't. Stepping down to the drive as soon as he disappeared inside, she took a seat on the edge of the fountain. The water fell in a soothing cascade of sound behind her, the breeze a caress over her cheek as she tried to understand the irrational depth of her anguish. She'd always known Dmitri was never going to be human in any sense.

He isn't my Dmitri.

Again that voice, from so very deep inside of her. As if it came from her soul itself. This time, rather than fighting it, she listened.

Always so strong, so protective. But never hurtful. Not to me. Never.

Whoever this figment of her imagination was, Honor thought, she truly was living in a fantasy world. Dmitri was no one's knight in shining armor and if it scraped her to bloody rawness to admit that, then she had only herself to blame. Because Dmitri had never lied to her, never pretended to be something he wasn't.

"Don't fool yourself about me, Honor. The human part of me died a long time ago."

"Where are we going?" she asked when the Ferrari pulled away from Jiana's estate.

"Angel Enclave—Jiana owns a house there." His words were cool, practical, and she wondered if he even understood how he'd damaged the fragile something between them. "It's standing empty, but I've had men watching it for a while. However, I think it's time I had a look inside."

Another thing he hadn't told her. Another illustration of the fact that while he might appreciate her skills in certain areas, when it came to treating her as an equal . . . But then the idea *was* laughable, wasn't it? She'd lived a mere twenty-nine years to his centuries, was mortal to his powerful vampire.

However, none of the logic seemed to matter, and she was no closer to understanding or corralling the violent depth of her emotions by the time Dmitri drove deep into the Angel Enclave, an exclusive settlement along the cliffs that hugged the Hudson. In most cases, the houses were set so far back from the road that it felt as if they were driving through uninhabited land, the trees on either side of the road ancient behemoths that almost blotted out the sky.

When Dmitri stopped, it was in front of gates watched over by a vampire Honor didn't recognize. Stepping out of the car, and to the ornate metal gates, she pushed them open while Dmitri spoke to the guard. Inside, she saw the drive was relatively short—though the gates disappeared from view when, walking forward alone, she turned a corner. It was beyond tempting to keep going, to see what might very well have been the lair of the monster who'd tortured her, but this wasn't like with Jewel Wan. She could still think, understood that to go in without backup would be foolhardy.

"Honor."

She turned to see Dmitri walking toward her—and suddenly the dam broke. "I have every right," she said, referring to the strange compulsion between them for the first time.

Not even a blink.

Stubborn, always so stubborn. So sure he is right.

On that, she agreed with the voice inside her mind.

The wind whispered slow and easy through the trees, through Dmitri's hair as she stood waiting for a response from a vampire used to explaining himself to no one. Her fingers spread, and she found herself closing the distance between them to stroke her hand through that thick dark silk. It was an intimate act, one for which she asked no permission, though he was a man no one would touch without invitation.

He didn't stop her, lifting his own finger to trace the line of her jaw. "You're asking me to act human," he said after a long, quiet moment untouched by time. "I'm not human, haven't been for a long time."

"And you," she said, fingers lingering at his nape, "are trying to make me believe you have no capacity for true emotion when I know different." Dmitri's heart wasn't dead, his soul not irrevocably tainted, of that she was certain.

Sliding his free hand down to her lower back, he tugged her closer. "Who are you, Honor St. Nicholas?" It was a strange question, but one to which Dmitri needed an answer. Because this mortal, her scent was that of wildflowers from a mountainside lost in time.

Haunting pools of emerald green met his as she shook her head. "I don't know."

Her answer made sense to him, though it was an impossibility. "Come. Let's explore this house."

"I thought you would've already done it."

"I had my men look through it, but it may be time for a deeper examination with everything else we know."

Walking beside him, Honor was both grace and a lush feminine beauty. But she also had a deep vein of strength that had well and truly awakened . . . and that intoxicated. He wanted to reach out, to touch her again, the unrelenting need far beyond simple lust. However, that would have to wait—her desire to enter the house, to run Amos to ground, was a pulse against his skin.

Unlocking the front door, he pushed it open. At first, there was nothing, only the slightly musty smell of a house that had been shut up for a while. Then he caught a whiff of the most putrid odor, that of rotting flesh.

Honor went motionless beside him, her gun smoothly in hand. "There's something dead inside."

"Long enough to have decomposed." Which meant that either Amos had somehow snuck back in past the guards and left a gruesome message, or something else was going on. "Yet not so long ago that the others who came here had reason to be suspicious."

"Dmitri."

Following the direction of Honor's raised arm, he saw her pointing at a flat-screen television on the wall. The power indicator was dead. And when Honor flicked on a light switch, nothing happened. "The electricity's down. Blown fuse maybe."

"It's an older home," Dmitri said, following the fetid scent. "Such things happen."

The rank smell took them not into a basement as he'd half expected, but to a large room at the back of the house. There was no lock, nothing to differentiate the door from any other along the corridor.

"God." Honor put a hand up over her mouth and nose as he pushed open that door—the odor was vile here, so concentrated it felt akin to soup.

The room itself was barren but for a wooden shelf that held a number of books and magazines, and a single armchair that looked as if it had been banished here because it was too ratty for the main living areas. Beside it sat a small burn-scarred table set with a crystal tumbler and a bottle filled with dark red liquid. The rug on the floor was threadbare.

It was the kind of shabby, comfortable den a man might create to get a little peace and quiet . . . except if you looked carefully, it became clear the armchair was angled toward a particular section of the wall. Normally, there would've been nothing to differentiate it from the rest of the room, the reason his men had missed it, but right now, water seeped from beneath that section to soak the rug.

"Fridge," Honor whispered. "There's a fridge behind there."

27

"I'll do this," he said, because though she'd demanded he not protect her, his need to do so was gut deep.

An intense look from those eyes that pierced him. "All right." She positioned her body in a way that gave her a sight line to the door, but allowed her to keep an eye on him as well. A slight shake of her head when their eyes met again and he knew that nothing he said would send her from this room. He was more than strong enough to force her compliance, but force was the one thing he couldn't use with this woman.

It would've been easy to explain his reluctance as part of the cold calculation necessary to get her into bed, but the lie would serve no purpose—not when she saw him in ways no other woman ever had. Ingrede, sweet, loving, strong Ingrede, wouldn't have understood the darkness that lived within him now. Honor did. It felt a betrayal to his wife's memory to think such a thing but that made it no less true. "Are you sure?"

No hesitation. "Yes."

Shifting his gaze to the wall, he ran his fingers along it until he found a small indentation. A single push and a section of the wall opened to expose a large, squat refrigeration unit, the water pooled below it mute evidence of the loss of power.

Trying not to smell the odor that spoke of putrid decay, he lifted the lid to brace it against the wall.

Then he looked down.

At the bodies.

The freezer was large enough that Amos hadn't had to cut off limbs or separate the torsos from the victims' lower halves. He'd simply bent the bodies into the fetal position and crushed them together like so many pieces of meat. "Detective Santiago is currently working on the serial abductions of tall, slender women of mixed race in the greater New York area, is he not? Specifically, women who have one black parent, one white."

Honor crossed the small distance between them to glance inside the freezer, her expressive face touched with horror. "Yes. Everyone's working on the theory that it's a human predator—no trace of feeding or any blood at the scenes. The women just vanish."

Dmitri ran his gaze over the body closest to the top. In spite of the putrefaction, her underlying bone structure was clear, enough undecomposed flesh visible that he could be certain of her skin color. "Such hatred," he said, recalculating everything he thought he knew about Jiana and Amos. "Toward the one being who has always protected him."

"Are you certain?"

Dmitri had made careful inquiries when the unnaturally close tie between mother and son became obvious and had been convinced the bond had formed as a result of Amos's madness, Jiana doing everything she could to help and protect her son. Now he wondered if he'd missed the far more sinister truth. "No longer as certain as I once was." He closed the lid.

"We'll call Santiago, get the cops involved." Everyone would assume Amos had gone insane with age. That facet of a long life was an unhidden truth, one that stopped none of those who wanted to be Made. Even two hundred years spent as a healthy, ageless vampire was a lot longer than the average human life span. "The more people we have watching for him, the better the chances of running him down."

Honor nodded, taking small, shallow breaths until they were back out in the corridor with the door closed. "Why did he take me? I don't fit the profile."

Cold rage pulsed through Dmitri's blood at the reminder of what Amos had done to Honor, but he gave the question serious thought. "He hates his mother, it seems, but he also wishes to please her." A flicker of memory, Jiana at a cocktail party she'd given four summers ago.

"Dmitri, I'm so glad you could come." A gracious smile, a kiss on his cheek. "Have you met Rebecca?" This time, the smile on her lips held an elegant sensuality.

"A pleasure," he said, inclining his head toward the curvy brunette beauty with skin of light golden brown who hung on Jiana's every word.

"You," he said to Honor, "are not his type, but you are Jiana's."

"That's sick . . . and put together with everything else, it raises certain questions." She glanced at the closed door to the room that spoke of Amos's twisted sexuality. "Let's head outside, call Santiago."

Dmitri let her lead them out through the back door. The sunshine was brilliant, the heat of it a slicing blade. As he watched, Honor strode down to the grass and used her cell to call the cop who had a way of ending up on cases linked to immortals. While she did that, he made a few calls of his own, including one to a senior vampire under his command. "Make certain Jiana doesn't leave the house," he ordered. "I need to have a chat with her." Hanging up, he waited for Honor to walk back to him.

She halted a foot away. He closed that distance to take her into his arms, careful not to imprison her, but she didn't freeze up at the contact. Instead, she sank into the embrace, her own arms tight around him. They stood there in silence for long sun-soaked minutes, Honor's pulse a steady, thudding beat against his vampiric senses.

The last time Dmitri had stood thus, simply holding a woman because it felt right, he'd been mortal. "My wife," he said, speaking words he'd spoken to no other, "loved the sunshine. She would come out into the fields with me, and while I worked them, she'd"—*rock our baby boy*—"work on the mending. I was always tearing my shirts."

Honor's laugh was soft, her voice gentle as she said, "A wonderful wife."

"She was," he continued, knowing that though the man In-grede had loved had been as different from him as night from day, he'd never stop mourning the loss of her smile, "but she also used to drive me mad at times. I'd tell her I'd fix some-thing in the cottage when I got home, and by the time I'd re-turn from the fields, she'd have done it and have the bruises to prove it." His heart had almost stopped the day he'd found her on the roof. "And she couldn't cook."

Honor looked up, eyes sparkling. "Did you ever say so to her?"

"You must have a low estimation of my intelligence." He bent until their foreheads touched. "She pretended to love to cook and I pretended to adore her cooking, and we both lived for the village festivals when we could buy from the stalls."

Honor's laughter was a deep, husky sound, twining into his very blood. And for a moment, he was . . . happy, in a way he hadn't been happy since the day the cottage turned to ash, tak-ing his heart with it. "Witch, you are," he said, dipping his head to claim her lips in a kiss that held both the sweetness of the sunshine—and a good dose of raw sex. "In my bed, Honor. That's where I want you."

Lips wet from his caress, she cupped his face. "I think"—a soft murmur—"that's where I want to be."

It was full dark by the time they arrived back at the Tower. Venom was waiting for them. "This came through the mail today." He handed over an envelope.

It proved to contain a note written in the same code as the tattoo that had originally brought Honor to the Tower.

"I'll be leaving to take the night watch on Sorrow in an-other fifteen minutes," Venom said while Honor scanned the note. "Do you want me to find someone else so I can go over to the Angel Enclave, keep an eye on the cops?"

"No. Illium's on-site."

Honor, already working the code in her mind, tuned out the rest of their conversation. It wouldn't take her long to translate this, she thought, not with the work she'd done on the tattoo.

An hour later, she looked up from where she sat on the sofa in Dmitri's office and passed him the translation.

You took what I loved. Now I will take what you treasure.

Honor rubbed her hands over her face as Dmitri read the message in silence. "He has to have known what Isis did to you. And still . . ."

"Love, it seems," he murmured, "is truly blind." Putting down the piece of paper, he picked up his phone. "Jason," he said when it was answered on the other end. "Describe Kallistos to me." A pause. "Yes, beyond a doubt."

Honor waited until he hung up to say, "Kallistos was Isis's lover?"

"Yes, though he had a different name then. A youth, only decades into his Contract. He was bleeding from her attentions when we found him." Letting him live had been an easy decision. "We believed him another victim." But Kallistos, it seemed, had loved his mistress regardless of her cruelty.

"A young angel," he said, choosing his words with care so as not to put Honor at risk of having her memory wiped, as had happened to Illium's mortal lover, "has gone missing from Neha's court. No one is quite certain when he disappeared." Especially given this next fact. "Ask me the name of the senior vampire who was in charge of him."

"Kallistos," Honor said, blowing out a breath. "It's how he's making those protovampires." A question in her eyes. "I know you won't tell me the process, since even Candidates are put to sleep during the initial stages, but everyone knows it's the angels who Make the vamps. I always thought it was the older ones."

While the angels did nothing to negate that view, it was in fact the younger adults who built up the toxin more quickly in their bodies. The older the angel, the higher his level of tolerance—though even archangels weren't immune, as Uram had proved. "Jason just told me that the angel was last seen by someone other than Kallistos a year ago," he said, not answering her implied question. "If we assume he was abducted soon afterward, and taking his age into account, he would've been able to successfully Make one vampire."

"Kallistos tried to Make more," Honor said, walking to the plate glass of his window, the rain that had begun to fall forty minutes ago turning the city into a mist-shrouded mirage, "and it diluted the effect." Brow furrowed, she recrossed the carpet.

"Quite likely." Not only that, Kallistos hadn't followed the correct procedures, the reason for the mutation in the dead males' blood cells. "It should be far easier to run him to ground now that we have a name and a face."

Having come to stand beside him, Honor leaned back against his desk, nodded. However, her expression was troubled. "I can't stop thinking about Jiana. She seemed so loving, maternal."

"There's nothing as yet to say that she isn't—Amos's madness may be his own." But Dmitri had deep doubts about that, because from what he'd seen over the years, this depth of hatred mingled with warped love had its roots in something that should never have been, an ugliness that seeded a twisted kernel deep within the soul.

Midnight green eyes met his, haunting and promising him an impossible dream. "You don't believe that."

Closing the distance between them, he stroked his fingers over her jaw, the softness of her skin an irresistible enticement. "Do you think you can read me?"

"I think"—her hand closing over his wrist—"I know you far better than I should."

Yes. Too often, he saw knowledge in her eyes that shouldn't have been there, felt a familiarity in her kiss, her laughter that made him ache, and he wondered if he wasn't giving in to a subtle insanity of his own. And yet he couldn't pull away, pull back. "There's nothing more to do tonight." The phone call to Jason had set the search for Kallistos in motion, and as for Jiana's son, Dmitri had already put the entire region on alert.

And sometimes a man had to seize the moment, regardless of the consequences. To allow it to pass might mean it would never again come.

"Dmitri, come dance with me."

"My feet ache from the fields, Ingrede. After I return from the markets?"

A smile that lit up the room, though fear lurked a silent intruder in her eyes. "After you return."

Except Isis's men had taken him when he returned. His last memory of his wife was of her holding their children and trying not to betray the terror that had turned her warm brown eyes an impossible ebony.

He could never go back, never dance with his wife while

Misha laughed and the baby kicked her legs in the air, but he could kiss this woman who had somehow become a part of him, her gaze holding mysteries he was driven to solve. "It's time, Honor."

He saw the skin pull tight over her cheekbones, knew she wasn't certain she wouldn't panic, slash out at him in self-defensive violence, but her answer was a simple, powerful, "Yes."

Honor took in her surroundings in silence as Dmitri led her up off the level painted that gleaming, dangerous black and to the top floor of the Tower. It proved to be carpeted in white with glittering threads of gold, the paint on the walls that same gold-flecked white, the artwork a mix of old and new—a brilliant tapestry of a place of mountain and sky, on which perched dwellings whose doors opened out into thin air; a gleaming sword sharp as a razor; a framed poster of the ridiculous television show *Hunter's Prey*, complete with the muscle-bound lead and his "vampire vixen."

"Illium bought it for Elena," Dmitri said, following her gaze. "It should be interesting to see her reaction."

Honor's lips twitched. "They're good friends."

A shadow drifted across Dmitri's expression, but all he said was, "Yes," before adding, "Raphael's suite occupies half the floor. The rest of the area is divided into quarters for the Seven, though mine takes up double the space of the others since I spend the most time in the city."

She hesitated. "You don't have another home?"

"It never seemed necessary."

Honor heard a thousand unsaid things in that statement, understood that the idea of home held a pain for him he would never seek to re-create.

"Don't worry," he said before she could say anything, "the square footage of each apartment is larger than that of most stand-alone houses, and the walls are soundproofed to ensure total privacy."

Honor had nothing against the setup and was quite certain his apartment was a sprawling space ten times the size of her own. But— "No, Dmitri. Not here."

"Why?" A question asked with a cool sophistication that might've intimidated her once, but now made her wonder what Dmitri didn't want her to see that he'd put up those silken shields.

"It isn't right." Honor stood her ground, the voice inside of her whispering that this moment was critical to how Dmitri would see her. "I refuse to be just another woman you take to your bed."

Dmitri rubbed his thumb across her knuckles, no hint of any readable emotion on his face. "You think which bed it is makes a difference?"

There was, she thought, such cruelty in him at that moment. He could hurt her badly and walk away as if it mattered nothing. "Perhaps not for you," she whispered, knowing the time for breaking things off, for protecting herself, had long passed, "but for me, yes."

A silence. As taut, as dangerous, as the garrote worked into Dmitri's belt.

28

It was the sound of the elevator opening down the hallway that seemed to decide Dmitri. "Yes, interruptions are far more likely here."

Such a practical reason, but one she was willing to accept for the present.

Leaving the Tower, they drove to her building and headed up to the apartment that she was slowly, carefully making into a home. Hunters did that. Ashwini's apartment was a lush place full of color—cushions of gold-shot silk, sculptures picked up here and there, postcards of spice-heavy stalls in faraway markets. Honor's was less exuberant, but she'd taken her personal mementos out of boxes—items Ash had left as they were—started to unpack them.

Now, framed snapshots cascaded down one wall of her living room—a laughing grandmother snapped during a hunt in Mexico, a mountain storm captured in Colorado, a single elk against the snow in Alaska—while her battered but beloved camera sat on the dining table, ready to be checked after its time in storage. Her bedroom, too, she'd begun to make her own. The sheets were a fine blue cotton, the pale cream walls hung with more photographs from her personal collection.

"Wildflowers," Dmitri said, halting on the doorstep. "Those weren't here last time."

Startled that he'd focused on the photographs when the sexual tension between them was at fever pitch, she said, "I just put them up. I was tracking a vampire across Russia a few years ago when I found this field." The memory of it had haunted her for months, until she'd put up the photos where she could see them before she closed her eyes, again when she woke.

Dmitri walked to stand in front of the array of fine black frames, touching his finger to one particular shot with a bright blue flower nodding in the corner. "There was a ruin here once."

Spine tingling, she crossed the carpet to join him. "I had the strangest feeling something had once stood there, even though there was no evidence of it." She'd also had the insistent sense that she'd be disturbing something precious should she cross the border of tiny blue flowers that separated one small section of the riotous field of color from the rest.

"How did you find out, Honor?" Dmitri's eyes were hard black stones, his tone the same one he'd used on Valeria, on Jewel Wan.

They'd stripped themselves of weapons as they entered, neither wanting a violent interruption, but now instinct had Honor calculating how fast she could get to the knife hidden down the side of the bedstand.

"I was," she said, forcing herself not to act on the instinct, "driving through a fairly isolated area when I lost my way." The truth was, she'd driven off the path and into an uncharted wilderness on purpose, unable *not* to follow the painful tug that drew her onward.

"I must've driven for hours, and this is where I stopped." She shrugged, trying to make light of an experience that had pierced with such aching sorrow, she'd cried for hours after she finally returned to civilization. "I'd never seen a place as beautiful." As eerie, as heartrending.

Dmitri continued to stare at her, such lethal calculation in his eyes that it took all her control to stay in position, to not lunge for the bed and the blade so close. "What do you see in the photos?" she asked instead, feeling as if she stood on a precipice, her entire life balanced on this moment. "Dmitri?"

Face stripped of all sophistication, until he was only the

sleekest of predators, he reached up to tuck her hair behind her ears. "If this is a game, you won't like the price you'll have to pay."

The hairs rose on the back of her neck. This time she stepped away . . . but didn't go for a weapon. She couldn't. She *had* to trust him, because if she couldn't . . . if she couldn't, then her world would simply shatter into a thousand fragments. "Threats aren't sexy." *Don't do this. Please.* "Take your black mood and leave."

He stalked her instead, trapping her against the corner, the body she'd looked forward to caressing suddenly a stifling wall. It took every ounce of her will to keep from striking out, from kicking and clawing. But when he bent his head and very deliberately put his mouth over her pulse, she couldn't stand it anymore.

She stabbed her fingers into the exposed side of his neck.

Or would have, if he hadn't manacled her wrist with a steel-strong grip. *No, no, no!* The restraint threw her back into the pit where she'd spent so many weeks, the pit she now realized she'd never escaped—but twined through with her terror was a crushing sense of betrayal.

Not my Dmitri. This isn't him.

And then there was no more thought.

Dmitri had never been as angry as he was at that instant, riding a vicious edge where he hungered only to hurt the woman in his arms. He didn't know what game Honor was playing, but he would get the answer out of her, even if he had to break her into a million tiny pieces. That field, what it represented, it was not to be touched, *not by anyone.*

Squeezing her wrist as she froze against him, he went to touch her with his fangs in an act that he knew was cruel, but then again, she'd been playing him from the start. There was no chance in hell that she'd just *happened* to come upon the field where his wife and baby girl had died, where he'd brought his son afterward, so that Misha wouldn't be alone, where he'd stood vigil for an entire turn of the seasons.

"My beautiful Dmitri." Big brown eyes filled with worry. *"Don't let her change you. Don't let her make you cruel."*

Ingrede's words had been unable to halt the change, not after she was gone. Nothing would reverse it. So he would make use of it.

A burst of movement from the hunter who had thought to make him a fool.

He had no trouble pinning her to the wall. But Honor didn't stop fighting, twisting and wrenching her body with a strength that would break something soon if she didn't stop.

When he pinioned her arms above her head with a grip on her wrists, and pressed her lower body against the wall with his own, she bit him on the neck. Hard enough to draw blood. Jerking away, he tightened the hand he had around her wrists. "Foreplay already, Honor?"

No response, only that furious twisting and pulling and fighting even though she had no hope of escaping him. She made not a sound, her breath tightly controlled.

That was when he looked into those eyes of mysterious green.

There was no one there.

No personality, no hint of the woman who had laughed and pleasured him with such sexual confidence that morning, nothing but the animal instinct to survive. And he knew she would kill herself trying to get free.

"Dmitri, I'm scared."

"I'll never hurt you. Trust me."

Trembling under the whisper of memory, a memory that didn't belong to Honor and yet spoke for her, he released her hands, lifted his body off hers. She came at him like a tempest unleashed, slamming her elbow into his face, her fisted hand into his larynx, her booted foot against his knee.

Crashing down onto the bed on his back, he blocked some of her most brutal strikes, but did nothing to halt her. Her rage rained down on him, bloodying his nose, his mouth, putting bruises on his body that healed almost as soon as they were made.

"Bastard." It was the first thing she'd said since he'd trapped her in the corner. "You goddamn bastard." A savage blow to his jaw that had his teeth snapping together.

Blocking her next blow, he looked into her eyes . . . and saw Honor looking back at him again. The brilliant green was washed in a sheen of wet, and her next blow when it came lacked the power of the others. She thumped both fists on his chest over and over and over again. "I hate you! I hate you! I hate you!" It was a furious litany that turned into sobs so harsh they spoke of unimaginable anguish, her body crumpling over his own. "I hate you." A whisper.

Right then, he hated himself.

Lying motionless until she stopped moving, those painfully raw sobs turning into heartbreakingly silent tears against his chest, he dared put a hand on her hair, stroking her now tangled curls. He didn't know what to say to her, how to explain the rage she'd incited within him.

But there was one thing he could say, something he hadn't said to a woman in near to a thousand years. "I'm sorry, Honor. Forgive me."

Sitting perched up on the sink in the large bathroom off her bedroom, Honor watched in silence as Dmitri ran the disinfectant over her scraped and bruised knuckles. She bit back a hiss at the sting, her eyes lingering on the cut on his lip, the bruises on his face. Part of her, horrified by her own violence, wanted to cup that sinful masculine face in her hands, kiss each and every bruise in gentle apology. But the rest of her was curled up into a tiny ball deep within, watchful, wary.

The light glinted off the black of his hair as he ministered to her and she remembered the heavy silk of it against her palms. She remembered, too, the force of his grip as he'd pinned her arms above her head.

"I bruised you." He slid his hands under her wrists, his skin darker against the paler hue of her own—now marked by bands of dull red.

Fairness made her break her silence. "I did worse." She'd hit him hard enough that the bruises were going to take at least an hour to heal, in spite of his vampirism. More, the cut on his lip wasn't a shallow gash. His shirt, ripped at the shoulder seam, betrayed faint red marks that were almost healed, but on the whole—"I came out of it better than you."

Dark, dark eyes met her own. "The physical hurt isn't the core of it, is it?"

Her stomach grew tight, acid burning her throat. "All of it," she said in a voice turned rough from the force of her earlier sobs, "everything we've done to this point . . . I think it's gone." Lost under the shock and terror that had reduced her to a clawing animal, a biting, hitting, trapped creature who had once more been made a helpless victim.

Dmitri had made a mockery of her hard-won strength, crushed her faith in her own judgment, but most of all, he'd taken the pride she'd rebuilt scrap by scrap, and she wasn't sure she could forgive him for that.

Not saying a word, he threw away the cotton swab after taking care of all the scrapes and made sure not to crowd her as she left the bathroom. Chilled deep within by a sense of loss that made her feel hollow, as if her entire existence had been wiped away, she stumbled into the living room and to the window that looked out over a city lashed by rain.

The lights were muted, hazy through the water, until it felt as if she was all alone in the world, trapped in a glass cage. It was a feeling with which she was intimately familiar. The friends she'd made, the relationships she'd forged, it had made the loneliness bearable, but it had always been there, inside of her, this strange "missing." It was Dmitri who'd filled that hole, and Dmitri who'd made it even bigger.

A whisper of the darkest of scents and she knew he'd walked into the living room on silent feet. But he didn't come to her, and a minute later she heard him in the kitchen area. Looking across the open-plan space divided only by the smooth curve of the counter, she saw him put together a plate and bring it to the table after clearing away her camera.

Walking around the table toward her, he kept a distance between them. It made the ice in her chest impossibly colder . . . and then she knew it was her heart that was frozen. "Eat, Honor," he said. "You haven't for hours." There was something in his voice she couldn't read, an element she'd never before heard from him.

Angling her body so she could look him full in the face, she saw only the walls of an almost-immortal who had lived longer than she could imagine. "You should go." She couldn't stand it, having him here with this impassable gulf between them. It was undoubtedly idiotic to feel this lost by the end of a relationship that hadn't ever really begun, but it felt as if he'd reached inside her and crushed her soul, then ground it under his boot.

A bleak shadow in those eyes of so deep a brown they were almost black, and with such age in them. "You send me away."

Would you send me away?

She blinked at the strange echo, focused on the man who stood so close and so distant. "I have to." To survive, to scrape the tattered remnants of her pride, her self, back together.

Dmitri said nothing for long moments as the rain fell against the glass in a melody of sound she'd always before found soothing. Today the tone felt jarring, the beat too jagged against her oversensitized nerves. When Dmitri raised a hand, then dropped it, she felt the loss like a stab to the heart, and she understood he could hurt her worse than he already had. But then he did the one thing she'd never, ever have expected.

Holding her gaze, he closed the final distance between them and went down to his knees, that beautiful bruised face looking up at her.

When he placed his arms around her waist and pressed the side of his face to her abdomen, the tears started flowing again, slow and quiet, over her cheeks. Dmitri didn't bow his head to anyone; he didn't surrender or submit. But he was on his knees before her, vulnerable to a kick, a stab to the neck, the most violent rejection. "Oh, Dmitri." Trembling, she ran her fingers through his hair, this man who had been scarred so badly that distrust was an instinctive response.

She knew the wildflowers had set him off in the bedroom, but she still had no idea why. However, now was not the time to ask. Now was the time to decide.

"Forgive me."

Did she have that in her? The strength to forgive him for the horror he'd brought back to life just when she'd begun to believe she'd beaten her abusers after all, for the hurt he'd done to her heart, but most of all for the humiliation of being reduced to a scrabbling animal?

Honor's hand fisted in his hair.

The rain continued to fall outside, but inside there was only silence—and an acuteness of clarity that told her the decision she made in this instant, about this man, would resonate throughout her life. If she stepped off the edge on which she currently stood, she could fall hard, perhaps shatter forever . . . or she could find her way home.

Home.

The idea of it was nothing but a fantasy built out of her intense and inexorable loneliness, many would say. But they didn't understand the incomprehensible strength of what she felt for this man who knelt before her, giving her something he gave no one. *All her life* she'd searched for him, even when she hadn't known his name. He wasn't who she'd imagined him to be—was a far more deadly, hardened creature.

Still mine. Still my Dmitri. Wounded, changed . . . but not lost. I will not believe him lost.

Honor didn't fight the voice that wasn't her own and yet came from her soul. It was a familiar madness by now.

Dmitri's hand spread on her lower back. "Don't end this."

"Would you go?" she asked, unclenching her hand, stroking her fingers through that black silk again as she wiped away her tears with her free hand.

A long, long pause. "Yes." A single harsh word. "If you want your freedom, I'll give it to you."

So . . . the choice was hers and hers alone.

29

In the end, the decision wasn't so difficult after all, because when it came to Dmitri, she had no sense of self-preservation. And that, too, was a madness, as relentless as the need she had to touch him, hold him . . . love him. "Stay," she said, and felt the shudder in the powerful body of the man who'd offered her freedom.

It broke her a little.

Sliding down to her knees, she wrapped her arms tight around his neck and buried her face against the heated warmth of his skin. His own arms came around her an instant later. Fear, that insidious intruder, that silent shadow, she waited for it . . . but it didn't come, as if the raw brutality of their fight had purged it out of her system, leaving her bruised and battered but whole.

"Never again," Dmitri whispered into her hair, his voice naked, his shields stripped to nothing. "I swear to you."

Cupping his neck at the nape, she caressed him with tender strokes, and it was an act of gentling for both of them. For this harsh, dangerous man who was her own, and for the ragged, lonely girl within her. "Tell me why." She needed to understand, to see into the shadows of his heart.

One of his hands fisted in her hair. "It's a memorial," he said, his voice so rough, it was difficult to understand. "No one other than Raphael knows of its existence."

Her heart thudded, a huge wave of *knowing* pushing at her mind, but it slithered out of her grasp to fade away like so much mist when she tried to reach for it, to hold it. Letting it go for the moment, she thought of the wildflowers, so many colors, so many shades, all of them bobbing their heads in welcome as she parked her vehicle far off in the distance to avoid crushing them. She'd walked, slow but certain, through the riot of color, drawn to the invisible ruin—as if her body were a compass and the ruin true north.

The melancholy of the place had weighed down her limbs, but she'd been certain she heard the echo of laughter, too . . . of a child's delight. "It's a place with memory," she whispered. "There isn't only sadness, Dmitri. You must remember." The words weren't her own, and yet they were. "You *must*."

"I remember everything." A laugh created of jagged metal and broken glass. "Sometimes I wish I didn't. But those memories, they're set in stone, never to be forgotten."

Honor thought of what it must be like to carry such sorrow through the ages, to mourn for nearly a thousand years, and felt an ache so vast it had no end. "She wouldn't have wanted this for you," she said, so certain that she didn't stop to question it. "You know that."

Honor was right, Dmitri thought. Ingrede would have been horrified to see who—what—he had become, how he'd let the loss of her and the children twist him. But he also knew another thing. "Some things, no man can resist. Some losses, no husband"—no father—"can ever forget."

"Dmitri—"

"I don't know what I can give you, Honor," he said because she deserved honesty, "but I know I've felt nothing like this since the moment she died."

Honor cupped his face. "It's all right." The gentlest of kisses.

He didn't know how she'd become the one to offer comfort when he'd caused the harm, but his soul, cold for so long, basked in the warmth of her.

* * *

"I once fed Elena," he told her a long time later, as her lips closed over the forkful of rice he'd lifted to her mouth, as she allowed him to take care of her in a way he hadn't earlier.

Curiosity turned the deep green of her gaze to sparkling gemstones. "Were there knives involved?"

"No, but she was tied up at the time." It seemed an eon ago that he'd taunted Elena while she remained restrained for her own safety. "She'd shot Raphael." The others in the Seven had been ready for blood, Dmitri bound by a vow to keep her safe.

Honor leaned forward, brows lowering. "I heard rumors . . . she really did?"

So he told her the story, and managed to get most of the food into her at the same time, wondering if she'd noticed the fruit and honey he'd added to the table.

"I do have hands, husband."

Lifting a slice of fruit up to those beautiful lips as she sat on his lap, one arm around his neck. "You can use those hands to thank me for taking such good care of you."

Small white teeth biting into the fruit, slender throat swallowing the juicy flesh. "Dmitri?"

"Yes?" He ran the fruit down that throat, licked up the juice.

She shivered. "I hope I'm sitting in your lap when I'm a toothless crone and you a wrinkled old man."

Putting down her wineglass, Honor rose to slide into his lap and memory and reality collided in a kaleidoscope that made his head spin. Her lips touching his only escalated the fracture of time, the taste of her hot and sweet and painfully familiar even as it was not. Stroking his hand up to the back of her neck, he forced himself to hold her with conscious gentleness as she opened her mouth over his and explored him with slow, sinful decadence.

The tenderness of the moment destroyed him, singing to parts of him he'd thought long dead. The scent of her, wildflowers in bloom, the feel of her under his hands, the way she laughed, it all fit him like a key into a lock. Ingrede had been so very different on the surface—a woman who loved home and hearth, who wouldn't know how to use a blade except in the kitchen, but she'd had the heart of a lion, his wife.

So did Honor.

"Yes," he said to her when she broke the kiss on a soft suck of sound.

Honor angled her head in a silent question.

Locking his eyes with those the shade of mist-laden forests, he very deliberately ran his hand down to close it over her breast. "Now, Honor."

Her heartbeat thudded against his hand, her voice raspy with the storm that had just passed . . . and with a passion that flushed her full lips until he wanted to use his teeth on her. "The windows," she whispered.

This high up, there was no chance of being overlooked . . . except, of course, by immortals with wings. "Close the blinds." The quiet command slipped out.

Honor's lips tugged upward at the corners. "As you wish."

Knowing he was being teased and quite content with the state of affairs, he watched her rise and walk to shut the blinds, enclosing them in the soft intimacy created by the quiet shield of rain beyond the glass. "What do you need?" he asked when she turned back to face him.

It was the first time in centuries upon centuries that he'd put a lover's needs above his own. Oh, he'd never left a bedmate unsatisfied, even if the pleasure he'd been inclined to give had been a razor-edged thing almost brutal in its intensity, but care . . . no, he hadn't taken care of a lover since the day he left his wife with a promise to return.

If Honor asked him to temper himself, he'd find a way to do it. But what she said was, "I won't break," and it was a solemn statement.

He thought of how she'd gone mad in his arms, her mind trapped in a nightmare. Fractures existed inside of her, and tonight, bastard that he was, he'd helped widen them. But they would heal—because Honor had come out swinging. Raising his hand to his jaw, he rubbed the tender bruise. "You almost broke me."

A smile, slow and heartbreaking in its beauty. "You deserved it."

He felt his own lips curve. "I did." Scanning his eyes up

and down her body, he said, "I still intend to have my wicked way with you," in a deliberate attempt to gauge how far she'd allow him to go.

"No kinky stuff till later."

Surprised she'd even entertain the thought after what he'd done, he lifted his gaze to her own—and saw an understanding that stunned him. She knew she had power over him, this mortal who was so much weaker and yet who had brought him to his knees. Honor wasn't like him, hadn't been turned cynical by an experience that would've twisted many only toward bitterness and hate, would never use that power in a malicious way. But the knowledge, it allowed her to play these games with him.

Good.

Pushing back his chair just a fraction, he crooked a finger.

She kicked off her boots before crossing the carpet to straddle him. Her hands lifted to the buttons of his shirt. "I love the color of your skin," she murmured, leaning forward to press a kiss on the bared skin of his breastbone.

It was the sweetest of caresses, and it made him weave his fingers into her hair and insist on another. Laughing, she peppered his chest with kisses, the shirt gaping to his waist now. "Such beautiful, pretty skin. Does the shade change over your body?"

He tugged at the bottom of her top, waited until she raised her arms to pull it off over her head. "I told you. You'll have to"—clenching his abdomen against the impact of her—"wait and see." It was his turn to lean forward, press his lips to the sun-kissed honey of her skin, his hands possessive on her hips.

"I have scars."

Those responsible for creating those scars would pay for decades to come, because Dmitri had no mercy or forgiveness in him. Not for this crime. "I see only you." Another lingering kiss before he drew back. "And you're my own personal addiction."

Cupped in black lace, her breasts were lush curves that made his mouth water, his fangs aching to sink into that sweet flesh. He wouldn't do it, not until she issued the invitation, but that made no difference to his cock. It was as rigid as rock, blood pulsing hot and thick. And that was before he allowed himself to think of the tight, wet sheath of her core.

"I want to be inside you." He sucked on the upper slope of her breast, licked the red mark. "So deep you feel branded."

Honor's fingernails dug into his nape, her voice a husky whisper. "You make me want to do things no good girl would ever do."

Her words relaxed the final relics of the twisted knot inside him. "I'm never going to stop you." Raising his head, he claimed her, stroking his hands along the dip of her waist and over her rib cage to cup both breasts at the same time. The generous mounds were teasingly covered by the fine lace of her bra, a small red bow in the center. "I thought a hunter would be more practical." He ran his thumbs across nipples pebbled and tempting.

"Complaining?"

Squeezing her taut flesh, he took her lips in an open-mouthed kiss in answer.

Her head fell back when he released her mouth, the position exposing the slope of her neck. His blood hummed, his gaze locking on the pulse in her throat. Teeth gritted, he distracted himself by focusing on her breasts. It worked. They were luscious, a little too large for a hunter's active life, and perfect for Dmitri's hands.

Sliding his hands to just below the exquisite curves, he was bending his head to indulge himself with her when Honor tugged on his hair. "Kiss my throat." A whisper as soft as the air itself.

His hands spasmed on her rib cage. "That might not be the best of ideas." He was starving for her, his entire body one big pulse.

"You're old enough to control it." A sensual challenge. "I'm sensitive there." Raising her hand, she ran her fingers down the arch of her throat.

His cock jerked, his mind full of a thousand debauched images of what he wanted those strong fingers to do to him.

"I hate that I've lost that pleasure because of what they did," she said. "I want it back."

Instead of obeying the order, he filled his hands with her breasts once more, her nipples hard points against his palms, glorying in the escalation of her heartbeat, the jerking cadence of her breath. "Sensitive here, too, aren't you, Honor?" Plumping her up for his delectation, he lowered his head to grip one of her nipples with his teeth, knowing the lace would rasp against her flesh, an exquisite pain.

A hotly feminine sound of frustration. "That whip of yours"—breathy words—"ever felt it on your own body?"

Releasing her nipple with a flick of his tongue, dampening the lace and increasing the friction, he looked up. "No." He was always in control. That was who he was. But— "Maybe we could trade."

Narrowed eyes. "I know you're getting something over me, but I can't figure out what."

That was when he shifted forward to press a hot, wet kiss to the side of her neck, high up near her jaw. She froze in his arms, but he kept his mouth where it was— even as he stroked the line of her body from breast to hip, hip to breast, over and over again with one hand, spreading the other on her lower back. "Feel the wetness," he whispered, then blew against her damp skin.

When she shivered, he licked at her. "Choose, Honor. Tell me what you like." It was taking all of his experience to keep himself in check with this woman who destroyed him. "Tell me," he said again, locking down his instincts to take, to possess. "You hold the reins."

Fingers sliding over his nape and into his hair, she said, "Long, wet kisses."

It was no hardship to indulge her—he could feast on every inch of her and start all over again within seconds. Her body remained stiff for a long time, but the fingers on his nape, they dug in a little, her pulse accelerating until his own sang with the erotic beat of it. And then she said, "Harder, Dmitri."

He liked his name on her lips when she was half naked on top of him, her body so lush and open. He'd like it even better when he was driving his cock into her. Blowing on the skin he'd just kissed, he drank in her responding shiver before giving her what she'd asked for—long, hard kisses that left her with dark red marks on her neck—at the same time that he used one of his hands to squeeze and mold the heavy warmth of her breasts. He had every intention of marking those, too.

When he finally lifted his head from her throat, her eyes were hazy with pleasure, her body relaxed. It wasn't a "fix," but the experience would give her a weapon against the night-mares—he was more than willing to suck on her sweet body anytime she needed a refresher. "I want," he murmured, "to put my mouth here." He rocked up against her, pressing into the heated vee of her thighs. "Is that going to be a problem?"

Wide eyes, languorous with a healthy, decadent lust. "No. They— Nobody seemed interested in that. But no bites on the inner thighs. I . . . it hurt."

Rage roared through him, so savage and brutal he had to dip his head for a second in case she saw it. But then Honor rolled her hips over him, sliding her fingers under the loose fabric of his collar to caress his back, and he was in the mo-ment again, with a beautiful, sexy woman who had been mis-used and who was now his to pleasure. "Do the panties match?" he asked, tracing the scalloped edge of her bra.

"Yes." Her chest rose and fell in a ragged rhythm. "They're red with a black bow."

"Witch."

She laughed, confirming his supposition that she was teas-ing him again. No one had done that for an eon. "Take off this shirt, Dmitri"—a nibbling kiss on the sensitive curve of his earlobe—"or I'll tear it to pieces."

Hissing at the caress, he made quick work of the shirt, throwing it to the side and shoving his hands between their bodies to rid himself of his belt at the same time. His cock was a steel rod in his pants, pressing in urgent demand against the fabric—he undid the top button for relief, but resisted the urge to release his turgid flesh. If he did, this would end far too fast.

And he wanted to savor.

It had been so long.

The thought whispering out of reach before he truly heard it, he traced the strap of Honor's bra to the cup, nudged it down to bare the swollen pout of her nipple. Leaving the lace tucked just under it, he repeated the process with her other breast. Then he leaned back and drank in the sight of her dis-played for him like an erotic feast.

30

Her breath, already ragged, turned fast and shallow, her hands dropping to her thighs. Then she did something unexpected. Pushing in with her upper arms, she plumped up her breasts for him, serving up the feast. He groaned, dipped his head to suck one tightly furled nipple into his mouth while he rolled the other between his fingertips.

Luxuriating in the taste of her, he alternated between one luscious breast and the other, until she pulled at his hair. "What?" He heard the arrogance, decided she was strong enough to deal.

"I can't breathe." Face flushed, heartbeat erratic, hair tumbled, and nipples hot and wet from his caresses, she was a sexual fantasy come to life.

"You aren't planning to rush me, are you, Honor?" He flicked his thumb over one nipple before reaching back to unhook her bra and peel it off, revealing the full beauty of her breasts. The honey gold of her skin was creamier here, more delicate, until he knew his fangs would leave two perfect tiny bruises on her flesh—he could heal a bite completely, but as he'd already proven, he wasn't exactly a civilized sophisticate when it came to Honor. He wanted her to bear the intimate brand.

But not until she was ready. However, there were other ways to mark a woman. "Lean back with your elbows on the table." Another command.

One she obeyed.

The position not only left her at his mercy, it pushed up her breasts for his pleasure. "I want to feed from you," he said, and saw the immediate terror in her eyes, "but I won't. Not until you give me an unmistakable verbal invitation, so push that fear out of your mind." He held the deep green of her gaze until the terror was washed away by relief . . . and a smoldering sensuality that told him this was a woman who'd match him in bed stroke for stroke, kiss for kiss.

"Honor?"

"Yes."

"I'm going to do things to you now that a good girl *definitely* shouldn't let a man do to her."

The words made Honor's body turn liquid.

Then Dmitri put that sinful, dangerous mouth on her breast, sucking hard enough to leave a love-bruise, before dipping his head to suckle her nipple with strong tugs that made her womb clench. If his earlier caresses had been painfully tender, this was pure, raw sex. Nothing in his touch said he considered her fractured, considered her damaged goods, and that gave her a freedom she wouldn't have believed possible.

Pushing upward into the merciless knowledge of that mouth, she was rewarded with his tongue swirling around her nipple, doing things to her that she hadn't known were possible. Squeezing her thighs around his powerful body, she watched him lift his head. Lick his lips. And move to her neglected breast.

A kiss of teeth.

Not until you give me an unmistakable verbal invitation . . .

Chanting that promise in her mind, she rode out the spike of fear to drown in the rush of pleasure. "Don't stop," she said when he raised his head.

He leaned forward to press a kiss just below the hollow of her throat in answer, eyes of sin and darkness holding a look of satisfaction he made no attempt to hide. "Can you reach the honey?"

Twisting slightly, she grabbed the squeeze bottle of honey

he'd put out with the fruit and handed it to him, knowing full well she was giving him a weapon with which to torment her further.

He flicked open the cap and, continuing to maintain the intimate eye contact, leaned forward to lick her nipple—just once, just enough to tantalize, to have her sucking in a breath—before upending the bottle and squeezing the sticky liquid not onto her body as she'd expected, but into his hand. He flicked the top closed after he was done, and gave it to her.

She managed to put it somewhere on the table without ever taking her eyes from him.

Dipping a single finger into the thick golden liquid, he lifted it to her lips to trace her with honey sweetness. She sucked his finger into her mouth, swirled her tongue around it as she'd done to his cock in the car. Those sexy eyes told her exactly what he wanted to do to her, but the heat was a slow-burning ember, Dmitri's fuse apparently very long.

Lucky her.

"Keep doing that," he murmured in a voice that was the most opulent fur over her skin, "and I'll have you kneeling between my legs sucking on something much harder."

She caught his finger between her teeth, a sensual punishment for words that might as well have come from some uncivilized barbarian. "Floor would be tough on the knees," she said after releasing him, feeling hotly, gloriously female. "Next time I suck you, I want to be kneeling on a nice comfy sofa."

"I live to grant your wishes." Finger glistening from her mouth, he dipped it back in the honey and painted both her nipples with a precise, near-delicate touch, before beginning to create an intricate curving pattern on the slopes of her breasts. "Don't move."

It was pure torture to sit motionless as he caressed her with long, slow, sticky motions of his finger, his body big and hard and aroused beneath her, his erection so very close that she had fantasies of ripping off his pants and mounting him, his thick flesh pushing into her in rigid demand.

Dmitri's eyes glittered as they met hers and she wondered what he saw. But all he said was, "Be a good girl, Honor, or I'll have to punish you."

A big, rough hand spanking her with erotic heat between her thighs, his fingers becoming slick with her need as she tugged against the bonds that tied her to the bed . . . and allowed her no room to defend herself.

She shuddered as the fantasy formed full-blown in her mind. "Maybe I"—she swallowed as he painted a line down to her navel, drawing a curving design a half inch above the low waistband of her jeans—"would enjoy your version of punishment."

"Hmm." He ran his finger back up. "It wouldn't be punishment then, would it?" A sensual threat from a dangerous creature who knew how to play every facet of a woman's body. "Now, come here." Curving his hand around her body, he pressed his palm onto her back.

She gasped as the honey met her skin. "I'm all sticky."

"Come make me sticky."

Having no objection to pasting herself against his body, she crushed her breasts to his chest. "We're going to make an awful mess." She couldn't help but claim his mouth, that beautiful, sexy mouth that was becoming her most sinful indulgence.

He let her take him, let her suck on his tongue and ride her body against his cock, but the material of her jeans was thick and she couldn't feel him like she wanted. When his hands clenched on her thighs, it was a silent demand. Breaking the kiss, she separated their honey-coated bodies with a husky moan and rose to her feet to undo her belt, throw it to the side.

Then, as Dmitri watched, she flicked open the button at the waistband of her jeans and pushed down the zipper to reveal the front of her red panties. Urging her forward with his hands on her hips, Dmitri reached in to trace the tiny black bow, the intimate touch making her want to beg him to move that hand lower, rub harder. Except— "What if I—"

He kissed her navel, right above her panties, the kiss hot and wet.

Her toes curled, and the only reason she remained upright was because of his hold.

"Then," he said, answering the question he hadn't let her complete, "we try again. We try all night because I have every intention of taking what's mine."

She ran her fingers through the heavy black silk of his hair. "Possessive much?"

The smile he gave her was lethal in its impact. She'd known from the start that she was perilously vulnerable to him, but it was at that moment that she realized she could deny him nothing. It was a terrible weakness, but one that was fused so very deep into her psyche, she knew there was no fighting it, no ignoring it.

My Dmitri.

Stepping back, she shimmied out of her jeans and threw them aside. But when she would've straddled him again, he shook his head, nudged her toward the table. A blush crept up her body as she perched on the smooth pine, her knees demurely closed. Shifting his chair closer, he slid his hands down her thighs to cup the backs of her knees, her calves, and it was a tormenting pleasure. She allowed those knowing hands to caress her, to part her knees and spread her thighs as he directed her to put her feet on the chair on either side of his body.

She felt exposed, naked, though she still wore her panties. "Dmitri." Stroking up honey from her body, she shaped his lips with her fingertip. His jaw was hard under her hand as she cupped his face and kissed him, slow and sweet and a little bit wicked, biting down on that slightly full lower lip.

He moved his hands over her thighs, squeezed. And then he nipped back.

It zinged a ripple of pleasure right through her. Eyes wide, she stared at him, this gorgeous creature more dangerous than any vampire she'd ever before known. She'd thought any hint of a bite would make her freak out. Swallowing, she looked down at his hands. "My thigh," she whispered. "Do it."

Not saying a word, he wiped up honey from his chest and ran a line down the sensitive flesh of her inner thigh. It made her tremble, but the tremor wasn't caused by fear. Not yet. However, the instant he bent his head to her flesh, she froze. Not stopping, he closed his teeth on her. The bite was more a tease than anything, with not even a hint of fang. Trembling, she said, "Do it again."

He gave her another teasing kiss. Another.

Until her body couldn't hold the tension any longer and she

shuddered, melting into his touch, his seduction. Long, slow
licks, small, playful bites, hard sucks, he gave her all of them.
But he didn't sink his fangs into her flesh, didn't draw up her
blood. "When I feed from you," he murmured, "it won't be a
rushed thing. I plan to savor every hot second of it." He tugged
her forward, reaching up to play with the thin black ribbons on
the sides of her panties, his lips a little swollen from her kisses,
his bones sharply defined against that warm, beautiful skin.
"Lie back."

Shivering at the dark seduction of him, she took a deep
breath and bent over to lie on the table, laughing when her
back met the warmth of the wood. "Sticky."

Lifting up her legs until her knees were hooked up over his
shoulders, he ran a finger down the very center of her panties.
"Hmm, yes."

Her brain couldn't quite process his statement, her nerves
short-circuited by that single touch. Again, she waited for the
fear. Again, it didn't come. That was when she made the connection. This, with Dmitri, it was about pleasure.

"Forgive me."

Never again would he unleash the honed blade of cruelty
on her. She knew that to the depths of her soul, had heard it in
the cadence of his voice, felt it in that moment when he knelt
before her, this man of power and pride, the moment that had
been the dividing line between the past and the future.

So this was about pleasure.

The assault had been about pain.

"Are you ready, Honor?"

Yes. But she didn't have the chance to answer, because that
was when he put his mouth on her through the damp fabric of
her panties. *"Dmitri."*

Half of Dmitri wanted to tear off the last flimsy scrap of
Honor's clothing and plow into her in a single deep thrust,
claiming her in that most elemental of ways. The other half of
him wanted to use every bit of the sensual skill he'd gained
over the centuries to make her his slave.

Her panties stuck to the plump, flushed curves of her intimate flesh when he drew back, slid his hands under those silly

little ribbons that made him insane, and tugged. She lifted up her body and he was peeling that scrap of nothing down her thighs an instant later. He stood to get them completely off, and when he looked up at her, he knew he'd reached the limit of his patience. Leaning down, he licked at the honey over her breasts.

"So now I'm your serving dish," she said with a smile that kicked him right in the heart. "I knew you had an ulterior motive."

Laughing—and when had he last done that with a lover?—he kissed his way down her body, to the damp curls between her thighs. And found he had a little more patience after all. Enough to retake his seat, part her, and kiss her, hot and slow and with exquisite care, laving his tongue against the hard nub at the apex of her thighs.

Her back arched, her fingernails scrabbling on the wood. "Dmitri." Her breath escaped her in a choked-off scream that made him tuck his thumb against the slick entrance to her body and push inside a mere fraction as he covered her with his mouth once more. It was enough. She came apart for him, a sweet burst of feminine spice against his senses.

Rising to his feet even as the final tremors shimmered over her body, he stripped off his remaining clothing and sat back down before pulling her to the edge of the table. "On me, Honor."

"I can't move." It was a breathless complaint.

He kissed her hip bone, felt her shiver. Tugged a little more. She flowed into his arms, all liquid and pleasured and boneless, her legs spreading to either side of his body. Lazy, she kissed him before reaching down to squeeze his turgid arousal with strong, knowing fingers.

Hissing out a breath, he tugged off her hands. "Later." He pulled her forward, lifted her using his considerable strength . . . and slid her down oh-so-slow onto his cock. Scalding heat and exquisite tightness.

His mind blanked for an instant.

"Oh." A long, breathy moan. "You feel . . ." Hands thrusting into his hair, cupping the back of his head as she settled more firmly onto him, rolling her hips and using tiny inner muscles to squeeze his cock.

Dmitri swore a quiet blue streak, his hands clenching on her hips. When she continued to make the small sensual movements about to rip his control to shreds, he dipped his head and sucked one taut nipple into his mouth. She cried out and lost her rhythm, letting him regain a piece of his sanity. Licking her one more time, he insinuated his hand between their bodies to lightly circle her clitoris as he began to move inside her in the shallowest of strokes.

"You'll kill me." With that, Honor found his mouth.

Lost in the wild passion of her kiss, he stood, taking her with him, and perched her on the edge of the table, their bodies still joined. Her legs were wrapped around him, her mouth fused to his, one hand cupping his jaw, the other in his hair. He felt surrounded by her, adored by her. A startling thought . . . but welcome.

Kissing his way across her cheek and down her jaw when she broke the kiss, he moved his hand to her hip, angling her exactly how he liked. Then he began to move. Their gazes locked. Stayed locked.

Her eyes were shimmering midnight forests, her cry a single word. His name. He fell with her, so much pleasure rocking through him that it felt as if he'd broken into a million iridescent pieces.

31

A very sexy shower later—Lord, but Dmitri was inventive—
Honor cuddled up next to him, amused at the thought of cud-
dling up to a vampire so lethal he scared others of his kind.
"You're a very clever man."

He ran the fingers of one hand down the side of her face. "I
know."

Honor laughed because what else could a woman do when
the man in bed with her had driven her to so many orgasms,
she was still seeing stars? "That position—letting me be on
top, while handing you all the power. I'm playing way out of
my sexual league, aren't I?"

"Don't worry." He wove his fingers into her hair. "I'm an
excellent coach."

Yes, she bet he was. Kissing her way up his body, she snug-
gled her face into his neck and drew in the warm scent of him.
It felt like coming home.

The awakening was as rude as the sleep had been pleasurable.

"Amos has been spotted," Dmitri told her after reaching out to answer his cell just before a misty gray dawn.

The vampire wasn't on the grounds of Jiana's Stamford estate when they arrived, but he'd left pieces behind—several of his organs sat in a glistening pile on the grass, covered with droplets of the fine, fine rain that beaded on their hair, dampened their clothing. Heavy steel spikes encrusted with blood betrayed where he'd been pinned to the earth, purple zinnias and sunny chrysanthemums crushed and splattered with blood congealed to black in pockets where the rain couldn't reach.

"Whatever I might have dreamed of doing to him," Honor murmured to Dmitri as they stood on the small rise overlooking Jiana's home, the moisture-laden early morning wind lifting their hair off their faces, "this is worse."

"He had to have been otherwise compromised or he'd have escaped those steel pegs before he was gutted, his intestines removed," Dmitri said, eyes on the flesh and blood ropes that looked obscene surrounded by flowers struggling to reach for sunlight that wasn't there.

"Or maybe," Honor said, looking at the blood-soaked woman who sat rocking not far from the site of the carnage, runnels of red dripping from her arms and legs into the earth, "he didn't want to escape . . . not until he realized she wasn't planning to stop." And still he'd been unable to end the life of his attacker, this woman he both loved and hated.

Dmitri's gaze followed her own, but there was a cold consideration in it that didn't seem to fit the circumstances. Jiana had, after all, attempted to execute her son in the most brutal fashion. The only reason Amos wasn't dead was because he'd apparently managed to rip out one of the spikes and hit Jiana so hard across the face with it she'd ended up unconscious with a broken cheekbone, a deep gash marring that mocha skin. He was long gone by the time she alerted the guards.

"Payment for his crimes," the female vampire had whispered when Honor and Dmitri arrived on the scene.

Honor wouldn't have believed the woman's violent change of heart if not for the fact that quite aside from the damage done by Amos during his escape, Jiana's face was horribly bruised, the elegant silk and lace of her nightgown all but torn off her, her ribs cracked.

"He looked at me," Jiana had added, eyes dull, "in a way no man should look at his mother."

That, Honor thought, was what had pushed her over the edge—it seemed there were some things even the most devoted of mothers couldn't accept. However, it was clear Dmitri had a different view of matters. Waiting until he shifted his attention back to her, she said, "What do you see?"

"It's not what I see. It's what I smell."

Rather than asking him to elaborate, she considered all the facts, hazarded a guess. "Some kind of a sedative or tranquilizer in his blood." There was more than enough of the latter splashed around, thinned though it was by the rain, to make a determination.

A clipped nod. "This was no act done in unthinking rage. It was calm, cold, *calculated.*" His eyes lingered on Jiana. "Consider the fact that in spite of her 'cooperation' earlier, she made no mention of the culvert that allows covert access to this property."

"A mother's instinct to protect trumping her rational mind," she said, playing devil's advocate. "As for the drugs, could be she's lying and he didn't only say or do something she couldn't accept, but actually succeeded in assaulting her.

"Traumatized, she put something in his drink, waited for him to get disoriented, weak, and then she did this." Amos could've easily stumbled to this part of the estate, even drugged and less than lucid. It was less than a hundred yards from the house, and with the guard at the front door having been knocked unconscious, while the others were situated around the perimeter, no one could refute that version of events.

"Plausible." Dmitri's eyes lingered on the pile of organs that were still pink with health, evidence of the vampirism that meant Amos would recover as long as he had a steady supply of fresh blood and a place to hide.

"Except," Dmitri continued, interrupting her thoughts about how a man came back from being gutted by his own mother, "whatever happened here, it wasn't simply about execution, was it?"

She looked at the scene again, consciously putting aside her impression of Jiana as a loving mother pushed to the brink, and focused only on the facts. One of which was that this had taken time. A lot of time. Because the organs . . . they'd been removed with neat precision, sat in a tidy pile.

Heart chilling at the realization, she was about to turn toward Dmitri when she glimpsed the torn and bloody piece of cloth flung a couple of feet away. "He was gagged." And from the near-black quality of the blood caught in the wrinkles the rain hadn't penetrated, he'd bitten through his tongue, likely shredded his lips. The ground where he'd been pinned was drenched in so much of that same blood it appeared wetter than the surrounding area, pale pink dew gleaming on some of the chrysanthemums hanging from broken stems.

The conclusion wasn't an easy one, but it had to be said. "She enjoyed this."

"There is every indication." Turning, Dmitri walked to Jiana, a sleek shadow in the black jeans, boots, and black T-shirt he'd pulled on during a quick stop at the Tower.

Honor forced herself to follow, though it tormented her to think of a mother taking pleasure in the murder of her child, no matter the evil done by that child. It was something she simply had trouble comprehending, the maternal instinct within her a staggering force . . . though she had no children of her own.

Shaking her head to clear it, she came to a standstill beside Dmitri as he looked down at Jiana's apparently tormented form. "You were too clever, Jiana," he said in a purr of a voice that wrapped ice around Honor's throat.

Jiana continued to rock back and forth, her tattered nightgown clinging to her slender body, the bruises on her face having turned a sickly yellow-green at the edges as she healed. She gripped a serrated blade in one hand, the entire thing encrusted with dried blood that resisted the rain.

In a whiplash-fast move Honor didn't see coming, Dmitri slid out a razor-sharp hunting knife from his boot and went as if to slice off Jiana's head. The female vampire was flowing up and striking a defensive pose in the blink of an eye, her own knife slashing out toward Dmitri. He knocked it to the ground with inhuman speed, and, gripping Jiana's wrist, held her in place as he put the edge of his deadly blade to her throat. "Now," he said, "you will talk."

Jiana's gaze skittered to Honor. "Help me." Such torment in her eyes, such a black depth of sorrow . . . and behind it, a prowling viciousness Honor would've missed if Dmitri hadn't pushed the blade a fraction deeper, startling Jiana into dropping her mask of emotional pain for a single split second.

"You created him," Honor said, sickened. "Whatever his madness, you took advantage of it to twist him even further."

Jiana's face morphed, the frail beauty of her transforming into something contemptuous and sneering. "He is my son." No remorse. "Mine to do with as I choose."

At that instant, Honor understood the depth of both Jiana's malevolence and her intelligence. She'd had the foresight to play them from the start, her "penance" with the blood junkies a smokescreen set up just in case anyone came looking. Even if that hadn't happened till months or years in the future, Jiana would've always been able to point back to her apparent distress at the time to lend credence to her protestations of being guilty of nothing except loving her child too much—a child she'd clearly always been ready to sacrifice.

And yet, Honor was certain the love Jiana had professed for Amos wasn't all a lie. Something had tipped the balance— perhaps the fact that Amos had not only slipped the leash and begun to act on his own, rather than as Jiana's creature, but that he'd started to attract the wrong kind of attention. "He'd become a liability," she murmured, "might've betrayed you if he was taken." Surrounded by the carnage Jiana had done—had *enjoyed* doing—Honor was convinced the female vampire's hands were stained with far more evil than anyone other than Amos realized. "He learned everything he knew from you."

A flash of vicious rage in those onyx-dark eyes that turned Honor's guess into truth even before Jiana said, "I would've forgiven his taking of you—it was an intriguing amusement after all." Words designed to stab and cut. "But the stupid boy planned to take two more hunters after I *warned* him to stay quiet and out of sight."

So Jiana had set out to torture, then execute him. If she had succeeded, Amos's death would've been far more painful than anything Honor could've ever devised . . . for he would've died looking into the pitiless face of the one woman who was meant to love him without corruption or condition.

A woman whose mouth now curved into a nasty smile. "I did so enjoy being *kind* to you in the pit. I had plans to return, to earn your trust. Your anguish would've been all the sweeter when I turned on you."

"Enough," Dmitri said, cutting Jiana off when she would've continued. "Where is Amos?"

"If I knew, do you think I would've alerted the guards?" Not giving any warning, Jiana lunged at the blade against her throat, but Dmitri was faster, dancing the weapon out of her way.

"There will be no easy death for you," he said, gripping the vampire by the throat and lifting her up off her feet. "You will come before Raphael."

Jiana began to kick and scream. "We fall under your purview, Dmitri! You must mete out the punishment!"

"First we must know all of what you have done." With those words, he snapped his hand.

Jiana's head lolled, her body going limp, and Honor realized he'd broken her neck as he'd done Jewel Wan's. "It'll be easier to transport her this way," he said when he saw her staring.

The violence of his world staggered her, but she was no innocent. She'd known from the instant she decided to step onto this path that it would be no gentle ride. That didn't mean she had to accept everything as it was. "She would've gone anyway."

Dmitri passed Jiana's limp body over to another vampire, with orders for her to be taken to the Tower under constant guard. "I was getting sick of her voice."

"Dmitri."

A dark glance, fine jewel-like beads of water collecting on lashes black as the night. "Trying to gentle me?"

"That line you walk," she said, knowing he was pushing her on purpose, "it's very thin. I'm trying to stop you from crossing it. Everything you do, every decision you make, it has a cumulative effect."

He strode to the edge of the rise, a black silhouette against the chill gray of the morning, his eyes on the gracious home below. "Near to a thousand years, Honor."

"You're an almost-immortal." Moving to join him, she

touched her fingers to his. "You have another thousand to step away from that line."

Dmitri's expression was unreadable when he looked at her, his thoughts hidden. "Can you track Amos?"

Aware she couldn't hope to convince him to take another path when their relationship was barely formed, she held her peace for the moment. "The blood here survived, but I'm guessing the rain will have made a mess of any smaller traces. However, Amos was bleeding badly so there's a chance if he didn't manage to get to a vehicle."

"It should be safe, but take someone with you." He raised his hand and she felt a rush of air above her head as wings of sooty black streaked across to land lower down the rise. "Jason will keep you company. I have something to attend to."

She caught the edge in his tone. "Dmitri."

"I'm going to personally tear apart Jiana's Enclave property, and I'll set Tower personnel to ensuring Amos has no hidden bolt-holes. If there are any files naming those who accepted his invitation, I'll find them."

Drawing in a deep breath, she looked out over the flowers. "I think we tracked them all." There were no unknown scents or bodies in her memories, no voices that didn't fit. "Thank you."

A brush over her hair, and then he was gone, leaving her to her task.

She used every ounce of her skill, even asked Elena to drop by and confirm, but her instincts proved correct—Amos had bled through the culvert, but his trail ended there.

"Car," Elena agreed when Honor showed her the tracks, her words crisp regardless of the dark circles under her eyes. "No hint of any further scent. You want me to tell the Tower to put out an alert on vehicles owned by him?"

"He's too smart to have used anything that can be traced back to him." Amos's cunning was a vicious thing.

A single bead of water rolled off the white-gold of a primary feather as the other hunter spread her wings a fraction. "Never know with immortals—arrogance can sometimes blind them to reality."

"Yes." Honor took in the dark circles again, the lines of strain. "Tough night?"

The other woman blew out a breath, strands of her hair escaping her braid to whisper across her face. "Was up until five a.m. talking with one of my sisters. She's going through some stuff." A shake of her head. "Love can kick you in the gut sometimes."

Honor thought of Dmitri, of how vulnerable she was to him, and couldn't disagree. "But when it's right . . ."

"Yes." Elena's eyes met her own, the silver shimmering despite the lack of sunlight. "I'm in no position to throw stones about getting involved with dangerous men, so I'll just say— living in the world of immortals can be brutal. You ever need anything, including support to tie Dmitri up so you can torment him with a fork, call me."

Honor's lips twitched, an unexpected respite. "You still haven't forgiven him for that."

"I intend to carry the grudge into eternity." Those pale, striking eyes returned to the culvert, to the blood trail, all humor fading. "I'm not a mother, but to do what you say Jiana did . . ."

"Yes."

Elena left soon afterward, her wings a splash of brilliance against the steel of the sky, but Honor didn't return to the city. Instead, she walked to join Jason where he stood in the shadow of an old magnolia tree, its leaves a thick waxy green. "I'd like a look through the house." It was an itch at the back of her neck, a sense that she'd missed something . . . or perhaps seen something she hadn't understood at the time.

The house was as elegant as the last time she'd stepped inside it—except for the evidence of a violent fight.

Holes in the walls, bloody palm prints, broken furniture, and paintings skewed crooked where they hadn't been pulled off and thrown to the ground. "If Amos was sedated," she said, "how did he do all this, manage to beat Jiana?"

Jason, his presence so silent that she was almost startled to hear the rustle of his wings, spoke for the first time. "A slow-acting or mild sedative would have left him with some awareness of what was happening—enough that he tried to fight it."

"Jiana would have known," she murmured, "how to calculate any dose to her son's size and strength. Then all she'd have had to do was taunt him into a rage." She could see the weaving, staggering pattern clearly now. He'd crashed into the wall there, skewed the ornamental mirror, tipped over the wooden table with its delicate legs, then kicked his way free and done something that sprayed blood over the wall.

"A blow to Jiana's mouth," she said, nodding at the spray.

"We'll know for certain soon enough," he said, his wings a whisper of darkness as he walked into a room off the main hall. "Raphael will take the memory from her mind."

Honor shivered at the idea of such a violation. "How do you stand it?" she asked, aware it was an intimate question, but compelled to ask. "Knowing he could do the same to you?"

"Trust." He gave her an unreadable look over his shoulder, his eyes as dark as his wings. "The kind of trust that allows you to take Dmitri to your bed even knowing what he's capable of doing to women who edge his temper."

Startled by the response, and by the fact that he'd picked up that piece of information though it appeared he'd just returned to the city, she looked with more care at that face marked by the swirling lines of a tattoo that should've made him stand out no matter his surroundings. And yet . . . Shadows, she thought, clung to Jason.

"Whatever it is you are to Dmitri, Honor," he said in that voice as deep and quiet as the heart of night, "it's not like Carmen or the others." Lush black lashes came down over near-black eyes, then rose again.

Fascinated by this angel who she knew instinctively rarely spoke to those he didn't know, she touched her hand to a shattered figurine and waited, knowing he had more to say.

"He won't brush you off like an annoyance or let you walk away." Spreading his wings to block the rest of the room from her view, he held her gaze. "It's too late. Do you understand that?"

32

With her gaze Honor traced the lines of the incredible tattoo that covered the left side of his face, the ink ebony against warm brown skin. Hair pulled off his face into a neat queue, he was both sexy and remote. "Are you trying to warn me or protect him?"

"It doesn't have to be one or the other."

"I don't need to be warned off Dmitri, Jason," she said, wondering if this dark angel lowered his guard with anyone. "I see him as he is. As for the other . . . it's not necessary." The truth was, Dmitri owned her heart.

Jason's eyes seemed, like his wings, to reflect nothing though he looked straight at her. "Many would've curled up and died after what you experienced."

An intimate observation, but then, he'd answered her question. "I almost did," she said, wondering why her answer would matter to an angel, yet she knew in her gut it did to Jason. "But turns out, spite is a damn good motivator—I didn't want the bastards to win."

Jason's expression didn't move off her, and she had the powerful sense he wanted to pursue the topic, but his next words were pragmatic. "Things are as expected in this home."

"Yes—no, wait." Turning, she went back to a painting she'd righted on the way in. It was the nude of Jiana in bed, her slumberous eyes looking at the artist as a woman looks at a lover. "This was what I saw," she whispered, tracing the *A* in the bottom right-hand corner, nausea churning inside her at the implications. "Amos painted this."

"Perhaps."

Nodding, she glanced up. "You're right. It's not conclusive. Let's keep looking."

The black-winged angel was a silent presence by her side as she explored hallways covered by a rich, cream-colored carpet, thick and lush where it wasn't crushed by broken and overturned furniture or matted with blood. The farther they got into the house, the less aggressive the carnage, until at last they were at the very end of the second floor, where nothing had been disturbed.

It was there they discovered evidence Honor would've been happier never to find. The fine sheets on the large bed were tumbled, a bottle of sensual massage oil on the bedside table. On the floor lay not only a robe of bronze satin and lace that Honor recognized immediately, but a man's jacket and gleaming leather shoes. "Amos wasn't wearing shoes." His bloody footprints had made that clear.

One of Jason's wings brushed her back as he spread them behind her, a warm, startling weight. "Some things should simply not be."

"Yes." Amos, she thought, had never had a chance. Then again, so many in the world had overcome the terrible crimes done against them without needing to torture others. Still, she couldn't help but imagine the man who was her nightmare as a scared, defenseless child. "Do you have any idea of when this may have begun?"

"Amos and Jiana were always close, to a degree that was noticed." A pause. "We did a quiet investigation, found nothing amiss."

"They were clever." Honor thought of Jiana's tears, how very convincing she'd been in her despair. "*She* was clever."

Turning away from the silent accusation of the tumbled sheets, she said, "If this had come to light, would it have led to a severe punishment?" If so, it might well prove to be the strongest motive for Jiana's attempted murder of her son.

"Yes—an endless one. Even amongst the most dissolute immortals," Jason added, a dark heat to his tone she realized was rage, "some things are deeply taboo. To subject a child to such depravity, it's beyond our comprehension."

"So sweet and soft." A tone chilling in its gentleness. "I have heard such blood is a delicacy."

Hot breath on her face. "No! Please!" she screamed, her body pinned, helpless.

Laughter. Followed by a thick, wet sound and then her baby's screams rending the air.

Honor jerked back to the present with a cry of horror locked in her throat. Pushing past Jason's wing, the feel of his feathers liquid silk, she ran through the corridors until she stumbled out into unexpected sunshine, the rain having passed with whispering swiftness. The golden early morning light poured over her, a luminous counterpoint to the terrible sorrow within.

That ugly thought inside the house, that slice of words and sound, hadn't felt like a dream but a memory. *Her* memory, though she'd never been in such a horrific situation. Her heart ached with such pain she couldn't bear it, the infant girl's frightened screams tearing her soul to pieces.

"Honor."

It took conscious effort to close off the ripping chasm of a memory that reverberated inside her mind and turn to speak to Jason. "There's nothing to find here." Instead of the joy she'd expected to feel at this instant, when the hunt for her abusers was reaching its final stage, there was a hollowness inside her, a sense of loss that erased such petty things as vengeance. "I'm heading to the Guild."

Jason flared out his wings, the midnight shade so absolute, it absorbed the sunlight. "There is a car waiting for you by the gate."

"Dmitri," she murmured, knowing he had to have arranged it.

Jason gave her a penetrating look. "He's a vampire of old.

It is instinct for him to treat his woman with such care." He was gone in a wash of wind moments later, flying hard and fast up above the cloud layer, until she could no longer see even a glimmer of black.

But he'd left her with a crucial piece of knowledge when it came to dealing with Dmitri in a relationship.

His woman.

She had no doubt that that had been a deliberate word choice on Jason's part, another hint as to how Dmitri's brain worked. As she walked to the gate, she considered the issue with care—because Dmitri was the most important part of her life and she wasn't about to lie to herself about that.

She could reject the car he'd organized and call up a cab, making it clear that she wasn't about to allow him to treat her like a butterfly in a jar. Or she could accept the ride and the fact that her lover was a thousand-year-old vampire, give or take a few years, who came from a time in which his act would've raised no eyebrows.

To be utterly honest, it was nice to feel wanted, to feel cared for after a lifetime spent taking care of herself. While she couldn't define the relationship between her and Dmitri, she knew he would protect her with brutal ferocity until it was over.

Reaching the car, she slid in. Not only was having a chauffeur in New York nothing to sniff at, but acquiescing to it didn't do her any harm, while it allowed Dmitri to do what he needed to do: take care of her.

A smile bloomed over her face, a silly kind of happiness infusing her blood. She didn't fight it, even as she thought that her capitulation when it came to the car would give her an excellent negotiation tool when a bigger battle loomed.

Strategy, that was the key to dealing with a man as intelligent and as harshly practical as Dmitri.

My Dmitri.

Dmitri glanced at Raphael as they stood along the cliff behind Raphael's home, above the relatively calm waters of the Hudson and across from a Manhattan that had become a shining mirage in the morning sunlight. "Was I wrong?" he asked, knowing Raphael had already spoken to Jiana.

He wanted to be wrong, the need coming from the part of him that believed a mother should always care for her child, the part that knew Ingrede had spent her last breaths trying to save Misha and Caterina.

"Your wife fought to protect your daughter, Dmitri. Such a tiny rag doll of a thing."

Raphael's voice overrode the memory of Isis's cruel whisper, the raw echo of his broken cries. "No, you weren't wrong. Jason's information has also been confirmed."

"And Jiana?"

"I will take care of her." Absolute cold in those words, a reminder that the Archangel of New York had no mercy in him for those who committed such crimes—and that though his consort had awakened a vein of humanity in him, he remained a being of terrible power.

"Jiana was correct—that should be my task." It was a punishment he would have no compunction in delivering personally. Because Amos was what Jiana had made him. And Amos had hurt Honor so badly that Dmitri couldn't think of it without a blood haze across his vision. *Honor would never know,* he said to Raphael. *If I broke Jiana.*

The archangel took his time replying. *Are you sure you do not want your hunter to know you?*

No one, not even Raphael, had truly known Dmitri since Ingrede's death—he'd put away the heart of him the day he'd snapped his son's neck; he'd believed it dead. The fact that it wasn't . . . he wasn't sure how he felt about that. Only one thing was certain—he'd never give Honor up.

"If something ever happens to me, how long will you wait before you marry again?" A laughing question as his wife leaned on his bare chest. *"Try and be decent and wait at least a season."*

He knew she was teasing him, but he couldn't laugh, not about this. Thrusting his hand into hair he'd already tangled when he loved her, he tugged her down for a kiss that left her mouth kiss-bruised, her eyes wide.

"Dmitri." Fingers touching his lips, her voice a whisper.

"Never," he answered. "I will never again marry."

Her hand on his cheek, soft skin scraping over his morning stubble. "You mustn't say such a thing."

Closing his fingers over her wrist, he brought her palm to his mouth, pressing a gentle kiss to the warmth of her. "Are you planning on leaving me, Ingrede?" She owned him body and soul; she was his reason for being.

"Never." A nuzzle, nose to nose, that was such a silly thing she did, one that made him smile each and every time. *"But I wouldn't have you be lonely should we be parted. I couldn't bear you so sad."* Before he could speak, she added, *"But you can't marry that Tatiana. I don't like the way she looks at you."*

He laughed, kissed her again. *"Wicked woman."* But when the laughter faded, he spoke the indelible truth. *"I won't take any other woman into my heart."* He pressed a finger to her lips when distress colored her eyes. *"I'll wait for you to find me again. So don't take too long."*

Now, he was close to breaking his promise. "Am I betraying her?"

"I think," Raphael said, his wings shimmering gold in the sun, "your Ingrede was a woman of generous heart."

Yes, he thought, she had been. Ingrede had never been openly possessive—except when it came to Tatiana, who had indeed looked at Dmitri with an invitation in her eyes that should've been directed at no married man. The memory made him smile. "She was also a jealous thing."

Raphael laughed. "She gave me the most fierce look when she thought I was attempting to seduce you."

And then, Dmitri remembered, when she'd realized the angel was nothing but a friend, she had invited Raphael to dinner. So gentle had been Ingrede, but she'd spoken without fear to an immortal as they all stood in a newly sown field, and that immortal had come to their humble table. "I don't think we've ever again laughed as we did at that table."

"It is a cherished memory," Raphael said. "One I've never forgotten, one that has never faded."

It helped, he thought, to know that someone else remembered her. Remembered their children. Misha and Caterina had had such fleeting lives, but those lives had burned themselves into Dmitri's soul. And now, another name was starting to make its mark there, that of a hunter who awakened memories of a time long gone even as she began to shadow his wife's smile from his mind. *Forgive me, Ingrede.*

"Kallistos," Raphael said after long minutes of silence, his eyes on the angels flying across the river to land on the Tower roof.

Dmitri forced his mind off the only two women—one so sweet and of the hearth, the other a hunter but with those same gentle hands—who had laid claim to his heart in his near thousand years of existence. "I've alerted every one of our people in the region." He knew the vampire was close—the taunts had been too personal. At least in Times Square, Kallistos had to have been lingering nearby to witness Dmitri's reaction. "But he's old, and he's intelligent." However, Isis's lover didn't concern him as much as the angel who had been taken. "Will the boy survive the constant use Kallistos is making of him?"

Raphael's expression was grim, his bones sharp lines against his skin. "He's young, still vulnerable. There is no knowing how much damage Kallistos has caused." *Do you have a watch on your hunter?*

Of course. If Kallistos truly was mad enough to attempt the vengeance he'd threatened, she would be his target—because Honor was mortal, far easier to hurt and kill. As Ingrede had been mortal. "Not this time," he said, the words a vow.

33

Sorrow welcomed Honor with a bright smile when she dropped by the young woman's home a couple of hours after returning from Jiana's estate, and she was delighted when Honor told her it was time for her first self-defense lesson. "I'll go get out of my jeans."

Having stopped by her apartment to change into long black exercise pants paired with a simple deep green tank top, Honor began to warm up on the private lawn behind the house while the other woman ran inside.

The vampire who watched her from his relaxed seat on the back steps wore wraparound shades and a black suit with a crisp white shirt, his hair brushed back into perfect lines. If she didn't know better, she'd have thought he'd stepped out of some Fifth Avenue salon and wouldn't know one end of a blade from the other. Except she did know better. She'd seen the way Venom moved—that kind of grace a man only had if he danced. And she wasn't talking about the ballroom.

"Want a partner?" he asked, taking off his shades to reveal those startling eyes, so very alien. "I promise I'll be gentle."

Honor was almost certain she would now be okay with unfamiliar male contact, especially in a combat situation, but she shook her head. "Sorrow should be out soon."

Venom leaned forward with his elbows on his knees, the sun caressing brown skin that had enough warmth in it that it was extremely strokable. Not as strokable as that of the lethally sexy man Honor had had in her bed not long ago, but she bet Venom didn't have trouble getting dates, even with those eyes.

Now, his lips curved just a fraction. "I always thought Dmitri would choose someone a little more . . . sophisticated."

Taunting her, she thought, the viper-eyed male was taunting her to amuse himself. "You remind me of an eight-year-old foster brother I once had," she said, continuing her stretching routine. "He used to throw mudballs at me after I showered because he thought it was hilarious." There had been no meanness in Jared and she'd actually kept in touch with him for a while until age and time had faded the relationship. "He didn't find it funny after I dropped one down his back."

Venom's expression turned disgruntled. "I'm hardly a child."

Strange—she was decades, centuries younger, and at that moment, she wanted to cross the distance between them, rumple his hair, and kiss him on the cheek in amused affection. Before she could shake off the inexplicable feeling, Sorrow ran down the steps, dressed in pants similar to Honor's and a navy T-shirt bearing the name of a famous Irish bar.

"Are you going to pull out your cock to prove it now?" the girl asked with mock sweetness, having obviously overheard Venom's declaration.

The vampire's eerie pupils contracted to hard pinpoints. "Be careful your claws don't get you eaten, kitty."

Making a hissing sound at him, Sorrow stalked to join Honor on the grass. "Dmitri must really hate me," she muttered. "All the men at his command and he sends me Poison."

"Kitty?"

Sorrow bared her teeth to expose tiny fangs about half the normal size. "He calls them little kitten teeth."

Venom, Honor thought, glimpsing the rage in Sorrow's changing eyes, either had no idea what he was playing with . . .

or he had a very good idea. "We'll start with basic moves," she said, making a mental note to ask Dmitri to confirm if she was right about the fact that Venom was pushing the girl on purpose to gauge her level of control.

Sorrow leaned closer, lowered her voice. "Does he have to watch?"

"If you tell him to leave, he'll take even more pleasure in staying." As it was, Venom was answering a call on his cell phone, his body in a languid position she had no doubt could change in the blink of an eye. One of these days, Honor would spar with the vampire—after first taking Dmitri on in a session.

Her thighs clenched at the idea of tangling with her sexy, dangerous lover in that arena, their bodies sweaty and straining. "Just ignore him," she said, wrenching her mind back to the present.

Sorrow took a deep breath. "Okay," she said on the exhale. "Show me."

It was twenty minutes into a relatively undemanding session that the young woman swayed and collapsed.

Venom was beside her with such speed that Honor's breath caught in her throat. Jerking the semiconscious woman into a half-sitting position, he shoved back the left cuff of his shirt, having removed his jacket earlier, and said, "Feed," in a voice that was a whip.

Sorrow tried to shove him away but she was frighteningly weak, to Honor's worried gaze. "Fuck you." Her voice slurred on the curse.

"Stand in line, kitty." He shoved his wrist to her mouth. "Feed or I will pin you down and pour my blood down your throat. After which I will take you to the Tower so you can be placed under twenty-four-hour supervision as a spoiled brat should be."

Sorrow bit down on his wrist. Hard, judging from the vicious glint in eyes ringed by glowing green—though Venom showed no reaction. Realizing the young woman had allowed her power reserves to run low to the point of endangering herself, Honor said nothing until Sorrow shoved at Venom's arm again. This time he allowed her to break the blood kiss.

Wiping the back of her hand over her mouth, Sorrow said, "I suppose you're going to tattle."

Venom used a handkerchief to clean off the neat puncture marks on his wrist before redoing his cuff. "You want this to be our secret?" It was a steel-edged question, his eyes hidden behind mirrored sunglasses an instant later. "Too bad you've got nothing that would interest me when it comes to bartering."

Honor would've ignored the taunt, having caught on to Venom's games. But Sorrow gave a sharp scream and jumped on the vampire. Laughing, he plucked her off and rose to his feet with a fluidity that was as reptilian as his eyes. "Careful," he said, brushing off his shirt as the young woman pushed herself upright, "or you might hurt my feelings."

Sorrow went very, very quiet. Then she *moved*.

Sucking in a breath, Honor ran to grab her gun out of her practice bag, but she didn't know which one of them to aim for once she had it in hand—or even if she'd hit the intended target. It was like watching two feral cats in the most deadly of dances. They moved so fast the eye couldn't quite track them, their strikes and counterstrikes flowing from one to the other with a grace that was breathtaking.

But while Sorrow fought with instinct born of primal rage, Venom was a cold, quiet predator who was playing with his prey.

Honor's eyes narrowed but she didn't lift the gun.

Games or not, the vampire wasn't hurting Sorrow. Not only that, he was allowing her to express the terrible fury inside her, an anger that had its roots in something far more sadistic than Venom's barbs. The young woman kicked, tried to claw and punch, even went airborne a couple of times, but she made no impact on the vampire, who simply *wasn't there*, his reaction time not human in any way, shape, or form.

It was beautiful. In a terrifying sort of way. "Can you move that fast?" she asked the man who'd come to stand beside her with a dark grace as old as Venom's power was young.

Dmitri slid his hands into the pockets of his stone-gray suit pants, his white shirt open at the collar to expose skin she wanted to lick and suck and bite. "Venom has a particular way of moving," he murmured in a voice that was pure sex, though he kept his attention on the fight. "Comes from the same place as his eyes."

It was difficult to breathe with him so close, and in a mood that wrapped her in warm honey and champagne and promises of sin dipped in chocolate. "Stop spreading sex pheromones around."

A faint smile that promised all sorts of debauched, decadent deeds. "I think we should spar, Honor. Winner gets to do whatever he or she likes to the loser."

Uh-huh. "You're an almost-immortal," she said, able to see that Sorrow was slowing down, "and you're Raphael's second in command."

"I'll keep to human speed." The kiss of exotic spice against her skin. "Give you your choice of blades while I have only my hands."

Knowing she was a sucker, but unable to get the image of dancing with Dmitri out of her head, she nodded. "You're on." That was when she saw Sorrow stagger.

Venom pulled back at the same instant, and suddenly they were no longer two feral creatures in motion, but a shockingly sexy vampire, with his hair messed up, his sunglasses gone, and his shirt ripped, and a petite Asian woman covered in sweat, her chest heaving as she braced her palms on her knees.

Striding closer, Honor showed Sorrow no mercy. "He kicked your ass."

Sorrow's head jerked up, long, silken strands of hair having escaped her ponytail to stick to her face. "I—"

"Be quiet." She flicked a hand at Venom. "Go away."

Whether he would've obeyed had Dmitri not been present was a moot question, because he inclined his head and left without a word.

"If you were an Academy student," Honor said, realizing this young woman needed a type of guidance no man could provide—not without slamming into Sorrow's jagged pride, "you'd be on your ass now because your instructor would've put you there."

Honor knew about pride, about clutching at the tattered shreds of it when you had nothing else left. But she also knew about survival. "Then you would've run or crawled twenty laps of the practice field before dragging yourself into bed, only to run twenty more when you woke."

"He—"

"Was taunting you, mocking you." She raised an eyebrow. "And you lost control. That loss of control will get you killed one day." Sorrow was dangerous, but without discipline, that strength could turn into a lethal liability. "Before we do any more sparring, we're going to work on your discipline."

Sorrow clenched her jaw, but managed to contain her temper this time.

Good girl. "Have you ever meditated?" The skill of dissociating her mind from the horrors inflicted on her body was one of the reasons Honor had come out of the assault sane.

Sorrow gave a stiff nod. "My grandmother taught me. I haven't tried it since . . ."

"I think you should." Honor put her hand on the young woman's shoulder. "I want you to go inside, have a long, hot bath, do whatever else it is that relaxes you, makes you happy."

Those brown eyes being overtaken by vivid green were bleak, all defiance leached away until she was suddenly heartbreakingly young. "Nothing does anymore."

"Do your best." Nightmares couldn't be vanquished overnight, and Sorrow's had altered her on a fundamental level. "Then sit down and attempt to meditate. Next time I'm here, we'll talk things over—because, Sorrow? You can't keep it all bottled up inside. I know." The notebook she'd never intended to use had become so important, a cathartic release that drew away the poison. "We'll find something that'll help you cope."

Sorrow swallowed. "Do you think I can?"

"Yes." Sorrow needed someone to have faith in her. "Oh, *yes,* sweetheart."

"Elena wanted to come see me," the other woman blurted out without warning. "I know she saved me . . . but she has wings." A shiver that shook her entire frame. "I couldn't."

"I'm sure she understands." Squeezing her shoulder, Honor had another thought. "How much time are you spending alone?"

"I'm never alone."

"Sorrow."

"It's not too bad. My family . . ." Her lip wobbled and she bit it hard enough to leave red crescents in the delicate flesh. "They don't know about Uram—the story is that I was attacked by a human crazy and infected with a dangerous virus.

I thought they'd reject me when the changes started to show, but they've been wonderful. Mom would be here every day if I'd let her."

"Then let her," Honor said, touching her hand to the girl's cheek. "Family builds a foundation, one that'll help you stand, fight." Honor had never had that foundation, so she understood its value on a level Sorrow couldn't comprehend.

Nodding, the young woman reached out with an impulsive hug. Honor returned the embrace, happy she was at the point where such sudden actions didn't cause her to flash back to the pit where Amos had trapped her. As she stroked her hand over the girl's back, her eyes met Dmitri's and something unsaid but understood passed between them—Sorrow was no longer simply his to watch over, but theirs.

It was as Dmitri and Honor were driving away from Sorrow's that he got the call.

"Dmitri." The rough male voice brought an ancient memory to life.

"Please." A lifted hand, the boy's back bloody from a vicious whipping.

"It's all right," Dmitri said, unable to feel pity, his heart stone, but aware this boy was another victim, no threat. "We won't hurt you."

"Is she dead?"

"Yes, the bitch is dead."

"Kallistos." He pulled over.

A rusty, painful-sounding laugh. "Very good."

Dead air for several seconds.

Dmitri waited, knowing Kallistos would get impatient—according to the people Jason had in Neha's court, this vampire, with his face and body that had mesmerized men and women alike over the centuries, had never quite mastered his temper.

"I hold the reins today, Dmitri." Kallistos's voice would never be smooth, his throat having been damaged at a critical juncture during his Making, but now it lost the veneer of sophistication. "You'll do as I say or this rather pretty angel will die a slow and painful death."

"Tell me what you want."

"I'm sending you directions. Drive. If I see any hint of wings, I'll gut him."

Directions came into Dmitri's in-box as the call ended. "This is only part of the route," he said, after giving Honor a précis of the conversation.

"He doesn't want to chance an angel flying ahead of you."

Dmitri considered his options, made a call to Illium. "Alert Raphael as soon as he's back in the city." The archangel was on his way back from a meeting. "You're too distinctive, Jason's gone, and I don't trust anyone else not to muck this up."

Illium cursed. "I'll fly out, meet Raphael partway."

Hanging up, Dmitri turned to Honor. "Are you armed?"

"Always."

Punching up the speed, he raced out of New Jersey and toward Philadelphia. More instructions came in as he drove, and it was seven hours later, the sky beginning to darken with the first faint streaks of the time between sunset and true night, that he found himself back in Manhattan. Mouth grim, he picked up the call as it came in.

"Have fun on your little drive?" Kallistos laughed, and it was the sound of metal grating.

Dmitri maintained his silence, guessing Kallistos would believe him to be in the grip of a rage that would disallow rational thinking. It didn't. Dmitri's hatred for Isis didn't blind him—not now, not after he'd bathed in her blood.

"I left you a present." Kallistos was almost giggling. "In one of the New York properties you own." The other vampire hung up.

Telling Honor what Kallistos had said, he did an illegal U-turn and headed out toward Englewood Cliffs. *Sire,* he said, able to speak to Raphael since the archangel was directly overhead. *If you and Illium will take these three*—he relayed the addresses—*I'll take care of the fourth.* He sent through the final address as well.

"We're taking the closest property," he said to Honor. "Raphael and Illium will reach the other locations much faster." Kallistos, he thought, was long gone.

"What are the chances this might be the spot?"

He considered the high fences, the lane in the back that

could be used to sneak onto the property. "It's relatively private, and decaying enough to suit Kallistos's sense of theater, from what we've seen so far." Increasing his speed, he blew past startled motorists.

If it had been an older angel at risk, Dmitri wouldn't have felt the overriding alarm he did now, but the one who'd been taken was young, his immortality not yet set in stone. Of course, most mortals or vampires would still be unable to cause him a fatal injury, but Kallistos was older than Dmitri; he had both the strength and the knowledge to murder an angel so vulnerable.

34

"We're here." Dark hair whipped off Dmitri's forehead as he took them down a somewhat derelict street, before turning in through a pair of open gates that led to a decaying apartment complex.

"I'm guessing the value is in the land?"

"Millions." Bringing the car to a halt behind the protective barrier of a pile of rubble, Dmitri got out and opened the trunk to retrieve a stunning blade too big to be covertly carried. No, this weapon was about power and intimidation.

It was, if she wasn't mistaken, a scimitar. However, she didn't get much of a good look at it before he was striding back, the weapon held to his side, his eyes flat with lethal intent. "Stay at my back, Honor. Kallistos is most likely gone, but we can't assume that."

"I'll cover you," she said, not arguing with the order because she knew about confronting your own monsters, and Kallistos was Dmitri's.

"No, stay literally at my back. A gunshot won't do me any significant damage, but could kill you."

The idea of Dmitri bleeding for her made Honor's hand

clench brutally on the butt of her gun, but again, she kept her silence, knowing time was of the essence. "Let's go."

He was a sleek shadow in front of her, one who ensured she was never exposed to anyone who might be watching them from the building. Honor didn't breathe until they'd traversed the open section to reach the door. He went in first, while she kept her eyes forward as she backed in behind him, gun pointed outward.

The only thing that met them inside was silence . . . and a broken angel. The boy—and yes, he was a boy still, his deathly pale face holding the fading softness of childhood—had been dumped on his front in the dusty lobby, his pale brown wings streaked with blood and dirt as they lay limp and crumpled on either side of him.

Wrong, there was something wrong with those wings.

Broken.

It was, she realized, feeling sick to her stomach, the only way to transport an unconscious angel if you didn't want to use a huge truck and draw unwelcome attention.

"Honor."

"I've got you covered."

Crouching down, Dmitri touched his fingers to the angel's cheek.

"He's warm." Putting down the scimitar, he used utmost care to turn the body, making sure not to further damage the boy's wings. "No heartbeat." But that didn't mean all hope was lost. *Raphael, how close are you?* he asked, having felt the archangel's mind touch his as he turned in through the gates.

Minutes away. Show me.

Dmitri opened his mind enough that Raphael was able to see through his eyes, assess the damage. *Give him your breath, Dmitri. He will not survive otherwise.*

Trusting Honor to maintain the guard, Dmitri began to breathe for the young angel, feeling that chest, heavy with the muscle necessary for flight, rise and fall under his touch. It wasn't more than five minutes later that Raphael walked into the building. The archangel didn't hesitate in kneeling on the dirty floor, his wings trailing in the accumulated dust and debris, to take the boy into his arms—replacing Dmitri's lips with his own.

An archangel's breath held incredible power.

As Dmitri watched, a faint blue glow suffused the place where Raphael's lips met the young angel's.

Rising, he picked up the scimitar and turned to glance at Honor, a hard-eyed hunter with a gun in her hands she wouldn't hesitate to use to protect the vulnerable—yet one who had the heart to feel pity for what her abuser had suffered as a child. Dmitri had no such softness inside him, but he accepted that it was an integral part of Honor, this complex woman with ancient knowledge in those eyes of midnight green.

Nodding at her to hold her position, he began to check the area to see if he could glean anything that might speak to Kallistos's whereabouts. Nothing but scuff marks in the dust from where the other vampire had dragged the young angel's body inside. Kallistos had left the same way he'd entered, making no effort to hide his prints. *Will he live?* he asked, seeing Raphael break the life-giving kiss.

Eyes of unearthly blue locked with his. *Yes. And he'll be whole once more. But he will need care of a kind the mortal world cannot provide.*

Dmitri nodded. *I'll organize transport to the Refuge.*

No, Dmitri. I must take him myself. The archangel rose, the angel's limp body in his arms. *We'll leave three days hence, after he has had a chance to regain a little strength.*

Elena?

She is my heart. She comes with me.

Dmitri had expected nothing else. *I will watch over your city, Sire.*

It was as Raphael was leaving that Honor stepped forward. "Wait."

Walking around to the archangel's other side as if she hadn't just halted the most powerful being in the country, she lifted up the young angel's hand. It was fisted. "He's hiding something in his palm."

Raphael glanced at Dmitri. "Force it open."

Dmitri managed not to break any bones, but he did have to bruise the boy to peel apart his fingers. To reveal the crushed but still recognizable remains of two sugar maple leaves. "Nothing to differentiate them from any other similar leaves," he said, picking up the remains of the greenery.

Cupping the angel's hand, Honor leaned closer. "He's written something on his palm."

"Eris," Raphael said, his vision acute. "The word is 'Eris.' "

Dmitri frowned. "Neha's consort? No one has seen him for centuries." Even as he spoke, his eyes fell once more on the leaves from the sugar maple tree. "Neha," he said, an old piece of knowledge jarred loose in his mind, "has no properties in this territory, but Eris had a liking for it before he went into seclusion." Whether that seclusion had been by choice was debatable, for Dmitri had heard rumors that Neha's consort had betrayed her with another woman, been punished for it for the past three hundred years.

It wasn't impossible that Kallistos's position in Neha's court had allowed him access to Eris, and, whatever else he had become, Isis's lover had proven intelligent. More so perhaps than Eris—who had always been Neha's gleaming ornament of a consort, a beloved plumed bird the archangel had showered with jewels and silks. "Kallistos must be using Eris's estate as his base."

"Go," Raphael said, gathering the hurt angel's body closer to his own. "Take all the men you need."

"Sire." *I won't leave the city vulnerable. There's still a chance Neha's hand is behind this.* The archangel hated everyone who had helped execute her daughter, Anoushka—Raphael was amongst that number. *This may be a trap to draw us away.*

I'm more than capable of defending my city, Dmitri.

And she is more than capable of poisoning the air itself if it suits her purpose. I'll go alone. I'm strong enough to handle Kallistos, even if he has more of his protovampires with him.

Raphael's blue eyes were relentless. *You will take Illium.*

I am not blinded by the past. His decisions were rational, coldly so.

Nevertheless. Raphael's expression changed the barest fraction. *I would not lose my second.*

Dmitri bowed his head in a slight nod. "Honor," he said after the archangel walked out with his living cargo, "I'm going to take the chopper to Vermont—"

Stalking to stand face-to-face with him, she pushed at his chest. "If you're even thinking about leaving me behind, think again."

He should've stood firm, would have had it been any other woman. But Honor . . . she had her hooks so deep into him that it made the *old*, merciless part of him go motionless, examine the situation—and his sudden vulnerability—with icy focus. To destroy this strange, wonderful something between them, all it would take were a few well-chosen words of utmost cruelty.

Honor was smart, but she was also tender of heart. She didn't know the depths to which he could go, the wounds he could inflict. He could make her bleed without ever raising a hand. "I am not a good man, Honor," he said, touching his fingers to her jaw.

Instead of shying, she leaned into the touch. "You're my man."

You're my man.

The echo of Ingrede's words tangled with Honor's, but then, his wife had been tender of heart, too. He'd protected that heart with all his strength . . . and he knew that despite the deep weakness she created in him, he would do so once more with Honor. It was a strange thing, to feel such tenderness again, to know he was capable of it. "Come. It's time to beard the monster in his den."

V enom was the one who most often piloted the chopper for use by the Seven, but Dmitri knew how to do it—he'd been curious when the machines had been invented. Though he found more pleasure in handling cars, he'd kept up the useful skill. Now, having delayed only long enough to change and gather weapons, he lifted the black machine off the helipad situated not on top of the Tower, but several floors below, on a balcony cut *into* part of the building.

"Illium?" Honor's voice came through crystal clear, both of them miked, ears protected against the noise of the blades.

"He's already on his way." The blue-winged angel was one of the fastest fliers amongst his kind and would beat them to Vermont. "I've been in contact with the Made who live in and around the general region of Eris's property."

"I rang a couple of hunter friends nearby, too." Her scent twined around him in the confines of the cockpit, fine ropes he knew he'd never break. "None of them had heard anything."

"Neither had my people—but Kallistos is no youth." He wouldn't have done anything to draw attention to himself near his lair. "I'm certain we'll find him there."

"One way or another," Honor said, reaching out to brush her fingers over his jaw in an unexpected caress, "tonight will finish this."

"How do you understand?" That it savaged him to realize this small piece of Isis survived when his family's ashes had been scattered by the wind so long ago, entire civilizations had risen and fallen in that time.

No longer touching him, she said, "I know you, Dmitri." A fisted hand over her heart, her voice soft, potent with raw emotion. "Right here, so deep it feels as if you've been a part of me since the instant I took my first breath."

Reaching out, he brought her fist to his lips, pressed a kiss to the knuckles. She robbed him of words, of sophistication, until he was once more the man he'd been with his wife— harder, deadlier, but with the capacity to feel emotions both beautiful and terrifying. He would spill blood for the mortal by his side, split open his veins if she asked, slay demons and enemies until the world shivered at the sound of his name.

But he would not mourn her. Because a man didn't survive such a loss twice.

Having landed far enough from the house that their arrival should've gone unnoticed, Dmitri looked up as they began to navigate the heavy woods that led to Eris's estate, attempting to spot Illium. Not even a hint against the starless night sky, but when Dmitri said, *Illium*, the response was immediate.

I see you. I've scouted the house—it's silent, but there's no way to know if Kallistos lies within.

Even if he isn't there now, he'll return to his lair sooner or later.

Breaking the mental contact, he relayed Illium's words to Honor. She nodded, the gun she'd chosen as her main weapon held to her side. He preferred the blade. The scimitar he carried was an old favorite, and it often sat on display in Raphael's home at the Refuge—but the last time he'd been at the angelic stronghold, Dmitri had felt driven to take it down, bring it to New York.

"The runes on your blade," Honor asked as they continued to walk through the thick quiet of the woods, the rustling of the leaves the only sound. "What do they mean?"

"You should know," he said with a provocative smile. "It was another witch who put them on the blade for me, after all."

A green-eyed glance as sharp as the gleaming edge on his scimitar. "Careful, or I might decide to turn you into a toad."

Hell with it.

Gripping the back of her neck, he brought her to him for the kiss he'd been wanting to claim for hours. A long dark tangling of tongues, he indulged in her until she shuddered, her lips ripe and swollen. "After this is over," she said, touching her fingers to her kiss-wet mouth, "I think I want to spend a month locked in a bedroom with you."

His lips curved. "That could be arranged." The bedroom games he wanted to play with Honor were beyond decadent, beyond sinful. "The house should be coming up soon."

"There," Honor whispered a bare two minutes later.

Hidden in the midst of what felt like thousands of sugar maple trees shivering in the whispering night wind, the house sat private and cocooned from the outside world. Though they'd come out behind it, Honor had no doubt what she was seeing accurately reflected the overall architecture. Despite the serene setting, it was no fairy tale, no elegant retreat. It reminded Honor of nothing so much as a hulking beast, a monument to gothic excess.

Two snarling gargoyles guarded the back steps, their fangs bared and claws unsheathed. From what she could make out in the dark, that was simply the beginning—she was fairly certain more gargoyles peered out from the roof, including a giant batlike creature silhouetted against the pitch-black sky.

The ivy that covered most of the building added to the impression of decaying menace, as did the spread of leaves deep on the ground. As if decades' worth of forest debris had collected on top of each other, until now, the ground was forever lost. Walking across the leaves—soft this time of year, concealing rather than betraying their passage—Honor kept her gun in hand as Dmitri's blade cut a dark wound through the night, his stride as confident and quiet as a hunting cat's.

She touched his arm when they reached the bottom of steps that led onto a narrow porch, pointed. "Look."

No ivy or moss covered the central part of the stone steps. As if they had been used recently and often. When she bent down and cautiously flicked on her flashlight, shielding the beam with her palm, she was able to glean a faint path in amongst the organic matter that covered what may once have been a manicured lawn. A single nod to Dmitri, before she flicked off the flashlight and they headed slowly and silently up the steps and to the back door of the monstrosity of a house.

Dmitri angled his head.

It was strange—in a wonderful kind of way—how perfectly she understood him. Bending, she duckwalked to the nearest window. She could see nothing beyond, but she kept going, checking window after window.

The only thing that lay beyond was a stygian darkness.

Since the house was enormous, that meant nothing, but she turned and straightened up enough to shake her head at Dmitri before moving past him to check the other side, while he kept watch, a silent, dangerous predator almost indistinguishable from the night. It was at the third window that she saw it.

35

Heading back to Dmitri, she whispered the results in his ear, his scent familiar, welcome. "Light appeared a second ago. Flickering, as if from a candle." The glow of it had been diffuse in a way no electric lamp could mimic. "Deep inside the house."

Dmitri raised his hand . . . toward one of the gargoyles on the roof.

Wings unfurled and Illium flew in silence toward the front, ready to block any attempt at escape.

"Could be a diversion," she said, heart pounding from the rush of adrenaline caused by the unexpected sight. "Kallistos might be waiting behind the door."

Dmitri shook his head. "I smell nothing to indicate that, and my senses are acute." Reaching out, he twisted the door-knob with care. When it opened under his hand, he said, "A trap then." His lips held a faint smile. "Don't get hurt, Honor, or you'll be waking up with fangs."

She froze. "I haven't been tested." All short-listed Candidates were tested for *something* during the acceptance process. Theories as to what ranged the gamut, but the tests themselves were compulsory.

"Blood," Dmitri murmured, "is not difficult to obtain, especially when it comes to active hunters."

"Ever heard of privacy?" she muttered under her breath as he pushed the door wide and slid inside.

She followed him—into unrelieved darkness, the light she'd glimpsed hidden by the arrangement of the walls. Cutting through it with an unerring step, Dmitri made his way to the hallway. She shadowed him, rising up on tiptoe when he lowered his lips to her ear. "Stay out of sight. There's no reason for him to believe I brought you." At her nod, he added, "And privacy is such a modern concept."

Deciding she'd yell at him later, she used every ounce of her skill to conceal her presence as they moved down the hallway, while Dmitri did the opposite, striding down with heavy, booted footsteps until the light came into view. It originated from a room that flowed off the hall toward the front of the house, had been reflected by the ornamental mirror opposite.

That mirror, carved with grapes and mythical creatures covered in gold, showed her nothing beyond a candle flame as Dmitri passed out of the doorway and into the dark beyond, while she pressed her back to the wall, ready to go in when needed.

"Dmitri." A rough kind of a voice, raspy yet deep.

"Your throat never recovered."

"I shouldn't have displeased her as I did." A sound that might have been a sigh.

"Your mistress wasn't known for her patience—or the care with which she handled her toys."

The civility of the conversation made the hairs rise on the back of Honor's neck. She knew full well she was listening to two predators circling each other. Only one of them would survive the night.

Kallistos had lost none of his beauty in the intervening years. He had, in fact, grown further into that delicate bone structure that showcased eyes of brilliant copper, and lips so soft and well-shaped, more than one angel had been seduced by their perfection. His body, too, was a thing of beauty. Slender, but with incredible muscle tone—the air barely stirred when he moved, his tread that of a dancer.

"An exquisite creature," Isis had called him the day she took Dmitri to her bed—and forced Kallistos to watch.

"I have been an ill host." Kallistos waved his hand toward a tray set with a crystal decanter filled with bloodred liquid that shimmered in the candlelight. "We are two sophisticated men, are we not?"

Dmitri took in the flush high on Kallistos's cheekbones, the glitter in those copper eyes, asked, "How long since you slept?"

The other man leaned back against the wall beside a massive fireplace. Sliding his hands into the pockets of suit pants of a deep brown that appeared almost black in the candlelight, he angled his face to its best advantage. It was, Dmitri knew, an automatic act, but not an unconscious one—because as Dmitri had learned to use the scent lure as an offensive weapon, Kallistos had learned to use his face and body.

Now, he parted those perfect lips the slightest fraction. "There is a large bed upstairs . . . quite ready for use." Sensual invitation in every word, the confidence of a man who had been able to bend both male and female to his advantage for centuries.

Even Isis, Dmitri thought, had cosseted him when she wasn't torturing him. It was no wonder the young human men the vampire had lured to his lair had come so sweetly to their deaths, surrendering their bodies for him to do with as he wished. "You failed in your attempt to Make vampires."

"I thought to build an army." A smile designed to make his audience smile with him, to see him as a pretty adornment, no threat at all. "A silly premise, I soon came to realize, but why not use the slaves I already had? It was fun leaving presents on your doorstep."

Pushing off the wall with a look full of delight, he circled around the sofa until they stood only a few feet apart, his gait elegant. "Then it struck me—I didn't need to have an army to destroy you." He spread his hands. "All I had to do was take someone you loved and make you watch while I slaughtered her."

Memories, painful and brutal, threatened to roar to the surface, but Dmitri had had almost a thousand years to learn to think past the pain. "You were lying in a pool of your own blood when we discovered you." It was a quiet reminder, a final chance. "She'd whipped you until she'd shredded the skin off your back, then ridden your cock while you screamed."

A jagged anger marred the flawless lines of Kallistos's face. "You didn't understand her, peasant that you were."

"And you were naught to her but a pretty toy," Dmitri said with cruel honesty, "something she would have perhaps regretted breaking, but only for as long as it took her to find a new bauble."

Copper burned hot, but Kallistos didn't strike, didn't react. "She broke your bauble, didn't she?" A vicious smile. "They said your wife squealed like a stuck pig while they rutted on her."

Rage seared his bloodstream, but he would never give Kallistos the satisfaction of seeing what it did to him to think of his gentle, loving Ingrede's final moments on the earth. "Do you still love her, Kallistos?"

A dark silence, followed by a simple, "Yes."

"Then there is nothing more to say." He struck out with the scimitar, aiming to decapitate.

But Kallistos was no longer there, having moved with feline grace to shield himself behind a sofa. "Careful," the vampire said, pulling a gleaming sword from its hiding place by the heavy piece of furniture, "or you'll never find out where she is."

Dmitri breathed deep, caught Honor's scent near the doorway. "You have nothing."

A mocking smile. "It wasn't difficult to take her. All I had to do was make a phone call threatening her younger brothers." A smug satisfaction that was as chilling as it was impossible. "She slipped out past your guard and right into my arms, the delicious little thing."

Honor didn't have younger brothers. But Sorrow did.

Ice steeled his blood. "Surrender to me now," he said, catching tendrils of unexpected scent that told him Kallistos still had living protovampires at his command, "and I'll make your death an easy one." Honor was out there alone, but the instant Dmitri went to her, he would give Kallistos another target.

Kallistos laughed again, a rough, broken, painful sound. "It amuses me to know you'll live the rest of your life knowing she died a slow, painful death—after servicing me until I tired of her. It's a pity you didn't arrive an hour earlier." A smile that aimed to draw heart's blood. "She screamed your name at the end."

Dmitri went after Kallistos without warning, shoving the raw fury of his emotions to the back of his mind. That would come later. After Kallistos was dead.

Avoiding the lethal strike, the other vampire twisted and almost flew over the sofa to land on his feet on the other side. "Neha," Kallistos said as Dmitri circled around to face him, "is many things. One of which is a master blade fighter."

"Her skills didn't help her daughter," Dmitri taunted, aware of sounds in the hallway, bodies starting to stream into the room behind him, blocking the exit.

"Anoushka was arrogant." Kallistos came at him in a blur that sliced a line across Dmitri's T-shirt, soaking the black material the dark red of his blood. "I, however, don't care about showing off. Only causing you pain."

Dmitri swept out again, slid the wrong way on a thick rug. Kallistos used the opportunity to cut a deep gash on his back, the blade skating agonizingly off his spine. "How does it feel to be the weaker one, Dmitri?" A hissing question. "She begged you to spare her life, *begged* you!"

Ten of the young, weak protovampires with guns. No more sounds in the hallway.

"She was a bitch who deserved to die." With those cold words, he began to move in earnest. But rather than heading toward Kallistos, he spun out toward the edges of the room, cutting down the protovampires who thought to gun him down. But he was too fast, his blade sweet fire through the air, spurting blood onto the walls as Kallistos screamed and lunged after him.

So, Isis's former lover bore some kind of a twisted love for his creations after all.

Using his feet to push off a wall splattered with red, he flipped over Kallistos and down into a crouch below the barrage of bullets. But one caught him in the arm nonetheless. Shaking off the pain, he sliced out with the scimitar again, amputating his attacker's legs at the knees. The vampire was too young, too badly Made to survive it, his screaming high-pitched, endless.

The survivors were already shooting . . . but their shots suddenly went wild, their hearts blown out from behind by a hunter with deep green eyes burning with a fiery center.

Raising his head to see Kallistos rushing toward Honor, lip curled into a snarl, he shifted position to block the other vampire. The clang of steel rang through the room, vibrated down his wounded arm, but Dmitri had fought with body parts missing. This was nothing.

Kicking out at Kallistos's knees, he grazed him with the blade as Kallistos twisted out of the way and ran not toward the doorway, but toward the windows of thick old-fashioned glass that looked out over the grounds. Not stopping his head-long momentum, the other vampire slammed through the glass and out into the yard in a shattering cascade of sound and blood.

"Honor!"

"I'm fine. Go!"

Jumping through the same hole in the glass, he rolled up into a standing position to find himself facing a Kallistos whose face bore a blood-soaked smile. "Clever, Dmitri. Manipulating me until I'd tipped my hand . . . or maybe I was manipulating you." Lifting two fingers to his mouth, he whistled.

Barking filled the air and suddenly hounds as black as night were boiling out from the woods toward the front of the house, their canines razor sharp and their aim obvious. Flowing around Kallistos, they came at Dmitri—but not all of them. Part of the pack headed into the house, likely drawn by the spilled blood . . . or by Honor's scent. Because Kallistos was laughing, a look in his eyes that said he'd played his endgame.

Seeing a flash of blue in his peripheral vision, Dmitri yelled, "Inside!" He sliced out at the hounds at the same time, cutting their thickly muscled bodies in half, but they continued to pour out of the woods. If he fell to the ground, they'd tear him to pieces, probably eventually succeed in the decapitation that was the only thing that would end his near-immortal life.

"A pity I won't get to personally kill your bitch," Kallistos spat. "But I'll enjoy the thought of her mauled body nonetheless."

Dmitri continued to cut down the hounds, the pile of bodies growing ever deeper around him. *Don't you dare die, Honor.*

He knew Illium would do everything in his power to protect her, but it destroyed him that he was once more unable to protect the woman he loved. That was when he heard rapid gunshots from inside the house and remembered that, while Honor might touch him with the same gentleness Ingrede once had, she was a hunter, honed and blooded, no one's victim.

He bared his teeth in a feral grin.

My Honor.

Slicing out with the scimitar in one hand as he pulled his own gun with the other, he took out so many of the hounds that the others turned wary.

Not enough to back away, but enough to hesitate.

Using their hesitation, he lifted the gun and shot Kallistos in the face.

The vampire screamed and went to his knees, having obviously not expected an assault from the modern weapon. Dmitri cut his way through the dogs to put the gun to Kallistos's temple. The vampire was broken on a fundamental level, would never recover.

Isis had done this to him.

And so Dmitri would give him mercy.

But Kallistos clawed out with his hands before Dmitri could pull the trigger, smashing the gun from his hand and unbalancing him enough that he fell to the ground with Kallistos's mutilated face above him. Dropping the scimitar because it was no use in such close quarters, he fought bare-handed as Kallistos gouged and tore at him with hands that weren't human.

Feeling those nails cut into his flesh, he realized the man had been hiding some kind of a weapon tipped with short but razor sharp, serrated points and worn over his knuckles. Now it acted as a shredder, ripping through Dmitri's chest and the side of his neck. He blocked Kallistos when the blinded vampire would've clamped his hand around Dmitri's neck and, pulling a short knife from his belt, cut Kallistos's throat.

Blood gushed hot and wet onto his face, but Kallistos was older than Dmitri by about two decades. He didn't go down. Instead, clamping his free hand over his throat, he slashed out with the one he'd turned lethal. "I'll end you." Spittle bubbled around his mouth, a fine red foam. "Like you ended her."

Dmitri managed to grab Kallistos's wrist, halting his strike. That was when he felt a hound's teeth on his foot, beyond where Kallistos straddled his body.

36

Kicking out and hitting a thick, solid body, he dropped his grip on Kallistos's arm, leaving his face and throat unprotected as he put all his strength behind thrusting the knife he still held into the spot just below Kallistos's heart. Hitting it, he wrenched upward, cutting the other vampire's heart in half.

Agony seared into him as those rough metal points dug into his face, raking across, but the impact of the blow faded toward the end as Kallistos jerked, blood pouring out of his chest and his throat at the same time. Twisting the knife deeper, until the vampire's heart was nothing but pulp, Dmitri pushed the body off himself, snarling at the dogs at the same time.

They retreated . . . but their eyes were on the fallen Kallistos, who twitched as he tried to heal himself. Dmitri knew that if he was left undisturbed, he would rise again. Vampires of their power and strength weren't easy to kill. However, if Dmitri walked away, the hounds would tear Kallistos apart like a hunk of butchered meat.

"This one is my special pet." A smile as Isis stroked long, gleaming nails over the slender body of a boy barely become a man. That boy, tied to the bed, arched up into her touch . . .

then screamed as she dug her nails into his balls and ripped them off.

No, Dmitri thought. He could not leave Kallistos to suffer—even after the horrors the vampire had committed.

Sorrow.

His gut clenched, anguish and rage burning in his throat, and he almost walked away, leaving the other vampire to the hounds' slavering hunger.

A flicker of memory, of Kallistos at the start of Dmitri's imprisonment.

A soothing balm over his back.

"She can be demanding, I know, but she is a good mistress."

The young vampire had tried to make his life easier, even distracted Isis from landing a blow that would've taken Dmitri's eye at a stage that meant it might not have healed.

"Help me."

Kallistos had said that to Dmitri once, after Isis had hurt him so badly, he hadn't been able to rise to feed. Dmitri, in chains, had been helpless to do anything at the time, but today he would.

Grabbing the discarded scimitar, he brought the blade down on Kallistos's throat. A single hard strike was all it took to separate the head from the body, but Dmitri made extra certain Kallistos would never again rise, using a shorter blade to carve out the vampire's damaged heart. As he turned to head toward Honor, having no choice but to leave Kallistos's body to the dogs, he saw her run out of the house with Illium, guns blazing.

The hounds stood no chance.

"No one can know of this," he said to Honor as he examined the nascent fangs of one of the protovampires inside the house, no longer surprised at what some would chance for immortality.

"I understand." She crouched down beside him, that strange compassion on her face. "It wouldn't only rock the power structure of the world if angels were seen to be vulnerable, it might give someone else ideas."

"Yes." So intelligent, he thought, and with such a clarity to her thinking, Honor was a woman who would be an asset by his side, quite aside from the fact that he wanted only to hold her, breathe in her scent, hear the living beat of her heart. But first they had to examine the house room by room. It proved to be empty of living inhabitants, but they discovered several decaying bodies buried in shallow graves below the house, evidence of Kallistos's failed attempts to Make vampires.

However, that wasn't the biggest discovery.

"Dmitri?" The questioning female voice came on the line as he stood with Illium and Honor surrounded by the dark scent of death. "I missed your call—I was at my brothers' music recital."

A kick to his chest, radiating out through his body. "You're safe."

"Is everything okay?"

"Yes." He passed the phone to Honor, needing a minute to rebuild the emotional shields that had somehow crashed at the sound of Sorrow's voice.

It wasn't until evening the next day that they returned to New York, having stayed behind to ensure everything was processed and cleaned up, until no one would ever know what had taken place in that quiet spot surrounded by the bright green of hundreds of sugar maples. However, he didn't pilot the chopper to Manhattan and the Tower, but to a derelict condemned building not far from the New York–Connecticut border. "Are you sure?" he asked the woman with eyes full of mysteries he wanted to explore as she lay tumbled, pleasured, and smiling in his bed.

"Yes," Honor said. Amos, she'd realized, wasn't the monster who haunted her.

It was the cage he'd put her in.

Getting out of the gleaming machine, she waited for Dmitri to join her and then she led them into the bowels of hell. The building was stickered with Do Not Enter signs, but she strode forward and through to an internal door that led to a cement-floored basement.

"He told me," she whispered, nausea churning in her stomach, "that he planned to do up the place, turn it into an old-fashioned *salon* where only the privileged would gather, but

first he had to make sure all his guests had the right appetites."
Appetites that meant Honor had almost died before Amos ever
got the walls painted, much less replaced the mildewed carpet
and broken floorboards.

A male hand closing over the doorknob. "I'll go first."

"I need to—"

"Face your demons." Dmitri brushed her hair off her face
with unexpected tenderness. "That doesn't mean you have to
do it alone and unshielded."

Looking into that face that still bore remnants of the brutal
gouges from the fight, she realized that he needed to do this,
too, to protect her. She couldn't pretend his protectiveness, his
care, was unwelcome. Not here. Not when it was Dmitri.
But— "Together." She touched her hand to his. "I won't hide
from any part of this, not even behind your broad shoulders."

A long, taut pause before he nodded and opened the door
that led down into her own personal hellhole. But as she navigated the steps, Dmitri by her side, her nausea was wiped out
by anger, cutting and bright . . . and then, as she stepped into
the pitch-black room where she'd been held and tortured for
two long months, by pride.

I survived this.

The thought had barely passed through her mind when the
thing came at her out of the dark, teeth bared and fingers
clawed, eyes glowing red.

She began to shoot, yelling, "No!" when Dmitri would've
lunged past her. "I have it!"

The creature kept coming and she kept shooting, the noise
deafening in the enclosed space. Finally it lay wheezing on the
floor. Taking out her flashlight, she aimed the beam at whatever it was that had made this foul place its lair, never moving
her gun off it.

"You." A bubbling, blood-filled word.

He no longer looked anything like the photos Dmitri had
shown her, his elegance buried under animalistic hunger. The
skin had retracted from his mouth to bare his gums, his fangs;
his face was hollow, falling into itself. As was his body under
the tattered remains of his shirt, his broken ribs not yet completely fused, other parts of his torso pulverized with bullet
wounds.

"I had you," Amos whispered.

"No," she said again, speaking to Dmitri.

"Honor."

"He's no danger." Walking to look down at Amos's emaciated form, she realized he'd somehow gotten himself here after Jiana carved him up. However, once safely hidden, he hadn't had the strength to go out to feed, even as his body cannibalized itself to heal his massive injuries.

A pitiful creature.

But one with a reservoir of strength.

He lunged up at her with a hissing roar. Not losing her cool, she emptied her clip into his heart, blowing it to smithereens. "Will he rise again?"

"No. He was too weak." Dmitri's hand touched her hair. "It's done."

Turning, she looked around the smoke-filled room and saw just that. A room. "Yes. It's done."

Exhausted and emotionally drained, she didn't protest when Dmitri flew them to the Tower and took her to his suite.

"I had a new bed delivered," he told her as he drew her into the shower and began to help her strip. "You'll be the only woman who ever sleeps in it."

He owned her heart, this vampire with his scars and his darkness. "Come here." Cupping his face as he leaned down toward her, she rubbed her nose against his, felt his body stiffen for an inexplicable second before he took her mouth in a raw claiming of a kiss, the kind of sinful, debauched kiss no good man would ever give to his woman. The resulting shower was decadent and welcome, but her body gave out when she hit the bed.

They wanted to dishonor her, the vampires with the hot eyes and the hands that roamed over her flesh as they pinned her to the wall. She knew that, understood that. "Forgive me, Dmitri," she whispered inside her mind, and turned quiescent.

They laughed. "There, she wants it. I knew these peasants were all happy to spread their thighs for a real man." Rough, clawing hands pushing up her skirts, another pair mauling her breasts.

In spite of her shame, her rage, she told herself to be quiet, to not fight.

But then the third vampire walked into the nursery and came out with Caterina in his arms. "So sweet and soft," he murmured, his tone chilling in its gentleness. "I have heard such blood is a delicacy."

Quiet, quiet, she told herself even as fury turned her blood to flame. If she protested, the monster would know he held a piece of her heart in his hands and he would hurt Caterina even more. But her silence couldn't protect her child, and she screamed in horror—"No! Please!—as the vampire lowered his head to Caterina's tiny neck and began to shred it like a dog. Her baby's terrified cry pierced the air, pierced the silence, pierced her until she bled.

Jamming her elbow into the nose of one of the vampires who held her, she stabbed the other with the kitchen knife she'd hidden in her skirts when they came into her home with such evil in their eyes. "Let her go!" Escaping because they hadn't expected defiance, she wrenched Caterina from the feeding vampire's arms. "No, no. Oh, no." Her poor baby was dead, her throat so much meat, her little body already cooling.

"No!" It was the keening cry of a mother as the monsters tore at her again, but she would not release Caterina. Not even when they broke her ribs, shoved her to the ground, and pushed up her skirts. She didn't care what they did to her, not as long as they didn't touch Caterina . . . and didn't discover Misha.

"Stay quiet, Misha," she pleaded in her mind. "Stay quiet, so quiet." He'd been playing in the little space below the roof that was his "secret" place, and she'd yelled for him to hide when she'd first seen the vampires. There had been no time to get to Caterina, but she had hoped they would not be so vicious as to harm a babe.

She felt no pain when they hurt her, felt nothing, every ounce of her being concentrated on listening for her son, on holding her daughter close. "I couldn't protect her, Dmitri," she whispered in a soundless voice as the vampires used her.

"I'm sorry." She would die here, she knew that. And whatever else, he would not forgive that. He was so stubborn, would carry the wound in his heart till the day he took his last breath, her beautiful, loyal husband who had loved her even when an angel came to woo her.

A whisper of sound.

Looking up, she saw Misha peering over the edge of the roof space. With her eyes, she told him to be quiet, to be still. But he was his father's son. Screaming in rage, he jumped on the back of one of her attackers, sinking strong little teeth into the vampire's neck. The vampire went to rip off her son and throw him to the floor as she fought to escape, to protect him.

"No!" One of the others caught Misha's screaming, twisting form in his arms. "She wants the older child alive!" He squeezed her sweet boy tight as she begged him not to hurt her child. But the monster only laughed, continuing to crush Misha until his tiny, fierce body went limp.

Then, finished with her, they broke her spine so she couldn't escape as the house filled with smoke, with flame. She died with her baby in her arms, holding on to the end. But there was no peace for her soul, her mind filled with the echo of Misha's screams, the sight of Caterina's ravaged neck, and Dmitri's haunting words when Isis's men came for him. "Will you forgive me, Ingrede? For what I must do?"

Such a proud man, her husband. So very, very proud. "You fight a battle," she'd whispered, touching her hand to his cheek. "You do this to protect us. There is nothing to forgive."

So he had gone, her Dmitri, gone to the bed of a being who saw him only as a thing to be used. And he had promised to come back, no matter what it took. But now, she wouldn't be waiting for him.

His heart would break.

"Honor!" Dmitri shook the woman who had slept so warm beside him through the night, trying to wake her as she cried great, hiccuping tears.

Then she turned, burying her face into his chest, and he knew she was already awake. Her tears, they were those of a woman who had lost everything. Utter devastation in every hot, wet drop as she cried and cried and cried, her body shaking so hard, he worried she would shatter.

She wouldn't hear his words, wouldn't be gentled, so he simply held her, tighter than he ever had before. She didn't fight him, didn't do anything but cry—until his chest was wet with her desolation and he wanted to tear something apart. But he didn't tell her to stop. Amos's death, he thought, had been the catalyst for this, and if she needed it to complete her healing, so be it.

So he held this hunter whose midnight green eyes said she saw him, shadows and all, who touched him as Ingrede used to do, who made him imagine an impossible truth, held her so close that she was a part of his very soul.

37

Honor sat with her legs dangling over the side of the rail-ingless balcony outside Dmitri's office. It would be a terrify-ing plunge if she fell, but she figured one of the angels below would catch her. Of course, she wasn't about to take the chance—there was no way in hell she planned to die anytime soon.

Not after it had taken her so long to come back from the last time.

Her breath caught in her throat at her conscious acceptance of an impossible idea . . . except it wasn't. It was as real as the Manhattan skyline in front of her, steel against a cerulean sky streaked with white. The memories had cascaded one on top of the other since she woke in the early hours of this morning, crying so hard that her chest remained sore, her eyes swollen and her throat raw.

He is my husband.

Perhaps not in law, but as far as her soul was concerned, Dmitri belonged to her.

Always.

When the door slid open at her back, she glanced over, expecting the man at the center of her thoughts. It wasn't. She smiled at the hunter who came to sit beside her. "How did you get up here?" Security was airtight.

Ashwini swung her feet. "I sweet-talked Illium."

"I didn't know you knew him."

"I didn't. Now I do." Dark brown eyes full of liquid intensity settled on Honor. "He said you needed a friend. I knew that already, but I pretended it was news. What's wrong?"

Honor turned her face to the wind, letting it push back her unbound hair, tangle it into as wild a mess as Dmitri made of it in bed. "You'll never believe me."

A long silence before Ashwini said, "Remember the first time we met?"

The memory was crystal clear. It had been in a raucous bar filled with hunters and mercenaries. They'd laughed over drinks, eaten deep-fried everything, sowed the seeds of a deep, abiding friendship. And then, as they were walking out the door— "You called me an old soul," she whispered. "A lost soul."

"Still so old you make my chest hurt"—Ash leaned in so their shoulders touched for a moment—"but no longer lost."

Shuddering, she braced her palms on the rough surface on which they sat. There would be no more whispers, she knew, from a life long gone—there was no longer any need, the barrier between past and present wiped out in the storm of her tears until she saw the woman she'd been as clearly as the one she was now.

The reawakened memories caused her agonizing pain. The thought of losing Caterina and Misha . . . she couldn't bear it. But she'd remembered, understood something far more beautiful, too. Loved, she had been *loved*. And, she thought, remembering the arms that had held her so very tight this morning, she was loved again. He might never be able to say it, the lethal blade her husband had become, but she knew.

What she didn't know was whether her beautiful, wounded Dmitri was ready to hear what she had to tell him.

Dmitri watched the two women sitting out on the balcony and checked for the third time to ensure the wing of angels waiting below were on alert to catch if necessary. "I should go out there and drag them both inside," he said to Raphael when the archangel walked in to stand beside him.

"Yes," Raphael said. "It should be a most amusing sight."

Dmitri shot the archangel a dark look. "Your consort is a bad influence."

"My consort is now joining your woman."

Turning, Dmitri saw Elena come to a somewhat wobbly but safe landing on the balcony. She pumped her fist in the air before sitting down next to the long-legged hunter with the dark eyes who was Honor's best friend—and, according to the reports they had on her, an extremely gifted individual when it came to those senses that weren't accepted by most humans. Immortals, however, had been alive too long to dismiss such things as fancy. And so they kept watch on Ashwini. "Janvier courts her."

"I think it's time to pull him in." *It'll give Venom a long enough period to ensure a smooth transfer.*

Dmitri nodded, feeling a wild kind of peace within him when Honor laughed, her body half hidden behind the midnight and dawn spread of Elena's wings. "It'll be good for Venom to work alongside Galen." The vampire was strong but young and could be impulsive; while Galen was as stable and centered as a rock.

"I agree." Raphael's own wings rustled as he resettled them. "I spoke to Aodhan—he hasn't changed his mind."

Dmitri thought about the extraordinary, fractured angel, wondered if he'd find what he sought in this bold, brash city with its pulsing heartbeat of life. "Do you think this is the start of his healing?"

"Perhaps." A quiet pause. "We will be his shield, Dmitri."

"Yes." *The young angel?*

Resting. His will is strong—this won't break him.

Good.

Outside, the women continued to talk, their hair tangling together in the playful wind, Elena's brilliant near-white strands against Ashwini's sleek black and Honor's softer ebony curls. It was a sight that would make any man take notice. "We aren't who we were even two years ago, Raphael."

"Are you sorry about this change?"

"No."

*   *   *

Honor challenged Dmitri to a sparring session that afternoon and lost. He took her to his bed that night, laid her out for his delectation. When she bit her lower lip and whispered, "I thought you said something about a velvet whip?" in a voice that held both anticipation and the tang of sensual nervousness, he took her mouth with a voracious need that had her scenting the air with the sweet musk of her arousal.

Drawing it in, he made her lie on her back—her unbound hands holding on to the bars of the headboard—and began to kiss, to taste, every tiny inch of her, from the smooth warmth of her brow to the hollow of her throat and the tight furl of her nipples. There, he stopped, took his time, until her nipples were wet and pouting, before moving to the dip of her navel, the quivering nub of flesh between her thighs, the curve of her knee, and finally, the graceful arch of her foot.

Breath coming out in ragged gasps, she shook her head when he told her to turn over.

"Honor." It was a command.

"No." Haunting eyes full of defiance that was an invitation, her body so sensitized that when he ran his finger lightly between her legs, she jerked up, her eyes clenched tight and her muscles tensed in readiness for a shattering peak. *"Dmitri."*

"No," he said, removing his touch and dipping his head to speak with his lips against her ear. "You don't get rewarded for misbehavior."

Unrepentant, she kissed the side of his face, his jaw. Soft, wet kisses that made his cock throb in the black pants he still wore, while she lay bare to him, her skin hot silk, her blood warm and aroused and whispering to him of an erotic addiction he couldn't afford to indulge.

"Does bribery work?" Another kiss.

He pressed his hand to her abdomen, nudging her flat onto her back again. "That's another rule you've broken." He'd ordered her to lie motionless.

"You're not going to have mercy on me, are you?" It was a husky question as he rose from the bed and went to a closet . . . but she kept the promise she'd made to him at the start, stayed in bed.

"You should know better than to expect it from me," he said, closing his hand around the handle of a soft velvet whip he'd never before used, as he hadn't used anything in this room. He'd built a bed for Ingrede, and in the same way, he'd put this room together for Honor.

Now, running his hand over the whip, he flicked the tails over his arm to ensure it would cause her no pain, only the most excruciating pleasure. Her eyes went to the whip when he turned to walk back to her, and he saw her hips twist in a way that told him she was very close to the edge. Allowing his lips to curve just a little, he ran the soft tails over her body from chest to thigh.

"Where," he murmured, "would you like to take your licks?" He circled the strands around her breasts. "Here?" Stroking lower, over her thighs. "Here?" Going back up, switching his hold to run the handle through her delicate folds. "Or maybe here?"

She cried out, and he knew she was on the precipice. Drawing back, he switched his hold again and flicked out with his hand. The velvet tails kissed the flushed skin of her thighs and her whimper turned into a throaty moan.

"Wider," he ordered.

Spreading her thighs, she locked gazes with him.

His next stroke hit her inner thighs and he saw the storm rising in those eyes akin to midnight forests. Gauging it precisely, he flicked out his hand again . . . so the velvet fell on the damp folds between her thighs.

She came with a scream, her arms straining as she continued to cling to the iron bars of the headboard, her breasts flushed and her back arched.

Wanting her to ride it, to squeeze every drop of ecstasy out of it, he flicked the whip again, over her breasts.

Her pleasure took her over, and she was beautiful. Dropping the whip, he got rid of the remainder of his clothes and settled himself between her thighs, pushing inside her as she came down from the high, her flesh quivering with aftershocks. Tiny inner muscles spasmed around him, almost stealing his control. But he'd had centuries to hone it and he intended to draw out the night's pleasure.

Groaning, Honor held him tight as he rocked inside her in slow, shallow thrusts that tempted but never delivered. Sweat slicked their bodies ten long minutes later and the woman who was his lay on her back, clawing at the sheets and attempting to force him deeper with her ankles locked around his back. "Faster."

"I won the sparring session," he reminded her. "I get to do whatever I like." Leaning down, he licked up a droplet of sweat from along her throat. "Right now, I want to take you slow and easy."

Her chest heaving, she tried to thrust a hand between their bodies. Grabbing it, he pinned it above her head, before taking her other one and pinioning them both at the wrists with one hand. "Bad girl." Holding her gaze, he stroked again, heard her frustration in the low moan at the back of her throat. "Scared?" It was a serious question, because he had her restrained.

"No." Arching up, she bit his jaw. "You should be, though."

Rolling his hips, he loved her in ways that had her eyes closing and her breasts rising up toward his mouth. He took advantage, sucking and playing with her nipples as he continued to torment her with his cock. When he lifted his head and claimed a kiss, she sucked on his tongue . . . then she did the one thing that had always made him lose control, even before he was Made. Nuzzling her way down to his throat, she clamped her teeth over his pulse and licked out with her tongue.

Snarling, he released her wrists to fist a hand in her hair, pulling her off his throat—taking care so she felt no hurt—even as he seated his cock balls-deep inside her in the same motion.

She gasped. "Oh, God."

"How," he whispered, using his other hand to push up one of her knees, spreading her wider for him, "did you know to do that?" It was a very specific caress, one he'd discovered with Ingrede. In the years since, other women—Favashi included—had tried to go for his throat, but he'd never, ever left it unprotected.

Until Honor.

"You refused to fall in love with anyone else, Dmitri." A whisper with the impact of a gunshot. "So I had to come back for you . . . husband."

Every muscle in his body locked. *"No."*

Honor's response to that single harsh word was nothing he could've predicted. "It's okay." Cupping his face with gentle hands, she smiled crookedly, her eyes luminous with a love so deep, he thought he'd drown in the shimmering midnight green. "You don't have to believe me, or even think me sane. Just let me love you."

Her next words were whispered in an ancient, forgotten language, the dialect one that had been spoken only in a tiny village long since crumbled to the earth—a dialect Dmitri alone remembered. Except the lilting rhythm of it fell from Honor's lips as if she'd run wild through the same fields, danced under the same brilliant sun. "I've always been a little bit crazy when it comes to you."

"I can't—" he began, because what she was offering, it was too much, a gift too painful.

"Shh." She ran her fingers through his hair. "It's okay."

"No." It wasn't okay, wouldn't be okay until he had the answers he needed.

"So stubborn." Kissing him slow and deep, she held him to her with her legs around his hips when he would've pulled out. "I should've expected it from the man who once clambered up a mountainside at dawn to bring me wildflowers."

His entire body shuddered under the weight of the knowledge in her eyes, in her touch, in her voice. All the tiny things she'd done that had nudged at his memory, the echo of Ingrede's joy breaking his heart when it was Honor who laughed, the way she *knew* him, it crashed against the chaos inside him, leaving only a raw need in its wake.

"Let me give you what you need, husband. I've waited so very long." Haunting words tangled with an exquisite desire that sang to his blood. *"Drink."*

The final thread of his control snapped.

Roaring, he drove into her again and again and again, until she was clenching around him with feminine power and he was coming with such satisfaction that he had no memory of sinking his fangs into her neck. Then the tart, wild taste of her blood hit him with the ferocity of a windstorm, and suddenly he was hard once more.

Honor felt her eyes grow wide as Dmitri began to move again, his fangs sending a wave of sultry pleasure through her system—languid, persuasive, tasting of sin and sex and everything deliciously bad . . . and so unlike what she'd experienced in the basement that a comparison would've been laughable.

Moaning at the opulent swell of it through whimpering muscles and a pleasantly shattered body, she felt herself coating the hard intrusion of his arousal in lush need. "Oh, God, Dmitri."

The thick length of him pushed past swollen tissues, arcing ripples of ecstasy throughout her system, as he bent at her neck and fed. Thrusting her hand into his hair, she held him to her, the scorching sexuality of the moment cut with a wild tenderness. He sucked hard, and her body bucked.

Making a low, deep sound of satisfaction, he pulled out, pushed back in . . . and rode her to an orgasm that never seemed to stop.

Her muscles were still quivering from the erotic pleasure when, ending the blood kiss, he licked his tongue over the tiny wounds, sucked the skin again, and raised his head. "We're not done," he purred in her ear as her legs fell off his back, too exhausted to hold on. Reaching between them, he plucked at her clitoris with fingers that knew her far too well.

Another orgasm rocked through her, deep, so deep. "I can't take any more." It was a moan.

"Liar." A rolling move of his hips, and she was rising toward him, her hands caressing his chest, his arms.

He had endless patience, and he wasn't about to give her what she wanted this time. Not until half an hour later, when she was sucking on his throat, scratching his back, and threatening to use a blade on him. That was when he pulled out his cock to her frustrated scream, spread her thighs wide, and bent that dark head to suck her clitoris into his mouth.

The erotic shock was so intense, it seared her nerve endings, had lights exploding behind her eyes. She was fairly certain she lost consciousness for a blinding second. When she lifted her drugged eyelids at last, it was to feel her beautiful, dangerous Dmitri sliding into her in a primal thrust that was pure possession.

38

Freshly showered, they spoke sitting in bed, Honor lying against Dmitri's chest, her body soft and warm and his. Absolutely, categorically *his*.

"I couldn't hide this from you," she said as he ran his fingers through hair he'd dried as she sat slumped against him, lazy and sated, "but I was prepared for utter disbelief, thought it might take me years to prove it to you."

Taking her hand, he spread it over his heart. "Some part of me knew from the start." She was inside him, her soul forcing his own back to life. "I just wasn't ready to consciously accept it." Honor was the brave one, the one who had taken that leap of hope.

Her hand fisted. "I know this will hurt you so much, but I need to have this question answered." Eyes iridescent with tears, jewels in the rain. "Misha . . . what did they do to Misha?"

A searing burn on his chest, the scent of burning flesh and muscle and his body's silent screams. But his mouth he kept shut, though it cost him a piece of his sanity.

"There now, lover. You will never forget me." Isis's red lips pressing over the burned and scarred flesh, her tongue digging into the still painful wound. "Always, you will carry me

within." Her flawless face stayed serene as she took up the branding iron and pressed it to his flesh a second time to make certain of her words.

Blackness engulfed him and when he woke, his chest was ridged with a scar so heavy and thick, he thought nothing would ever erase it. Looking up, he saw Raphael staring at that brand with a cold intensity that spoke of death. The angel said nothing, but when their eyes met he jerked the chain that held his left hand cuffed to the wall. It took Dmitri's dazed mind a moment to see, to understand.

The stone was cracking. A year it had taken him, but Raphael had weakened his bonds enough to snap them—now, Dmitri simply had to survive, become strong again. So he did, though Isis had almost broken him. But he didn't do it to kill her, though that need was a fever in his blood. He did it so he could hold his son again, the only one of his family who remained.

"Shh, Misha," he said, his throat cracked and raw when his son screamed and convulsed, his tiny body attached to the wall by a cuff around his neck. "Papa will be there soon and he'll make it all right."

He'd kept his promise. He'd given his son peace.

The guilt of what he'd done clawed him bloody. "Isis tried to Make him."

A horrified sound. "He was too young."

"Yes." Dmitri couldn't put this pain into words, but when Honor's hands came up to cup his cheeks, he bent his head toward her, let her press her lips to his closed eyes, to his lips.

"I understand." Her voice was a husky whisper. "It is all right, Dmitri. It was the only thing you could've done."

Dmitri hadn't cried, not for near to a thousand years. But the remembered agony of cradling his son's body in his arms, of looking into those trusting eyes fevered and full of suffering and a madness that had already made Misha gnaw at his own flesh, of holding that gaze until the very end, when he ended the life of his brave, beautiful boy . . . it tore through him now, creating cutting rivers of pain.

He would've drowned but for the woman who held him through the storm, whose tears mixed with his own, whose gentle hands gave him forgiveness for a crime for which he'd never forgiven himself. "I was their father," he said at long last. "Caterina, Misha . . . I couldn't protect either of them. I couldn't protect you."

Honor shook her head. "You *fought* for us. You surrendered your pride, your body, your freedom. But most of all, you loved us until none of us knew what it was to live without being adored." Cupping his face again, she touched her forehead to his. "If I got a second chance, don't you think our babies must have, too?"

Her whisper didn't wipe out his grief over their loss, but it touched it with the glow of hope. And having this woman in his arms, that was a gift no one could ever take away. "Ingrede or Honor?" It mattered not to him, the essence of her indelibly inked on his soul.

"Ingrede lived another life, was another woman." A kiss on his jaw, followed by a scowl. "I'm Honor, so don't suddenly start thinking I'm going to put on skirts and be a stay-at-home wife."

"You can do whatever you wish to," he said. "So long as you don't go far from me." He wouldn't allow that, couldn't stand it. "Almost a thousand years I've waited for you. I can't give you that distance."

"Dmitri." It was a long time later that they spoke again, his need for her a deep well that would never run dry. "I've got no desire to put distance between us," she said, brushing his hair back, caressing his jaw, constant touches of love. "The position at Guild Academy for a teacher of ancient languages is still open. I'm going to go for it."

"Good." Lifting her hand to his lips, he kissed her knuckles. "We'll marry at daybreak." His wife would wear his ring, be his in every way.

"Old-fashioned." Laughter, familiar and new, wrapping around him, binding him. "I hope you know you'll be wearing gold, too."

"I've waited an eternity to wear it again." Body and soul, she owned him. "I'm yours. Always."

Mists in her eyes. "I *love* you."

"Even if I'm no longer as good a man as you once knew?" Never again would be, his soul too battered, too threaded through with violence and darkness.

"We're both of us a little beat up—that's what makes us interesting."

He wanted to laugh, but his chest ached. "Do you wish to be Made, Honor?" If she chose the firefly life span of a mortal, this time he would go with her. It was no choice, but a simple truth.

Honor went motionless. "I can't be anyone's slave, Dmitri. Not ever."

"That won't be a problem." Then, because this was Honor, who knew him as no other did on this earth, he said, "You'll only ever serve me."

"Arrogant man." Rising to straddle him, she touched her nose to his, rubbed in that familiar way. "At the start, I thought no, I could never be one of the monsters. But we never had a chance, Dmitri. I *want* that chance. I want a hundred lifetimes with you."

He didn't give her the opportunity to change her mind, greedy for every instant, every second. "We'll begin the process after the marriage ceremony."

"Do you think the Guild will still accept me?" It was a worried question. "The Academy's never been prejudiced against vampiric instructors, but . . . my friends."

"If they are your friends, they'll stand with you."

Yes. Having faith in the strength of the relationships she'd built, she laid her head against him, this man she'd fought death itself to find. "Tell me what you did, what you saw, after I was gone."

A strong hand fisting in her hair, possessive and dark. "I've lived many years."

"That's okay," she said, spreading her fingers over his heart. "We have eternity."

Turn the page for a special preview of
Nalini Singh's next book in the
Psy-Changeling Series
Now available
from Berkley Sensation!

R~iaz~ caught a flash of midnight hair and a long-legged stride and called out, "Indigo!" However, he realized his mistake the instant he turned the corner. "Adria."

Eyes of deepest blue met his, the frost in them threatening to give him hypothermia. "Indigo's in her office." The words were helpful, but the tone might as well have been a serrated blade.

That did it. "Did I kill your dog?"

Frown lines marred her smooth forehead. "Excuse me?"

God, that *tone*. "It's the only reason," he said, holding on to his temper by a very thin thread, "I can think of to explain why you're so damn pissy with me." Adria had been pulled into den territory during the hostilities with Councilor Henry Scott and his Pure Psy army a month ago, had remained behind to take up a permanent position as a senior soldier. She had fought with focused determination by Riaz's side, followed his orders on the field without hesitation.

However, off the field?

Ice.

Absolute.

Unrelenting.

Frigid.

Folding his arms when she didn't reply, he stepped into her personal space, caught the subtle scent of crushed berries and frost. A strangely delicate scent for this hard-ass of a woman, he thought, before his wolf's anger overrode all else. "You haven't answered my question." It came out a growl.

Eyes narrowed, she stepped closer with a slow deliberation that was pure, calculated provocation. She was a tall woman, but he was taller. That didn't seem to stop her from looking down her nose at him. "I didn't realize," she said in a voice so polite it drew blood, "that fawning over you was part of the job requirement."

"Now I know where Indigo learned her mean face from." But where his fellow lieutenant's heart beat warm and generous beneath that tough exterior, he wasn't sure Adria had any emotions that registered above zero on the thermometer.

Adria's response was scalpel sharp. "I don't know what she ever saw in you, but I suppose every woman has mistakes in her past." The slightest change in her expression, the tiniest fracture, before it was sealed up again, her face an impenetrable rock face.

Scowling, Riaz was about to tell her exactly what he thought of her and her judgmental gaze when his cell phone rang. He answered without moving an inch away from the woman who was sandpaper across his temper, rubbing him raw with her mere presence. "Yeah?"

"My office," Hawke said. "Need you to head out to check on something."

"Be there in two." Snapping the phone shut, he closed the remaining distance between them, forcing Adria to tip back her head. "We will," he said, realizing those striking blue eyes with an edge of purple had streaks of gold running through them, beautiful and exotic, "continue this later."

That was when Adria's cell phone rang. "Yes?" she answered without breaking eye contact with the big, muscled wolf who thought he could intimidate her.

"In my office," Hawke ordered.

"On my way." Hanging up, she raised an eyebrow at Riaz in a consciously insolent action. "My alpha has requested my

presence, so get out of my fucking way," she said with utmost
sweetness.

Eyes a brilliant dark gold that were more wolf than human,
narrowed again. "Guess we'll be walking together."

Not giving an inch until he stepped back and turned to head
to Hawke's office, she walked in silence beside him, though
her wolf bared its teeth, hungry to draw blood, to bite and claw
and mark. Damn him. *Damn him.* She'd been doing fine, cop-
ing after her final separation from Martin. That had been a
bloody battle, too.

*"You'll come crawling back to me. Maybe I'll be waiting.
Maybe I won't."*

Adria bit back a raw laugh. Martin didn't understand that it
was over. Done. Forever. It had been over the night a year ago
when he'd stormed out of their home, not to return for four
months. The truly stunning thing was that he'd had the gall to
be shocked when she'd told him to go find someplace else to
sleep and slammed the door on his face.

"Cat got your tongue?" An acerbic comment made in a
deep male voice that ruffled her fur the wrong way.

"Go bite yourself," she muttered, in no mood to play
games. Her skin felt too sensitive, as if she'd lost a protective
layer, her blood too hot.

"Someone should bite you," Riaz muttered. "Pull that stick
out of your ass at the same time."

Adria growled, just as they reached the open door to
Hawke's office. The alpha looked up at their entrance, unhidden speculation in blue eyes so pale, they were those of a wolf
given human form. However, when he spoke, his words were
pragmatic. "You two free to go for a drive?"

Adria nodded, saw Riaz do the same. "What do you need
done?" Riaz asked.

"Mack and one of his trainee techs went up to do a routine
service of the hydro station," Hawke told them, "but their vehicle's not starting, and they've got components that need to
be brought back to the den for repairs."

"No problem," Riaz said. "I'll take one of the SUVs, pick
them up."

Even as Adria was thinking the task was a one-person job,
Hawke turned to her. "You're now one of the most senior peo-

ple in the den." His dominance was staggering, demanding her wolf's absolute attention. "I'd like you to get reacquainted with the region, given that you haven't spent an extended period of time here since you turned eighteen."

She nodded. Ranking just below the lieutenants in the hierarchy, senior soldiers were often called upon to lead, and as a leader she had to know every inch of this land, not just the section she'd been assigned to during the battle. "It'd be better if I do it on foot."

"You can explore in detail later on." Hawke pushed back strands of hair that had fallen over his forehead, the color a distinctive silver-gold that echoed his coat in wolf form. "I want you to have a good working knowledge of the area as soon as possible." He handed her a thin plastic map. "The trip up to the hydro station will take you through some critical sections—and you have certification in mechanics, correct?"

"Yes." It had been an interest she'd turned into the secondary qualification all soldiers were required to possess. "I'll take a look at the vehicle."

"What about the replanting?" Riaz asked, his voice clawing over her skin like nails on one of those old-fashioned chalkboards the pups liked to draw on. "Felix's team have enough security?"

"They're fine." Walking to the territorial map on the stone wall of his office, Hawke tapped a large cross-hatched section below what had been SnowDancer's defensive line in the fight against Pure Psy. "Felix's volunteers and conscripts"—a sharp grin—"are planting the area with fast-growing natives, but for now, it's so open it's easy to monitor, especially with the cats sharing the watch."

Adria thought of what she'd seen on that battlefield filled with the screams of wounded SnowDancers, the cold amber and red of a flame so hypnotic and deadly, and wondered at the cost paid by the young Psy woman who held all that power—and their alpha's heart. "What are the chances of another Pure Psy attack?" she asked, intrigued on the innermost level by a relationship that appeared so very unbalanced on the outside, and yet one that was as solid as the stone of the den.

It was Riaz who answered. "According to Judd's sources, close to nil. They've got worse problems."

"Civil war," Hawke said, shaking his head. "If he's right, there'll be no avoiding the impact—so we make sure we're prepared to weather any storms."

Nodding in agreement, she left the office with the man whose very scent—dark, woodsy, with a sharp citrus tone—made her skin itch. "We should get some food." The drive wouldn't be quick, plus Mack and his tech, who had probably not planned to be up there this long either, would be hungry.

"Should be something in here," Riaz said, walking into the senior soldiers' break room.

They worked with honed efficiency to slap together some sandwiches and were ready to go ten minutes later. Clenching her abdominal muscles as she got into the vehicle with Riaz, Adria told herself to focus on the route, the geography, anything but the potent, masculine scent of the man in the driver's seat . . . because she knew full well why he incited such vio lence in her.

Riaz drove them out of the garage, and into the mountains, very aware of the cool silence of the woman with him. The more time he spent with her, the more he realized how unlike Indigo she was, in spite of the superficial similarity of their looks. One of the reasons he'd always enjoyed the other woman's company was her upfront nature—Adria, by comparison, was a closed box with Do Not Enter signs pasted on every surface.

He understood that. Hell, he had his own "no go" zones, but with Adria, it was armor of broken glass that drew blood. "This track," he said, doing his job because personality clash or not, he knew his responsibilities, "is the most direct route to the hydro station."

"Not according to the map Hawke gave us." A quick, penetrating glance. "So what's wrong with the other road?"

Man and wolf both appreciated her intelligence, something neither part of him had ever doubted, even when she was slicing into him with her verbal claws. "Sheer cliff face right in the middle." Making two tight turns, he continued onward. "Meant to delay any aggressors if they ever get that far."

Adria didn't say anything for several long minutes, studying the map and their passage into the mountains. "I'll need to request another senior soldier go with me on some of my exploratory trips, so I don't miss things like that."

"I'll take you," Riaz said, because damn it, he was a lieutenant, even when it came to a prickly piece of cactus like Adria. "Indigo made sure I was familiar with the details after I came back from my posting in Europe. It'll be good for me to go over the knowledge."

Adria blinked, taken by surprise. "I appreciate it." It was the only thing she could say without giving everything away.

Riaz snorted, his hands strong and competent on the manual steering wheel as he navigated a particularly steep embankment. "About as much as you appreciate a root canal, but whatever your problem with me, we have to work together."

Setting her jaw, she focused on the view beyond the window—of the most magnificent scenery on this earth. Summer was fading, though autumn hadn't yet arrived, and the land was swathed in dark green, the peaks in the distance touched with white.

A flash of movement.

"Who's that?" She jerked forward to watch a big tan-colored wolf race across a meadow to the left, chasing a sleek silver wolf she immediately recognized. "He's being rough with Evie." Fury boiled in her blood. "Stop the car."

Riaz's chuckle held pure male amusement, fuel to her temper. "That's Tai, and Evie won't appreciate the interruption, Aunt Adria."

Biting back her harsh response, Adria glanced at the two wolves again, saw what she'd missed at first glance. They were playing, all teeth and claws, but with no real aggression to it. Just as Riaz turned a corner, cutting off the view, the two wolves nuzzled one another and Adria realized Tai and Evie weren't just playing, they were courting. "She's too young." While Indigo was very close to Adria in age, Evie was much younger.

"She's still a wolf, an adult female wolf," Riaz said, pushing the car into hover drive to negotiate a damaged section of the road. "You might have forgotten, Ms. Frost, but touch is necessary for most of our kind."

Her hand fisted, that nerve far too close to the surface.

A year.

It had been a year since she'd been in a sexual relationship, a rawly painful kind of isolation for a wolf in the prime of her life. But she'd been handling it, until Riaz and the raging storm of a sudden, visceral sexual attraction that terrified her.

"If we're throwing stones," she said, protecting herself by going on the offensive, "I'm not the only one who prefers a cold bed." Riaz was a highly eligible male—the fact he'd taken no lovers was a point of irritation with the women who wanted nothing better than to tussle with him. "Maybe that's why you're such a prick."

Riaz's snarl was low, rolling over her skin with the power of his dominance. Wrenching the wheel, he brought the SUV to a stop on the side of the road. "I've had it." Turning off the engine, he turned to her. "What the *hell* is your problem with me?"

"Drive," she said, almost ready to crawl out of her skin with the need to rip off his T-shirt and use her teeth on all that hot, firm muscle. "Mack is waiting for us."

"He can wait a few more minutes." Golden eyes that were no longer in any way human slammed into hers. "You've had a hard-on for me since you transferred to the den. I want to know why."

Gut twisting, she snapped off her safety belt and pushed open her door to step out into the cold mountain air. The chill did nothing to cool the fever in her blood, the need ravaging her body, threatening to make her a slave when she'd finally found freedom. Desperate, she concentrated on the majesty of her surroundings in an effort to fight the tumult inside her. In front of her lay tumbled glacial rocks, huge and imposing, beyond them the dark green of the firs that dominated this area. Above it all was a sky so blue it hurt.

The slam of a door, followed by the thud of boots on the earth shattered her fragile attempt at control, and then Riaz was standing in front of her, blocking the view. "We are not leaving," he said, his skin caressed by the sunlight that gilded his hair a gleaming blue-black, "until we work this out."

Feeling trapped, suffocated, she shoved at his chest and slipped out to stand beside the car rather than with her back to

it. "I'm not the only one who has a problem. You've been picking at me since the day I was pulled into the den."

He growled and the rough sound rasped over her nipples,
wrapped around her throat. "Self-fucking-defense. You took
one look at me and decided you hated my guts. I want to
know why."

Jesus, Adria thought, how had she gotten herself into this?
"Look," she said, deciding to back down before her wolf took
control and she found herself feasting on male lips currently
thin with anger, "it's nothing personal. I'm generally a bitch."
According to Martin, she was one with a stone heart.

"Nice try"—a harsh laugh that held nothing of humor—
"but I've seen you with others in the pack." He took another
step toward her, invading her space and her senses.

Hell if she was going to allow him to walk all over her.
"Get out of my face."

"You sure you want me to?" he asked, a dangerous look to
him. "Maybe the reason you react like a hissing cat around me
is because you want me even closer."

She sucked in a breath.

Riaz's eyes widened.

Look for

Angels' Flight

A Guild Hunter anthology
by Nalini Singh
Coming March 2012 from Berkley Sensation!

From New York Times *Bestselling Author*

NALINI SINGH

Kiss of Snow

A Psy-Changeling Novel

Since the moment of her defection from the PsyNet and into the SnowDancer wolf pack, Sienna Lauren has had one weakness. *Hawke.* Alpha and dangerous, he compels her to madness.

Hawke is used to walking alone, having lost the woman who would've been his mate long ago. But Sienna fascinates the primal heart of him, even as he tells himself she is far too young to handle the wild fury of the wolf.

Then Sienna changes the rules, and suddenly, there is no more distance, only the most intimate of battles between two people who were never meant to meet. Yet as they strip away each other's secrets in a storm of raw emotion, they must also ready themselves for a far more vicious fight . . .

A deadly enemy is out to destroy SnowDancer, striking at everything the pack holds dear, but it is Sienna's darkest secret that may yet savage the pack that is her home . . . and the alpha who is its heartbeat.

penguin.com

LOOK FOR THE NEW GUILD HUNTER NOVEL FROM
NEW YORK TIMES BESTSELLING AUTHOR

NALINI SINGH

ARCHANGEL'S CONSORT

Vampire hunter Elena Deveraux and her lover, the lethally beautiful archangel Raphael, have returned home to New York—only to face an uncompromising new evil…

A vampire has attacked a girls' school—the assault one of sheer, vicious madness—and it is only the first act. Rampant bloodlust takes vampire after vampire, threatening to leave the streets running with blood. Then Raphael himself begins to show signs of an uncontrolled rage, as inexplicable storms darken the city skyline and the earth itself shudders.

An ancient and malevolent immortal is rising. The violent winds whisper her name: *Caliane*. She has returned to reclaim her son, Raphael. Only one thing stands in her way: Elena, the consort who must be destroyed…

M758T0810

As Tracker for the SnowDancer pack, it's up to
Drew Kincaid to rein in rogue changelings who
have lost control of their animal halves. But nothing in his life has prepared him for the battle he
must now wage to win the heart of a woman who
makes his body ignite...and who threatens to en-
slave his wolf.

Lieutenant Indigo Riviere doesn't easily allow
skin privileges, especially of the sensual kind—and
the last person she expects to find herself craving
is the most wickedly playful male in the den. Everything she knows tells her to pull back...but she
hasn't counted on Drew's will.

Now, two of SnowDancer's most stubborn
wolves find themselves playing a hotly sexy game
even as lethal danger stalks the very place they call
home...